Somewhere
East of Life

Fiction

The Brightfount Diaries
Nonstop
Hothouse
Greybeard
Frankenstein Unbound
The Malacia Tapestry
The Horatio Stubbs Saga
The Helliconia Trilogy
A Tupolev Too Far
The Secret of This Book

The Squire Quartet

Life in the West
Forgotten Life
Remembrance Day
Somewhere East of Life

Non-fiction

Cities and Stories
The Detached Retina
The Twinkling of an Eye

Poems

At the Caligula Hotel
Songs From the Steppes of Central America

Somewhere East of Life

BRIAN ALDISS

Ship me somewheres east of Suez,
   where the best is like the worst,
Where there aren't no Ten Commandments,
   an' a man can raise a thirst.

RUDYARD KIPLING, 'The "Mary Gloster"'

An *Abacus* Book

First published in Great Britain in 1994
by HarperCollins
This edition published by Abacus in 1999

A CIP catalogue record for this book is
available from the British Library.

ISBN 0 349 11148 0

Typeset in Bembo by M Rules
Printed and bound in Great Britain by Clays Ltd, St Ives plc

Abacus
A Division of
Little, Brown and Company (UK)
Brettenham House
Lancaster Place
London
London WC2E 7EN

With love
to
Felicity and Alex –
Bearers of fruits
from
Kidlington and Osh

Acknowledgments

My gratitude goes to Editor David S. Garnett, who has published portions of this novel in *New Worlds*: as 'FOAM', 'Friendship Bridge' and 'To the Krasnovodsk Station', respectively in *New Worlds I*, *New Worlds 3* and *New Worlds 4*. Another portion, 'The Madonna of Futurity', was published simultaneously by editors Robert Silverberg and Karen Haber in *Universe 3*, and in *Heyne Science Fiction Jahresband 1994*, edited by Wolfgang Jeschke, in Germany, and also in завтра in Moscow.

As a member of the Society of Makhtumkuli, I wish to thank Dr Youssef Azemoun for his assistance in the matter of Turkmen poetry.

Thanks also go to Djumageldiev Tirkish in Ashkhabad for his advice – although this is an entire work of fiction, as readers may discover. (Amanda Schäfer is real.)

Contents

1	Friends in Sly Places	1
2	Murder in a Cathedral	18
3	Bishops Linctus	28
4	FOAM	39
5	Some Expensive Bullets	51
6	Soss City	72
7	'The Dead One'	84
8	Looking for a Postcard	112
9	A Head Among the Throng	123
10	'Time Had Run Out'	136
11	'The Madonna of Futurity'	157
12	A Crowded Stage	173
13	Richard and Blanche	183
14	In the Korean Fast Foot	198
15	Makhtumkuli Day	224
16	Burnell Speaks!	241
17	Glimpse of Airing Cupboard	260
18	The Friendship Bridge	277
19	A Toe and a Tow	290
20	PRICC Strikes	298
21	Subterfuge	314
22	A Brief Discourse on Justice	315
23	To the Krasnovodsk Station	316
24	Singing in the Train	331
25	Snow in the Desert	346
26	The Executioner	354
27	Squire Ad Libs	361
28	Open to the Public	370
29	'Newcastle'	385

When you reach the point of no return there's nothing
for it but to go back

Old Goklan saying

1
Friends in Sly Places

It seemed right to take flowers. A gesture had to be made. A nurse accepted them from Burnell and stuck them in a glass vase. Burnell went and sat by his friend's bedside.

Peter Remenyi was still in a coma. He lay propped on pillows, looking the picture of health, his skin tanned, his jaw firm. So he had lain for two weeks, fed by drip, completely unaware of the outside world. Yesterday's flowers drooped on a side table.

Burnell had escaped from the car crash with nothing more than a bruised arm. He visited the hospital every day. He had taken to reading aloud to Remenyi, from Montaigne or the poets, hoping that something might penetrate that deep silence into which his friend had fallen.

He stayed for half an hour. Rising to leave, he patted the patient's cheek.

'You always were a mad bugger at the wheel, Peter,' he said, with some tenderness. 'Stay put, old pal. Never give up the struggle. I'll be back tomorrow. I have to go now. I have a date this evening with a beautiful lady, a star in the firmament of her sex.'

It was the evening of all evenings. The sun went down in glory, the lights came up in competition. Budapest's Hilton Hotel, installed in the ruins of a sacred site, piled on extra floodlighting. A reception was being held by World Antiquities and Cultural Heritage, which several important functionaries from several important countries were attending.

Everything was on a lavish scale, slightly tatty only round the edges. Gipsy orchestras raced through their notes in every available space. Their violins swooped through *czardas* after *czardas*, just as drink poured down throat after throat. A Ukrainian dance group threw themselves about with abandon in the centre of the main ballroom.

Undeterred by wars in the Caucasus, the East, the Far East, and several points West, the guests paraded in finest array, embracing or snubbing one another. Powdered shoulders, jewels, and luxuriant moustaches were on display. Many smiled, some meant it. Suave waiters, Hungarian and Vietnamese, moved among the crowds, delivering messages, pouring Crimean champagne into ever ready glasses. Conversations surged and popped like the bubbles in the champagne. Some who talked looked over the shoulders of their partners, in search of escape; others moved in closer. Loving, lingering glances were exchanged. Formality increasingly gave way to something more physical. The most recent jokes circulated, political or scabrous in content. Gossip chased itself among the international guests, the potted palms.

The air-conditioned atmosphere, as time wore on, became charged with alcoholic fumes, excitement, innuendo, enzymes, exaggeration, assignations, assassinations of character, and the most fragrant of sweats. Couples started to slip away. And Burnell looked deep into the green eyes of Blanche Bretesche, breathing faster while trying to keep his usual cool.

He, she, and some of her friends, left the reception and went together into the warm night. Music came faintly to them. They climbed into taxis, to be whisked downhill and across the great glittering city of Budapest. Streets, shops, restaurants sped by. The extravagant elephantine Danubian city prospered, fat on arms sales and many wickednesses, as befitted the over-ripe heart of Europe.

Burnell never quite learned the names of all his noisy new friends. His senses were alert to Blanche Bretesche, to her eyes, her lips, her breasts. Blanche was Director of the Spanish Section of WACH. One of her friends – the one in full evening dress – directed them to a restaurant he knew in Maijakovszki Street, near the opera house. Here were more crowds, more musics.

The restaurant was neo-baroque, ornate inside and out. Though it was late, the place was crowded with a confusion of people, laughing, eating, drinking. Two inner courtyards were filled with tables. Burnell's party found a free table in the second courtyard. Above them, along flower-draped balconies, a woman sang passionate Hungarian love songs. The man in evening dress, summoning a waiter, ordered wild game specialities, which were not available. Without argument, they settled for *lecso* all round, accompanied by mineral water and a red wine from Eger. Although the main point of the gathering was to enjoy each other's company, the food was also excellent. The warm evening held its breath in the courtyard.

Saying little as usual, Burnell allowed his gaze to alight on the flower of Blanche's face as she talked. The quick wit of her replies always pleased him. Her contributions to subjects under discussion were shrewd, often dismissive. He liked that. She was as much a citizen of the talk as any of the men, though they did not defer to her. While the conversation grew wild and ribald, it remained magically on course, contributing, like all friendly talk, to a general understanding.

When the question turned to a scientific paper of Blanche's, he saw her quick look, sheltered under long dark lashes, turning more frequently to him, as if questioning. A signal flashed unspoken between them. Round the convivial table, between spates of talk, they applauded every song the resin-voiced woman sang, calling up to the balcony in acclamation, though they had scarcely listened to a note. And at two-thirty in the morning, Burnell summoned a taxi. The taxi carried him back through the scurrying town, with his right arm about Blanche Bretesche, to his hotel.

Even before he woke next morning, he was conscious of her warmth. He found himself lying on his stomach. Her arm was across his back. Turning his head cautiously, he was able to watch her sleeping. Happiness flooded him.

He had always admired the look of her, from the alert walk – much like a stalk, he thought – to the well-shaped intellectual head. With those closed green eyes went a dark colouring particularly to his taste, though her hair was now cut fashionably shorter than when they had first met, some six years ago. She had been Stephanie's friend, and was about Stephanie's age, thirty-four or so. Now she was his friend – truly a friend, trusting and direct.

Raising himself gently, he surveyed her sprawling body. Nothing was one quarter as beautiful as the female body, no sky, no landscape.

Blanche was calm about her lovemaking, not stormy. The affirmatives she had uttered still sounded in his ears. There was another sound now, in their shared room. Not merely the distant hum of traffic as it crossed the bridge from Buda to Pest. A fly buzzed against one of the window panes.

Cautiously, Burnell manoeuvred himself out from under that arm with its lashes of dark hair chasing themselves from mid-forearm to elbow. Padding over to the window, he opened it. The bluebottle, after raging against the pane a minute longer, was caught by the breeze and made its escape into the open air.

Perhaps it said to itself, 'Ha, I figured my way out of that . . .' But flies had no hold on truth. For all their countless generations born since glass was invented, they had never comprehended its nature, and so remained continually trapped by it.

When he turned back into the room, Blanche's eyes were open.

'All the time I was asleep, one of that woman's songs was going through my brain. What do you think she was singing about? Did you understand a word of it?'

'It would be the usual things,' he said, closing the window. 'Love betrayed, a starry night, a white glove dropped in a garden . . .'

She smiled. 'I wonder what Neanderthals sang about, if they sang at all.'

'Oh, I'd guess love betrayed, a starry night, and a white mammoth tusk dumped in the cave. Why?'

'Some Catalan archaeologists have found an undisturbed cave in the mountains near Burgos, the home of early man. I'm interested in the way primates turned into men and women. When did speech develop, when did simple simian games of tig become

4

elaborate human games with rules, and aggression codified. That kind of thing.'

He went towards the bed. 'Who sang the first love song. Who invented the wheel. Why did the English invent marmalade from Seville oranges.'

She reached out and took his hand. 'Talking of the English, Roy, come and screw me again, please, just a little, will you?'

'There's no breakfast for you until you let me.'

The breakfast was good too. They ate in the room, talking mainly of their work. WACH both brought them together and generally kept them apart. Burnell had recently been in Milan, documenting the restoration of the Duomo. He was due to report to his superior in Frankfurt, where WACH had its headquarters, in two days. Blanche was now mostly at her desk in Madrid, able to get out on field work infrequently. She had to catch a flight back to Spain the following day.

'I speak German and Spanish – in fact, Castilian – more frequently than I do French. I don't regard myself as particularly French any more. I belong to the Community.'

'You're an enlightened woman.'

'Don't be silly. I know you speak half a dozen languages, you footloose creature. Why didn't you go back to England for your leave, instead of pottering about Europe? Do you like the German domination of the EU?'

'I don't mind it. It was inevitable. One reason I'm here and not in England is there's something I want to check in the anthropological museum. No, whenever I go back to England . . . well, everything seems to come in quotes nowadays. It all seems old fashioned. You know, things maintained for tourists, like "The Changing of the Guard". People still have, insist on, "toast and marmalade" for breakfast. They "drive down to the coast". They go to "the RA private view" and in "the season" they attend what they still call "Royal Ascot", despite all that's happened to the royal family. My father still likes his "cup of tea", and talks of Europe as "the Continent". That kind of thing.'

She laughed over her second croissant. 'They only do that kind of thing in exalted Burnell circles. Oh, I remember you dislike those circles, but they're bred in you. That's why you're so self-contained. I like that, really. It's quaint . . .'

He put a hand over hers and laughed with her. 'Quaint! Yes. The French also have their traditions, if I remember correctly. Listen, my boss has a bungalow on Lake Balaton. I've got a hire-car. Let's drive down to Balaton for the day. We can swim and sail. You can tell me about your latest paper. Come on.'

She smiled at him, with slight mockery. 'You look a little more boyish than you did yesterday. And I feel a little more girlish. Is that a word? Girlish? There are several things I am supposed to do today. I could cancel them. Let me make a few phone calls . . .' Setting down her coffee cup, she gave a sudden exclamation. 'Oh, Roy, come to Madrid and live with me. I'm sure we'd be so happy, truly.'

He lowered his gaze. 'You know I don't speak Spanish.'

They drove through hectares of sunflowers to Lake Balaton. They had chosen a perfect day for the jaunt. At one point they passed a refugee camp, protected by razor wire. Hungarian and Croatian flags hung limply from flagpoles. They were past it immediately.

At a minor crossroads, Burnell slowed the car. This was where the crash had occurred which left Peter Remenyi in a coma. Both cars involved had been wrecked. No sign remained of the collision. He reminded Blanche that the previous summer, he, Remenyi, and another friend had gone horse-riding in the Alps, bivouacking most nights.

'What did you read him today, when you were sitting with him?'

'Oh, whatever's to hand – just in case it gets through to him, wherever he is. Shelley. "Whence are we, and why are we? Of what scene The actors or spectators?"'

Blanche gave an appalled laugh. 'Oh, that's awful. Isn't that a lament for someone dead?'

He speeded up again. 'In this case, the nearly dead.'

The bungalow was situated in the diplomatic strip, away from the crowds. It proved to be a mansion built in ornate mock-art-nouveau style. Its verandah overlooked the blue waters of Balaton.

They admired the frightful taste of its decor, joked about the garish nude paintings, sailed, swam, sunned themselves, and made love on the reindeer rug in the living-room to the music of Smetana. Although the forests and rivers the composer had celebrated were destroyed by pollution, his music remained pristine. The hairs of the rug came off on their damp bodies.

Sometimes she looked up at the mock-Mucha ceiling, sometimes he did.

At sunset, they strolled arm in arm to the nearest restaurant. Foal was on the menu, so they ordered foal.

As if an earlier conversation was in Blanche's mind, she said, 'Spain's the most successful part of the Community, except maybe Sweden. Outside of Germany, that is. It's a wonderful noble country. At least you might come and visit me, meet some of my friends. Drive down to Cordoba, meet the statue of Averroës.'

'I hear Spain is rather autocratic, nowadays.'

'Oh, that! They've banned this e-mnemonicvision craze, if that's what you mean. EMV is treated as if it was – were, do you say? – the subjunctive? – a drug. I am inclined to agree. Violent videos were bad enough, but to experience other people's actual memories – isn't it a kind of rape? – it's regarded as obscene in a Catholic state.'

'You've never tried EMV? Properly used, it can be a good learning tool. I ran a bullet of Umberto Benjamin's memories of cathedral building. It's in the WACH library in Frankfurt. The insights were startling. It was as if for half an hour I really was Benjamin. EMV is mind talking to mind. There's nothing like it.'

'I would have guessed e-mnemonicvision would be too invasive for you.'

The waiter was pouring wine into their glasses, red and randy. As they toasted each other, Blanche said, 'Mainly EMV is used for second-hand sex and misery and violence, not learning. I'm inclined to think it is demeaning to human nature.' She laughed. '"If God had meant us to pry into other people's minds, He'd have given us telepathy" . . .'

7

'It may prove in the end to allow us better insights into others. God knows, we could use that. While you're experiencing the false memory, you do seem to be the other person. You know the old Indian saying, "Don't criticize your neighbour till you've walked a mile in his moccasins".'

'Well, I still prefer reading. Old fashioned of me, I know. I also think it's an abuse that people – poor people – are forced to sell their memories. It's selling your past, a new form of prostitution, worse than selling a kidney . . . Where's that hunk of foal? I'm hungry.'

'But lovers, exchanging memories . . .'

'And becoming confused and neurotic. EMV is not a decade old and already it's causing all kinds of psychoses. But not in Spain, happily.'

He saw it was time to change the subject. Besides, a violinist was sawing his way towards their table, eyes levelled at them along his instrument, a marksman aligning his sights on a target. A burst of 'Elegaila' was due. 'Tell me more about your work. I'm so ignorant, spending my time in decaying places of worship. I've lost touch with the modern world.'

'Lucky Roy! Well, my work is more interesting to me than its description would be. Let's talk about you. I know you've got problems. We all have. You've heard about my mother's lawsuit before. It goes on . . . It's your quality of remoteness I like, do you understand? Everyone is so bloody *engagé* these days. To take a position, a stance. You don't have a stance, do you?'

'I'm ruled by circumstance. Blanche, I don't know how you put up with me.'

'I'm an idiot, that's the reason.' They laughed.

As the waiters began to load their table with plates, she began to talk about Spain, its recent past, its distant past. The full-bodied wine, the tender foal steak, the cry of the violin, robbed what Blanche was saying of its nuances.

Next morning, he drove her to Ferihagy airport. As they embraced and kissed each other goodbye, she said, 'I'll think of you – and remember we shall need more of one another very soon. Just bear my invitation in mind.'

'Blanche – of course. Of course I will. It's just . . .'

'It's still Stephanie, isn't it?' Lines of gathering frown appeared on her forehead. 'I thought you might have stopped that foolishness.'

He shook his head, not in denial but in impatience with his own nature. The green eyes were suddenly luminous with anger.

'Why don't you bloody well forget Stephanie? She's bloody well forgotten you.'

Then she was off, raising her boarding card above her head as she swept past the official at the entrance to the departures lounge. Elegant, in full control, moderately famous, one of the modern ladies of a united Europe.

He made his way up to the observation deck. Tall tails of planes like sails of yachts moved their insignia past his vision: Malev, Lufthansa, KLM, United British, EuroUnion, Singapore Airlines, SAS, Aeroflot, EuroBerlin, Alitalia, Bulgair, and her airline, her flight, Iberia, about to carry her back through Europe's skies to the place where she lived and moved and spoke Castilian.

At last Burnell turned away. He jingled his keys abstractedly as he made his way to the short-term car park. Nothing for it now but the museum and old things, relics connected with death. His milieu.

He let self-hatred gnaw within him as he eased himself into the hired BMW.

Under genuine regret at Blanche's departure, he tried to stifle some relief. Supposing he went to live with her, what then? What would he *do*? *Find* to do? Shouldn't Castles in Spain – *Châteaux en Asie*, as the French called them – remain splendidly imaginary? What would it feel like to love, to have continuous intercourse with, another woman, while Stephanie remained as much part of his interior monologue as a separating language? He could ask himself the question even with Blanche's physical presence still aromatically close. As he drove to the museum, he attempted a macrocosmic analogy. How could England ever become genuinely part of the European Community while its language kept the USA ever in mind?

By such linguistic artifice, he tried to distract himself from that ignoble sense of relief at Blanche's departure. But self-knowledge is generally a traitor.

The dead were driving the living to the grave. The dead were represented by skeletons, frisky and grinning, unaware they were anatomically incorrect. The line of the living began with prelates in grand robes, the Pope in the lead. Following the prelates came a procession of merchants, hands on purses, then ordinary men and women, a soldier, then a prostitute in a low-cut, tight-laced dress; lastly, a crippled beggar bringing up the rear. Thus most ranks of medieval society were represented, together with inescapable gradations of decay.

This *danse macabre* had once formed an integral part of the stonework of the cathedral at Nogykanizsa. The slab on which it was carved had been saved when the cathedral was partially destroyed, to repose in the grandly named National Museum of Hungarian Anthropology and Religion.

'Sorry, to do photographs is strickly forbidden,' said the guide, seeing Burnell unzip his camera bag. 'Better give it me your camera.'

She was a narrow bent woman in her fifties. A dewdrop pended at the end of her narrow nose. Her attitude suggested that nobody knew the trouble she'd seen, or that she was preparing to see in the near future. Her clothes – the nearest thing possible to a uniform – indicated that she neither shared nor approved the prosperity the new order of things had brought to her city.

She jangled her keys in best gaoler fashion. This part of the museum was officially closed for alterations, on the principle all museums adhere to, that some sections should always remain inaccessible. Only when Burnell had shown his World Antiquities and Cultural Heritage pass had he been reluctantly allowed entry.

He took a few measurements. In his black notebook he made notes and sketches. Could it conceivably be that the Pope was a representation of one of the sixteenth-century Clements whose portrait hung in the Uffizi in Florence? He made a more careful drawing of the papal figure. The frieze, severed and displayed on a bench, had suffered from weathering. Yet it was possible that the emblem carved on the Pope's pocket represented the Castle of St Angelo, in which the pontiff Clement had been incarcerated. If so, Burnell had established an important connection hitherto overlooked.

Steering herself in her heavy shoes, the guide came to stare over Burnell's shoulder. 'It's a disgust, *der Todten Tantz*. These skeleton, pah!' She gestured towards the stone with an open hand.

'Mortality – Christian stock-in-trade. But elegant rather than repulsive, to my mind.'

'Repulsive, you say? Yes.'

He admired the way the leading Death gestured with some gallantry towards the open grave, its skull bizarrely decked with flags. The gesture could have been copied from a painting of skeletons disrupting a rural scene in a painting in the Campo Santo in Pisa. The helpful guidebook to the museum, published in Hungarian and German, attributed to the sportive Death the saying, 'In this doleful jeste of Life, I shew the state of Manne, and how he is called at uncertayne tymes by Me to forget all that he hath and lose All.'

For a while, as Burnell measured and sketched, silence prevailed. The only sound was the footsteps of the guide, as she walked to the end of the gallery and back. She sighed in her progress, jangling her keys like a gaoler in a novel by Zola. The two were alone in the gallery, confined within the museum's stone walls. The woman paused to stare from a narrow window at the city below. Then she called to her visitor from a distance, her voice echoing in the empty space.

'Theme of *Todten Tantz* is much popular in Mittel Ages. In the *stadt* of Nogykanizsa, half of the population is wipe out by the Plague only one year after building of the cathedral. Only one year!' She gave a harsh laugh, her larynx rattling in her throat. 'Now we know better than this, praise be.'

Approaching Burnell step by step to punctuate her sentences, she launched into a discourse regarding the horrors of the Middle Ages. She concluded by saying, 'Why you draw bad dead things? In those times was much misery here in Budapest. In these times now, everyone makes many money. Christianity and

Communism, both is finish, forgotten. God and Marx – gone away! So the world is better place. People have more enlightenment than previous times.' She sighed so that her breath reached Burnell. 'I am old woman, of course – too late to benefit.'

It is always unwise to argue with guides. Burnell rejected both her assumption and her breath. 'Can you really suppose people have become more enlightened? On what grounds do you suppose that, madam? Have you forgotten all the fratricidal wars at present in progress on the fringes of Europe?'

The guide gave a wicked smile, pointing a large key at Burnell as if it were a gun. 'We kill off all the Russians. Then the world is a better place. Forget about every bad things.'

Burnell closed the black notebook with a snap. 'It's the living who distress me, not the dead. Kindly let me out of here.'

Burnell took a light lunch in his hotel room. He ordered a small honeycomb, which he ate with butter and brown bread rolls, and goat's cheese.

He could not but contrast the day with the happiness of the previous day with Blanche. Nevertheless, as he was never continuously happy – and did not expect to be – he was rarely continuously sad.

He enjoyed good health. Burnell in his mid-thirties was a muscular man of above average height who spent a good part of life outdoors. As a boy he had enjoyed riding, mainly on the family estate in Norfolk, while at school he had excelled at sport, cricket in particular. He had lost interest in such competitive activities after his mother's death.

His expression was generally set, but he smiled readily. When he did so, he became almost handsome. There were women, including Blanche, who waited on that smile, so honest, so conceding of the world's frailties. Burnell's view of himself was harsh: he saw himself as a wanderer, without vision. In that, he seemed a typical man of his time, 'The Era of the Question Mark', as one political commentator had dubbed it. The dreadful inheritance of the twentieth century rumbled about everyone's heads.

A major interest in Burnell's life, perhaps strangely for such a passive nature, was travel. The sort of travel he engaged in on behalf of WACH hardly involved the idea of escape. His consignments involved him in the usual discomforts travellers experience, particularly those who travel alone: delay, disappointment, indifferent rooms, poor food, the insolence of petty officials, and sometimes even danger. Although Burnell gave no indication that he willingly embraced such discomforts, his friends observed how he volunteered for work in those parts of the world where such discomforts were most readily available. Italy, and Milan, had been for him, as he said, 'an easy number'.

He scarcely realized that to his English and foreign friends he was already something of a legend. They saw him as the cool Englishman of tradition. Those who knew him in the field discovered his preoccupation with trivia: airline timetables, various states of the prints of Piranesi's *Carceri*, the alcoholic strengths of various Hungarian *raki*, the perfumes used by whores, details of brickwork, barrel vaulting and buttresses, and the flavour of a *samsa* eaten in an ex-Soviet republic.

He was cool under fire and in love. He was kind in a weak way, though certainly never intentionally cruel to women. Being well born, he had a mistrust of others well born.

He had no vision. He regretted his divorce. He was cynical. But he ate his honeycomb with slow pleasure. Sitting in the sun by his window, he drank coffee and read the newspaper.

The main headline of the paper ran: 'STAVROPOL AIRPORT BATTLE. First Use of Tactical Nukes: Crimea "Ablaze".' The accompanying photo consisted mainly of smoke and men running, like the cover of a lowbrow thriller.

There was as yet no admission by the EU that war had broken out in the Crimea. It was represented merely as a disagreement between Russia and the Ukraine. The disruptions would cease after various threats and admonitions from the EU Security Council. It was the form of words that that admonition would take which was currently being discussed in Brussels and Berlin.

He set the newspaper aside to gaze vacantly at the window. He admitted to himself he was feeling lonely. Blanche would be back in Madrid by now. Perhaps one of her many friends would have met her. She moved in cultivated circles. He looked at the photograph of his ex-wife on his bedside table, without seeing it. He just moved in circles.

In the afternoon, he visited Remenyi, still silent in his coma, and read to him as usual.

The grand steam baths under the Gellert Hotel were choked with bodies, male and female. Many of the bathers exhibited the bulk and the posture of wallowing hippopotami. Encompassing steam provided some kind of cloak for the torpid anatomies, while reinforcing a general impression of a bacchanalia or, more accurately, a post-bacchanalia.

The baths had been in use since Roman times; occupying Turks had enlarged them. Allowing himself his usual afternoon soak, Burnell reflected that little had changed since then. Everyone was taking it easy. The hairy stomachs surrounding him, the monumental buttocks, belonged to affluent members of Hungarian and European society. Next to him, Swedish was being languidly spoken. What with wars and trouble in the old Soviet Union republics, in the Caucasus and beyond the Caspian Sea, Swedes were prospering. Hungary was neutral, the Switzerland, the crooked casino, of Central Europe. It sold Swedish-made armaments to all sides with business-like impartiality.

Surveying hirsute figures wantonly reclining, Burnell thought, 'That one could have made Pope; he has the nose for it. And there's Messalina, with the cruel and creamy thighs, and that one could be Theodora, her blue rinse beginning to run a little in the heat. That little rat is Iago to the life . . . Blanche would be amused.' It was Blake, it was Doré, it was also super-heating. He thought of Blanche's nakedness, and was embarrassed to find an erection developing. He climbed from the sulphurous waters, wrapping himself with English discretion in a white towelling bathrobe.

On the way back to his room, Burnell encountered a lean bearded man clad only in a towel and hotel slippers. He was moving towards the baths, head forward in something between a slouch and a run, one eyebrow raised as if it were the proprioceptor by which he navigated. He and Burnell looked at each other. Burnell recognized the haggard lineaments, the eroded temples, the eyebrows. They belonged to a distant acquaintance from university days, Monty Broadwell-Smith.

Monty, eyebrow swivelling, locked on to Burnell at once.

'Roy, old chap! How jolly to see you.'

'Hello, Monty.' Burnell knotted the bathrobe more tightly. Monty had been sacked from his post at the University of East Anglia some while ago. There had been a small scandal. Finances had gone missing. Burnell, not caring about the matter, had forgotten the details. 'What are you doing in Budapest?'

'Little private matter, old chum.' He had a dated way of addressing people, smiling and nodding as he did so, as if agreeing with something off-stage. 'Helping out a bit at what they call the "Korszinhaz", the round theatre in the park. Scenery, you know. Well, scene-shifting. To tell the truth, only been here four days. Wandered round in a daze at first. Didn't know where I was . . .' He paused and then, seeing Burnell was about to speak, went on hastily, leaning a little nearer. 'Between you and me, old boy, I'm here consulting a very clever chap, sort of a . . . well . . . a *specialist*. You see, something rather strange has happened to me. To say the least. I'd like to tell you about it, as an old friend. You still with WACH, I presume? Perhaps you'd care to buy us a drink? Fellow countryman and all that kind of stuff, compatriot . . . Excuse the towel.'

They went up to Burnell's room. After opening the mini-bar, Burnell slipped into a shell-suit. He handed Monty a sweater to wear.

'Fits me to a T,' said his visitor. 'You wouldn't mind if I hung on to it, would you? Bit short of clothing, to tell the truth – here in Budapest, I mean. Some crook nicked all my luggage at the airport. You know what it's like . . . They're a dodgy lot.'

Burnell poured two generous Smirnoffs on the rocks. They raised their glasses to each other.

'That's better.' Monty Broadwell-Smith sighed. He licked his lips. 'I'll come straight to the point, old pal. "Music when soft voices die Vibrates in the memory . . ." So says the poet. I expect

15

you remember the quotation. But let's suppose there's no memory in which those soft voices can vibrate . . .'

Burnell stood by the window, saying nothing, contemplating Monty with distrust.

'I'm forty, or so I believe. Four days ago, I found myself in an unknown place. You'll never credit this. I found myself in an unknown place – not a clue how I got there. Absolutely at a loss, mind blank. Turned out that I was here, in Budapest. Budapest! Never been here before in my natural.'

He was already contradicting himself, Burnell thought. If he were lost, how had he known his luggage was stolen at the air-port?

'So now you're staying in the Gellert?' Burnell spoke challeng-ingly, determined not to be touched for Monty's air fare to England. Knowing something of the man's background, he felt no particular inclination to help.

Monty leaned back in his chair so as to look as much the invalid as possible. 'Terrible state poor old England's in. Read the papers. To what do you ascribe it, Roy?'

'Neglect of education, lack of statesmen. What's your problem?'

'Couldn't agree more. I suppose that's why someone like you has to scout round for a job abroad?'

'No doubt. What's your problem?'

'It's very serious. I know you're a sympathetic chap. I'm attend-ing the Antonescu Clinic. Mircea Antonescu is a foremost specialist, right at the cutting edge of psycho-technology. Well, he's Romanian. They're a clever race . . .' He gave Burnell a side-long glance under the eyebrow before hurrying on. 'I'm not staying at the Gellert. Couldn't afford it. Too expensive for some-one like me. I'm renting a cheap room in Pest – view of the gasworks, ha ha . . . You see, Roy, old pal, this is the bottom line: I've lost ten years of my memory. Just lost them. Wiped clean. Can't remember a thing.'

Burnell uttered a word of condolence. Monty looked slightly annoyed.

'Perhaps you don't understand. The last thing I can really ember is, I was thirty. Ten and a bit years have passed since then and I've absolutely no notion what I was doing all that time. No notion at all.'

'How terrible.' Burnell suspected a catch was coming, and was loath to commit himself.

'FOAM. That's Antonescu's term. FOAM – Free Of All Memory. He sees it as a kind of, well, liberty. There I beg to differ. You know what it feels like to lose your memory?'

Despite himself, Burnell was interested.

'It's like an ocean, old chum. A wide wide ocean with a small island here and there. No continents. The continents have disappeared, sunk without trace. I suppose I couldn't have a top-up of vodka, could I?' He held out his glass.

As he poured, Burnell admitted he had seen Monty once or twice during the previous ten years, before his sacking; perhaps he could help to fill the gaps in his memory. Monty Broadwell-Smith made moderately grateful noises. There was no one else he could turn to in Budapest.

When asked if his memory-loss was caused by a virus, Monty professed ignorance. 'No one knows – as yet at least. Could have been a car crash, causing amnesia. No bones broken if so. Lucky to be alive, I suppose you might say. But what's going to happen to me, I've no idea.'

'Your wife isn't with you?'

Monty slapped his forehead with his free hand. A look of amazement crossed his face. 'Oh my sainted aunt! Don't say I was married!'

He drank the vodka, he kept the sweater, he shook Burnell's hand. The next morning, Burnell went round to the Antonescu Clinic as he had promised. Monty wanted one of the specialists at the clinic to question Burnell, in order to construct a few points of identification. Monty suggested that this would help towards a restoration of his memory.

Burnell had agreed. He felt ashamed that he had so grudgingly given his old sweater to a friend in distress.

2

Murder in a Cathedral

'Nothing to worry about, old chum,' Monty Broadwell-Smith had said. 'They're masters of the healing art.'

The Antonescu Clinic was not as Burnell had imagined it. Cumbersome nineteenth-century apartment blocks, built of stone expressly quarried to grind the faces of the poor, lined a section of Fo Street. Secretive Hungarian lives were lived among heavy furniture in these blocks. They parted at one point to permit entrance to a small nameless square.

The buildings in the square huddled against each other, like teeth in a too-crowded mouth. Instead of dentistry, they had suffered the exhalations from lignite still burnt in the city. A nicotiney taint gave the façades an ancient aspect, as if they had been retrieved from a period long before the Dual Monarchy.

The exception to this antiquity was a leprous concrete structure, a contribution from the Communist era which announced itself as the Ministry of Light Industry. Next to it was wedged a small shop hoping to sell used computers. Above the shop, when Burnell ascended a narrow stair, he found a huddle of rooms partitioned out of a loft. A dated modernity had been achieved with track-lighting and interior glass. Tinkling Muzak proved the Age of the Foxtrot was not entirely dead.

Burnell sat in a windowless waiting-room, looking at a post-Rothko poster which displayed a large black cross with wavery edges on a dark grey background.

A man with a thin cigar in his mouth looked round the door,

sketched a salute in greeting and said, 'Antonescu not here. Business elsewhere. Meet Dr Maté. Maté Joszef, Joszef Maté.'

He then entered the cubicle and proffered a long wiry hand.

In jerky English, Dr Maté explained that he was Mircea Antonescu's second-in-command. They could get to work immediately. The best procedure would be for Burnell to ascend to a room where a series of questions concerning the forgotten years of Monty Broadwell-Smith could be put to him and the answers recorded electronically.

'You understand me, Dr Burnell? Here using most modern proprietary methods. Dealing extensively with brain-injury cases. Exclusive. Special to our clinic. To produce best results in Europe, satisfied customers . . .' Maté's thick furry voice was as chewed as his cigar. As he bustled Burnell from the room, his haste almost precluded the use of finite verbs.

Burnell was shown up a spiral stair to a room with a skylight and technical equipment. Here stood a uniformed nurse with grey hair and eyes. She came forward, shaking Burnell's hand in a friendly manner, requesting him in good German to remove his anorak.

As he did so, and handed the garment to the woman, he caught her expression. She was still smiling, but the smile had become fixed; he read something between pity and contempt in her cold eye.

At once, he felt premonitions of danger. They came on him like a stab of sorrow. He saw, seating himself as directed in an enveloping black chair, what clear-sighted men sometimes see. His life, until now modestly successful, was about to dip into a darkness beyond his control. In that moment there came to him a fear not for but of his own existence. He knew little about medical practice, but the operating table and anaesthetic apparatus were familiar enough, with black tubes of gas waiting like torpedoes for launch. On the other side of the crowded room, e-mnemonicvision equipment stood like glum secretary birds, their crenellated helmets ready to be swung down and fixed to the cranium. These birds were tethered to computerized controls, already humming, showing their pimples of red light.

Maté bustled about, muttering to the nurse, stubbing out his cigar in an overflowing ashtray.

'If you're busy, I will come back tomorrow,' Burnell said. The nurse pushed him gently into the depths of the chair, telling him soothingly to relax.

'Like wartime,' said Maté. 'Still too many difficulties. Too many problems. Is not good, *nicht gut*. Many problems unknown.' Switching on a VDU, he biffed it with the heel of his left hand.

'Large inflation rate problems, too high taxes . . . Too many gipsy in town. All time . . . The Germans of course . . . The Poles . . . Vietnamese minority . . . How we get all work done . . .'

He swung abruptly into another mode, suddenly looming over Burnell. 'Just some questions, Dr Burnell. You are nervous, no?'

As his long stained fingers chased themselves through Burnell's hair, he attempted reassurance. The clinic had developed a method of inserting memories into regions of the brains, to restore amnesiacs to health. The method was a development of e-mnemonicvision. First, those memories had to be recorded with full sensory data on microchip, and then projected into the brain. While he gave a somewhat technical explanation, the nurse gave Burnell an injection in his arm. He felt it as little more than a bee sting.

'But I don't know Monty Broadwell-Smith well . . .'

'Good, good, Dr Burnell. Now we must append electrodes to the head . . . Obtain full data in response to my questioning . . . No dancer will rival you, but every step you take will be as if you were treading on sharp nights . . .'

Burnell tried to struggle, as the words became confused with the heat.

He could still hear Dr Maté, but the man's words had become mixed with a colourful ball, which bounced erratically away into the distance. Burnell tried to get out the word 'discomfort', but it was too mountainous.

He was walking with Maté in a cathedral, huge and unlit. Their steps were ponderous, as if they waded up to their thighs in water. To confuse the issue further, Maté was smoking a cigar he referred to as 'The Trial'.

Offended, Burnell attempted a defence of Franz Kafka, distinguished Czech author of a novel of the same name.

'As a psychologist, you must understand that there are men like Kafka for whom existence is an entanglement, while for others – why, they sail through life like your torpedoes.'

'These differences are accounted for by minute biochemical changes in the brain. Neither state is more truthful than the other. For some people like the author to whom you refer, truth lies in mystery, for others in clarity. We have the science of medicine now, but prayer used to be the great clarifier. The old Christian churches used to serve as clarifying machines.'

'You mean they helped you to think straight in what you might call "this doleful jeste of life".'

'I've just got to get a millimetre further in.'

They continued to walk in a darkness the extent of which Burnell could hardly comprehend.

'Anyhow, you're good company,' Maté said, affectionately. 'Is there anything I can do for you in return?'

'More oxygen,' Burnell said. 'It's hot in this . . .' Uncertain between the words 'chair' and 'cathedral', he came out with 'chairch'. 'As a chairch architect, I've visited most of the cathedrals in Europe – Chartres, Burgos, Canterbury, Cologne, Saragossa, Milano, Ely, Zagreb, Gozo, Rheims . . .'

He listened to his voice going on and on. When it too had faded into the distance, he added, 'But this is the first time I've ever been in a hot and stuffy cathedral or chairch.'

'I'll put this match out. There are new ways. What we medicos call newral pathwise. Your friend Kafka – personally I'd have lobotomized him – he said that "all protective walls are smashed by the iron fist of technology". Whingeing, of course, the fucker was always whingeing. But it's the tiny little fist of nanotechnology which is smashing the walls between human and human. In the future, we shall all be able to share memories and understandings. Everything will be common property. Private thought will be a thing of the past.'

Burnell laughed. He had not realized that Maté was such good company. To continue the joke, he said, 'In that connection, Jesus Christ was pretty au fait with nanotechnology. You remember? That resurrection of the body stuff? Strictly Frankenstein stuff. Dead one day, up and running the next.'

Maté professed himself puzzled. They halted under a statue of Averroës. He had heard of Frankenstein. It was the other great Christian myth which puzzled him. This was almost the first time Burnell had ever encountered anyone walking in a cathedral who had never heard of Jesus Christ.

Since the man was interested, Burnell tried to deliver a brief résumé of the Saviour's life. The heat and darkness confused him. He could not recall how exactly Jesus was related to John the Baptist and the Virgin Mary. Nor could he remember whether Christ was his surname or Christian name.

'I see, so they hanged him in the end, did they?' said Maté. 'You'd be better not to remember such depressing things.'

It seemed sacrilegious to mention the name of Jesus in such a place.

The cathedral was constructed in the form of a T, the horizontal limb being much longer than the vertical, stretching away into the dark. The weight of masonry pressed down on Burnell's head and shoulders. Great columns like fossil vertebrae reared up on every side, humming with the extreme messages they carried. In defiance of the laws of physics, they writhed like the vital parts of the chordata, click–clack, clickety–clack, climbing lizard–tailed into the deeper darknesses of the vaulting overhead. He could feel them entwined up there.

Burnell and Maté had come to the junction of the great T. The vertical limb of this overpowering masterpiece sloped downwards. Burnell stopped to stare down the slope, though it was more sensed than seen. Instead of imagining that hordes of women were passing by in the gloom, he giggled at Maté's latest joke; the demon claimed not to have heard of the Virgin Mary either. He was now sitting on Burnell's shoulder in an uncomfortable posture.

'The devil's about to appear,' he said. 'Hold tight.'

'The devil? But you hadn't heard of the –'

'Forget reality, Roy. It's one of the universe's dead ends . . .'

'But would you happen to know if this is Sainsbury Cathedral?'

At the far distant end of the slope, the sallopian tube, a stage became wanly illuminated. In infinite time. The. Pause. Stage. Pause. Be. Pause. Came. Pause. Wan. Pause. Lee. Pause. Ill. Pause. You. Pause. Min. Pause. Ay. Pause. Ted. Trumpets. It was flushed with a dull diseased Doppler shift red.

Funebrial music had begun, mushroom-shaped bass predominating, like a Tibetan at his best prayers.

For a few eons, these low levels of consciousness were in keeping with the old red sandstone silences of the Duomo-like structure. They were shattered by the incursion of a resounding bass voice breaking into song.

That timbre! That mingled threat and exultation!

It was unmistakable even to a layman.

'The devil you know!' Burnell exclaimed.

'I'd better shove off now,' said Maté.

'Hey, what about those playing cods?' But the man had gone.

Until that moment, the devil had been represented only as a vocal outpouring roughly equivalent to Niagara. Now he appeared on the wine-dark stage.

The devil was ludicrously out of scale, far too large to be credible, thought Burnell – even if it was disrespectful to think the thought. In the confused dark – weren't those lost women somehow still pouring by? – it was hard to see the devil properly. He was an articulation, and approaching, black and gleaming, his outline as smooth as a dolphin's, right down to the hint of rubber. Nor was the stench of brimstone, as pungent as Maté's cigar, forgotten.

He advanced slowly up the ramp towards Burnell, raising the rafters with his voice as he came.

Striving to break from the networks of his terror, Burnell threw out his arms and peered along the wide lateral arm of the cathedral.

'Anyone there? Help! Help! Taxi!'

To the left, in the direction from which they had come, everything had been amputated by night, the black from which ignorance and imagination is fashioned. Towards the right, how-ever, along that other orbit, something was materializing. A stain of uninvented liquid. An ox-bow of the Styx. Light with its back turned to the electromagnetic spectrum.

'Help! My hour is almost come!'

The devil still singing was approaching still.

Atheist Burnell certainly was, in an age when no courage was denoted by the term. But too many years had been spent in his capacity as church custodian for WACH, investigating the mortal remains, the fossils, of the old faith of Christendom, for something of the old superstitions not to have rubbed off on him. He also had some belief in the Jungian notion of the way in which traits of human personality became dramatized as personages – as gods or demons, as Jekylls or Hydes. This singing devil, this bugaboo of bel canto, could well be an embodiment of the dark side of his own character. In which case, Burnell was the less likely to escape him.

Nor did he.

Burnell took a glutinous pace or two to his right. He began to begin to paddle towards that dull deceitful promise of escape. Violet was the vision reviving there. Fading into sight came a magnificent Palladian façade: a stream of perfection that scarcely could brook human visitation. Doric columns, porticoes, blind doorways. No man – however worthy of this unwedding cake – was there to answer Burnell's gurgle for help.

If the burrow to the left represented the squalors of the sub-conscious, to the right towered the refrigerated glory of the super-ego.

Still Burnell swam for it, convulsing his body into action.

'Mountebank!' he screamed as he went.

But the black monster was there, reaching out a hand, reaching him. Now Burnell's scream was even higher, even more sincere. The thing caught him by his hair. Snatched him up . . .

. . . and bit off his head.

Blanche Bretesche was drinking steadily. She was in her Madrid apartment with friends. It was late. The red wine of Andalucia was

24

slipping down her red gullet as she talked to her friend Teresa Cabaroccas. The two women were discussing love in an age without faith. They'd been in a Madrid back street, watching a performance by a once famous flamenco dancer, now a little past it and married to an innkeeper. The singing had been in progress after midnight.

'Oh, one more damned passionate wail!' – suddenly Blanche had screamed and stood up. She practically dragged Teresa from the crowded tavern.

'Why have these people some kind of licence to yell their sufferings?'

'The audience empathizes, Blanche. You can wallow in it for a bit, can't you? And with the suffering – that spirited arrogance! Oh, it's the arrogance I admire, not the suffering. The defiance of poverty, misery, betrayal, fate. The body says it, not just the voice . . .' Annoyed at being pulled from the entertainment she had not greatly enjoyed, Teresa was drinking as rapidly as Blanche.

'Why shouldn't *I* get up and wail my sufferings?' Blanche asked. 'My bloody discontents? Wail them from – oh, the square, the mountains, the TV studios . . .' She kicked her shoes to the far end of the room and put her bare feet up on the table.

'But your whole life – that speaks out for women, for fulfilment.'

'Fulfilment. I spit on the word. When was anyone really fulfilled? When did anyone ever have enough? Tell me that. Go on, tell me when anyone ever had *enough*. I mean there's not enough to have. The imagination's always greedy for more. Like that Madame Fotril when I was a girl – she lived next door to us and she ate her five-year-old daughter, cooked – with cabbage, of all vile things. Cabbage! I've never eaten cabbage since. The mere thought makes me sick. And then my parents took me with them to the funeral. Funeral! What could have been in the coffin, I kept asking myself. I was possibly twelve, just growing breasts like unripe apricots and hair between the legs, and all I could think was that maybe the priest had thrown the saucepan into the coffin with the bones.

'There was a woman – a fearsome woman – who wasn't afraid

25

of her imagination, who demanded enough, whatever it cost. Well, I feel like that. It's love – no, it's not really even love, it's wanting something I can't have, almost like a principle, the principle that we should never ever in this life be satisfied –'

'Oh, calm down, we've all got problems,' said Teresa. She got up and walked unsteadily to the balcony, trying to cool her cheek against a stone pillar. 'Who is this guy you were talking about, anyway? A Hungarian?'

'Not a Hungarian,' said Blanche. She looked down into her glass, afraid to say 'English' in case her Spanish friend laughed. She didn't wish to spoil the drama of the moment.

A pompous-looking man had accompanied them to the performance. He sat in a cane lounger with a lager on the table by his side, giving every appearance of lassitude. When he could be sure of being heard, he said, in his carefully enunciated tone, 'What we're talking about here in a secular age is a hunger for God. God or the Breast. You can have enough sex, Blanche, believe it or believe it not. You can never have enough of God. God's the giant breast in the sky.'

Only Teresa felt qualified to comment on these remarks. From her vantage point on the balcony, overlooking the square, she said, 'It's a divine dissatisfaction.'

The man stretched his legs. 'I wouldn't put it like that, dear. More gross, quite honestly, than divine. Do you realize how much of every day is taken up with food, with the belly? The pursuit of food, the eating of food, the recovering from its after-effects? The stomach's as much a tyrant as the genitals.'

'Not in my case,' said Teresa, who was dieting.

Taking a rein on herself, Blanche said in a low desperate voice, 'I was a friend of his wife's. I loved him then . . . Was it just a case of "can't have"? He looks so lovely. And he thinks I look lovely. And he's good and pleasant to be with in bed. Isn't pleasant better than good? The number of men I know who're good in bed and nothing else. Good – and shits. Roy . . . Roy's a decent man, and when I saw him again –'

'Did that woman really eat her daughter or are you just tipsy and making it all up?'

'If only he wasn't so caught up with the past . . .' Blanche half rose. She set her glass down unsteadily on the marble top of the table.

'Christ!' she said. She sat down again, suddenly sober, suddenly bereft of words. Somewhere, a long way away, an evil thing had befallen her lover.

3
Bishops Linctus

You don't find it odd to discover gradually that you're sort of running. Or more a jog-trot. You can see the legs going, and they're yours. And the scrubby grass below your shoes, resilient, springing up again when you've passed. That's not odd. But something's odd.

Imagine yourself in an art cinema. The movie begins without titles or proem. The opening shot is of some character walking or jogging across a featureless landscape. Photography: grainy, bleached. Camera: perhaps hand-held in an old-fashioned twentieth-century way.

The sequence immediately holds your interest, although there's little enough to see. Perhaps some kind of tribal memory comes back, if anyone believes in tribal memory – or anything else – any more. Our ancestors were great walkers, right back to the Ice Age and beyond. If you can walk along a glacier with bare feet, you deserve to succeed.

Now imagine you're not in a comfortable seat watching the movie. You are that jogging character. Only you're not in a movie. You're real, or what we label real for convenience, according to our limited sensory equipment. (Anyone who walks on a glacier with bare feet needs his head looking at . . .)

Head . . . Yes, that's still there . . .

You're not surprised even at that.

Your life appears to have begun anew, and you're progressing across what will turn out to be . . . a rather unappetizing stretch of England . . . Salisbury Plain. Salisbury Plain is a) flat, b) plain,

c) cold, and d) preparing to receive sweeping gusts of rain. You register these facts one by one.

But walking is no trouble. It's everything else that's trouble.

Like how you got where you are. Like what happened. Like who you are. Even minor details like – where do you think you're going?

Night is closing in. It comes in early, rising out of the ground to meet the lowering cloud.

So what do you do? You go on walking.

There's a landmark distantly to your right. Half-concealed by a fold in the ground stands a broken circle of stone monoliths. You imagine it's the ruin of some bizarre Stone Age cathedral which was taken out in the war against the Neanderthals. It stands cobalt and unintelligible against the outlines of the over-praised English countryside.

Cathedrals . . . Something stirs in the mind.

Now wait . . . but you continue, limping as you walk, while darkness filters into the saucer of land like a neap tide. You continue, more slowly now, whispering words to yourself under your breath. You feel gradually more in command of yourself. As if in confirmation, a line appears along the featureless wastes ahead. When you reach it, you find a fence, with a road on the far side of it. Darkness now gathers about you like an illness.

When you have climbed the fence, you flounder through a ditch, to stand by the roadside. Almost no traffic passes along the road. You wait.

You? You?

Me. I.

The dissociation of personality closes. A blurry zoom lens shrinks back into focus. He realizes he is one Roy Burnell.

Or used to be. Something is missing.

With these slow realizations comes the first angry drop of rain. He realizes that he needs shelter before anything.

He knows he has a father, but cannot remember his name, or where he lives. As he stands there shivering, he recalls the loss of his mother. And was there someone else?

He tries to thumb a lift from cars as they approach from either direction. Their headlights sweep over him. Past they swish in the increasing downpour, never pausing.

Bastards.

He remembers that word.

A long while later, in hospital, Burnell is to remember the dream of the devil who bit his head off. It really happened. Someone stole part of his memory.

At last, when the rain is dwindling, a car stops. A woman is driving. A man sits beside her in the passenger seat. It is an old car. She puts a big blunt face out of the window and asks him where he wants to go. Burnell says anywhere. They laugh and say that is where they are going. He climbs into the back of the car.

All he can see is that the woman is heavy, middle-aged, and has a head of frizzy hair. The man might be her father. He is old, sharp-nosed, stoop-shouldered, wearing a cap. As the car roars on its way, the man turns stiffly and asks Burnell a few questions in a friendly way.

Burnell wishes to be silent. He is cold and frightened, being reduced to near anonymity. He cannot frame any answers. He remembers he can't remember a car crash.

The couple fear he is a loony, and kick him out in the nearest village. He is inclined to agree with their judgement. Why can't he remember how he came to be on Salisbury Plain?

The rain has stopped. He stands where they dropped him, outside a row of cottages showing no signs of life. Prodding himself into action – he is tired now – he walks along the road, out of the village. It is pitch-dark. A wood fringes the road. The wood drips. He thinks he hears mysterious footsteps. He turns round and goes back to the village.

A sign tells him he is in Bishops Linctus. A few widely spaced lights burn here and there. No one is about. He passes a Shell filling station, a builder's yard, an EMV and video shop. Still it might be the Middle Ages.

He reaches a pub called the Gun Dog. Its sign depicts a ferocious hound showing its teeth at a partridge. Burnell has no money in his pocket, and consequently is afraid to enter the pub.

There are countries whose names he does not for the moment recall where one might enter a hostelry when down on one's luck, and be treated in a considerate manner; he is not confident this would happen in England.

He stands indecisively in the middle of the road.

Unexpectedly, someone is standing close by. Burnell starts, and gives an exclamation of surprise. The silent newcomer is a young man in leather gear and high boots, with a shotgun of some kind tucked under his arm. Hearing Burnell exclaim, he backs away. He steps briskly past Burnell, to walk away along the road.

After going no more than ten paces, he halts. Burnell stands where he is. The young man comes back, not too close, to inspect Burnell.

'You OK, mate?'

By the glow from the pub, Burnell sees a strange round head, on which sits a thin young face, twisted into seriousness, with fair eyebrows and stubble on the jaw. Also a bad case of acne.

'Not too good. I may have been in a car crash.'

The young man is guarded, his manner hardly friendly. He characterizes Burnell's claim to have lost his memory as 'all balls'. Nevertheless, after a few questions, he opines that his old ma will help.

With that, he walks on, adopting a kind of swagger, looking back once to see that Burnell is following.

Burnell follows. Little option but to follow. Head hanging, shoulders slumped. No idea what's going on.

Bishops Linctus street lighting stops where the road begins to curve upwards. Somewhere beyond the lighting stands a line of council houses, back from the road, with cars and lorries parked in front of them. The young man heads for the nearest house, where a light burns in the uncurtained front room.

They push in through a recalcitrant back door, into a passage obstructed by a mountain bike. A sound of firing fills the house. The TV is on in the front room, from which emerges a woman shrieking, 'Larry, Larry, you back?'

'What's it look like?' he replies.

In close-up – she bringing a plump face close to Burnell's – Larry's mother is a well-cushioned little person in her early fifties, her lower quarters stuffed into jeans. The shriek was a protective device; the voice sinks back to a lower key when her son brushes past her and switches off the TV programme.

The woman immediately takes charge of Burnell, giving him the kitchen towel to dry himself on, and a pair of worker's cords and shirt to wear. While he removes his wet clothes and dries himself as in a trance, she prepares him a cup of instant coffee, chattering all the while. As he drinks the coffee, she prepares him a slice of white bread, buttered and spread with thick honey. He eats it with gratitude, and is so choked with emotion he can only squeeze her hand.

'Don't worry, love. We know all about the bloody police in this house. Knock you about, did they?'

The picture keeps going out of focus.

Perhaps he has passed out from fatigue. Rousing, he finds he is sitting on the grubby kitchen floor. He looks up at a poster advertising a can of something called '*Vectan Poudres de Tir*, Highly Flammable'. He looks down at ten red-painted toenails protruding from gold sandals. A hand comes within his line of sight. A voice says, 'Oops, dear, you OK? It's the drink, is it? Terrible stuff. I don't know what God was thinking of.'

'Leave him alone, Ma!' roars Larry from the passage.

As he is helped up, Burnell thinks he hears a bird singing.

'Take no notice,' says Ma, almost whispering. 'It's just his manner. He's a very nice quiet boy really.'

Shock shot. Larry appears suddenly into the kitchen doorway, in a gunman's crouch, both hands together in a shootist position, clasping an imaginary gun. 'Bang, bang. Got you both.'

Ma laughs, says to Burnell, 'He's daft.' Burnell wonders if events are registering on him, or whether he might still be running across an endless plain. A bird twitters in his head.

He steadies himself against the sink, which is crammed with the remains of Indian take-aways. He cannot speak.

Larry unlocks the door of the room at the rear of the house. A large notice on the door, painted in red paint, says 'My Room.

Keep Out. DANGER.' On it is a poster of Marilyn Monroe with a pencilled-in moustache and teeth blackened, and a large photograph of howitzers firing in World War I.

'You need a good night's sleep, that's what you need,' Ma tells him, looking concerned. She gives him a toffee. As Burnell chews the toffee, Larry sticks his head round the door of His Room and calls Burnell in. He locks the door from the inside.

'Sleep here. It's OK. Don't listen to her. She's nuts.'

Burnell says nothing, chewing on the toffee. The sporting gun previously tucked under Larry's arm keeps company with a large six-shooter on a box by the window. However, when Larry pulls a rug and cushion off his bed, throwing them on the floor, a semi-automatic rifle is revealed, snuggled among the blankets.

A slow panning shot reveals the narrow room to be full of magazines about guns. They are piled up in corners and spill out of a half-closed cupboard. They are stacked under the bed among cartridge boxes. Used targets are wedged behind a strip of mirror: black outlines of men in bowler hats, their hearts shot out, macabre Magrittes.

'Are you a gamekeeper?' Jaws automatically munching as he forms the question.

'Work on Thorne's farm. Sometimes I'm a brickie, aren't I? Out of work. You can doss down there, right?'

Doubtfully, Burnell settles on the floor. He knows nothing and feels miserable. He cannot remember if he met Larry before. He hopes that if so they are not related. Cousins. Anything.

Something hard he recognizes as the muzzle of a gun is thrust into his ear. He laughs nervously. Looks up.

'Any monkey business in the night and you get it, right?' Larry withdraws the weapon and shows the pistol to his guest, innocent in his grimy hand. 'Look at this little beauty. You know what this is?'

Larry kneels on the edge of his bed, glaring down at Burnell, who makes a feeble reply. Larry is not a great listener. He goes on without pausing for answers. 'It's a sweet little performer. I bet you never saw one like it. It's a Makarov PSM. A Makarov PSM, illegal in this country, a KGB pistol, a Makarov PSM.' He pronounces the name like a lamb voicing its mother tongue. He removes the magazine from the gun to demonstrate eight rounds of a gleaming bottle-neck appearance. He makes a curious noise in the back of his throat. 'See them rounds? Under an inch long. Know what they can do? Bust through body armour, OK? Good as .44 Magnum bullets. Blow a man's guts out through his arse. Old KGB knew what it was doing. No kidding.'

Suddenly the pistol is gone from his hand. 'Concealment weapon, see. That's why it's so little. KGB knew what it was about, right?'

Smiling weakly, Burnell says, 'I have to sleep now, Larry.' The toffee has gone.

A second later he is staring down the barrel of Larry's semi-automatic, which Larry, kneeling up, cradles in a professional way under his right arm. It is a cold steely piece of goods he is aiming.

'You try anything funny in the night, you get a dose of this. Get it?' His little face withers. 'This is my big baby.'

Reaction shot of Burnell, sitting up, alarmed. 'No, no, I just want to sleep.'

Larry asks him challengingly if he's a bloody lunatic, and Burnell says he thinks he must have banged his head.

Loud banging on the door. Larry swings the semi-automatic in that direction. Ma yells from the passage, 'Go to sleep. You got to go to Swindon tomorrer.' He makes shooting noises in his throat, raking her with imaginary gunfire before turning back to Burnell.

'You try anything funny, you get a dose of this, right?' Relenting slightly, he explains that this impressive weapon, his big baby, is an American .50 calibre Barrett M90, weighing only twenty-two pounds. He assures Burnell he could hold off an army with it.

'I hope you aren't expecting an army.'

'Muslims, Blacks, Police – let 'em all come. See what they get.' There is a tense silence. Burnell feels unwell.

'What Muslims do you mean?'

'My dad comes back here, he's going to be in trouble.' As he settles down, Larry says with a sob, 'That bastard.' He cradles the Barrett in his arms. He reaches out and switches off the light.

Sitting huddled nervously on the floor, Burnell hears an intermittent sob. Or perhaps Larry is just sniffing.

Longing to go to sleep but afraid to lie down, Burnell says in a small voice that he appreciates Larry's kindness.

He half expects to have the muzzle of the Barrett back in his ear. Larry merely says, 'I like helping people, Roy.' Gentle as a dove.

Burnell is comforted. He murmurs those decent words to himself like a mantra; 'I like helping people . . .'

He falls back in a troubled cataleptic sleep. Rats gnaw in the depths of the cathedral. He wakes to find it is the sound of Larry scratching his acned cheeks in his sleep. So the movie ends. But Burnell is for real and his troubles are becoming more real as dawn sneaks in to dozy Bishops Linctus.

Morning was hardly a spectacular affair: old and grey and broken, like an overworked carthorse out to grass, to find its way by accident into the back yards of the council houses.

Larry had left the room when Burnell emerged from the entanglements of his rug. What roused him from limbo was the sound of Ma shouting at her son. Encouragement and admonition, carrot and stick. He sat up, aching all over. His predicament rushed back and took him by the throat. But he was undeniably feeling a little better.

Leaning back against a distempered wall, he fished about in his brain for an identity.

Larry entered the room, carrying a mug with no handle. 'Thought you'd like some char, mate, OK?'

The unrivalled powers of hot sweet tea served to clear Burnell's head. He rose and sat on the side of the bed. From there, he stood up and went into the kitchen, where he sluiced his face under the cold tap. The debris of the take-away had gone. Instead, pairs of socks were soaking sludgily in the sink. He no longer felt so dissociated from himself, and smiled at Ma as he wiped his face on a grimy towel.

'You're a bit more perky this morning, I see,' Ma said. 'The washing machine's gone on the blink again. Of course he's not much use round the house. The black bloke next door will fix it for me. Have you said hello to Kevin?'

A yellow canary sat in a cage on top of the fridge. It cocked its head on one side, looking at Burnell while trying out a few notes.

Ma went over to the cage. She stuck a finger through the bars. The canary lifted one wing in a defensive gesture. 'There's a good boy. He likes you, don't you, Kev? I think it's a girl actually. One of the family, aren't you, love? Keeps me company, any rate. Say hello to Kevin, Roy. I wash her under the hot tap every Saturday morning, don't I, Kev? It likes that – sings her little heart out, bless her. You like a nice wash under the tap, don't you? It's one of the family, aren't you? I'll find her a bit of groundsel in a while. Who's a good boy then?'

While this monologue was in progress, Burnell was keeping an eye on Larry. Larry was dressed in a padded military jacket without sleeves. He had wedged the front door open and was marching back and forth between his room and an old Land Rover standing in front of the house, loading boxes of ammunition into the back of the vehicle.

Seeing Burnell's glance, Ma said, 'He's got to go into Swindon. There's a job prospect. You better stay here with me – I don't like the way he drives. Much too fast on them country roads. You and me'll go down and see Dr Ramakrishna in the village. She's – you know, what I call discreet. She was trained in London, she was telling me. She'll help you. She told me once she liked helping lame dogs over stiles, she said.'

'That's me.' He spoke vaguely. Something about Larry's movements disturbed him. Larry had left the house by the front door, which remained open. He put up the tailgate of the Land Rover, locking it into place. His movements were performed in slow motion. Once he looked back into the house with abstracted gaze, as if he were inwardly composing a poem. Burnell raised a hand in greeting. He received no response.

Walking ponderously, head down, Larry went round to the cab of the Land Rover and climbed in. He sat in the driver's seat. Nothing happened.

More curious than alarmed, Burnell, still nursing his tea mug, went forward into the small front room, from the window of which he had a clear view.

He could see the back of Larry's head. It did not stir. It resembled a cannonball which had succumbed to a parasitic yellow grass. Larry was making no attempt to start his vehicle. He merely sat in the driver's seat. Burnell was about to turn away when a movement up the road caught his eye.

The highway leading from this side of the village was an anonymous semi-rural stretch of road. A field opposite the houses awaited building permission. The curve of the road wound up a slight incline. The road surface remained damp from overnight mists. Behind and beyond the houses lay open agricultural land, at present looking pale and inert. The houses followed the curve of the road. Most of the vehicles which Burnell remembered to have been parked there last night were gone about their owners' business, leaving the houses and front doors in plain view.

From the door of the furthest council house, two hundred yards distant, a man had emerged. He came out, went inside again, to re-emerge pulling a push-chair. He steered this object through the front gate and started down the slight hill towards the village.

In the push-chair sat a small child dressed in a blue overall. Burnell saw its arms waving, possibly in excitement. Perhaps it was two years old. The man could have been the child's grandfather. He had grey hair and wore an old nondescript raincoat. It looked as if he was talking to the child. Possibly he was going to the village to shop. Possibly, thought Burnell, idly, his daughter, the child's mother, was unwell.

Larry stirred in the driving-seat as the push-chair drew nearer. His window wound slowly down. A gun barrel protruded, pointing up the road. Burnell could see enough of the chevron-style muzzle brake to recognize the Barrett semi-automatic which Larry had shown him the previous evening. He took a deep breath to call out. As he did so, a shot sounded.

The man in the nondescript raincoat sank down on his knees in the road, still holding on to the handle of the push-chair.

Three more shots rang out. The push-chair blew apart. The

man's head and shoulders were covered in shreds of baby as he fell over on his side, to roll against the grass verge.

Larry's Ma had seen at least something of this, or had heard the shots. She was drying a plate. This she dropped as she ran from the kitchen into the front hall.

'No, no, Larry. Stop that at once, you idiot! What do you think you're doing? Come in immediately.'

After firing the shots, Larry kicked open the Land Rover's door and planted his boots on the gravel with a crunch, left then right. He was moving slowly with a sleepwalker's lethargy. He carried his semi-automatic at the port, its muzzle at his left shoulder. As he turned to face the house, he brought the weapon expertly to his hip and fired a rapid burst.

His mother was blown from the porch back into the passage. Still moving, he fired more shots into the house. The back door splintered.

Burnell was also in motion, rushing from the front room as soon as the firing stopped. To his relief, he saw that Larry in his abstraction had left the key in the lock of his door. He turned the key and rushed into the room. Desperate as he was, he saw a blue metal gun barrel protruding from under a cushion on the bed. He flung himself under the bed, taking the Makarov with him. Fighting to thrust the bundles of magazines and cartridge boxes out of his way, he turned about so that he was concealed, facing the door. He was convinced that Larry was about to finish him off too.

He could hear Larry in the front hall, and the business-like click of a fresh magazine locking into place on his weapon.

Steadying the pistol with both hands, Burnell levelled it at the door.

'You come in here, I'll blow your guts out through your arse,' he muttered.

4

FOAM

In Ward One on the third floor of Swindon Hospital lay Roy Burnell. Of the four beds in the ward, only his was occupied. He felt no great inclination to get up.

Nevertheless, even the horizontal position could not stem a swirl of events around him. There were, first and foremost, the visits from the police, and in particular from an Inspector Chan, an Asian member of the Wiltshire anti-terrorist squad.

The police had discovered Burnell in a house with a dead woman. He had been armed, and surrounded by boxes of bullets and much literature of an incendiary nature, as the official phrase went. He had been disarmed, handcuffed, and taken none too gently to the police station in Swindon. There he had been interrogated for some hours. It was then that Inspector Chan had been called in. Burnell's plea that he had somehow lost his memory had been taken as additional reason to suspect his motives.

Only slowly had Burnell, dazed by events, realized that the police had initially been frightened men. The presence of a psychotic killer in Bishops Linctus had been alarming enough; the possibility that there might be two of them, the second armed with an illegal KGB murder weapon, had driven them mad.

Forensic evidence supported Burnell's statement. The bullets which had killed the dead woman, Mrs Beryl Foot, were fired from the Barrett . 50 calibre semi-automatic now in their possession. Not only did the Makarov PSM use 5.45mm rounds, but examination showed it had not been fired recently.

Released and installed in hospital, suffering from exposure,

Burnell discovered that what was now known as the Bishops Linctus Massacre had attracted world-wide attention. The specialist in charge of his ward, a friendly Dr Rosemary Kepepwe, brought him newspapers, where he was able to see what had happened that terrible morning

After shooting the old man, Stanley Burrows, 58, and his stepgrandson, Charles Dilwara, 1½, and his own mother in rapid succession, Lawrence 'Mad Dog' Foot had walked armed into the village. There he shot dead the first three people he saw outside the Spar supermarket. Several other people had been wounded and a plate-glass window valued at £2,000 had been broken. 'BISHOPS BLOODBATH' screamed the tabloids.

Mrs Renée Ash, blonde, 22, had witnessed the events from the window of her hairdressing establishment. She had her photograph in the paper, sitting coyly on a low wall, legs crossed. 'It was awful,' she said. 'There was blood all over the pavement. And on a Saturday morning, too.'

The shooting aroused more excitement than the war in the Crimea, in which British troops, the Cheshires, were involved. Everyone expected trouble in the Crimea, but in a quiet little spot like Bishops Linctus, in the peaceful British countryside . . . The Prime Minister himself was driven down to the scene of the crime to shake a few hands.

As for Larry 'Mad Dog' Foot – as his friends reportedly called him – armed police from Bishops Magnum and Salisbury had shot him down behind the Shell garage. Some papers carried photographs of his body covered by a blanket being taken away on a stretcher. Burnell thought of Larry saying gently, 'I like helping people'. Perhaps his help had been refused once too often.

Burnell's melancholy was deepened by a sense of having fallen off a wall. He felt no power on earth could put him together again. Pieces of the past floated in his mind like fish in a bowl, without destination.

He was sedated and slept for long periods. At one point he woke to find a doctor with a maternal bust encased in a white apron at his bedside. This was the comforting Dr Rosemary Kepepwe. She sat by his side and talked soothingly.

'I've been in a coma, haven't I?'

'We think you have fallen victim to memory-thieves. It's one of the mushroom industries of the modern world . . . Anything's stealable nowadays,' she said, smiling down at him. 'Don't worry. Did you hear of e-mnemonicvision?'

'Was there some kind of crash?'

'Don't worry. We'll do a few tests on you and soon you will feel better.'

He trailed about the hospital from room to room, comparing diagrams, playing with bricks, having blood samples and brain scans taken, helpless in expert hands. A neurosurgeon jokingly offered to lend him a copy of Proust's *Remembrance of Things Past*.

Dr Kepepwe came back to see him shortly after an orderly had delivered Burnell's tea. 'Now, don't worry about anything. The Neurology Department is piecing together a map of your brain with indications of lesions there. They know that a section of your memory has been stolen from you.'

He grappled feebly with the idea. Visions of scalpels and silver handsaws rose to his mind.

The doctor said firmly, 'Memory has no one location in the brain. It's not a department. The thieves in your case have covered the hippocampus and regions of the cortex. We'll know more precisely soon. It's a delicate operation.'

He groaned. 'You mean they've cut me up, destroyed my brain?'

She wagged a finger, smiling. 'It's an electronic method, well established these last five years. I don't want to hear too many complaints from you, sir! You're lucky that your period of memory was evidently stolen by an expert, not just some cowboy. First look at your brain suggests that you are pretty OK otherwise. You might easily be in PVS.'

For some reason he could not make out, he longed to hold her hand. Gazing up at her, he said, 'I'd be less inclined to complain if I knew what PVS was.'

'When they started doing e-mnemonicvision operations on the human brain, accidents occurred. That's where EMV has got its bad name, why it's still limited. Some volunteers became cases

41

of PVS – which stands for Persistent Vegetative State. PVS. Of course you are experiencing a terrible loss, but you seem otherwise fully functional. You talk OK, for instance.'

'Hope so,' he muttered.

'What about sexual functions, then? Do you still have erections?'

'Hadn't you better research that area yourself, Doctor?'

When she laughed, most of her body shook. 'You're a naughty boy, that I can see. We shall return to that subject later. Drink your tea and don't worry about things.'

'Do you want a raspberry jam sandwich, Doctor? I've lost my appetite as well as my memory. Will my memory return? You're sure I wasn't in an accident – a car crash or something?'

She shook her head. 'Everything's as I tell you. We'll soon find out more about you. That will help. You're going to counselling every morning, starting tomorrow, and that will help too. We can find out how many years of memory you've lost.'

'Years? Shit!' He said he could recall that there was an opera he had seen in which a man had his reflection stolen. This was worse, like a kind of evil magic.

'You see, you remember some things, like the opera. Now don't worry. Rest today. You're still in shock. Eat up that sandwich.'

He obliged the doctor by taking a bite before asking her what EMV was.

'You don't even recall that? It's a scourge of modern life, like video shockers only a few years back. You know that tumours can be removed from the brain without old-fashioned surgery, and now it's possible to remove selected memories. Those memories can be stored electronically and so reproduced any number of times.

'Oh, it's a huge industry.' While he munched at the limp sandwich, she explained how EMV was a sport for amateurs, just as television had been invaded by amateur videos. Anyone with a striking memory or experience could sell it to the EMV companies, 'the way poor people used to sell a kidney for a bit of money'. Of course they would lose that memory for ever but, if it was valuable to them, it could be reinserted once it was recorded.

'So I could get my memory back if I could find the thieves?'

'You can't catch these people.' She went on to say that for EMV-viewers, the memories projected into their heads were as transient as dreams although, projected at greater power, they could become as permanent and 'real' as genuine memories. A vogue for the permanent insertion of seemingly life-enhancing memory implants was yielding up a new generation of mental cases whose assumed memories did not fit their own personality patterns.

Burnell was sunk in introspection. His gaze fixed itself on a malevolent square of cherry fruit cake lying on the white plate before him. He became convinced that he could read its mind: and somewhere in the warped mental processes of the fruit was an ambition to eat him, rather than vice versa. Only with an effort did he manage to look away and stare into the friendly black face by the bedside.

'I can't remember where I was before I found myself running on Salisbury Plain.'

This time, she put her hand reassuringly over his. 'We shall find out all about you. Don't worry. Tomorrow, our psychotherapist, Rebecca Rosebottom, will see you. And she is an absolute guru.'

Smiling, she rose to go.

'Would you take this piece of fruit cake away with you?' he bleated.

Searching about in his head proved to be a strange process. He could recall his early life easily. The death of his mother was vivid. It was possible to trace the chain of events until he was in his mid-twenties, when he had grown a small moustache to impress a girlfriend. That would mean the memory was probably ten years old. After that, nothing.

The last thing he could remember clearly was standing in a building in a foreign city waiting for a lift. He was in the foyer of an ornate hotel, all white and gilt and potted cheese plants. The lift cage descended from an upper floor. He walked into it and pressed a button to go up. After that – nothing. The dreaded white-out, the feared abyss. The thieves had got the rest.

The following morning, Dr Kepepwe entered Ward One with a broad smile on her face and her hands behind her broad back.

Burnell was propped up in bed, having just finished breakfast. She came and contemplated him for a moment before speaking.

'You are Dr Roy Edward Burnell, AIBA. Those are letters after your name. You have been a university lecturer. You are a specialist in the architecture of religious structures such as cathedrals. You are currently an Area Supervisor for the World Antiquities and Cultural Heritage organization in Frankfurt in Germany. You have responsibility for threatened buildings of architectural and religious merit over a wide area.

'And how do I know all this? Because you have also published a learned book, in which you contrast human aspirations with human-designed structures. The book is called *Architrave and Archetype* and –' she brought her hands from behind her – 'here's a copy, just tracked down!'

He took the book from her. It carried his photograph on the inner flap of the dust-jacket. He stared at it as if the title were written in letters of fire. In the photograph he had no moustache, praise be.

'We're getting somewhere,' Dr Kepepwe said proudly. 'We hope to contact your wife next.'

He smote his forehead. 'My God, don't say I'm married.'

She laughed. 'Well, you certainly were. Current marital status unknown.'

He closed his eyes, trying to think. No memory came through, only the tears under the eyelids. Whoever his wife might be, she constituted a vital part of the vault the memory-thieves had robbed. It was lonely, knowing nothing about her. Leafing through the copy of the book Dr Kepepwe had brought, he found her name. There it stood, alone on the printed page, the dedication page:

For

STEPHANIE

'Nothing is superlative that has its like'

Michel de Montaigne

Tears came again. He had a wife. Stephanie Burnell. The line from Montaigne, if it was more than mere courtesy, suggested love and admiration. How was it he was unable, with his memory of her gone, to feel no love and admiration?

'We can't have you moping,' said Dr Kepepwe, bustling in, to find him staring into space. 'Are you well enough for a game of tennis? There's a good indoor court on the top floor. I'm a demon. I'll play you when I'm off duty at five-thirty.'

To kill the afternoon, he wandered about the great white memorial to human sickness. The few staff he encountered were Asiatics. He found his way into what the hospital called its library, where ping pong was played. The room was deserted; but the whole hospital was strangely deserted, as if the world's sick had miraculously healed themselves. The library shelves, like the shelves of a derelict pantry, held nothing by way of sustenance. Almost no non-fiction, books on dieting excluded, no travel worth a second look. Fiction of the poorest quality, all formula stuff – romances chiefly, thrillers, also fantasy: *The Dragon at Rainbow Bridge* and similar titles, featuring pictures of brave men, women, and gnomes in funny armour.

In a neglected corner where ping pong balls could not reach lay a clutch of Penguin Classics. Zola, Carpentier, Balzac, Ibsen, Dostoevsky. He remembered the names. Also the *Essays* of Montaigne.

Burnell picked up the volume almost with a sense of destiny, having so recently come across Montaigne's name in his own book. Carrying it over to a bench, he read undisturbed while the best part of an hour stole away, drowsy and silent. He believed he had heard the cadences of Montaigne's prose before. Nostalgia rose in him, to think he might once have read it in the company of the unknown Stephanie. They must have enjoyed the way the sixteenth-century Frenchman spoke directly to his reader:

I admire the assurance and confidence that everyone has in himself, while there is hardly anything that I am sure of knowing, or that I dare answer to myself that I can do. I never have my means marshalled and at my service, and am aware of them only after the event . . . For in my studies, the subject of which is man, I find an extreme variety of opinions, an intricate labyrinth of difficulties, one on top of another, and a very great uncertainty and diversity in the school of wisdom itself . . .

Perhaps that is how I was, Burnell thought. Uncertain. Perhaps it was my nature – and not despicable in Montaigne's eyes. In which case, my dilemma at present is but a special instance of a more general one. He turned the word 'certain' over in his mind, as if it were a curious stone found on a seashore. The great conquerors of history had all been certain. Alexander, Genghis Khan, Napoleon, Shi Huang Di, the First Emperor of China. He wasn't sure but he thought he had never been built in that mould. His father's tyranny had been enough.

One sign of his lack of the tyrannical gene was that he could not beat Dr Kepepwe at tennis.

After they had played in the echoing court, they drank lemonade together in a deserted canteen. She said she must get along home, but seemed in no hurry to go. On the contrary, she tried to discover how much he knew of recent history, exclaiming with a mixture of delight and dismay when he did not know who was Britain's Prime Minister, or what had happened recently to the royal family.

Her view of England was that it had now become like Ireland, a country with so much unemployment and such a lack of manufacturing base that many people were forced to go abroad for a living. Blacks and Asiatics, in consequence, claimed a greater role in running the country; it was they, by and large, who were fighting a Muslim insurrection in the Midlands. Dr Kepepwe portrayed the Midlands as an alien land; she was, she explained, a Southerner.

When she asked Burnell what he could remember, he told her of a boyhood trekking holiday in Iceland on which his father had taken him and his brother. It remained as a landmark in misery and humiliation.

She asked him how he enjoyed working in Germany. She had

a fear of Germany. Did he not think continually of Hitler's Final Solution and the terrible crime of murdering six million Jews, gipsies, blacks, and other harmless people?

'I used to think about it, I suppose,' Burnell told her. 'But your question is part of a wider question. Watch the TV news. Terrible slaughter is taking place today in the Crimea, the Caucasus, Bosnia, and elsewhere. The wider question is why humanity is so appallingly cruel – man against man, man against woman, individually and en masse. If there were a God, he would have thrown up his hands in despair by now.'

'No, no,' said Dr Kepepwe, shaking her head and much of her body. 'God never gives up.'

As she was leaving, the doctor said, 'I'm alone at present while my husband David is away. How I miss him.' She represented him as the best husband a woman could have, saying proudly that he had won the Isle of Wight Sea-Fishing Trophy two years in succession. He was a brain surgeon and everyone respected him.

David Kepepwe had volunteered to serve under General Stalinbrass in Russia, where surgeons and doctors were badly needed; he was in the Crimea at present. She hoped he was still alive.

'Well, maybe I've talked too much to my prize patient. Tell me honestly how you feel in yourself.'

Without thinking, he said, 'An ocean, Doctor. A wide ocean with only a small island here and there. No continents. The continents have sunk into the depths . . .'

That quizzical regard again. 'FOAM, that's what they call it. "Free Of All Memory". You were lucky the villains didn't steal everything. And there are advantages. I have bad things I'd like to forget. Think of the foam on that private ocean of yours. Remember, "oceanic" has good connotations, so don't worry. I'll see you in the morning.'

In her office, Dr Kepepwe kept a well-behaved dog which waited patiently for her throughout her spells of duty. It was at least in part a long-haired terrier. Burnell learnt later its name was Barker. He saw the doctor collect Barker as she picked up her things to go home. The dog needed no lead. It was a dignified little animal, and gave Burnell a hard sidelong look to indicate that any patting would be regarded as condescending: also somewhat animalist.

As Dr Kepepwe left with a wave of the hand, Barker followed at unhurried pace, walking stiffly, looking terribly English. Burnell could imagine it with a copy of *The Times* tucked under one arm. It and its mistress vanished into the dark to her car and a little unknown nook somewhere.

'Whatever crimes and errors I committed over the past ten years, they've been wiped cleaner than if I'd been in a confessional. The Catholics should rig up EMV in all their confessionals. The forgiveness of sins could then be followed by the forgetfulness of sins . . . Which might make human life easier . . .'

Once the doctor and her dog had left, loneliness overcame him. He knew no one, not even himself.

Switching on his TV set, he found the movie channel was about to show a fantasy film of ancient vintage. Obispo Artists presented *Brute of Kerinth*, which he began indolently to watch. The film had immediate appeal in his anomic condition since the action was set on a planet and its moon far from Earth. The special effects pleased him, but the happenings, centring on a lost heir and a throne, were those of an historic costume drama. He lost interest, switched off, and gazed at the ceiling instead.

When a half-hour had dragged by, he got himself on the move.

Walking about the echoing hospital in his white gown, calm, savouring his own ghostliness, he imagined himself in an empty fishtank. Active steps were being taken to trace anyone who had known him during those ten lost years. Colleagues, parents. The confusions of war, the tight security now covering Britain, made ordinary communication difficult. But all would be well. He would be reunited with Stephanie in due course.

In the long antiseptic corridors, green LCDs winked, often accompanied by hums and growls. The entrails of a glacier received him.

Under cover of his ghostliness, he invaded Rosemary Kepepwe's office. All there was neat and anonymous, conventional down to the stained coffee mug on the filing cabinet. On the desk beside a monitor screen stood a framed photograph of husband David. Shining black, he smiled into the camera, standing beside a large fish on a weighing-scale. Burnell recognized an Isle of Wight Sea-Fishing Trophy when he saw one. Another photograph showed two smiling boys in their early teens, with Barker standing meditatively beside them. He wondered about their lives. There was small ground on which to speculate. Dr Kepepwe was little more than an embodiment of kindness and a fast backhand.

Burnell's steps were solitary on the antiseptic tiled stairs. No use to question who had lived, survived, faded away under painkillers, within these walls. The quota of patients had been cleared out. He was almost alone.

The news was bad. The hospital awaited a new intake: dying and wounded from a fatal engagement in the Crimea. Military men from all the armies involved were being flown here for treatment. Together with the soldiers heading for the Radioactivity Unit would be sick scientists – scientists, Burnell had been told, who had flown out to Bulgaria to deal with a nuclear plant going critical, and had suffered high doses of radiation. The emergency militarization of the hospital was being carried out under a cloak of secrecy, as all Swindon knew.

Taking a service lift up to the roof, he reflected that at any day now the wards would be filled with men harpooned by their wounds, poised on the brink of final white-out. What of the dead Larry? Had something in his cannonball head been moved to imitate the wider carnage taking place across the Crimea, Georgia and elsewhere? Had poor Larry mistaken Bishops Linctus for Stavropol, and died believing in his own gallantry?

On the roof of the hospital stood air-conditioning plants, breathing out their stale breath. The grimy air of Swindon had painted them black. Burnell went to the parapet and looked over. In the darkness, evidence for the town was mainly electric; lines of street lights, glows from houses, beams of car headlights. By such tokens, the presence of humanity could be hypothesized.

A cat approached him, daintily balancing along the parapet. It came without fear, to manoeuvre under one of his arms. As soon as he stroked it, the cat began to purr. Burnell put a cheek against the neat little head and addressed it affectionately.

Overhead the stars shone, remotely promising something better than the brief rush of biological existence. Engines sounded somewhere below them. Three heavy transport planes passed over Swindon, heading from the West towards the eastern stars. Burnell kept an arm protectively round the cat in case it was scared.

When he returned to his ward, to his nest in the glacier, the cat followed. In clear light, the animal was seen to be a bundle of long black fur. From its forward extremity, like glowworms in a thicket, the odd eye or two winked out now and again. Burnell stroked its more accessible parts, and it spent that night on his bed. He slept badly, harassed by thoughts of Larry and his mother.

In a fit of loneliness in the small hours, he held the warm body of the cat to his chest, comforted by it. He consoled himself by telling himself that the days would pass.

And so they did. And they brought Stephanie to him.

5

Some Expensive Bullets

By the time Stephanie arrived, Burnell was acclimatized to hospital routine. He exercised early in the morning before visiting the psychotherapist and underwent tests in the afternoon. In the evenings he read. To awaken and find the stray cat had gone was the least of Burnell's worries. Yet the animal's absence reinforced a sense of emptiness. The humble creature, unable to bear his company, he supposed, had disappeared into the warren of the building.

After much hesitation, he phoned his father in Norfolk. It was Laura, his stepmother, who answered the call.

'Your father is somewhere in the garden, dear, talking to the gardener, showing him what's what. He had to sack the last man. They're so unreliable. The new man seems rather promising. He comes with wide experience, although he's lame. I suppose that doesn't matter. I've spoken to his wife.

'The garden's not at its best, though the iris bed looks splendid. Irises don't mind the drought so much. We need rain badly.'

He listened to that precise theatrical voice. It conjured up the distant world of Diddisham Abbey, and the life lived by his father and Laura. When he had the chance, he explained to Laura what had happened to him.

'Oh dear!' she exclaimed. 'What pickles people do get into. To have one's memory stolen. Well, you'll just have to try and get it back, dear. Do you want me to come over and visit you? I suppose I could do that. I suppose I should. You know your father isn't able to come.'

'That's all right, Laura, thanks. I'll manage.'

'You do sound terribly depressed. I don't wonder. Poor soul. Look, ring me again soon, is that a promise?'

The visits to Dr Rebecca Rosebottom were no more comforting. To maintain his morale, Burnell woke early and exercised in the empty gym for an hour. He showered, shaved, and breakfasted, to present himself in the Rosebottom clinic on the second floor at nine-thirty.

Burnell sat on one side of her cold hearth, Rosebottom on the other, in not particularly uncomfortable chairs.

Rebecca Rosebottom reeked of ancient wisdom and more recent things. She dressed, she mentioned in an aside, in astrological fashion. Old portions of embroidered curtain material were draped across her body in contradictory directions, presumably to indicate this in the ascendant and that in the descendant, and the other undecided over the bosom. She could have been in her fifties or sixties, her head being spare of flesh and of an apple-and-thyme jelly colour, above which rose a wreath of matted grey hair. Her disinclination for movement reinforced a mummified appearance.

She told Burnell on the second morning that she knew he was a Buddhist.

'I don't think so, Rebecca.'

She encouraged him to talk. Burnell had always regarded himself as a listener. His architectural pursuits had not been an encouragement to conversation. After his mother had died, he had never been able to get close to his father. He had thought his father always involved with international business affairs. Unexpectedly, he now found himself pouring out the troubles of those adolescent years: how his brother had been classified as schizophrenic, how his father had married again, how confused he was about the new wife.

'You felt it was natural that you should feel antagonistic to Laura.'

He plunged into his complicated feelings for the beautiful actress his father had brought home unannounced. Laura was kind and amusing; yet to accept a replacement for his mother was disloyal. Then came his father's accident in Rome, when he had broken his spine in a car crash and lost the use of both legs.

He had considered himself haunted by bad luck. He had tried to commit suicide. In some strange way, he felt an identification with Larry Foot, the killer of Bishops Linctus. He could only wonder if he had committed any crimes during the years for which memory was missing. He was sure Stephanie would know.

'You're dependent on her and what she says.'

'How should I know?'

Through questioning, they established that it was an entire ten years which had been stolen. Rosebottom ventured the thought that the theft had taken place abroad, since EMV was strictly regulated in Britain.

'From what you say, I gather you are sorry that your marriage has been wiped from memory.'

He became impatient. It was not the marriage alone. He did not know what kind of man he had been, how his professional reputation stood, or how much money he earned. Her mummified presence and occasional comments served merely to make him more aware of his predicament, while resolving nothing. It was bad enough facing life; facing Rebecca Rosebottom was worse.

Before going to the second floor for his third session, he found the little black cat again. He cradled it in his arms and took it into the clinic with him.

Once more, Larry Foot forced his way into the confessions. Rosebottom remarked on it.

'I've suffered two traumatic shocks, Rebecca. Unconnected, but one after the other. I probably need proper counselling on both. Though counselling is not going to get my memory back.' He looked hopelessly out of the window as silence fell between them. A convoy of three military vehicles was entering the car park, billowing out a blue haze of pollution as they lined themselves up.

Turning his attention back to the fine immobile Egyptian head, he said that he was troubled by a contradiction he could not resolve. Of course he understood the terrible nature of Larry's crime, for which he had paid with his life; but there was also the factor of Larry's innocence. Larry had said he liked to help people. He seemed not to have understood that even his mother was real. Burnell elaborated on this for some while without making himself clearer, only half aware that what had puzzled him was the nature of cruelty and of pain, the titbit that followed cruelty.

When Rosebottom indicated that Larry was just an incidental misfortune, with nothing to do with Burnell's personal predicament, Burnell disagreed. Privately, he thought that whoever had stolen part of his memory was also no better than a murderer; the cruelty factor had operated.

All he brought himself to say was, 'I was threatened with death, Rebecca. I was shit-scared.'

'I sympathize, believe me. You can keep on telling me if it makes you happier. I'm no ordinary shrink. EMV cases always have attitudes.'

As often happened, silence fell between them. He felt he had never known such a conversation stopper as this lady who was supposed to promote the flow of talk.

And, as so often happened, he then began talking in an unpremeditated way, telling her that, as he had said, he had suffered two traumatic shocks. He woke in the middle of the night after a nightmare, wondering if he had become schizophrenic.

Rosebottom invited him to tell her what he meant by schizophrenic.

He said, 'That's what my brother's got. I have a brother called Adrian. At present he's under medication in Leeds.'

After a protracted silence, in which Rosebottom maintained an attitude almost beyond stillness, Burnell said he did not want to talk about it.

Her smile stretched her lips sideways to a great extent.

'Time's up, I'm afraid. Perhaps you will feel more like saying something tomorrow.'

'Just tell me whether I am schizophrenic or not.'

She shook her head, slightly. 'You have a long way to go yet.'

As he rose to leave, Rebecca Rosebottom said, 'There's just one thing.'

'What?'

'I am allergic. Also my star sign is against black animals of any kind. So just don't bring that frigging creature in here next session. OK? You don't need any kind of baby surrogate. OK?'

Burnell turned and stared at her. 'Do you think there's going to be a next session?'

Hurrying from the clinic, letting the little cat free in the corridor, he made his way back to the ward, taking a route that led him past Dr Kepepwe's office.

He looked through her glass door. Rosemary Kepepwe was sprawled at the desk with her face buried in her arms. For an instant, he thought she was crying. Barker sat by her on the desk, regarding his mistress thoughtfully, wondering what action to take. Burnell went in.

'Oh, these people!' the doctor exclaimed, without being more specific. She ranted about them for some while before stating exactly what it was that had upset her. The military administration who would be taking over the hospital had just visited and left their orders. The first instalment of wounded from the Crimea was expected to arrive at first light on the following day. But before that – in just an hour or two – a squad of men from the RASC were going to arrive to repaint the interior of the hospital.

'Does it need repainting?'

'I always liked it blue and white. So fresh, you know.' Dr Kepepwe mopped her eyes. 'I like this hospital. I like working here. Barker likes it here, don't you, Barker, my love? Blue and white create a cheerful healing atmosphere. These horrible army men are going to paint it all green today.'

'Green! Why on earth?'

'Dark green. Khaki green.' She looked piteously at Burnell. 'They say it's for camouflage purposes.'

Barker looked extremely serious.

The corridors were already beginning to smell of paint when one of the small Asians showed Stephanie into Ward One.

He heard her footsteps before he saw her. She entered with the air of someone determined to perform a duty not to her taste, with a firm jut to her jaw. Stephanie was tall, fair-haired, walking with ease inside a fawn linen suit, with a handbag slung over one shoulder. She held out a hand to Burnell, stepping back when he had shaken it. The hand was slender and cool. He liked the feel of it. Stephanie was fine-boned, delicate of countenance and strikingly attractive, he saw, only a slightly heavy jaw detracting from full beauty.

He invited her to take the one chair in the room. Sitting on the end of the bed, he scrutinized her, trying to see behind the cautious smile.

Keeping the pain from his voice, he explained that sections of his memory had been stolen by persons unknown. He had no idea where this had happened. It felt as if his head had been bitten off.

'So I was told when Laura called me,' Stephanie said. 'By chance I was in Britain, so I came along. That's what Laura said to do . . .' She chattered for a while, possibly to cover nervousness. Suddenly she said, 'Do you remember that my home is in California?'

Burnell frowned. 'We live in California? What for? Whereabouts? My work's in Europe.'

She rose from her chair to walk about the room. She complained of the smell of paint. He stood up politely, half-afraid she was about to leave.

'This is terribly embarrassing for me, Roy. If Laura called you, she should have explained.' She looked at him, then down at the floor, then towards the door.

'Well? Explained what?'

'Our divorce came through over four years ago.' With a burst of impatience, 'You mean you've even forgotten that?'

Burnell sat down on the bed. 'What are you telling me? You want to sit down or you want to walk about like a caged tiger?'

She began to walk about like a caged tiger. 'We got married. We got unmarried. Surely to God you must remember that! I live in Santa Barbara now, with Humbert Stuckmann. It just so happened I was over here in the Orkneys and I called Laura. Laura's remained a friend. She told me you were here.'

'So you came to see me.'

'That's obvious, isn't it? I called the hospital and spoke to some-one or other. They suggested I might trigger off a missing memory.'

'If it's missing, how can it be triggered off?' He spoke abstract-edly. The ocean was stormy indeed; indeed there was not a continent in sight. The Atlantis of his marriage was gone. Somehow he had loved this lady, won her, and lost her. By what fatal flaws of character?

Stephanie had settled again in the chair and was talking in a formal way of crofters and dyes and looms far away. He was not hearing her. All he could find to say was 'Humbert Stickmann? What kind of name is that?'

'Don't be superior. I hated it when you were superior. You used to treat me as if I was a child.' She said he must have heard of Stuckmann Fabrics. Stuckmann fabrics and ceramics were famous world-wide. People worked for him in Scotland and even in Central Asia. Humbert, she did not mind saying it, was a genius. OK, so he was a bit older than her but he was a magical person-ality. Real genius. Loved colour. Always surrounded by admirers. Full to overflowing with occult knowledge which he beamed into his creations.

When her outpourings had ceased, he spoke again.

'This guy's rich, Steff? Is that what you're saying?'

Stephanie brushed the envious question aside. She spoke of how a certain phase of the moon had led Humbert to design the pattern which crofters were now weaving for him in the Orkney islands.

He interrupted to pose the question which could no longer be postponed: as to whether he and Stephanie had children.

'Of course not.' Her tone was cold. 'I have a son by Humbert. And you may recall I have fought all my life to be called by my proper name of Stephanie. Not "Steff". No one calls my man "Humb". He'd kill them if they did. And by the way I have reverted to my maiden name of Hillington. I'm Stephanie Hillington.'

And I don't know you, Burnell thought. Nor do you wish to know me any more. He remarked on something else that must have changed: she had picked up an American accent. She gave him no answer.

Looking defiantly at him, she made him drop his gaze. With a mixture of compassion and spite, she said, 'Poor old Roy! So much for the past. Maybe you'll find you're better without it, as I am. I never think of it. Life's rewarding and I live right smack in the present day.'

She stood up as if to leave. In his confusion, he could think of no way to try to bridge the gulf between them.

'This must be difficult for you, Stephanie. You must find this strange. Me, I mean. A crime has been committed against me. Apparently it happens. It's a new sort of crime – people can always think up new ways to offend against decency . . . Tell me, when did we first meet?'

'What a vile smell of paint. In the States, paint has no smell. What are they doing?'

'When did we first meet?'

She spoke gently enough and gave him a kindly glance which transformed her face. 'We met in your father's offices, one day in April, nine years ago. I was being interviewed for a job I didn't get. You took me out to lunch.' She smiled. 'You ordered champagne.'

'And we were in love? We must have been. Please . . .'

The smile went. She was on her guard again. 'Look, Roy, you've had other women since we split up. Laura tells me. You were a great chaser of women. But yes, if it satisfies your male pride, yes, we were in love. Quite a bit. It was fun while it lasted.' Her laugh was uncertain. 'I've got a car waiting outside.'

Keeping very still, he asked her how it had ended and what spoilt it. Even, more daringly, if the break had been his fault. She evaded the question, giving every impression of a woman about to take to her heels, saying it was foolish of her to have come. Perhaps she had been driven by . . . But she withheld the word 'curiosity'. She should have mailed Burnell a photocopy of the divorce certificate. Her flight back to Los Angeles had been delayed. As he had probably heard, someone had put a bomb aboard one of the 777s flying on the LA–New York–London route and blown it clean out of the skies. No one had yet claimed responsibility, though a terrorist group in the Middle East was suspected. She regarded Europe as an unsafe place nowadays. It was terrible what was happening in the world.

She ran out of things to say, to stand there looking downcast, half turned away from him. A silence ensued in which Burnell felt he could have crossed the Gobi Desert.

He managed to make himself say, 'But I've not remarried – I mean, as far as you know?'

Stephanie attempted to laugh at the idiocy of the question, then sighed. 'You're always travelling the globe on your World Heritage errands . . . You never wanted to go any place glamorous. You liked the tacky dumps where no one had heard of American Express. Well, you were always the self-contained type, didn't like shopping. Life's just fine for me in Santa Barbara. Lots of friends, lots of fun . . .'

'Do you realize how self-centred you sound? Is that what spoilt things between us?'

'You're being superior again. I must go. I have to protect myself, don't you understand that? The divorce . . .' A shake of the head hardly disturbed her elegantly styled hair. 'Of course I'm sorry about – you know, what's happened to you, or I'd not be here, would I? I don't mean to sound unkind but I don't wish to know about you any more. What's past is past.'

'Oh, no, never!'

'Yes, and for you especially. Start again, Roy.' Now she was half laughing. 'You keep sending me postcards from some of these dumps you go to, you know that?'

'Postcards? What postcards?'

'Sure. Draughty old churches some place or other. Town squares. I don't need them. The kind of dumps you used to drag me into.'

'You can't beat a draughty old church.' He forced a smile, which was not returned.

'It happens I've a couple of your cards along in my purse.' She placed her handbag on the window sill and began to rummage through it. As she did so, he thought, 'She must care something for me if she takes these cards up to the Orkneys with her . . .' He said nothing, conscious of his own heartbeat.

She produced a card, glancing at it before handing it over between two outstretched fingers, as if she suspected amnesia was catching.

She caught his eye as he took it. 'Too bad. Just the one card. Arrived the morning I left home. The others got torn up, I guess.'

Steff didn't have to say that, he told himself. Either she was protecting herself or being deliberately cruel – to hold me off? What if I grabbed her and kissed the bitch? No – I'm afraid to do so . . .

The postcard carried a colour picture of a church labelled as St Stephen's Basilica. Something informed him that architecturally it was not a basilica.

He turned it over as she watched him intently. 'You don't recall mailing that?'

He recognized his own handwriting. The card was addressed to Stephanie Hillington in Santa Barbara. He had known. The memory had been stolen.

The postcard bore a Hungarian stamp. His message had been written only sixteen days before. It was brief. 'Budapest. Brief visit here before returning to Frankfurt. Making notes for a lecture. As usual. Need some florid Hungarian architecture. Trust you're well. Have met ghastly old friend here. Just going round to Antonescu's clinic to do him a favour. Weather fine. Love, Roy.'

He jumped up and kissed Stephanie.

Stephanie found her way back to the car park and climbed into the Protean she had hired, startled to find how upset she felt. She sat grasping the steering wheel, unable to do anything. To her disgust, tears welled up in her and poured forth.

Why am I crying? What could have provoked it? My life has changed. I've grown away from him. I feel nothing for him any more. I live in an entirely different climate.

Of course he looked awful.

EMV must be a new thing in this country – we're freer in LA. We've got everything. Everything. Humbert goes for it, says he's lived a hundred lives, shooting EMV.

Yet she was angry and could not understand her own mood. While the divorce was pending, she had flown out to California, hired a camper, lived in Palm Beach with a stud of whom she soon tired. She hated the memory; perhaps it meant she had hated herself at the time. *Sex may be the cure for many things but it is no cure for misery; not in my case. Oh, no, Steff – cease this soul-searching. You know it's sick.*

But her recent freer past – her past since the divorce – rose up against her as if in accusation. There seemed no way of stopping it.

In a seafood restaurant in Santa Barbara one day, she had come across an older woman called Ann Summerfield, tanned like everyone else at the white tables. They drank margaritas together and talked. Ann had divorced and not remarried. She had a lover who was on the fringe of the film world, Sam de Souto. Ann too was English, despite her American accent. She and Stephanie became friends. Initiating her into West Coast ways, Ann taught her to sail.

Only a block away from Ann and Sam's apartment lived Ann's younger sister, Jane Barrieros. Jane was undergoing a divorce of unusual bitterness, and fighting for the custody of her son.

When Stephanie was introduced to Jane, the latter was a pale worried creature dependent on a then fashionable shrink, plus every known drug. She was, however, well established in a soft-ware company, Micromanser. Neuroticism fuelled her drive to excel. When at last she won her battle in the courts on grounds of cruelty, and collected several million dollars, Jane bought into Micromanser and married the boss.

Stephanie and Ann looked on in admiration – and cared for Page, the disputed son – as Jane's fortunes spiralled upwards in truly Californian fashion.

Jane bought a small computer company, building it up rapidly with the latest technical advances, slanting it towards the greying end of the population, and producing a revolutionary new game series, Loveranger, laced with plenty of VR sex. Loveranger soon became the leading trade name across the nation. The ladies lived a life of sun, fun, and success.

Loveranger computers came in tough ceramic cases. It was during a party at Ann's new place that Stephanie met the ceramics designer, blue-jowled Humbert Stuckmann. And fell for his line of talk . . . Humbert, too, with a name practically synonymous with quality fabrics, was also a part of the good life of sun and success. That he had already run through three wives seemed to Stephanie, at the time, to be a part of Humbert's charm.

They were married in Hawaii the next New Year's Day.

Humbert flew in his favourite group, Ceren Aid, to sing at the wedding.

And poor scholarly Roy has nothing to do with all that. I've just left him behind, as I've left England behind. Everything over here seems so small and drab. I ask myself how I ever . . .

She dabbed at her eyes with a tissue, staring out into the deserted car park.

Why am I going on at myself like this? I need to get back to the sun and the beaches. I must lose a pound or two – I'm getting too hefty for those glittering shores. Roy – I don't know him any more. It's a different life . . .

Then a traitorous thought, unexpected. *And do I know myself any more?*

But she swiftly negotiated that thought, not wishing to remind herself how she had once been a tidy little English housewife, doting on her husband and her house . . . She had even enjoyed 'doing the ironing'. The old-fashioned phrase came back to her with emetic force.

Shit . . . She started the car engine. All that was a different lifetime. Could it have been an EMV experience – what they called 'lietime'? Her Now was real, with the sun blazing above their aircond beach hut. *And Humbert standing naked on the bed with a great erection, one of his scuzzies coming on. Ceren Aid playing over the 8D. Humbert's fave disk.*

> *Dance and screw, get the bug so fine.*
> *Screw and dance, yee-hew, surf the style*
> *Surf then dance, shed it, shed your mind*

He shouting at her, roaring, kindalaughing. 'Kid, you and I we are the future, know that? The future in flames, all experience open to us. We've inherited the globe, it's our fruit to squeeze and drink right up, down the throat, right down your gullet like champagne.'

She lapped up this stuff from him and his friends. Gleeing, it was called. It turned her on, drove her crazy, made her wet between the thighs, gleed her right up, all the way.

'We're the high, the privileged, every day's one long sunfuck. One long motherfucking sunfuck. What's our duty? What's our duty? What is it? To rejoice, kid, that's what. You realise America grows enough food to feed the whole planet twice over? Well, let me tell you, kid – that goes for semen too!'

Why had she then said – except to prompt him on – that if there was so much abundance, how come thirty million Americans were on the bread line?

Of course Humbert had an answer. He said there were always winners and losers. That was just good old Nature's way. Starvation was just a way of telling someone they had better get lost and make way for good men. If the losers didn't like it – why, they could go and live on Mars! He roared with laughter. Was still laughing when they played his game of Animal on the bed.

She was at a loss to understand why she now recollected those days of merriment with so little joy. Damn Roy Burnell! She should never have come to see him. She popped another upper from her purse, put a foot on the accelerator, and rapidly left the hospital behind, on the start of her journey back to California and happiness.

But she remembered a quiet rabbi friend in New York, who had said to her, 'Have a little happiness while you are young – but never forget how trivial happiness is.' Or had he been a part of someone's lietime?

Burnell ran Monty Broadwell-Smith to ground in a bar in Pest. Monty was drinking with a few cronies and did not see Burnell. Which was hardly surprising: every line of sight ran up against gilded statuary or supernumerary columns. This nest of rooms, given over to most of the pleasures of the flesh, had been somewhere wicked under an earlier regime, and in consequence was well — indeed floridly — furnished. The posturing plaster Venuses consorted oddly with the group of tousled heads nodding over their glasses of Beck. Burnell stood in an inner room and told a waiter to fetch Monty, saying a friend wished to see him.

Monty was still wearing Burnell's sweater. When he saw who was awaiting him, he raised his hands in mock-surrender. Burnell put a clenched fist under his nose.

'Pax, old man. No offence meant. Honest Injun.' He put a hand up and lowered Burnell's fist. Barely ruffled, he explained that since he had lost his job in England he had had to find work in Europe — like thousands of other chaps down on their luck. Eventually, he had found a job acting as decoy for Antonescu and his illegal EMV enterprise. His role as an Anglophone was to lure in innocent foreigners who arrived in Budapest to take advantage of low Hungarian prices. It was economic necessity that drove him to it. His eyebrows signalled sincerity.

He knew, he said, it was a bit of a shady enterprise. 'Rather like wreckers luring ships on the rocks in the old days.'

'So you've fallen so low you'd even prey on your friends.'

'Be fair, Roy, old man.' He breathed alcohol over Burnell. 'I have to pick and choose my clients. You've no idea, no idea, how uninteresting some people's memories are, all through life. Mine wouldn't be worth a sausage. But yours — well, perhaps you don't remember, but I met you and your wife at university. She was a real stunner, so I knew your memories would be worth having.'

'You little bastard! You had your paws in the till at university. Now you've had them in my mind. Stealing memory is a form of murder.'

Wincing slightly, Monty agreed. 'Wreckers again, you see. Poor old mariners . . . Look, come and have a drink with my friends. No doubt there will be tighter legislation in Hungary when e-mnemonicvision becomes less than a seven days' wonder. Until that time, Antonescu earns a modest dollar from his bootleg memory bullets and tosses me the occasional crust. Now then, let me stand you an aperitif. It's almost lunchtime.'

'It's three in the afternoon, you boozy git!'

Monty put a persuasive hand on Burnell's arm. Burnell wrenched his arm away. 'You've poisoned my life, you bastard. You'd probably poison my drink. Now I've got you, I'm going to turn you in – you and your precious Antonescu.' There was canned music in the room. Ravel's 'Bolero' was playing, dripping away like a tap.

Monty drew himself up and smoothed the sweater down. 'Don't threaten me. You have a contempt for me. Fair enough – you always were a supercilious bastard. But just think how I might feel about you! I've had to edit ten years of your stupid life down to make a presentable bullet. It wasn't too edifying, old sport, let me tell you. A ten-year plod down the recesses of your memory! A bit like looking down into a sewer at times – no offence meant.' He elaborated on this in some detail, concluding by saying, 'You ought to be glad to be rid of stuff like that. You're free of it – Free Of All Memory!'

'Oh, I see, Broadwell-Smith. The FOAM theory of history: never learn anything . . . Just bloody forget, is that it? Have you ever heard that saying about those who forget history being doomed to repeat it? Why do you think the world's in such a fucking mess?' With a quick move, he twisted Monty's arm and had him in a half-Nelson. 'It's retribution time, Monty, and a stinking Hungarian cell for you.' He gave Broadwell-Smith's arm an extra wrench, till the man howled. A waiter came to watch, without interfering.

'God, that's no way to treat . . . Listen Roy, Roy, look, stop this. Do you really want unpleasant publicity? This is what I'll do. I'll make a deal. A generous deal.'

'No deals, you sod. You caught me once – you aren't going to catch me again. Out of that door.'

'Wait, wait. Ouch! Listen, you sadist, here's the deal. Just let me go, savvy?'

'Don't let him go,' advised the waiter from the sidelines.

'Let me go and I will nip straight round to the clinic. It's locked but I've got a key. I'll nip straight round to the clinic and I'll steal the master-bullet and bring it back to you. Where are you staying?

The Gellert again, I suppose? You plutocrats . . . I'll bring you back the memory bullet we made.'

Burnell twisted the arm again. The waiter said, appreciatively, 'This man, he never pays a round.'

Another twist, more details. 'There are two bullets, to be honest. I'm being honest, Roy. Ow! I'll bring them *both* back to you. And you can then go somewhere – England, Germany, France – and get those squalid years of yours reinserted back in your noddle, if that's what you want. What do you say?'

Burnell relaxed his hold. 'I'll come with you.'

Straightening, Monty regained confidence.

'No, you won't. There's a guard on the clinic door these days. He'd kill you. I'll get the bullets. Promise. Bring them to the Gellert without fail at –' he looked at his watch '– give me two hours. Say six o'clock, OK. I think I can swing it.'

With some reluctance, Burnell agreed to this plan. He let go of Monty entirely. Recent sessions with Rebecca Rosebottom had made him, he felt, unusually alert to fraudulence. Accordingly, he watched to see what Monty might do when he left the bar.

Monty performed somewhat as expected. The moment he was in the street, he started to run. Burnell ran after him. Monty dodged along a side alley, down some steps, and into a main thoroughfare A tram car was approaching. As Monty rushed to get on, Burnell's hand fell on his shoulder.

Only for a moment did a look of anger cross Monty's face.

'Oh, Roy, dear old feller – how glad I am you're here. Thanks so much.' The tram sliced by within a few inches of them. He fell into Burnell's arms. The latter fended him off but, before he could speak, Monty was babbling on, eyebrows shooting up and down.

'Roy, I have such trouble. As I left that rotten drinking establishment, the ghost of Charles de Gaulle was waiting outside for me. You know, the French chappie with the big conk who made it to President? Charles de Gaulle – an airport named after him outside Paris. There he was again! Right in the street, in broad daylight. Did you see him? I ran like billy-oh. Thank God you saved me! Sometimes he follows me into the old W. Never knew a case like it.'

Burnell hailed a cab and bundled Monty in.

At the Gellert, Burnell paid off the cab and heaved Monty, now in a collapsible state, into the ornate foyer.

'All right, Broadwell-Smith, now let's have the truth. No bloody ghost stories. I have every reason to beat you up, so vex me no further. How do I get my memory back? How do you get it back for me?'

Pulling himself upright and tugging his little beard, Monty said, 'Please don't threaten me in a place I'm well respected. Besides, I'm feeling unwell after all the exertion. Let me be honest with you, Roy, your last ten years were crap. Full of crap . . . There, I don't want to be too hard on you. Everyone's last ten years were probably full of crap. I ought to know – I've edited enough of Antonescu's silly symphonies in the last few weeks. What utter shits men are . . . Now I think of it, I feel sorry for you.'

Burnell stuck his knuckles between the other's thin ribs.

'Stop bullshitting me, you little cheat. You robbed me. You buggered up my life and then had me dumped on Salisbury Plain.'

Shaking his head, Monty looked out miserably across the Danube to Pest with its dense Magyar thoroughfares where fat profiteers of many nations were sweating over their calculators. 'You were lucky. Believe me. As a compatriot, as an old friend far from home, I interceded for you. Generally our victims – well, *patients*, let's say – get dumped outside the city, still drugged, on a refuse-tip twenty kilometres away from here. And what happens to them then? Peasants rob 'em or kill 'em.

'You've had an easy time of it. You should be grateful. Your pater was always well heeled, not to mention being a bit of a crook, eh?

'In your case – Roy, old chap, I shouldn't be telling you this. It puts my very life in hazard. In your case, I interceded. "*Cedo, cedere, cessi, cessum*", to beg or something. A flight was being planned to deliver arms to the UK, to the BRI. British Revolutionary Islam, savvy? Totally secret of course. A secret arms drop on Salisbury Plain, paid for by Muslims over here. I pulled a few strings and got you flown over too. Drugged. You were dropped along with the weaponry. Better than the refuse-tip, admit it. You owe me a big favour.'

'I owe you nothing. You're going to give me back those memory bullets right now.' Knuckle in deeper. A passing sheikh, wafting perfume, looked surprised, but not extremely surprised.

'You're hurting me, Roy. I don't feel well. The drink in that place was poisoned. I need to go to the Gents. I am about to be sick.' He writhed realistically, and made appropriate noises in his throat.

Burnell got him up to his room. He bound Monty's hands behind his back with a tie.

'This talk about a master-bullet in Antonescu's clinic. Are you lying? You'd better tell me, Broadwell-Smith, or I'll lock you in the wardrobe and leave you there to die.'

By this time, Monty was the same shade of trampled grey as the carpet. 'Really, old boy, you can work that one out for yourself. Antonescu runs an illegal operation. Is he going to leave evidence lying about? He might be raided any day – not by the police, of course, but by a rival gang. From the master-bullets we make about five hundred copies. Not much profit in it, really. As soon as these are sold to a dealer, they're off our hands and the masters are destroyed.'

'Five hundred copies? You made five hundred copies of my precious memories?' He was almost bereft of speech. While he knew nothing of his recent past, the whole world could be laughing over it.

'You weren't exactly in the Casanova league, old chum, let's face it. We had a Pole in the clinic a couple of months ago . . . He was in the two-thousand-copy bracket, because –'

'Never mind the Poles. You said you made two bullets. Was that also a lie?'

Presenting an expression of blameless honesty, Monty explained that Mircea Antonescu dealt in more than one market. He extracted all Burnell's professional knowledge, editing it from the ten-year period. That knowledge was reproduced in an edition of maybe a hundred copies. A limited scholarly audience existed for such things, and paid well. Lazy students of architecture, teachers needing a short cut – such people formed a ready market. Pausing to gather courage, Monty added that Burnell's store of learning made up one bullet; his love life made up the other. All skilfully edited, of course – by himself.

'Oh God!' Burnell sat down and hid his face in his hands. 'You swear this is truth, you little chiseller?'

'Would I lie? Read my lips.' He started to go into details of what he referred to as 'the choice bits', but Burnell interrupted him.

'So where have all these copies of my memory – my life – gone?'

Monty declared that that was up to the dealer to whom Antonescu sold. Antonescu was naturally secretive about such matters, but he had heard that the dealer traded the bullets on promptly to Eastern Europe and beyond, where they could not be traced. 'Buchuresti is one market. Bootleg EMVs move from there further East. All the old nations and raggle-taggle once coerced into the Soviet Union are avid to feed on porn.'

'Porn! You call my sacred memories porn, you little skunk?'

'It's a matter of terminology, Roy, old boy. They want to know how the West performs in bed. Insatiable. Untie me, please. A drink wouldn't come amiss after all the excitement.'

Privately, Burnell agreed. He untied Monty and took some slap, inhaling the designer drug through a short plastic tube. Monty helped himself to a generous neat gin from the mini-bar.

'So where is this dealer?'

'Ahh . . . I've always liked gin. Reminds me of my childhood. I'd end up on the aforesaid rubbish-tip if I gave away his whereabouts. Honour among thieves, old pal. Generally enforced at gun-point. Besides, he'll have shifted all the copies by now. Incidentally – this'll amuse you – I heard over the grapevine that President Diyanizov has a fabulous collection of Western EMV "love" bullets. He may be plugging in to you this very moment.'

Monty's laughter involved coughing circumspectly. Seeing Burnell's expression, he added, 'Diyanizov. The current boss of Turkmenistan. Far enough from here.'

'Never heard of him. I suppose he's a ghost, like Charles de Gaulle!'

Monty looked pained. 'That was just a joke, dear boy. Tell you what I'll do. Give me a couple of hours and I'll contact this dealer and see if he's kept a couple of your bullets for himself. Stephanie's a pretty sight in the altogether when she's worked up . . . He might have hung on to them for his own entertainment.'

'Phone him from here.'

Another idea occurred to Monty. Antonescu had just put together an anthology bullet he called 'European Peasants'. Monty knew from what he had seen that Burnell was a sport. He could have a copy for a thousand. It featured country men and women who had done disgusting acts with every animal on the farm.

'Phone,' ordered Burnell, pointing to the instrument.

Burnell stood listening as Monty dialled and made an oblique and muttered call. He replaced the receiver and smiled. Burnell was in luck. The dealer had the spare bullets, and would send a minion round with them on a BMW bike. Instructions were that Monty had to be by the memorial in the park behind the Gellert Hotel in half an hour, when the package would be dropped off.

The arrangement sounded genuine. Burnell paced the room while his Dapertutto was away. Like Hoffmann, whose shadow was stolen from him in Offenbach's opera, he was living a half-life and would do so until his memory was restored.

At least the Gellert management had been helpful. When Burnell disappeared, the hotel had collected his belongings from his room and handed them over to the police. After he had settled his outstanding bill, the manager had retrieved his belongings. His electronic diary yielded useful information. The address of his apartment in Frankfurt-am-Main, near the offices of World Antiquities and Cultural Heritage, was no longer a mystery. He could resume his job immediately, provided Monty Broadwell-Smith returned as promised.

Monty did return, looking flushed and – as far as habit allowed – triumphant. He had two EMV bullets, lying snugly side by side in a plastic box of standard design.

'Here you are, old boy. Your bullets, the last in Budapest. Ready to be inserted into the projector. There's one on the ground floor, as you may have noticed.'

When Burnell stretched out his hand, Monty produced only one of his coughing laughs.

'No, no, my friend. Hold the line a tick. I didn't obtain these treasures for nothing. I had to stump up to the despatch rider. Honest Injun. The dealer is no pushover. He rushed me twelve hundred and fifty Deutschmarks the pair – five hundred for the academic bullet, seven hundred and fifty for the amorous one. Sorry, but you'll have to reimburse me. These babies contain your last ten years, remember! I'm just a poor exile, as you are aware . . .' Raising an impoverished eyebrow, he gave Burnell a look of innocent appeal.

Trembling, Burnell paid up. Monty Broadwell-Smith touched his forelock, drained his gin glass, and disappeared. Burnell went immediately down to the EMV cubicle on the ground floor, clutching the little plastic box. It was vacant. He could regain his past time – and possibly his past wife. He fed the bullets into the apparatus, sat back in the chair, pulled the projector over his head, and switched on. Nothing happened. He turned up the intensity. Still nothing happened. The bullets were blank and Monty had escaped.

6

Soss City

Fragments of various post-Soviet wars were continuing. A truce was arranged in the Crimea between Russia and Ukraine. It was the sixth such truce. Heavy fighting was reported in the Caucasus region, where Alliance troops were involved. What had been a peace force was now engaged in counter-offensive operations. The UN met every day.

Radio reports from Tbilisi claimed that the Alliance was using chemical and bacteriological weapons in the Kutasi area. There, Azeri irregulars stiffened by units of the Turkish army were fighting Armenians. Questioned, American General 'Gus' Stalinbrass said, 'What in hell else do we do? These assholes don't give up that easy.'

On the previous night, four Georgian soldiers had found their way through a minefield to give themselves up to a British journalist, Dicky Bowden, 20. One of the soldiers was a boy of fourteen.

Bowden said, 'Starved and disaffected troops such as these are all that stand between the Alliance and the Caspian Sea.'

He said he was confident that the war would be over in a week or two. Say a month. Maximum two months. Certainly by year's end.

Burnell switched off the television news. He settled down to read his own book in order to regain some of the professional knowledge stolen from him. He had reinstated himself in his apartment in the Schäfer Building. It was evening in Greater FAM, as

Frankfurt-am-Main was known among the travelling classes. Frankfurt, in becoming FAM, had taken its rightful place beside LA, HK, and KL, to be known by its initials like an American president of yesteryear, when American presidents had power.

At twenty minutes to three, he rose, closing his book. His appointment with his superior at the WACH offices was at three o'clock. He took a lift to the ground floor and left the Schäfer, passing under the marble bust of Amanda Schäfer, where two lines of her poetry were incised in Carrera marble:

> *Lass das Tal der Finsternesse,*
> *tritt in meinen Lichtkreis ein*

It was no more than a brief stroll along a grass-fringed sidewalk to the building which housed the WACH offices. The block was situated behind the brown mass of the Xerox block, built to resemble a child's interpretation of Viollet-le-Duc's reconstruction of Carcassonne. All the blocks here, because they had no real context, were architectural abnormalities – to Burnell's mind, the degenerate opposite of the structures that it was his duty to protect.

Walking here once with Burnell, a visiting friend had looked about him in dismay and exclaimed, 'God has his reasons.' But God remained unobtrusive in Sossenheim, unwilling to intrude on an elaborate organization.

Sossenheim City, its civic designation, was an aggregation within an all-embracing FAM, a *grave* accent stretching north–west from what remained of the Niederwald. Sossenheim was too big to be called a business park. It consisted of offices, shopping malls, urbstaks, hotels, apartment blocks, *Bienenhäuser*, parklets, autostaks, conference centres. These units might be expressed as three million square metres of offices, two million square metres of living accommodation, point nine million square metres of retailing, and point six million square metres of automobile parking. The population of Soss City was two point two million by day and point nine eight by night. Potted plants, point four million, static. Many official bodies – such as WACH, to name one of the poorest of them – had offices in Soss City.

Soss City possessed no centre, no spot where citizens might gather, should they be seized by such an aberrant desire. Of the old village, a community where once men gathered in the bars of the crooked streets, to discuss the relative merits of Eintracht Frankfurt versus Bayern München, and beat up their wives discreetly on returning home, nothing remained: the exception being a row of two-storey brick houses in Mombacher Platz. These had somehow escaped bombs in World War II and later the demolition gangs, and now formed part of a History Theme Park. The new city was divided, though in no systematic way, into national sectors. Giant *Bienenhäuser* or 'beehives' contained citizens of the member nations of the EU. In other hives lived Japanese, Korean, Malaysian, Californian, American, Arab, South African populations, and so on. All these hives, although basically engaged on international business, cleaved to their national idiosyncrasies, their national cooking – diversified in many cases by integral Indonesian and Chinese restaurants.

National diversity compensated slightly for ethnographic oddity. Everyone in Soss City was middle-class, aged between about sixteen and fifty-five. Retiring drones had to take themselves off elsewhere. Children were herded and not seen.

On his brief walk, Burnell passed not a single advertisement, such as enlivened the centre of cities everywhere. Nor did he pass another human being. Only armoured security vans prowled by.

The daily tidal flow of habitation was serviced by monorails, high-speed coaches, U-bahns and S-bahns. Most early traffic surged into the various centres of FAM, fish into a crocodile's maw. The attraction of Sossenheim was that it offered safety without the necessity of neighbourliness. Burnell had always liked that; it mattered to no one whether or not he was around; he could come and go as he pleased. Also, none of the crime rampant throughout much of the Western world affected Soss City. High-income residents invested in the best security systems.

Soss City needed no central meeting-place; the traditional square had disappeared beneath the power of indoor electronics. But in the gaudy Ginza Mall – where you showed an ID to enter – clowns and high-wire acts entertained punters every day, fountains splashed, bands played (strong on Mozart and Miles Davis), and two live white tigers were fed one live black pig every day prompt at noon, inside the Adventure Cathedral.

Organic cities of an older order are never completed, always in process, like the individuals who work and play in them. Sossenheim City was complete. A package deal.

It was no secret to Burnell that Soss City was a dull place, and that the Amanda Schäfer was a dull building. He did not mind. Dullness was good plain fare, like bread. For much of his time he was elsewhere. On the roof of the hive were various gymnasia and a large enclosed swimming pool, fringed with palms and the Copacabana Snackeria, where you could drink coconut milk or the Düsseldorf beer with the nostalgic name, Belsenbräu. A few expensive shops graced the mezzanine floor, a *pâtisserie*, a jeweller, an *Apotheke*. On the lower ground floor was a theatre which showed films every day and staged a live show once a week, when lean lightly clad transvestites cavorted for fat men in business suits. Entry to 'The Pink Pussycat' was free to those who showed their Schäfer ID.

A higher culture was preserved, if only as an echo of the past. The Amanda Schäfer was itself named after a German writer of the region, whose slender book of poems, *Zeichen am Wege*, had acquired cult status. On every floor were EMV cubicles; the system was due to invade individual apartments shortly, as its popularity grew. TV was increasingly given over to amateurism; anyone with a camcorder could secure a viewing. That was democracy. TV's feeblest jokes were greeted with rapturous applause by studio audiences. But nothing by way of a living art form actually took place in, or was inspired by, the Amanda Schäfer.

The fragmentation afflicting Western society from the 1980s onwards found its embodiment in edge cities like Sossenheim. Among a vast crowd of demographically separate people, it was easy to be alone.

Even within the WACH offices, a sense of isolation prevailed. Burnell was aware of it as a secretary showed him into a small conference room. The air-conditioning reduced voices to a whisper.

The very word 'culture', so vague and threatening, had a deadening effect.

Burnell's superior, Karl Leberecht, rose from his desk, rushed round it, and embraced Burnell, clapping him on the back. As usual, Leberecht was immaculately dressed, sporting a carnation in the buttonhole of his pinstripe suit. Rumour had it that he beat his large Scandinavian wife.

He sat Burnell down, ordered coffee, sent his equally immaculate secretary out of the room, and insisted on hearing all Burnell's troubles. Putting his feet up, leaning back, and gazing at a bust of Eugene Ionesco was Leberecht's way of concentrating. He did not speak until Burnell had finished.

In his sympathetic fashion, Leberecht brushed to one side the whole business of Stephanie and any other affairs of the heart (as he phrased it) which might be contained in the erotic EMV bullet. Burnell was still a young man and would have plenty of time to accumulate more memories of beautiful women. Having said which, he laughed heartily; Burnell joined in in doleful fashion. The two men had often gone out on the town together.

What worried Leberecht – and at this point he struggled up and put his feet in their polished shoes firmly on the carpet – was that all Burnell's professional knowledge should be so easily available on the second bullet. He felt strongly that knowledge should be accessible only to those who were prepared to work for it – 'like good fortune', he said. Knowledge should not be purchased in the street, like ice cream or the services of a prostitute. He promised he would do all he could through WACH channels to track down the offending bullets and have them destroyed. Meanwhile, he offered Burnell indefinite leave.

Burnell said he was rootless and restless. He would rather work. Work at least gave him some sense of identity. Any assignment would be welcome.

Peering into the VDU on his desk, Leberecht pressed a few keys.

'The Caucasus, Roy. Georgia, Armenia, Abkhazia . . . Lots of obscure people with obscure names: Chechens, Ossetians, Ingush, Adygs, in that general area. Mainly the states are run by terrible men – ex-bomber pilots, mass murderers. Fighting goes on all the time. Just the sort of place you would love. Not a toilet that flushes from the Black Sea to the Caspian, I'd guess – *but*, some little treasures from a WACH point of view, here and there. Those treasures need to be documented – well, frankly, before someone or other blows them up. Do you like the sound of all this?'

'Suits me,' Burnell said. 'If I don't have some action, I'll be in a coma.'

Leberecht gave him a hard look. 'You're not insane or anything? Frankly, I'd prefer my desk in Soss City.' They both laughed.

The immaculate secretary brought in a map of the Caucasus. Leberecht indicated an area near the Black Sea coast which had recently proclaimed itself to be West Georgia, under a leader by the name of Lazar Kaginovich.

'Kaginovich is one of the maggots who have risen to the surface since the body of the Soviet Union decayed. Don't worry, you won't meet him.' Leberecht put a well-manicured finger on the map. 'In this mountainous area somewhere here is a place called Ghvtism. It's not marked. It's very remote, which may mean it's peaceful. We're interested in documenting a church called – it's a bit of a mouthful – Ghvtismshobeli. Say "Gutism" and "Show belly" and you'll remember it.' He chuckled. 'The Georgians have long prided themselves on being the southernmost outpost of Christianity. Just a few miles south of Ghvtismshobeli, it's Islam. So this little church is something of an outpost.'

'When was the church last inspected?'

'It's been listed for years, never inspected. A Italian traveller called in there in the eighties of last century, reporting a legend of a valuable ikon. Go and see if it's still standing, document it before they blow it to hell in some petty war or other. You sure you like the sound of it?'

Nodding, Burnell said he would go. Leberecht told him that as usual he would be given a pack with cameras, camcorders, survey instruments, and so on. Also, some American protection might be forthcoming.

'Oh? Why's that?'

'Well, Roy, a) the area's dangerous, and b) the Americans are interested in oil and anything else they can get their hands on. Georgia is on the way to the resource-rich nations of Central Asia. I should add that there's also a hush-hush c). A big-noise American general is taking a personal interest. I can say nothing more.'

'And that's very little, Karl.'

'Everything connects, my friend. A flight leaves FAM for Tbilisi on Saturday afternoon. I'll come and see you off.'

Back in his apartment, he began slowly to make arrangements to pack. To unpack, to repack. He opened a window. That hole in his life moved in to occupy the centre of his being. In Georgia new difficulties would fill the hole.

He took some slap. A bumblebee flew in the window, landed on him, and clung to his shirt, seeming to fondle the fabric with its forelegs. It was a matter of wonder what this industrious creature might be doing in flowerless Soss.

The bee, seen through Burnell's temporary glow, was an angelic creation. Its lovely body, covered in yellow and black fur, seemed to blaze. By contrast, an armorial lustre slid along the chitinous combs of the insect's legs. Its wings lay glistening along its body. He regarded it with veneration.

As he looked, he saw a small brown dot move in the region of the bumblebee's neck. A parasite was crawling about its furry host.

The bee flew to the window and began an angry buzz against the pane. He shooshed it into the open with a shirt.

Beginning slowly to contemplate the shape of his journey, he noticed a blank business card tucked into the noticeboard in his kitchenette. Written on the card in red ink was a local phone number. No name. It meant nothing to him, although he was certain it was not the number of his dealer.

He stood with the card in his hand, admiring its sharp edges, so precisely cut. Going over to the phone he dialled the red figures. A recorded voice said in German, 'Who is it? You've probably dialled the wrong number.'

'Oh . . .' He stuttered a little. His responses were slow. Before he could hang up, a woman's voice said in German, 'That's you, Roy? Sorry, I'm here.' Not recognizing the voice, he did not know what to say.

'Is anything wrong? Are you alone? I cancelled all our appoint-ments since you didn't call. You want me to come round? I can still fit you in tonight.' It was a quiet voice, with an unusual accent.

'I – look, I've been away . . . Yes, come round. What time?'

A slight surprise entered her voice. 'Seven-thirty, I guess, as usual, OK? You sound funny.'

'I'm fine. I'll explain when I see you. *Wiederschön.*'

He put the phone down. He should have asked her who she was; but these things would be easier face to face. It was so wimp-ish to have to admit you had had your memory stolen; no one liked admitting loss of memory. Whoever she was, she must be a girlfriend. She might be able to fill in some of his past. They could eat in the Schäfer's Chinese restaurant, and maybe they would make love. It sounded like a good way to pass an evening in the Federal Republic.

Wandering about the apartment, he found himself unable to think. In the top drawer of his dresser was the photograph of a pretty woman in a large straw hat, smiling, as people felt com-pelled to do when they saw a camera about. Was it a photograph of the girl he had just phoned? But this one was standing in front of what looked like a Spanish building. He was baffled. He thought, 'It'll be better after Saturday afternoon. That's the future. In the future all men are equal – nobody has memories of the future . . .'

He began to look out a book to take on the journey. Gibbon, of course. Montaigne. From his travel shelf he pulled down Freshfield's *Travels in the Central Caucasus.*

As darkness was falling, Burnell's phone rang.

'Burnell?' A neutral voice.

'Yes. Who's that?'

'Tartary. Listen to this message. Georgia, in the Caucasus. A missing ikon, known as "The Madonna of Futurity". Could be it's at Ghvtismshobeli. Number One wants it back here. Do your best . . .'

'Who's that? Who's Number One?'

'Just get that ikon.'

The phone went dead. On several previous trips Burnell had carried out seemingly unimportant missions for Codename Tartary he believed: in this way he earned money to support his habit. He could not identify the voice; its owner probably spoke through a masker. Possibly it was a German voice speaking an American English. Many mysterious things went on in FAM.

For a while he worked on his personal computer, summoning up data he had forgotten.

Number One might refer to 'Gus' Stalinbrass himself, the crazed American general in charge of the EU peace corps who had somehow turned his troops into an invading force, apparently with the intention of carving out an empire of his own . . . Strange things happened these days.

Another theory was that WACH was part-funded by Stalinbrass monies. He had listed possible evidence of this. The Director of WACH might be involved – mainly in the theft of art works from the emergent nations with which WACH was principally concerned. Someone in WACH was using Burnell. He stared into the illusory depths of his screen.

Burnell believed evolutionary pressures determined that people exploited each other. Consequently, he tolerated being exploited unless he felt himself squeezed. In retrospect, even the trick Broadwell-Smith had played on him was amusing.

He looked again into his electronic diary for further details on Tartary which might have been lost with the extracted memories. There was nothing. Not even a phone number. They got in touch with him, not vice versa.

How deeply he was involved he did not know. However, if someone wanted an ikon which he might come across in Georgia, he was complaisant enough to oblige.

Flicking through the electronic index, he saw the name Remenyi. It was another unknown. He turned up the entry.

Peter Remenyi was thirty-two years old, a celebrated

Hungarian ski-jumper. It appeared he was a close friend, and that he and Burnell had been in the Alps the previous summer, travelling on horseback. A home address in Budapest was given. Vexed to think he had been in Budapest and not called his friend, Burnell immediately phoned Remenyi's number.

For a while, he listened to the phone ringing in Hungary. Nobody answered.

He switched off the processor, sitting back, trying to sort through the struggle of non-memory in his head. Whatever had happened in the recent past was a puzzle. The sections of the brain involved with memory retention contained many amacrine cells or microneurones. Yet non-localized storage of data also occurred; in consequence, ghost images rose up. Faceless men and women came and went. And was there not someone he knew, possibly this Peter Remenyi, lying somewhere in a coma?

The nightmare thought occurred to him that he might himself be Remenyi. But that was absurd. His colleagues in WACH had identified him as Roy Burnell.

As he was throwing some clothes into a pack, his doorbell buzzed. It was seven-thirty on the dot. Burnell went and opened the door.

A young woman entered his domain, self-possessed on her high heels. A man of unprepossessing aspect had accompanied her. He remained in the corridor, giving Burnell a hard look, not speaking. The woman was in her late twenties, well built, not quite plump. Her dyed blonde hair was cut short, bristly at the back of the head up to the occipital bone. Her eyes, fringed by long false lashes, were curiously masked by the application of shining scarlet make-up which curved to a point on the temples. Her lips were painted black. She wore a tight green plastic skin dress, buttoning up the front, which emphasized her generous bosom. The dress ceased just below the swell of her mons veneris.

He understood immediately.

'You'll have to tell me your name.'

She was looking about the apartment, very business-like. 'That's silly. You sounded strange on the phone. Not yourself.'

'Maybe. I've been robbed. It's the EMV craze. Someone has

stolen my memory. The immediate past is a blank. I hoped perhaps you might help me.'

'I don't offer that kind of therapy. Sorry. You've got ninety minutes of my time. You can still have erections? I guarantee I will leave you relaxed and happy. As always.'

'It's clear we've met before. Because of the theft – I just don't remember you.'

'Let me remind you.' She was wearing nothing under the dress. It fell open like a chest of drawers spilling out its goodies.

'Does this look familiar?'

Her pubic hair had been shaved off.

She insisted on checking his anti-AIDS status. The indicator on his watch showed green. She showed her indicator, also reading Safe. It was OK. They went briskly through into the bedroom. She led the way. Burnell followed, admiring the jaunty buttocks, smooth as machine parts.

He had always liked the Germans, not least because his father hated them. The neatness of German towns, where modernity sat comfortably with antiquity, had been achieved nowhere else in Europe. In the same way, a Teutonic drive towards success – success in all things – was moderated by an everyday courtesy. Earnestness was similarly moderated by a sense of humour. He found the Germans honest; or at least they retained a respect for honesty. They were good on respect. Wholeheartedness attracted him, perhaps because he had never possessed the quality: it formed an element in the life here which excited him, an intense secret eroticism buried under the surface of daily existence which foreigners rarely saw: an eroticism which differed from the flashiness of Italian, the polish of French, the bounciness of Scandinavian, and the salaciousness of English eroticism, in that particular culinary quality, Teutonic wholeheartedness. He understood well that national wholeheartedness had led Germany into disastrous follies in the past, just as it had led to leadership in Europe in the present; still he found that wholeheartedness admirable: not only in economic life, but in bed. He paid her before undressing.

German women brought to lovemaking the same kind of homely expertise they once brought to breadmaking, the sleeves of their blouses metaphorically rolled up, their hair piled out of the way, the smells of a warm hearth in the air, flour spreading up to their armpits, the dough kneaded into required shape under those dimpled practised hands.

After ninety minutes and three orgasms, Burnell was relaxed and happy.

As the woman was leaving, he said, perhaps trying to restore his reputation in her fringed eyes, 'I won't be here next week. I'm going to Georgia.'

'I too shall visit the USA one day.'

The bruiser was waiting for her in the corridor.

7

'The Dead One'

The high-wing Yak 40 laboured towards the landing-strip like an aged pterosaur, fighting against a headwind which poured through the mountains. Below the snowline, the landscape was a faded green, patched here and there with livelier colour. It rose up to embrace the light aircraft. A river glinted, hastening down a valley, and was lost to view.

The airstrip was laid out on a plateau. The plateau was dominated by cliffs above and below, set in an extreme landscape, shiftless, unthriving, lying under puffs of cloud. This was a territory of religion, ideology, blood-letting, a land forever fought over, passionately disputed.

The Yak circled, coming in again, lower, still rocking, then into calmer air under the great slopes. Now buildings could be made out below, in particular a circular structure of some kind, with a cluster of vehicles round it like ticks round a wart. The plane burst through another puff of cloud, unexpectedly low, and tore it to shreds. Someone was firing at the craft. A way of saying Welcome to Transcaucasia.

The pilot shouted something to his two passengers which Colonel Irving interpreted. 'We're going down. As if we hadn't guessed. He says to hold on. As if we weren't.'

Then the twin-engine was no longer the aerial creature which had swanned over mountains, but a kind of mad car, bumping over grit. Burnell and Irving fought against the deceleration. The plane rolled to a halt.

A vehicle was jolting towards them as Burnell and Irving

climbed down. Behind the Jeep came a truck. Two men jumped from the truck. They ran towards the plane, which carried supplies from Tbilisi, medical supplies, an intensive-care unit, flour, and sugar. All these items were more important to the fighters on the ground than Burnell or Irving.

Everyone moved at the double. Burnell and his companion, packs shouldered, were bundled into the Jeep, which made off at full speed. Above the roar of its engine, the crump of mortar shells could be heard.

The Jeep banged its way towards the building Burnell had seen from the air. It stood ruddy against a smear of shattered limestone hills in the distance. It was, or had been, a mosque, the minaret of which had been destroyed: only a stump remained. The mosque itself was a simple cube, capped by a dome resting on pendentives. Its open-arched porch supported three minor domes. Tiles on the main dome were missing.

Burnell knew from his WACH briefing that Ossetian occupation of this Georgian territory had endured for some while, until the hostility of their Christian neighbours, together with climatic changes, had forced the Muslim Ossetians to seek more hospitable territory to the north. Like the Balkans, Transcaucasia was a patchwork of conflicting ways of life.

A cluster of men, wearing a variety of uniforms, stood under the domed porch. All were armed. They watched alertly as Burnell and James Irving climbed from the Jeep and approached. One of the men took a step forward in order to detach himself from the others.

Burnell's senses were so roused, by the drinking the previous night in Tbilisi, by the flight over the Caucasus, and by the exhilaration of finding himself in this divided land, that he took in the leader at a gulp. This man, right down to his swagger, was as picturesque as anyone could have wished, his khaki greatcoat being draped about with pistols, magazines, and the traditional Kalashnikov. With his boots and sheepskin hat he made a familiar figure, who appeared regularly on TV news bulletins. This was the rebel, taking advantage of the upheavals in Nagorny-Karabakh, who fought to establish his own breakaway state. He was all the more real to Burnell because the latter had seen him on television.

The leader looked mountainous. It was only later, seeing him less showily equipped, that Burnell realized he was no taller than average.

He gave his visitors a nod and a cold eye.

'You're Lazar Kaginovich?' Irving enquired in his deep voice.

The other drew himself up. 'I am Captain Lazar Kaginovich. Commander of Armies of the West Georgian Republican Forces.' His English was accented but fluent. 'You are of course the brave American Commander Irving, once an astronaut to the Moon. You are welcome in West Georgia.'

'It's just James Irving now.'

Kaginovich smiled by the sly expedient of raising his moustached upper lip. His expression did not change as Irving introduced Burnell.

'Dr Roy Burnell, eh? We received a signal regarding you. But you are not a doctor of medicine.'

'That's correct. My subject is ecclesiastical architecture.'

'There is a war going on and you come to regard a church . . .' Kaginovich shrugged his shoulders. 'Well, that's understood. We make concessions in time of war. To receive EU aid – to have Commander Irving – we must accept also ecclesiastical architects. Come with me.' The words provoked his sneer.

A frozen look about Kaginovich made him a century older than his real years. He had yet to reach thirty. Already experience had etched itself on his brow and under his eyes.

The men in the porch gave way for the newcomers, while scrutinizing them mistrustfully. These were Kaginovich's officers. One, a large man with sandy hair, gave an affable nod in Burnell's direction. After a suspicious glance, the others returned to gazing across the airstrip, where the Yak's cargo was being unloaded into the lorry. A distant mortar was still pounding, apparently to little effect.

Kaginovich walked with a slight limp, clapping his right hand to his thigh. Irving followed, with Burnell close behind, humping his gear over one shoulder. The old mosque had been wrenched from its original sacred purpose; it now housed soldiers, animals, and ammunition. A racket of lowbrow music issued from a radio.

The air was greasy with the stink of men, their cooking, their piss, and their mules. A number of West Georgian soldiers lay about on blankets, smoking, indolently watching smoke rise from a fire to cobwebby beams far above their heads. Their weapons and boots lay beside them. In one corner, mules and donkeys were tethered. The mules, black and long-eared, mutiny always in mind, shook their long heads over the backs of the donkeys.

An armoury of weapons, including a small field gun, bombs, and ammunition boxes, was piled carelessly near the fire, on which a cook was stirring a dixie.

Sunlight slanted in from above, rendered cold and fishy-looking by dirty windows. It was a scene more from the nineteenth century than the twenty-first. The end of the Cold War, signalling an uprising of nationalisms and ethnic quarrels, had set the map back to an 1899 disposition.

Tokens of war – of the continuing fragmentation of what had been until little more than fifteen years ago the Soviet Union – were everywhere. A shell hole through the front wall of the mosque had been plugged with sacking. Much of the interior was blackened by fire. Mural quotations from the Koran had been defaced. Wounded men lay on stretchers, tended by a male nurse. The desk to which Lazar Kaginovich strode was piled with papers held down by a clip of grenades.

Burnell thought of an analysis of the woes of the world, heard from a woman's lips. Had those lips been Stephanie's? He could not remember. But he remembered the terms. Women had risen up to assert themselves after centuries of oppression. Pride injured by this challenge, men had turned to an ancient proof of manhood, war. An alluring analysis but incorrect: the regions where women remained oppressed, without security or suffrage, were among those most ready to take up arms.

But to accept the aggressive nature of men, and the destructive nature of their creeds, was hardly a diagnosis, Burnell reflected, looking about him with excitement.

Kaginovich threw himself down behind his desk. He gestured

to his two visitors to draw up stools. He shouted for the radio to be switched off.

'I welcome you, Commander Irving. We of course know of your heroic past. We are honoured you have joined the West Georgian Republic's struggle for independence, and freedom against its oppressors.' His English contained rich aspirates in the Russian manner. He ignored Burnell.

Irving's relaxed attitude to life had been demonstrated on the flight from Tbilisi.

Speaking in his easy way, he said, 'Captain Kaginovich, as you are aware, I am merely on a peace-keeping mission instigated by the EU Security Council. I have nothing to do with the forces of General Stalinbrass, or with the UN blue berets, who were drawn into this struggle when their convoy was ambushed by Azeri forces near Signakhi.'

'Those Azeris – they're rebels, murderers, ethnic cleansers!' Kaginovich said.

'I'm a fact-finder, Captain. My presence here is designed to work toward a truce between you and your present enemies, so that proper discussions can take place and –'

'None of discussions! Not until we have regained our stolen territories from here to the sea.'

Irving continued unperturbed. '– in Borzhomi, or elsewhere to be agreed. To this end, the EU Security Council will deliver at least a percentage of the aid requested. Dr Burnell and I have flown in with the first instalment.' From inside his military parka he drew a list of the supplies and handed it across the desk. 'No arms there, of course.'

'We can secure arms from Hungary. We have friends, you know.' Kaginovich grabbed the paper and read hastily down the list. 'Yes. Not bad. Good. Excellent. We need everything. When can we receive more?'

Jim Irving was a neat wiry man in his sixties, athletic, without a gram of spare fat. His tanned good-natured face with its blue-grey eyes was mid-Western in origin, his white hair cut short. He spoke in a deceptively casual way. 'You may receive more aid when my mission and Dr Burnell's are satisfactorily completed.

Also when proper courtesy is shown to Dr Burnell. You have our papers and know Dr Burnell to be one of the trustees of World Antiquities and Cultural Heritage. His directive is a simple one, requiring your co-operation: to make a survey of the ancient church of Ghvtismshobeli on Lake Tskavani.'

Burnell said, 'We understand that the Tskavani region is at present under your jurisdiction. Or have United Georgian forces reclaimed it?'

Kaginovich slapped his thigh under the table and said, 'We undergo a war for our survival. I regard this directive as an imposition. We have no time to worry about old churches.' He launched into a lecture in which the word 'liberty' figured largely.

Burnell broke in. 'I shall leave at once if you are unable to co-operate. Let me remind you that if WACH means little to you, Captain Kaginovich, I come under the command of General Augustus Stalinbrass of the EU Security Forces, who takes a personal interest in my mission.'

Irving did not so much as blink an eye at this claim. Kaginovich stood up. He summoned a nearby guard, who came hastily forward. 'Dr Burnell, maybe you are a stranger to war. I will show you the reality of war in our region. You shall see how hostilities are conducted.'

He marched off with the guard, to leave the building by a side door.

As Burnell well knew, 'Gus' Stalinbrass cared little more for religion and culture than did the ambitious Kaginovich. Nevertheless, the Church of Ghvtismshobeli had notched up notably longer staying power than the General; indeed, it had outlasted what had been until recent years the Socialist Republic of Georgia. For all its inefficiency, WACH had exerted pressure through Washington. As Burnell waited to board his flight at FAM airport, he had received a letter of authorization and support from Stalinbrass's command. Of the hidden agenda regarding the ikon, nothing was said, but Burnell did not doubt that 'Number One' was involved.

Burnell had flown from FAM to Israel by Lufthansa, and from Israel to Tbilisi by a military jet. Irving had met him in Tbilisi.

From Tbilisi to Kaginovich's temporary headquarters had been a hundred-and-fifty-kilometre hop. In truth, Kaginovich's so-called revolution was little but a guerrilla movement. A dozen small cities, of which Bogdanakhi was the largest, had fallen to Kaginovich. The supplies they had brought him in the Yak were deflected from Ethiopia.

Impatient with Kaginovich's abrupt departure, Burnell rose and walked about. Jim Irving sat tight. 'Looks like we're going to have a floor show to test our nerves,' he said.

Abstract patterns formed from Arabic scripts had once adorned the walls of the old mosque. They had been largely obliterated by fire and graffiti. Kicking about in some ashes near the *mihrab*, the niche on the mosque's Mecca-facing wall, Burnell came on fragments of unburnt polished wood. The *mimbar*, the high pulpit, had evidently been used to warm Kaginovich's troops on cold nights. The captain had put religion to practical use.

Harsh shouts sounded, screams, curses. A number of guards entered the mosque, bringing with them two prisoners at gunpoint. The prisoners were mere lads, dirty, ragged, wild. Both looked sick with terror. They stumbled as they came.

Kaginovich followed, looking grimly pleased. Directed by a sergeant, the West Georgian guards thrust their captives against a wall of the mosque. Kaginovich issued an order. The soldiery all round sat up and took notice, or stood silently.

The sergeant produced a bowie knife, severing the belt of the older of the prisoners. The man's cord breeches were dragged down, to reveal to all that he had shat himself with fright.

Irving calmly surveyed the scene. He strolled round the desk and sat down in Kaginovich's chair, hitching a leg up on the desk. Taking his cue, Burnell sat down too, folding his arms tightly together to put himself in an imaginary straitjacket.

Another order from Kaginovich. The sergeant now threw himself at the other prisoner, the younger of the two. The guards held the lad, dragging his arms behind his back. Terrible cries rang out as the lad's face was carved into. Burnell could bear neither to watch nor turn away. One of the lad's eyes was gouged out. It fell to the floor.

The sergeant wiped his bloodied hands on the prisoner's shirt. The prisoner collapsed in the straw and dirt, trapping his mutilated face between hands and knees. His companion, unwilling witness to this cruelty, had turned a frightful colour. Sweat poured down his unshaven face. He began to babble. Possibly he was praying. His body shook so badly it needed four men to hold him still. The severed eye was picked up and rammed into his mouth. He was beaten about his head until he swallowed it.

Both prisoners were then shot from behind. As their bodies were dragged away, hounds sprang forward and quizzed at the trails of blood and slime.

Kaginovich rubbed his hands with a washing movement. He said to Burnell, 'Warfare is serious business. All that and more we shall do to their wives and sisters when we get them.'

The whole contingent was due to move towards the town of Bogdanakhi at dawn. Burnell and Irving were given rope beds to sleep on in a barrack near the mosque. Each carried space blankets to protect them from the cold of night.

Greatly though he longed for sleep, Burnell remained on a rocky shore of wakefulness. The scene in the mosque kept returning like a malignant bluebottle. It would not leave him. The pain of the young prisoners seemed drawn on his retina in white lines. Sickly, he crept at last into the open, to stand under the stars and gulp in the night air like a man diseased.

After a while, he saw Irving was standing near by, a dark thin figure with hunched shoulders. The aroma of his cigarette reached Burnell.

'It'll be a long way to Ghvtismshobeli at this rate,' said Burnell. 'And with this company.'

Irving spoke in a nonchalant morning voice. 'We may come up against worse sights yet. Those executions were not designed to impress us two alone. They were aimed also at Kaginovich's officers. Loyalty here is reinforced by cruelty.'

'Hard to see why anyone should be loyal to that monster.'

'Kaginovich is a renegade from the Georgian National Guard, where he was cordially hated. His men probably hate him too, but they fight for a land they love. Kaginovich's nickname, incidentally, is "The Dead One".'

'Not very apt, I'd have thought.'

'Nope? Believe me, Roy, it's bang on target. I'll tell you the tale one day. We'd better sleep now. Dawn's not far off and it'll be a tough day ahead.'

They returned to their beds. Irving faced the wall. A slight mutter came from him as he said a prayer. Burnell knew Irving carried a revolver, although he himself was unarmed. He said no prayers. But listening to that whisper in the dark, taking comfort from it, he fell asleep.

Since the fatal day in Budapest, Burnell had suffered from nightmares.

The fan vaulting of Gloucester Cathedral, and the beauties of that carved fourteenth-century stone, faded into being. For a while he was transfixed by an angel eye, unwinking. But the stonework began to steam. He traversed again cartoon-cavernous cathedrals, followed the twist of cloister, transept, choir and nave, complex as a mesenchyme brain, flowing and changing like the undifferentiated tissue of which he had been composed in primal foetal life. He was drawn under elaborate lierne vaulting, rib intersecting rib intersecting ribbons of romanesque – grandiose, glutinous, ludicrous, lugubrious, the very intestines of dream. Ages passed in unholy umber illumination until caryatids came closer and their eyelids opened, to stream blood and tears as once more the frightened prisoner choked down an unclaimed eyeball. And Jim Irving was waking him.

A drab light, thick as mutton gravy, was filtering into the barracks. As they pulled on their boots, Burnell was shivering. He felt he would never unsee what he had seen.

Parading in a thin mist, the forces of West Georgia were a bedraggled lot. They mustered in the open, well wrapped and ill armed, saying little. The mules, protesting still, were led out from their stalls to be loaded with mortars and boxes of ammunition. Supervised by officers, cooks doled out a meat stew fortified by garlic, peppers, and tomatoes.

There followed one of those mysterious delays which afflict all armies. A radio signal had not arrived. Kaginovich, the Dead One, remained in the mosque. Everyone stood about in the open, smoking or sparring with a friend. The clouds crumbled, the mist cleared, and a yellow light flooded the scene, as if to spill forgiveness over the wicked ways of men. The quality of brightness enabled Burnell to put his dream behind him.

Illogically, he regretted they were leaving a spot he at least would never see again. The sensation was strong enough to prompt him to unhitch his pack and take out a camera. He walked about, photographing the battered mosque and its setting.

The Georgian officers began to take an interest. The big man with dull fair hair, whom Burnell had noticed the previous day, came forward. He wore a black SAS combat jacket. In tolerable English, he invited Burnell to photograph the officers. They all smiled ferociously and struck heroic poses for the camera, like a group of boys on an outing.

The vehicles started up with dramatic outbursts of smoke and noise. They left the camp in file, chugging off along a winding road that led eventually to Bogdanakhi. The infantry was to take a shorter, more precipitous route.

Kaginovich emerged at last. He shouted orders. The troops moved off, leaving a small detachment to guard the rear. Burnell and Irving went with the main body.

A copse of stunted trees had grown up round the mosque. As the file of men passed by, Burnell noticed field mortars among the trees, idly guarded by two soldiers from the rear detachment. The copse was terminated abruptly by a steep cliff, on the edge of which stood the mosque. Its *mihrab* wall faced due south over the precipice towards far-distant Mecca.

The force passed by the ruinous building, to pick its way over the lip of the cliff and down, on the first leg of a descent into the valley of the River Tskavani. That valley was as yet parcelled up in mist and shadow; there seemed no limit to its gloomy extent. The sound of running water filtered up, and the chipped song of a bird. So dramatic was the view, Burnell ran off several photographs, until he needed both hands for the descent, and put the camera away.

To some extent, Burnell was prepared for the rigours of the territory. After his phone call from 'Tartary' – a communication of which 'Gus' Stalinbrass no doubt had some knowledge – he had read up on the region. His oldest informant was Douglas W. Freshfield, whose book, *Travels in the Central Caucasus and Bashan: Including Visits to Ararat and Tabreeze and Ascents of Kazbek and Elbruz*, had been published by Longmans Green of London in 1869. The stalwart Victorian described the hardships of travel in the unlucky isthmus between Black and Caspian seas. But neither the hachures of Freshfield's maps, nor the elegance of Kronheim's illustrations, fortified Burnell sufficiently for the way in which the crumbling goat path they were now following threatened to pitch them down into the valley below.

Low scrub, often aromatic, grew underfoot. No flowering azaleas, which Freshfield had led Burnell to expect, flourished on these precipitous slopes. They had to progress at times on their bums, clutching at the scrub.

After half an hour of perilous progress, a dramatic change in the light altered the scene. Across the gulf of valley to the west, piled cumulus revealed themselves, their grey-blue mushrooms burgeoning from the compost of the Black Sea. No sooner had they materialized than they warmed from neutral colours into faded rose and then into bright pink. As the strengthening sun brought about this transformation, thunder sounded in the bellies of the clouds and they were lit from within by lightning – Japanese lanterns of a terrible beauty. They were in the world of the romantic artist, John Martin.

As progress improved, Burnell allowed his thoughts to wander. He recalled the boyhood trip to Iceland on which his father had taken him. It had been disastrous. As they scrambled up the slopes of Vatna Jokul, his father had said, 'You've always been afraid of getting your hands dirty, Roy.' They were filthy enough now to satisfy the old man.

His father belonged to 'the old school' – a school Burnell at once admired and resented. Earlier generations of Englishmen had regarded Transcaucasia as a legitimate part of the great globe with which the British were involved, to ruin or rule. Throughout the last century, British power had dwindled away. The British Isles were now a remote appendage of central EU power. So he found himself scrambling along under a petty warlord. Enjoying it, of course, he told himself.

Old Freshfield – a distant relation on Burnell's mother's side of the family – had travelled where he would in his day. He moved through Central Caucasus, grandly summoning up Russian colonels to mail his letters home, or post-chaising into the wilds at will. Among various travelling companions, Freshfield had numbered young Englishmen going to help build the Poti–Tiflis railway, then under construction. Now here was Burnell, with half his head missing, under the orders of an ambitious sadist known as the Dead One. A century and a half saw a change in everyone's fate.

All day long, the West Georgian army worked its way down the slopes, men and animals, mainly in single file. Flies buzzed about them as the heat increased. It was known that the Tskavani valley harboured belts of radioactivity seeping from a local water-cooled nuclear power station which had been forced to close down. Nothing could be done about that hazard. Birds of prey wheeled overhead. Their numbers had increased recently.

Towards evening, a halt was called. The sun disappeared early behind the great shoulders of land above them. The Tskavani had a louder voice by now. Guards were posted, no fires were permitted.

The friendly officer in the SAS combat jacket, who introduced himself as Lieutenant Ziviad Orpishurda, came over to talk to Burnell and Irving. His was a large and open face. When he gave his great brigand's smile, his eyes became almost lost in wrinkles and his strong teeth showed. He was perhaps forty years old. Grey tinged his temples. He wore a beret at a rakish angle.

After some halting conversation, concerned mainly with the difficulties of the day, Orpishurda produced a bottle. He carried a *khandzali*, the Georgian dagger. His jacket pockets were stuffed with bullets. He had loaded himself down with an ancient machine gun, weightier than most men could carry. This he set down beside him in order to produce the bottle. The liquor was called, he announced, *chacha*. Irving refused it. Burnell nearly choked on it and then, liking its sensation of setting his whole anatomy on fire, took turns with Orpishurda swigging from the bottle.

The day faded as they talked. Mists rose. The donkeys coughed like old pensionable men.

Orpishurda was from the province of Samegrelo. He had lived in Poti for many years, and extolled its virtues. 'Poti is magnificent city, a port. Since before Christ, many empires visit Poti – Roman, Persian, Byzantine, Arabic, Ottoman . . .' He shrugged, looking towards where Kaginovich's bodyguard had set up a tent for their leader. 'We march to Poti after Bogdanakhi, and must take the city for West Georgia Republic. Is it your General Stalinbrass will help us?'

There was clearly an advantage in claiming a closer connection than was the case with the ferocious American general. Irving gave a tactful answer which seemed to please Orpishurda.

Peals of thunder rolled down from above to fill the valley. Under cover of the noise, Orpishurda said, leaning closer, 'Many officers know the Dead One is nothing good. Is mad fellow. But our cause is good. Poti is held by Georgia. It is vital for us, for West Georgia Republic. Our way to the sea – you understand it?' He passed the bottle again. 'Our people have many bitter memories. Georgia men under present rule and Muslim Azerbaijan make great misfortune for us. Once we were rich, even last century under Moscow rule, still very rich. Now – all is ruin. EU must help us. You understand it? Maybe use nuclear weapon. We are Christian people many centuries.'

Jim Irving nodded. 'Europe has long-standing fears of Muslim extremism. Possibly exaggerated. There is wide sympathy for the problems of this area.'

Orpishurda smiled very hard, evidently disliking this response. 'Exaggerated not. How can you understand it, sir? Is old Caucasus saying, "Only friend of the men is the mountains".' He took a moody swig of the *chacha* and fell silent. The silence extended itself. Burnell said nothing; contrary to what Irving had said, he believed the EU had given up on Transcaucasia long ago.

96

'We'll be turning in,' Irving said. But Orpishurda squatted on his heels and pulled Irving down beside him.

'When you are young man, sir, you have take a walk on the Moon? Is it so?'

'It's a while ago now.'

'Holy mother of Jesus!' As more thunder sounded, he stared earnestly into the face of the older man. 'That was in different age, no? Much better time, more peaceful, when Josef Stalin lived?'

Irving laughed. 'Not quite that long ago.'

'How was it on the Moon? To walk there, I mean? You like it? You like to go again?'

'It's hard to explain . . . Also the experience itself has been obliterated by the number of times I've told about it. You're right, though, the world was quite different then. I have problems explaining it to the youngsters. I was brought up cheek by jowl with technology – right up against it. I subscribed to the entire American ethos . . . like there would always be progress and we were all Good People and America was the best place, the Land of the Free and so on . . . And it was our duty to fight for Democracy and the American Way of Life . . . Well, you don't need to hear all that, Lieutenant. Yeah, I liked being on Luna . . .'

He was reluctant to tell about it. He had told it a million times. But Orpishurda wanted to hear. This was his chance of wider horizons. So Irving proceeded as night closed in round them.

'OK, we got stuck on a nasty bit of Luna, in the Apennines. Our buggy turned over on its side. There was a good chance we might never get home – the first men to die on Luna.'

'Did you have great fear?'

Now their faces were growing dim. Burnell listened, letting the *chacha* burn within him like a lantern.

'Of a sudden,' said Irving, 'I found myself trusting in God, rather than Mission Control in Houston. It was a revelatory moment. There I stood on another world, and I was granted a perception of life as a miracle – not just my life, though that too, but the whole shebang, everything, *homo sapiens*, consciousness . . . The universe itself, I guess . . . As something wonderful that had been conceived in a mind countless times more powerful than any human mind – the mind of God. That was my great moment of vision.

'And I knew myself to be contained within the Mind of God . . . a much bigger concern than NASA.'

Orpishurda seemed disappointed. He stuck a finger into the curls beneath his beret. 'But we're all in the mind of God, sir. We know that much even on Earth, here in this valley . . .'

'Well, I didn't know it till that moment. And that's how I've felt ever since. It changed me.' For a moment he was silent, thinking over what he had said. 'We were able to heave the buggy upright again. It weighed less up there. Once we got the ship back to Earth, I quit NASA. Now I do what I can. I'm haunted by a religious sense of mission, to spread the word of God.'

Burnell asked, 'Was that your best moment, Jim? In your entire life? That moment of revelation?'

Irving said, 'It transformed my existence. Since then, I've had many such moments. I live within revelation.'

'Um.' Burnell was always uncomfortable with religion.

Orpishurda gave a laugh. 'Would you kill someone?' He patted his machine gun.

Irving gave a forced laugh. 'If it was God's will, I'd kill anyone. Killing is one of the auxiliaries of Brother Death, part of the Almighty's plan. You know what they say – you can't make an omelette without breaking eggs.'

'How about not making the fucking omelette?' Burnell asked.

He received a cool smile. 'Perhaps Death and Love are equal in God's eyes.'

'You can revere a God with eyesight like that?' Burnell asked. Hostility rose within him: he detested the easy confidence of people – generally men – who claimed God was on their side. Particularly when God went easy on killing.

Orpishurda was getting to his feet, and Irving with him. Orpishurda shook hands with them both, promising they would talk again in Bogdanakhi. The Mayor of Bogdanakhi, he said, had proclaimed his friendship towards the West Georgians, and life would be easy there for a day or two until they mustered forces and moved on to Poti. He clapped a broad hand on Irving's shoulder, before making off into the dimness.

As they turned in, Irving said quietly, 'You're not a Believer, are you, Roy? I can always tell.'

'Well – no offence meant. It was NASA who got you to the Moon and back, wasn't it? Not God.'

'Oh? How is that?' The voice was calm, tolerant.

'Tell you some time.' To himself, Burnell thought, 'Let's get to that historic wreck of a church, grab the ikon, and get back to good old Germany . . .' He settled down with his head on his precious pack, preparing for his disturbing dreams.

They came at once.

Next morning, more mountainside. Heavy rain soaked everyone. Cold heavy rain. The path turned to mud pudding beneath their boots. But the Dead One led on, and at last they reached the valley bottom.

There was the Tskavani, hammering its stony way to the distant Caspian, black, grey and yellow, by turns.

Only ten kilometres ahead lay the city of Bogdanakhi. After a two-hour slog through sodden undergrowth, the forces gathered in a grove of sweet chestnut trees. Fires were lit, a gruel was served with bread and a ration of local brandy. The rain petered out. The Dead One addressed his men. Rain had by no means dampened his savage spirit. Showing his irregular teeth, he reminded them all of the insults which had been heaped on West Georgia throughout the ages, from the time when Bagrat of Iveria had forced a union with eastern Georgia in the tenth century. Now they were able to strike back at all who had persecuted them. Soon the whole world would ring with the name of West Georgia. The entrails of the enemy would decorate a path from the valley of the Tskavani to the icy teeth of the Caucasus.

The men, content with something in their bellies and cigarettes on their lips, squatted or leaned against tree trunks, listening placidly, with every evidence of good nature that bandoliers and Kalashnikovs allowed.

Bogdanakhi, Kaginovich emphasized, was the gateway to Poti.

In Poti, friendly nations would bring them supplies and men to the docks. Armies! Armies! The docks would swarm with them. Bogdanakhi had been held by irregulars, Azeris and Ossetis among them. Now it was free. The Mayor, a friend of Kaginovich's, would welcome them.

'We are winning through, my heroes!' He repeated the phrase. 'We are winning through.'

Kaginovich was wise enough to keep the speech short, and to throw in a scatological joke, at which everyone laughed. Burnell studied the brown faces in the clearing. He read there looks of contentment, and nothing of the tension he met with on the faces of men in the city streets of FAM. Unlike those bread-winners, these soldiers had presumably convinced themselves of the justice of their cause. They had then settled for the guerrilla life, where office hours were unknown.

Smoke from the cooking-fire rose among the trees. While the sweet chestnuts still dripped, their upper branches became full of sunlight which, as the sun rose above the valley, worked its way downwards, just as the smoke struggled upwards. It was agreeable to be here, half listening to a speech they must have heard often before, sitting on their butt-ends with their mates.

They had, Burnell thought, justified their existence in their own eyes, if they bothered to think about such matters. They had food and drink. They were outdoors, on a kind of hunt. They did not have to wash. They cared about their weapons but not, judging by appearances, their clothes. No great deal of thought was required of them. This was the neolithic inheritance; they resisted the urbanization, the suburbanization, which was overtaking the world, including Georgia. Their idea of a city was a place to be taken, a place of only temporary refuge.

They were a gathering of males. No doubt it was a woman who put the first ruched curtain up in an Ice Age cave.

Well, all that was fine as far as it went. But war was its pretext. If only these struggles could be carried out with dummy rounds . . .

According to Irving's muttered translation, Kaginovich was now saying that there were dangers everywhere. Be alert, men. Only within the city will we be safe.

As if to emphasize the truth of his words, two shots sounded from the other side of the river. A West Georgian who had been sitting on a log fell over backwards, rose to his knees so that all could see a smashed erupting face, and then collapsed. Some of his comrades grabbed their guns and rushed towards the river. Their officers called them back. They could be running towards a trap.

In grimmer mood, they buried the dead man among the bushes – here were Freshfield's first azaleas – and a rough cross was hammered into place by his head. A prayer was said before they moved on.

The Dead One sent two pairs of scouts ahead of his column. The first pair returned and reported all clear. The column pushed alertly through dense vegetation which gave way to abandoned apple orchards. They were keeping beside the Tskavani, which now ran straight towards Bogdanakhi.

They came to a marshy area where recent rain had brought out an abundance of fat green frogs. Forgetting about the recent death of their comrade, the soldiers dropped their rifles and ran about catching the frogs, laughing as they did so. A fire was started in a hollow trunk. The officers cursed. But the men would not forgo the chance of a feast. They skinned, barbecued, and ate the frogs before they would advance another metre.

The going became stickier. The Tskavani, bringing down broken branches from the hills, had flooded and left behind pools of mud. As the column was skirting the largest of these pools, having to pick its way over fallen limbs of trees, a driver leading one of the provision donkeys slipped and fell into the stinking brown stuff. Dragging on the rein to save himself, he caused his animal also to lose its footing.

The donkey tumbled in upon its driver. It struggled fiercely, braying as it did so, in its struggles burying the driver and working itself deeper into the mud. Soon only the man's hand showed, still gripping the bridle. Burnell suffered the vision of a pensioner's hand clutching the handle of a push-chair. No one could reach him without being themselves engulfed in the glutinous muck. Loaded as it was, the donkey only sank deeper.

Its eyes, its great grey lips, were distended in terror. Men called encouragement to the animal. When it reared up and seemed about to free itself, they cheered. The creature must have become entangled with a concealed branch. It plunged down further. With a last broken cry, it was gone.

The officers bellowed orders, asking if everyone wanted to be shot where they stood. The column proceeded on its way.

The noise they had made brought more desultory sniping from the far side of the river. The column gave answering fire.

The second pair of scouts reported in. They had met up with Bogdanakhi's forward defences and identified themselves. The city was free and calm, and would welcome the great liberator Lazar Kaginovich.

Bogdanakhi came as a pleasant surprise to Burnell. Most of it remained standing. On its outskirts stood gallows, where hung an array of corpses of enemies of the people, all flaky like strangled chickens. Yet beyond this lay a semblance of civilization. That is, if paved streets and parking meters meant anything.

To come on such a large town in these remote parts was in itself an astonishment. It had grown because of its bridge over the Tskavani. And to the bridge had been added, much later in history, a station on the Poti–Tbilisi railway mentioned as being under construction in Freshfield's book. From then on Bogdanakhi had prospered. So it could boast wide streets and modest palazzi of Italianate design. Most palazzi were intact, if somewhat dilapidated. The main avenues were lined with trees. Shops and restaurants were open for business. The population, having heard of Kaginovich's earlier victories, came from their homes to greet the West Georgian force. Flags were waved.

As the force entered town, with Kaginovich marching at its head, his flag-bearer beside him, a town band struck up. It marched ahead as guide, its brass uncertain of the tempo, but leading surely to the main square. The road was lined by Kaginovich's armoured column, which had arrived ahead of him. There was much cheering.

The way was long from the outskirts. The sun was hot. Many of the people who came to stand in their doorways to watch the procession were old. The young had left to join the armed struggle. Of those remaining behind, some wore soiled bandages. An old woman walked alongside the column, trying to sell plums. A blind man came forward haltingly. His head and face were bandaged, and he held out an old saucepan for alms.

Irving and Burnell were walking at the rear of the parade. Irving touched Burnell's arm, gesturing to him to wait, and turned back to the blind man. The beggar had a notice written on cardboard and hung about his neck by a string. Irving read out the convoluted Georgian script to Burnell.

'It says, "My eyes were removed by Azeri torturers. I must support my children, my wife being dead. Please help me."'

'The local pastime, eh? Well, it's terrible, but we'd better not get left behind, Jim.'

Irving showed no sign of haste. He exchanged a few words with the beggar, which led to a diatribe from the man, the bandaged head tilted to heaven. Later, Irving said the man complained of his fellow-citizens, that they had lost any sense of compassion and put no money in his pot. He claimed the world had gone mad.

'Did you agree?' Burnell asked. 'Or did you tell him blindness was part of God's plan?'

Jim Irving had heard the man out. He then made a suggestion. The beggar allowed Irving to remove the notice from his neck, turn it over, and with some labour write something on the other side. The man then draped this new notice round his neck.

Greatly impressed, Burnell asked how well Irving knew Georgia. Irving replied merely that he knew Georgia well. 'And for your information, the Georgians don't call themselves that. They call themselves *kartvel-ebi*. What we call Georgia they call *Sakartvel-o*.'

'You told me that when we met in Tbilisi.'

'Well now, Roy, I'm reminding you now.'

The procession had left the two foreigners behind. They ran to catch up with the rear, and did so as Kaginovich's men were entering the main square. The unit formed up bravely while the tinpot band changed from Meyerbeer to something with a military air.

The Mayor of Bogdanakhi marched out on to a platform flanked by flags. Lazar Kaginovich marched forward to meet him. The two shook hands, embraced, kissed. Kaginovich stood rigidly at attention while the Mayor gave a brief address.

The Mayor was a grand-looking man of some corpulence, by name Tenguiz Sigua, his great head of hair barely suppressed under a military peaked cap. He welcomed the Army of the West Georgian Republic to his town with a flow of Georgian rhetoric, gesturing with both hands outwards as he did so, as if to demonstrate, over and over, the dimensions of a vast Christmas pudding.

According to Irving's rough and ready interpretation, Mayor Sigua had an especial word of welcome for the heroic Lazar Kaginovich. He also spoke of hardship and changing times.

'Our people are always poor and have become more poor. Many have no houses. Those who have a house welcome in a hundred others. We are a hospitable people. Those who have a room welcome in twenty others. We are a hospitable people. Those who have a corner of a room have no possessions. Our poor country is a house without possessions, forgotten by the world at large. Yet we are a generous people. We give our hearts to the Army of Liberation.'

The crowd cheered wildly. The army, who stood to benefit from this official declaration of hospitality, gave three cheers. The band blasted away, this time with 'Somewhere Over the Rainbow'. The newcomers, for all their muddy condition, were then embraced by most of the populace.

'But he didn't say anything about support for Kaginovich,' Irving said. Burnell barely caught the remark. Both of them were being swept away by the crowd. Burnell, for the first time since arriving in this corner of the world, found himself regarded as a person of importance.

'Is Englishman! Is Englishman!' went up the cry, almost as if the impoverished multitude remembered Douglas Freshfield.

Although Burnell liked to think himself invulnerable to rhetoric, he was no more immune than the next man. Sigua's talk was more to his taste than Kaginovich's; it said something about the traditional hospitality of Georgia. And it was by this hospitality that

Burnell and the others were now inundated. It broke over them suddenly, like a wave. Despite or because of its troubles, Bogdanakhi celebrated.

A banquet had been arranged in a public building used long ago by the Youth Arm of the KGB. Celebrities and others crowded in. The amiable Sigua acted as *tamadar*. He was seated at the head of the table with Lazar Kaginovich at his right hand. He called for toast after toast as a gluttonous meal was served with glutinous leisure, platter after platter. An air of hedonism prevailed. Sturdy waitresses often slipped titbits on to the plates of their most favoured guests. Huge meat dishes were humped in, innards on skewers, gigantic ebullient breads and little *blinis* covered with caviar, sour cream, and various grasses.

Amid cheers, a whole roast lamb couched in lentils was set before the diners. They fell to with patriotic determination, swabbing up gravy with fists full of bap. Even after that encounter there was no time for truce. In came, as a *bonne bouche*, great bowls of a turkey dish called *chakhokhbili*, cunningly composted with garlic, onions, and tomato, which elevated poultry to a mythic level – all issuing forth from steaming regions unknown. Profusion, confusion – course after course, course before course. While others gobbled, roared, quaffed, Kaginovich pingled with his plate, his bone-white face shining down the long table like a memento mori, like an Angel of Death as well plucked as the turkey before him. When the Angel's eye once caught Burnell's, it was as if a grey sea pebble had been flung in his direction. Still the sturdy waitresses pressed on, sweating with football-team eagerness, distributing food and favours, Rubens-like Goddesses of Plenty. The wine was an equally sturdy Akhasheni. It came bravishing out of its bottles, washed down with fizzy lemonade, Borzhomi mineral water and pear water; later with a local cognac. Orpishurda, sitting next to Burnell, was assiduous in filling their glasses till a meniscus twinkled. A waistcoated band played lively airs, coaxing ever onward the rhythm of military jaws. As the hour and the nutrition wore on, the guests became more and more familiar with each other, and more and more jocular with the waitresses, and the waitresses with them. Clothing and behaviour were becoming unbuttoned. After the shoulder-slapping, the buttock-patting. After Rubens, Rabelais.

A kind of bioluminescence infused the scene, reinforced by noise. Madness was intrinsic to the situation. The feast was a raft isolated on the dread ocean of time, as Bogdanakhi was isolated in space. Rich vineyards and orchards, only partly despoiled by war, surrounded the city, to stretch all the way to the coast, to celebrated Poti; but the influence of the contingent's approach along the Tskavani valley left Burnell with the impression of a destination in jungle, out of touch, embedded in wilderness, lost. The romance of this illusion excited him. He fell to greedily, as the tastes and the toasts went up and down the table, in a manner alien to his usual asceticism. One other person besides Kaginovich was not drinking: Jim Irving sat with a composed smile on his face as the flagons passed by his nose.

Amid the uproar, the kindly *tamadar* announced it was Burnell's turn to give a toast. Cries of 'English! English!' Burnell pushed back his chair and rose, clutching his glass. Raising the glass high above his head until its contents sparkled under the chandeliers, he announced, shouting to make himself heard, that he wished to toast the courage, the beauty, and above all the hospitality of the city, this pearly *urbs in ruse* – he stumbled over that one – hidden from the outside world, called Bogdanakhi. As his friend Jim Irving believed in astronomy, so he believed in gastronomy. He rambled on, concluding by saying he would express his happiness by quoting from the greatest poem of last century, 'The Waste Land', by England's greatest poet since Shakespeare, T.S. Eliot – who, he was certain, had written these words with Bogdanakhi in mind. And probably did. And, moreover, had.

> Now is the time of booting up and programming
> When the monitor screens of life brighten
> Between the controls
> And the final print-out
> Come alphabets from afar
> Strange fonts
> And the wind in the yews outside

These last two lines struck him as so lyrical that he repeated them – twice. Vociferous if perplexed applause broke out. The Georgians were such great ones for poetry, however incomprehensible, that Mayor Sigua himself rushed round and embraced Burnell, kissing him on both greasy cheeks. Only later – next morning – did Burnell realize that the lines he had recited were dismal rather than joyous, and not part of 'The Waste Land' in any case.

At about the time that cakes and puff pastries – oozing, as though mortally wounded, their entrails of jam and chocolate – were being borne in on the scrum of waitresses, the Georgian sitting on Burnell's left, who spoke no word of English, grasped Burnell's arm. He was a compact man, his face purple as an over-written novel, his beard still entangled with fragments of the *chakhokhbili* and lamb, giving to the phrase 'mutton-chop whiskers' a whole new savour. Grunting, he pushed back his chair and groped inside his blouse. From this nook he dragged up a leather bag containing a substance which, if inhaled, he showed by gesture and demonstration, could benefit a person immensely.

'*Kargi*,' he said, emphatically, rolling his eyes. '*Kargi*.' He snorted a palmful of the substance up nostrils well adapted to the task. In passing over the bag to Burnell, he was perhaps seeking to make amends for splashing during the liquid aspect of the *chakhokhbili*.

By this time, Burnell was too sunk in enjoyment to have refused even a bowl of hemlock, if courteously offered. He took the grainy stuff up right nostril, up left. It proved to be to his customary slap what nuclear fission is to gunpowder.

He was floating above the littered table, winged like Satan in Milton's poem, over the dark abyss, this abyss still flavoured with turkey and puff pastries sprouting like mushrooms. He saw the table below him as a carpet about which heads were symmetrically arranged. Flight depended on the up-draught of body heat arising from the proto-historic feast. Jim Irving could be sighted, white of noddle like a webbed cactus. Burnell called, or thought he called. Irving continued to sip a glass of lemonade. The sight was infinitely amusing, viewed from Biblical heights, in security, above the pestilence that walketh in darkness and the gluttony that stalketh in the noonday.

'I am the ghost of Charles de Gaulle,' he said, or thought he said, spreading his wings like a cloak, or vice versa. Mention of the great French general reminded him that he needed to visit what a friend from long ago had felicitously termed 'the old W'.

Events thereafter were confused. Had he, for instance, pushed a jam-laden puff in someone's face as they sought to prevent him leaving the hall? Had he wandered down the Prospekt Konstitutii amid laughing crowds? Had he attempted another winged flight, under the impression he was immune to the laws of physics? Had a well-meaning stranger taken him into a family home, beseeching him to rest on a red ottoman? Had he made an amatory attempt on a daughter of the house – and then, when her mother had rushed to her rescue, on the mother as well? Had he found himself flung out into an alley? Had darkness fallen with the noise of a supermarket trolley crashing down a flight of marble stairs on a Monday morning? Had the turkey ultimately returned?

Had he lain hour after hour, possibly for as long as a year, looking up at stars and broken guttering, laughing at something too profound for mere consciousness? The music raced round his head, violins, wild tempi – the plangent music which had first attracted him to Eastern Europe; the language of violins elicited by despised gipsies. It made the broken guttering look so – symbolic. He lay there turning the word over in his mind. Symbolic. Sinbolick. Sinbollicks. Maybe you could build a whole house out of broken guttering. In time he came to reject the notion as uncommercial, whispering to the alleyway, 'All that gutters is not gold.' Did he? Had he? Could he?

Beyond a surf of uncertainties lay a beach of fact. At some point, Burnell had raised himself to his feet. He had said aloud, '*Chakhokhbili!*' He then walked through the town seeking the mayor's house. An urge to thank Mayor Sigua for the hospitality was strong in his breast, and other parts.

He found himself before a stone house decorated in the baroque manner. How attractive everything – the town, the evening – looked in his eyes. Equally attractive was a lady standing on a balcony above his head, taking the evening air. She beckoned to him. He went through the 'Me?' routine, pointing questioningly to his solar plexus. She beckoned again.

Confident that she was the mayor's wife, he entered the house by double doors. Music was playing. He entered a small inner courtyard. Men and women were here, drinking. What fun Bogdanakhi was!

Amazingly, he still had his pack with him; it had lain like a dog at his banqueting feet. As he settled himself upon it, a woman came and, after some linguistic misunderstanding, led him upstairs. On an upper landing, the young lady from the balcony greeted him. She was highly painted and powdered, and wore remarkably little for the time of day.

'Madame Sigua?' Burnell enquired.

She spoke no word of English. Another woman was summoned. She spoke a smattering of French. She told Burnell he could have a bath. His clothes would be brushed. And the lady he called 'Madame Sigua' would bathe him. She assured him they were happy to entertain an Englishman. He was thrice welcome in the best house in town.

The house could hardly have been more hospitable, or the substitute Madame Sigua more assiduous. She made Burnell welcome in every way, even to the extent of venturing into the bath with him. What though it was a tin bath with scarcely room for one? By her lying on top of him, she showed how both of them could be accommodated.

Her touch was as soft as gypsophila.

Burnell could not resist such a warm welcome. And how finely the house was furnished – though with a plethora of beds. When she had towelled him, she led him into a shuttered room. The bed was almost as narrow as the bath but, by adopting roughly the same ruse as previously, they both managed together. The lady was sumptuous in every particular, and Burnell examined most of them. It was his privilege to sample the renowned beauty of Georgian women at his leisure. They locked themselves so tightly together they squeaked. By slow sensuous movements, instinct mingling with practice, they came together.

'*Kargi?*' she asked.

'Immensely *kargi*. More please . . .' Recalling the other Georgian word he knew, he added, 'Immensely *chakhokhbili*!'

He slept. They were still interlocked, he in her, she round him.

On the human inhabitants of Bogdanakhi, curfew had been imposed. Packs of dogs, having the town to themselves, raged about the streets till dawn, disrupting dreams, the good dreams, the bad dreams.

Burnell woke as lights came through the shutters of the little room. Miss Butterbuttocks had gone. His head was abnormally large; other parts of his body were similarly engorged. He climbed out of bed and opened the window to let in some fresh air. He shivered.

Outside, Bogdanakhi was woebegone. The golden city of yesterday had faded away. In its place were workaday streets and broken pavements. Most of the contents of Burnell's pack had also faded away. In particular, his valuable cameras and the camcorder, brought along to record the Church of Ghvtismshobeli in detail – the ostensible reason for his mission – had disappeared.

Late rising is the custom in whorehouses. The place was as silent as a cathedral; only the smells were different. Burnell knew better than to complain about the theft. Lies would be as thick on the ground as used condoms. He put on his tattered and still filthy jeans and went downstairs with the lightened pack. An old bouncer, roused to grumpiness, unlocked the door and let him into the street.

He was thoroughly out of sorts with himself. It was strange how every shred of moral fibre blew away like dead leaves at the chance of getting a woman's legs open. Where does it all end? he asked himself. His only duty was to get to the church by Lake Tskavani as soon as possible and then leave this benighted country before more fighting broke out. He didn't need Jim Irving, he certainly didn't need Kaginovich. All he needed was a guide, and that had been pre-arranged by signals from FAM and WACH offices. Or so he hoped.

Any later wave of local violence would be more savage, after various arms dealers had seized on their opportunities.

People were stirring, despite the early hour. Indeed, the dismal streets were busy with men – mainly men – going in this direction and that, looking worn.

Three planes flew over. They circled. They flew low enough for the insignia of the Tbilisi government to be seen. Everyone ran for cover. Burnell ran with them. He sheltered in a stinking cellar. Three bombs fell somewhere outside. An old man nudged Burnell to get his attention. He pointed to his wrist where a watch had been, then to the sky. Burnell thought him to mean, 'They always come over just when I'm about to have my breakfast.'

But it was doubtful if the old man, or any of the other poor-arsed people trooping slowly from the refuge, enjoyed the luxury of breakfast. The ordinary citizen of Bogdanakhi was pale and tired and decidedly under-fed. Such persons were not welcome at mayors' banquets. You had to be fat or foreign to get an invitation to a banquet. It was a law universally observed.

8
Looking for a Postcard

The Bogdanakhi airstrip, already out of action, had been bombed again. The bombs had missed and hit a row of houses on the outskirts of town, near the railway station. The houses burned in a leisurely way, sending drifts of smoke into the centre of town.

Burnell did not dislike this picturesque touch. It made him feel intrepid – something to tell Stephanie about. 'A pall is drifting across the table as I write . . .'

Like many of the city's inhabitants, he was in a ragged state. During the adventures of the previous night, he had ripped the leg of his jeans, so that his knee showed. In Europe, a certain kind of youth prided themselves in having knees or indeed buttocks protruding through tattered jeans: a folk gesture towards a vanished proletariat. Such tricks of sartorial fashion worked only in prosperous societies. Here, his naked knee served more as a badge of extinction than distinction, and all too well suited his low mood.

He found the mayor's office, situated in a building with a bullet-spattered façade on the main square, Ploshchad Dimbarza. The undusted interior presented a touching mix of battered filing-cabinets, some electronic equipment, and worn Second Empire furniture. The walls were hung with vast oils of peasant girls in kerchiefs on co-operatives. He noticed how their scythes followed you round the room.

Hardly surprisingly, Sigua was not there. The office and its staff looked tense. The girls were pale and nervous, huddling together under a faded portrait of Lenin glaring gloomily outwards at the intruder, like a musk ox protecting its young. No information was forthcoming. Burnell put this down to the air raid.

Sigua's deputy was finally induced to emerge from an inner cubbyhole: a scruffy young man smoking a cigarette and sniffing. He cringed and kept glancing at the girls, as if for assistance. His manner invited bullying; Burnell accepted. He stressed his friendship with Mayor Sigua, while refraining from mentioning the kiss at the banquet. This only caused the deputy to draw another cigarette out of a battered packet and burst into a smoke-filled explanation in Georgian.

After more persistence on Burnell's part, he fetched an official form from his cubbyhole. The form, completed in purple ink, stated that two functionaries, a priest and a protector, had been appointed for Dr Burnell's visit by Mayor Sigua. Sigua stated that civic funds had been issued on behalf of the WACH, in order that Dr Burnell should proceed in safety to the historic Church of Ghvtismshobeli, the Church of the Mother of God.

This was very satisfactory.

Questioned through one of the office women, who spoke schoolgirl French, the deputy told Burnell that Father Kadredin, the priest designated, had volunteered for the mission. She said, 'The Holy Father has engaged a gunman.' Burnell was not averse to this last statement; it had a truly Georgian ring to it.

He asked again about Mayor Sigua. Again he received an evasive answer. All looked nervous. One slip of a girl crossed herself. The French-speaker told Burnell what he already knew, that the airstrip was bombed and out of action.

'There is enemy everywhere. Everywhere enemy. Enemy in Bogdanakhi.' She looked suspiciously at Burnell. 'Have you passport?'

Burnell asked to send a cable to General Stalinbrass in FAM. This restored their confidence in his bona fides, and he was allowed to do so. In his message he asked for assistance and, if possible, a helicopter. The ladies offered a coffee, which he refused. He had determined to replace his tattered jeans with a good pair of trousers, if possible, and said he would return in an hour for a reply to the cable.

There were fewer people than before on the streets. Burnell was too low in mood to worry about that. The city was smaller than had appeared the previous day: smaller and more broken. Its magic had fled and no bands played. Along one of the two main avenues, the houses proved to be mere shells, burnt out, their façades mocking. Bomb craters made some streets impassable. A line of trees had been roughly hacked down, to serve as firewood when electricity failed.

Such shops as were open were practically empty of goods. On a patch of waste ground a few women stood behind stalls offering vegetables like museum pieces. A cock with its clockwork strut walked near by, crowing intermittently in almost human terms of complaint. Burnell went over to look at a booth selling newspapers. He hoped to find a postcard to send to his ex-wife in California, but there was no such thing.

As he turned back into the other main avenue, a man was running by. It was Jim Irving. When Burnell hailed him, Irving paused and then came over. He shook hands, asking concernedly if Burnell was all right.

'I want to get you out of town fast, OK? I'm just fixing details. The Dead One has made a fatal move.'

'What's the trouble?'

'Later. Tell you later. Going to attend a meeting.' He was about to press on when a beggar came over at a fast shuffle and seized his hand. It was the blind man to whom Irving had spoken on the previous day. His notice still hung round his neck. He had been standing in a doorway, and came when he heard the American's voice.

They shook hands. While Burnell stood by, they conversed in Georgian. The beggar showed Irving a saucepan full of money. Even as he held it out for inspection, a passer-by dropped another coin in it.

The beggar went off in one direction, Burnell and Irving in the other. Burnell asked why the beggar's luck had changed.

'His faith in the kindness of his fellow-men has been restored. He figures it's all on account of the new notice around his neck.'

'What exactly did you write on his notice?'

'I put, "Next week, the moon above us will be full – I shall not see it." That did the trick. As you maybe learnt at the banquet, these Georgians set great store by poetry. Some of 'em do, let's say.'

Giving himself a self-satisfied smile, he was off again.

Pretty smart, thought Burnell, and continued his search for trousers.

Douglas Freshfield in his book had praised the shops of Bogdanakhi. He noted that they contained a wealth of Western goods, including saddles, hip flasks, china dolls with eyes that closed, and opera glasses. But that had been almost a century and a half ago. Civilization had received many body blows since then, and was retreating under a tide of edicts, insurrections, orphans, invoices, and independence movements.

The only goods on display were cheap print dresses, more vegetables, and quantities of a small white enamel cooker made in Volgograd, with which several shops were over-stocked. There was no chance of replacing his cameras.

Turning into a side street, he discovered an old garage converted into a store. The owner, an Armenian, presided over a trove of junk, including furniture and clothing. Among the clothes were hats, boots, and garments from many cultures. At the murky back of the store, Burnell came on a pile of English cavalry twill trousers, well provided with pockets, and ginger in colour. He bought a pair which fitted, and strode out into the sunlight wearing them, his old jeans under his arm. The feeling of self-consciousness would pass; and perhaps the ginger would fade.

In Ploshchad Dimbarza was a bar, conveniently situated next to the mayor's offices. To determine whether it was open or not was a problem. No sign announced its function, its owner perhaps working on a Georgian ethical principle that those who could not detect the presence of drink unaided did not deserve any. Burnell went in.

A small terracotta-coloured space was filled with the officers of the West Georgian Republican Army. Among them was Ziviad Orpishurda in his black SAS jacket. Kaginovich was not present. The officers had their heads together in a conspiratorial way. Their heads went up, their glasses down, when Burnell entered. They immediately made preparations to leave.

'Look, I don't want to break things up,' Burnell protested.

All the cheer of yesterday had evaporated. The men's faces were pale and drawn. With a clatter, they gathered up their weapons from behind the bar, nodded to Burnell, who stood aside for them, and filed out into the square. Jim Irving was left, sitting alone at a round marble-topped table. Without quite erasing a frown, he motioned Burnell to sit down.

'Let me buy you an *arak*, Roy.' He had a Borzhomi mineral water in front of him. The dim room was now deserted except for the two of them and a short fat bartender in shirt-sleeves, who served up a drink with alacrity. He retired behind his bar, to stand under a fading portrait of the old king, Herekle II, who was looking reproachfully into the nostrils of a horse.

'There's going to be trouble,' Irving said. 'You'd better get out of town.'

He spoke in rather a curious way, out of the corner of his mouth.

To Burnell came a kind of folk memory of old Western movies seen on television. Whatever else was lost, old time-stained names returned; Clint Eastwood, John Wayne, Alan Ladd, Gary Cooper . . . This was a replay with Irving seeing himself in the lead. The bar, the barman, the lull before the storm, the sunlit square empty outside, the sheriff prepared for trouble, his Winchester out of sight under the table, uttering his immortal lines. 'We got till sunset . . . Go while the going's good . . .'

Nervously trying to act his part, Burnell tossed down the *arak*, right to the back of his throat. He felt no better afterwards. It tasted much like the *anis* he drank in Paris *bistros*. Only the glass was dirtier. 'Perhaps I need a Borzhomi too,' he said, with a plunge out of character.

'Kaginovich has to be killed,' Irving said, from under an imaginary stetson. He sipped his mineral water, the good man forced to take up his gun again.

'You were going to tell me how he acquired his nickname,' said Burnell, trying to force Irving from his self-imposed role.

Irving fixed his disconcerting eyes on Burnell before speaking.

'Moral emptiness. That's what the world's suffering from. That's what we'll die of, Roy. "Without vision, the people perish . . ." Moral emptiness. You can feel it round you all the time.'

'To be honest, I can't feel it, Jim. You mean here in Transcaucasia?'

'Everywhere. In you too, I'd say. Maybe that's why you can't feel it. That dissolute banquet yesterday – it disgusted me. You know a great deal about churches and mosques but they're just empty shells to you. You have no religion.' Of course the old Westerns often had a preacher to point a moral.

'Spare me, Jim, for I have sinned. Barman, *erti* Borzhomi please!'

Irving leaned forward, tapping the table with an index finger. 'Don't fool around with your soul! Try to understand the inner meaning of the situation here. Every human drama is also a theological drama. Lazar Kaginovich was born of the dead. That is why he is a leader in this part of the world, where all bar nationalistic creeds are dead. Hearts are dead. Oh yes, they pretend Christianity, but those decades under Communism have perverted their faith.'

'Look –' said Burnell. But Irving fixed him with blazing blue eyes and launched into a terrible story.

Thirty years earlier, he said, an epidemic of cholera swept through Georgia. The Soviet authorities kept quiet about the disaster – censored it, so that the outside world never heard of the epidemic. Mass graves were dug. Thousands of people, men, women, children, died. Prayers were illegal but were said nevertheless by the few surviving priests.

'OK. A young girl called Medea lived in Bogdanakhi. She was just twenty years old, well liked, very pretty, and a member of the Komsomol, the Communist Youth Movement. Medea fell ill. She was taken to hospital. There she appeared to die. Parents wept, gave her up for dead, and a priest performed last rites over her. An over-worked doctor signed her death certificate. She was laid out on a slab to be buried next morning.'

Medea was renowned for her prowess in gymnastics. She was

famous as far away as Tbilisi. News of her death caused a stir, even when so many people were going daily to their graves.

A Commissar in his sixties, white-haired, white-moustached, had had his eye on Medea and encouraged her career. As a token of respect, he volunteered on behalf of the Komsomol to stand vigil all night over Medea's corpse. The family didn't dare refuse the honour.

But the old fox's motives were not pious. Drinking in the morgue, alone in the small hours, the Commissar got to peeking at the beautiful corpse. He became excited. Ripping off the coverings, he had a good look, and copulated with Medea's dead body.

'That's what he did, Roy. The sin was well attested. Raped the dead body, front and rear . . .'

'Look, I'm not exactly feeling too great,' Burnell said.

Irving took a sip of his mineral water before continuing.

'Came the morning, Medea's parents found the body had been interfered with, the sheets ripped. They called in the doctor, they raised Cain, they rang through to Tbilisi to protest at the desecration. To save its face, the hospital backed them, for once. An order went out for the old monster's arrest. The penalty for such a crime was death.

'The Commissar fled for his life. He just disappeared. Some say he slipped across the frontier into Turkey, where such crimes are taken more lightly.

'But Medea was not dead. She had fallen into a coma. The cholera had vanished. It was a miracle. Even as her parents wept over her defiled body, Medea stirred and came to life!'

'I see,' said Burnell. 'So the old Commissar did some good after all – pumped life back into her . . .'

Irving looked pained. 'Nothing of the sort. Like I said, a miracle happened. The parents believed that God had spared their only child.'

'Wait a minute! In that case, God had also arranged for the Commissar to have a go at her.'

'Don't be facetious, Roy. Wickedness is wickedness. The poor girl was in some pain. The nurses washed her violated body before allowing the parents to take their daughter home. She soon recovered, was just a little brain-damaged . . . Lack of oxygen to the brain. On the whole she was unharmed, although she had lost the power of speech. Certainly unharmed enough to bear a child. An unwanted and illegitimate son . . .'

'Kaginovich?'

Irving nodded. 'Kaginovich. Lazar Kaginovich. They gave the child the surname of the malefactor and the first name of Lazarus risen from the dead. He was regarded as conceived in death. A miracle.'

'Another miracle!'

'See, it was a kind of virgin birth in reverse . . . The Dead One. As a kid, the community allowed him to do whatever he wanted, without check, because of the superstitious awe inherent in poor people. No father around to knock a little sense into him.'

'What happened to Medea?'

Irving's voice was stern with unspoken judgement. 'She died just two months ago, killed in the bombing. Only fifty, but an old woman, partly gaga. The army officers I was talking to say his mother's death tipped something in Kaginovich's mind. They can't get through to him.' Turning, he slipped momentarily from his preacher role to revert to Western mode, calling, 'Bartender, another drink for my friend.'

'No more, thanks. It's a pretty ghastly story,' said Burnell. 'What happens now?'

With a certain satisfaction, Irving said, 'It's happened. Kaginovich quarrelled with Mayor Tenguiz Sigua after the banquet yesterday. Some say Sigua punched Kaginovich. The Dead One had him arrested, and has announced that the mayor is to be executed, shot, here in Dimbarza Square.'

Burnell stood up. 'It can't be. They were friends.' In true cowpoke style, he downed the fiery *arak* the barman brought in one gulp, without thinking. The Dook would have hated *anis*. 'He can't shoot the mayor!'

'Kaginovich can shoot anyone.'

Irving put his hands behind his head and stretched out in lazy Gary Cooper fashion. 'Fact is, Sigua is some kind of distant relation of Medea's. They're all related to each other here. But Kaginovich is making an example of Sigua. Seems Sigua refused to permit any local men to be conscripted into Kaginovich's army. Kaginovich was relying on picking up a thousand reinforcements in Bogdanakhi. Sigua told him to get lost. He needs the men to defend the city against possible future ground attack from Tbilisi. So Kaginovich had him arrested. Sigua has been denounced as a traitor and is to be shot at twelve noon.'

Burnell felt only shock at this fresh evidence of man's ingenuity to man. 'What do Ziviad and the other officers make of it?'

'They believe the city will be up in arms against them.' Still in the sheriff role, Irving said dramatically, 'Shooting could break out at twelve. That's why I want you out of here. Pronto.'

Burnell looked at his watch. It was an hour to High Noon.

He returned to the mayor's office. The door was locked. He knocked and rang the bell. Finally the French-speaking woman looked out from an upper window.

'Go away, *m'sieu!*'

'My cable from Stalinbrass.'

She disappeared. She reappeared. A piece of paper fluttered down to him. He ran and grabbed it. The text of the cable from FAM was brief. It read: 'YOUR MESSAGE NOT UNDERSTOOD.'

Burnell looked up. But all the windows of the building were closed. The woman had gone. He began to knock and ring; it might have been the House of the Dead for all the response he received.

Faintly annoyed and considerably thirsty, he turned back to the bar he had left only a few minutes earlier. It too had closed. Of Irving there was no sign. He looked about the square. Every door was being shut, every shutter being locked in place.

As Burnell stood watching these preparations, a noise reached him as of the rats leaving Hamelin Town. The citizens of Bogdanakhi were coming, whispering along in boots, trainers, and bare feet. Already a crude platform had been built in the middle of the square. They were coming to watch – not yet having had enough of death – the execution of their mayor.

A terrifying blast of E flat major assailed him. He jumped. Piano notes like hammer blows ricocheted off the stone flags. From the metal throats of loudspeakers all round the square, Beethoven's 'Emperor' Concerto stormed out at polysaturated amplification, shaking Burnell like all the voices of the wilderness crying in one. He ran for it, being a music lover.

He found himself struggling against a tide of people, great men, small men, lean men, brawny men, brown men, white men, grey men, tawny men, grave old plodders, gay young friskers. Burnell stood in a doorway and let them flow by. Behind the mob marched a more organized one, the Army of the West Georgian Republic in file of threes, led by Ziviad Orpishurda. And bringing up the rear marched Jim Irving, head held high.

Burnell fell in with them, tightening his grip on the shoulder-strap of his pack and instinctively picking up on the step.

'I'll bet it wasn't like this on the Moon!'

'You've got to get out of here, Roy. Orpishurda agrees. He can't guarantee what will happen if the Dead One carries out his threat to shoot the mayor.'

'And you?'

'Oh, I'm just an observer. I'll continue with the column to the Black Sea, I guess. If there's no mutiny. If things get really bad, I can always call up a chopper to airlift me out.'

'And God? As before?'

Irving looked at Burnell with his grave grey-blue eyes. Burnell smiled apologetically, thinking that here, after all, was a good man. Maybe good men were always comic to the trivial-minded. Certainly Jim Irving had the measure of Burnell's self-indulgent nature. His greed at the banquet, the wallow in the brothel – these were known to Irving, were accepted, but pained him nevertheless. 'God may provide a chopper if it suits his plan,' Irving agreed, with his smile.

Perhaps only a saint or a lunatic could still trust in his lunar vision: that somehow it was possible for mankind to live less miserably – even when he had returned to a world that believed no such thing.

Ploshchad Dimbarza was already filling with the able-bodied of

Bogdanakhi. The 'Emperor' had been faded down. Most of the men were slung about with weaponry; many had with them dogs on leashes as savage-looking as themselves, as if attending a 'Bring Back the Neanderthals' demonstration. It was much like a cattle market, except that these cattle added shouting and cursing to the jostling. Jeeps of Russian manufacture rumbled forward, headlights glaring back at the sun. Across the bridge spanning the Tskavani came a line of tanks bedecked with branches of trees, bullying their way forward amid crowds which reluctantly gave way. Over the crackle of the loudspeakers came a crackle of bullets from a distant part of town: rehearsals for the real thing were in progress.

Before Burnell and Irving diverged, the latter announced he had a parting present. 'I'm glad to see you don't pack a gun, although Ghvtismshobeli is out in the wilds. Ziviad said the church is wired off, so you might need these. They're good and sharp.'

He produced a pair of wire-cutters. As he handed them over, he saluted. Burnell thanked him awkwardly, and tucked them in one of the rear pockets of the ginger trousers. 'I'll see you when I get back.'

'Hope so. God be with you.' Burnell put out a hand. Smiling, Irving shook it.

Burnell jumped on to a low stone wall and surveyed the crowd. His eye was caught by a gaunt man in black, waving to him from beside the bridge. He knew intuitively that this must be the priest who had volunteered to lead him to Ghvtismshobeli. He elbowed his way through the throng to the bridge.

The Moon had one attraction. It was less crowded.

9

A Head Among the Throng

The priest stood out from the mob as a film star stands out from a crowd of extras. Though not exceptionally tall, he was exceptionally thin, to the extent of appearing to have no stomach or buttocks. This boardlike aspect was emphasized by a black habit, which trailed almost to the ground. Over this he wore what had until recently been a sheep, or at least half a sheep. It still smelt of the dead animal. His hair was long and dark, though he had long since passed life's meridian, such as it was; this hair seemed to enjoy a luxury denied the rest of the priest's anatomy, spilling over at back and at front, exuberantly. Two bulging hyperthyroid eyes summed up Burnell with a melancholy scrutiny. They seemed to say, and his mouth was in total agreement, 'Here's another sinner, as bad as the rest, and foreign with it.'

He clasped his hands together rather than offering either one of them, and introduced himself as Father Nolin Kadredin. To pronounce the final syllables of his name, he pulled back his lips to show a few black teeth, coffin-shaped in receding gums. He addressed Burnell in French as he proclaimed his delight in being permitted to guide the Englishman to the Holy Church of the Mother of God.

After Burnell had made appreciative remarks, he was introduced to the youth who stood slightly to Father Kadredin's rear. This was the appointed gunman, an over-grown lad of fourteen, by name Khachi. Khachi was dressed in drab shorts and immense black boots. His arms were tattooed with women and spaceships. Over his T-shirt he had slung what was presumably the other half of Kadredin's sheep, fleece inwards. To make himself look more bloodthirsty, he had tied a red kerchief round his forehead. He was further burdened with a large pack and a Kalashnikov. When introduced, he seemed to take an immediate dislike to Burnell, swaggering round him twice and sneering, with sound effects, to show contempt for Burnell's unarmed state, or possibly the ginger trousers.

'Is the boy your – er, um, acolyte? You are a priest of the Orthodox Church, Father?' Burnell asked.

'No more,' said Kadredin, in a deep voice, bowing his head in such a way that made it uncertain which of the questions he was answering, if any.

An interesting and complex character, said Burnell to himself. Just what I need.

'Are you prepared to leave immediately?' Burnell asked. As he spoke, however, Beethoven was cut off in mid-bar, to be replaced by a booming voice. Although Burnell understood hardly a word of the Georgian language except *kargi*, he apprehended the effects of the announcement. With an amount of non-pacific shouting, the West Georgian Republican Army formed up to make a living avenue from the platform in the centre of the square to the main street leading from it. They clearly understood that Kaginovich, the Dead One, would approach from this direction with his prisoner, Mayor Sigua, the About-to-be-Dead One.

At the same time, citizens and soldiers faithful to Sigua formed up on the other side of the platform, swinging their weapons into the ready position, ominously clicking off safety catches. How Kaginovich would deal with this lethal situation, Burnell could not guess; nor did he want to stay and see. His life had in the main been spent in quiet places, up towers, measuring tombs, or slung in cradles photographing roof bosses. He wanted to get away from the smell of violence. But Father Kadredin clasped his shoulder, made a perfunctory gesture of raising finger to lips, and said, 'Peace.'

As if in obedience to the priest's injunction, silence fell in the square. Directly across from where Burnell, the priest, and the gunman stood was the grandiose building which housed the mayor's offices. Double doors leading on to the balcony over the main entrance were thrown open with a crash. All heads turned in that direction.

It was twelve o'clock. A bugler marched smartly on to the balcony and sounded a call. He then retired. The balcony was momentarily empty.

Lazar Kaginovich himself appeared.

Greeting him came a rumble like an approaching avalanche. It issued from the throats of the crowd. The rumble ascended the scale, lost its unanimity, and broke into individual shouts of hatred or support.

'Murderer!' screamed a woman near by.

Kaginovich made no attempt to speak. For a moment he remained motionless on the balcony. His pale death's head looked as if it never spoke. The crowd fell silent. Kaginovich raised high his right arm. By this action he exposed to everyone's view the prize exhibit he clutched by the hair. It was the freshly severed head of Mayor Tenguiz Sigua. He had duped everyone.

Sigua's eyes stared blindly ahead, feasting their sight on oblivion. Sigua's bearded jaw hung open. Sigua's torn throat dripped. Sigua's face was little paler than Kaginovich's.

'Sigua!' A roar from the crowd.

Kaginovich allowed them only a brief glimpse of his gruesome trophy. Time to identify it, no more. Then with demonic force he hurled it into the throng below.

Before it struck, he backed away and was gone from the balcony. Such was the shock value of his appearance that no man, not his most relentless enemy, would have had the wits to take aim and fire at him.

Fighting began in the square immediately.

'*Allons!*' said Father Kadredin, nudging Burnell.

He ran on his long skirted legs across the bridge, his robe rippling about him. Burnell followed, and the boy with the firepower followed Burnell. On the far side of the Tskavani they ran between houses down a filthy side alley. Over refuse and ordure they skipped. A mangy dog fled in fear, yelping. Firing sounded from the square behind them.

The priest led them into a house in a back street. They stood in a kitchen where a hound was tied to a table-leg. The gunman fondled the animal and in general showed signs of being better-intentioned than had hitherto been the case. Whose house it was, Burnell did not discover. Thankfully, he accepted water from a small cistern by the sink, and regained his breath.

'What will happen?' he asked Kadredin in his formal French. 'Will the people accept the rule of Captain Kaginovich?'

'Sigua allowed the people of Bogdanakhi no modernity. Though cruel, the Dead One will give them what they want.'

'Democracy?'

'Cable TV. VR. EMV.'

'Nintendos,' supplemented the gunman, catching his master's drift.

The church of Ghvtismshobeli had been built at a distance from habitation. At first their way led along the valley, through vineyards. They passed a burnt-out tank. No one was about; all had gone into town to see the execution. On isolated houses propitiatory slogans had been painted, large in red paint: 'LONG LIVE THE REPUBLIC' was evidently the safest slogan. It would serve as republics came and went, and vineyards remained.

Houses became more infrequent as they started to climb. They entered forests of oak and beech, following a faltering trail. Once they encountered three desperate-looking men on emaciated horses. The boy gunman handled his Kalashnikov ostentatiously. The riders passed by without a word.

'Mm, horses would be good,' said the priest. 'Do you ride?'

'I used to.'

They saved their breath for the climb.

Compensating for the steepness of the ascent, the views became more generous. Where the trees fell away, they could see back to Bogdanakhi, could see the gleam of the railway line and the serpentine glitter of the river. Happiness filled Burnell. Difficulties there might be; meanwhile there was the beauty and freedom of the world to enjoy. He wondered why Jim Irving, in search of God, had found Him on the barren Moon rather than here, where the abundance of nature suggested that a good-hearted deity might indeed have decided to show what He was made of.

As they climbed, all three assisting their knees by pressing down with their hands, Burnell recalled a legendary tale a drunk had told him in Tbilisi. He smiled to himself.

When the world was being parcelled out among the various nations, God gave to each nation according to its deserts, which was why the Russians got Siberia and the Arabs a load of barren sand. The Georgians didn't show up at all, because they were all away enjoying a huge celebratory banquet. When they arrived at God's place next morning, rather hung over, they were too late. God had given all the land away.

'Sorry,' God said. 'Never mind,' said the Georgians, 'we're just about to throw another party. Come along with us, God, and forget your sorrows.' So God went with them, and had such a good time and got so merry that when it was His turn to give a toast, He announced that He had been keeping the very best bit of the world for himself. He had called it 'Georgia' after an old flame; an old sweet song kept her on His mind. But they could have the land. So they accepted and moved in.

As God was leaving, the Georgians called out, 'Hey, where are You going to live?' And the Almighty replied, hand on door latch, 'I'm just going to pop out for a million years. So you lot will have to look after yourselves.'

And looking after themselves was what the Georgians had had to do ever since.

As the sun was sinking, Father Kadredin led them to a dilapidated wooden house, behind which several goats were tethered. They were greeted by an old lame woman dressed in black, looking much like a witch in a fairy tale, with a long nose and a long chin and only a line of whiskers to keep them apart. The priest addressed her respectfully as 'Babo'. She took them in and immediately made a fuss of Khachi, the gunman, removing his kerchief to stroke his head and pouring him a bowl of goat's milk.

The old biddy was bent double with rheumatics. As she moved back and forth across her room, it was arguable whether the creaking came from her bones or the boards underfoot. Nevertheless, she was sprightly enough to hobble quickly away from Burnell. As they seated themselves at her table that evening, the priest said she was afraid of foreigners. 'Babo' served them wine and a tough bread called *lavash*, together with a large goat's cheese. The priest thanked her and blessed her.

In answer to a question Kadredin posed over supper, Burnell told him of the WACH interest in recording for future preservation the church they were heading for. From reticence he said nothing of the ikon, the Madonna of Futurity.

'The Church of the Mother of God is ancient,' said Kadredin, with a cheek full of *lavash*. 'Many myths attach to it – myths involving the history of Transcaucasia as well as the Word of God. But you are interested only in the fabric, is that so?'

'Professionally, yes.' The wine was wonderfully rough and rich. He raised his cup to old 'Babo' and drank. '*Jos!*'

'The fabric, hah! The outside show. Of the histories, the sacred nature of the church as House of God, you care nothing, *n'est-ce pas?*'

'I understand that during the years of Communist rule the church was closed. It became derelict, didn't it? No one cared even for the fabric then. Who cares for it now? Only, as far as I can see, World Antiquities and Cultural Heritage.'

'No, no, is incorrect.' He tossed back his unruly hair in denial. 'Many of us care. But we have no means while the world is in such turmoil. We are so poor.' He exposed the blackened teeth, breathing deep. He took only a sip of his wine. 'Why does not the EU help Georgia? This old woman here, she is Miss Georgia, a symbol of how we have all become. Why do they leave us in such a terrible state? They care for the fabric of this church, yes, but what about our people and our terrible poverty? Why cannot we join the EU?'

Burnell saw that there might be a long evening ahead. He drank more deeply. The old woman came with a candle and placed it in the centre of the table. The flickering light increased the depth of the shadows gathering about them. Khachi said nothing. At the back of the house, the goats cried aloud to the Moon.

While not wishing to quarrel with the lanky priest, Burnell

128

would not let his questions pass unchallenged. With a chunk of the harsh bread halfway to his mouth, he said, 'The abuse of human rights in this part of the world, such as I have myself witnessed, precludes any possibility of Georgia joining the EU. That's quite apart from other factors.'

'Why does this man Stalinbrass come to our country? He kills too.'

Ignoring this, Burnell said, 'For the rest, my advice would be for you to help yourselves, and cease blaming the outside world. It is never sufficiently recognized that the epidemic of Communism includes the painful convalescence of Post-Communismitis. Somehow, you will get through that phase. You must not destroy our own infrastructure. The patient must be his own doctor.'

'Without wishing to be impolite, sir, you drink of *Babo*'s wine too much. Such nonsense could be spoken only by those who have not suffered under repressive regimes. I take it you are not yourself religious?'

Burnell regarded the long face with its protruding eyes and the hank of hair hanging over the forehead. It was a striking physiognomy. He was prepared to like it. But liking that particular question was another matter. He delayed answer while he tore off another mouthful of bread and cheese.

'Religion has nothing to do with economics, or with the questions you raise. I am an atheist, Father. I find the world's various beliefs in various gods – well, misguided.'

Kadredin continued to masticate, moving his wad of half-chewed bread from one cheek to the other.

Then he said, 'Faith is man's greatest gift. What do you offer in place of faith?'

Smiling, Burnell leaned forward, elbows on table. This was an argument through which he knew his way.

'The times are always troublous. What is faith, Father, tell me? Isn't it just a belief that can't be moved in something that can't be proved?'

A long conversation was launched. Kadredin looked miserable as he defended a faith he professed to have lost. Nor was Burnell as sure of his case as he pretended, for the fact remained, as he was aware, that he had nothing to offer in place of the religious impulse. For all their private reservations, both men enjoyed debate, speaking for the most part in low tones. The young gunman moved from the table, to listen to a small portable radio, which he jammed against his ear as he munched his food. The old woman sat on a box, staring vacantly into space, breathing noisily through her mouth.

Though a moon was rising, the Georgian night was so dark that the single window reflected the candle on the table and the faces of the two men, talking and talking.

Burnell was teasing the priest, who claimed that God was mighty and grieved to see the divisions among humans. Burnell asked how God got on with Allah and Baal and Mithras and the Homeric gods.

Kadredin replied that such questions refuted themselves by their own foolishness. So it went. Every so often, the old woman would recollect herself, cross the creaking floor, and refill their cups with the strong wine.

When Burnell praised intelligence and enquiry above faith, Kadredin countered by remarking that Lazar Kaginovich was intelligent; to which he was reminded that Kaginovich also accounted himself a Christian. Growing more excited, for he saw where to develop a more crushing line of argument, Burnell said that philosophers and poets had long since agreed that it was impossible to believe that the great Spirit – whatever you called it – which created the universe could possibly have thought of coming down to Earth to have intercourse with some unknown woman in Palestine. That was just a primitive Creation myth, along with the tales of Adam and Eve, and the Devil with great wings. To believe such mumbo-jumbo disqualified one from logical thought.

Bowing his head, the priest sat in silence after this for such a long while that Khachi came over to see that he was well. At last Kadredin spoke in a low voice.

'Then I shall not argue with you more. You defeat me, sir. You have been sent by whatever power from your modern country to abuse me here and bring my sin of doubt to confront me. Well, I won't blame you for arrogance. Instead, I blame myself for worthlessness. As you point out, the scriptures must be absolutely worthless also . . . All I and my people have believed in is illusion. It is best if I take Khachi's gun and shoot myself – not in here, but outside among the goats . . .'

At this Burnell was greatly alarmed. He saw that he had trespassed, whether or not the priest was sincere in what he said. He begged him to cheer up, to see that they were just two men, friends already, having a discussion over supper, one warm evening in the country.

In any case, he added, by way of excusing himself, he had understood the priest to say that he had lost his faith, and so rather expected he felt the way he, Burnell, did.

Kadredin gave no answer. He rose, tall and thin, hair falling about his face, to stare for a time at the candle flame, now burning low. Then he marched over and took the Kalashnikov from Khachi. Burnell got hastily to his feet.

Kadredin smacked the gun. He declared that with such weapons Georgia had defended the Christian faith against heathen enemy over many centuries. Was such faith to be insulted during a so-called 'discussion over supper'? He wished to say, without wanting to be offensive – that Burnell was an enemy of all the Orthodox Church stood for. How typically unfeeling of the West, to send such a man, who had blasphemed against the Mother of God, to inspect Ghvtismshobeli, the shrine of the Mother of God.

Lifting his cup, but not drinking from it, Burnell explained humbly that it must have been the wine which spoke. He apologized if he had given offence. He begged Kadredin to sit down and continue with the meal, and he promised to say nothing more on the subject.

With reluctance, Kadredin approached the table, while Burnell politely stood for him. He caught sight of his own face, pale, reflected in the glass of the window. Isn't this typical of you?, he thought; you must always have been like this; no wonder Steff left you.

As Kadredin sat down, he remarked in a sulky voice that it was evident Burnell had not had parents to show him what he referred to as the Way. He had been fortunate in that his dear father had been exceptionally devout.

'Ah ha!' said Burnell.

And before he could stop himself, he had launched into the argument that religion was similar to a virus.

'A virus, Father Kadredin. Which children can catch from their parents. Some people grow out of it when they're adult. They cure themselves – the body throws it off, as it throws off measles. But the religious virus is pretty contagious, and occasionally sweeps through a country like an illness. Like influenza, it mutates, causing worship of one god here, another god there. The sufferers are all equally fervent. The brain is affected, as a computer can be ruined by a virus invading its programme.

'In extreme fevers – and there are records of many such in history – nothing will convince you you are unwell. You go forth and kill all those who are not of your faith. Crusades, pogroms, inquisitions, *fatwas* . . . In this way, the virus ensures its survival and propagates.

'Of course, the virus has lived so long with humanity it's now something of a symbiote: how else would the Jews have survived innumerable persecutions without strong infectious beliefs?

'Religion is similar to a psychotic condition. Maybe this terrible virus is carried in the genes, which harbour other destructive viruses. The chief symptom of this virus in those who contract it is that they believe they are in touch with God – often in some kind of intimate relationship with Him. Why else were lunatics in earlier times believed by the devout to be touched by God?' He had a certain shame-faced pride in this speech.

Lavash in hand, Kadredin rose from his chair.

'Sir, I can't listen more to you. I feel compassion for you and for your incomprehension. You speak in a language of science which I do not understand. I know science presumes to explain away all the secrets of the universe. But the love of God cannot be explained away, any more than sunlight can be explained.'

Burnell raised a fist. 'Sunlight can be explained! Science explains it.'

'You are so confident. Perhaps you too suffer from a virus? Science may explain the physical properties of sunlight. No one can explain the miracle of it. The beauty of it.'

With that, he pulled open the frail door of the house and went into the darkness.

All this time, Khachi had been eating with his mouth open, stuffing food into it intently, looking from one man to the other and saying nothing. 'Oh God, I've been drinking too much wine,' Burnell said to him. 'Why didn't the idiot remind me that self-discipline is one useful effect of religion?'

He couldn't endure the gustatory silences of the gunman. Sitting at the table, arms folded against its rough wood, Burnell remained staring into the candle flame. He wondered what he was thinking about. If God bothered to look down into his thoughts, He would see his mind blowing from side to side, flickering, no more capable of illuminating a room than could the candle.

Still the priest did not return. Staggering, Burnell got up, went to the door, pulled it open, and propelled himself into the darkness.

Some distance away moonlight was sketching in pasturage and clumps of trees. They registered as his eyes adjusted. The Moon in the sky was hidden from view by mountain, and did not shine on the old woman's house. Scabrous cloud piled overhead, still as glaciers, rendering the world in pencil-sketch form. Kadredin was standing a short distance from the house, thin, upright, one arm out horizontally to steady himself against a tree. He was looking away from the house. Burnell went over to him. He cleared his throat like a butler to announce his presence.

'Father, I wish to apologize for what I said just now. The wine's rather strong. Got the better of what I like to call my judgement . . .'

Kadredin did not respond.

'I'm too fond of argument. Sometimes I say things . . . well, we all do . . . I don't mean . . . You understand what I'm saying? I'm sorry.'

'It's not your fault.' Kadredin spoke without looking round, still gazing to where the land was laden with silver. 'I profess faith in God. But that faith has gone from my heart. You sensed that?'

'Please don't be offended. I'm a real shit. I was in a brothel last night in Bogdanakhi, screwing a prostitute. I'm sinful, I'm a sinner . . .' Yet even as he spoke, he was accounting himself insincere, and remembering how much he had enjoyed the lady.

133

He could not tell where his sincerity or his cameras had gone. Changing gear with an effort, he continued, 'I didn't intend to be insulting. Only clever. So I made a fool of myself.'

'Sir, you became clever because you perceive me for a fool. Men in general find my presence hard to tolerate. The Lord too, doubtless . . .'

'No, don't say that! Perhaps you are wiser than I. I'm a hollow man, Father. I'm in awful trouble. Ten years of my memory have been stolen. My wife's left me. I'm no one. Really, I'd be enormously glad of that love of God you talk about.'

Then Kadredin turned. He put a hand for a moment on Burnell's shoulder, saying in a deep voice, 'Let's sleep now. We shall make an early start in the morning.'

'Shit,' Burnell said to himself as they went back into the house and the aroma of goat. 'He's no fool. My penitence is utterly insincere and he sussed that. Why can't I find the truth in myself? I sincerely meant to be sincere . . .'

He laughed. He felt slightly sick. The night air was chilly.

As usual the dreams were bad. The one about divine justice, with God furious and driving a Jeep, almost cracked Burnell's skull open. When he thought he was waking, he thought he opened his eyes. There was the Devil, his face close to Burnell's. The sardonic lips, the beard, the caprine slitted eyes, the horns – oh, yes, it was the Devil right enough, much easier to recognize than God. And about to take a bite out of Burnell's flimsy blanket.

He sat up and shooed the goat away. Mists cleared from his mind. This was Hypothermia House. He rose shivering.

From the rear of the house – it was just a shack, he realized – came the sound of coughing. Moderately attracted by it, creaking at every step he took, he went through to the back room. It served as lounge, kitchen, stable, chapel, bathroom, and, presumably, abattoir. The goats were there. Kadredin stood at the back door. It was he who was coughing into the dawn air. Khachi was wandering aimlessly about outside.

'There's some coffee,' the priest said. He looked pale and strained. 'Then we'll be on our way.'

'Any breakfast?'

'You ate it for supper last night.'

As they shouldered up their packs and left, Burnell asked where the old 'Babo' was. Kadredin said she was already in the woods, gathering sticks and pheasant eggs. He had paid her for their night's stay. He named the sum. Burnell was astounded at its modesty.

'She doesn't understand inflation. She lives in the past,' said Kadredin, between coughs.

'Shouldn't we have given the poor old girl more than that?'

'We have a duty not to spoil things for other travellers who may come here.' As he spoke, he regarded Burnell with his bulging eyes and an absolutely straight face.

Throughout the day they walked. Khachi was always some way ahead of them, looking alert. The silence of the countryside had a calming effect on Burnell's nerves. At midday, they rested under a tree from the heat of the sun. Kadredin produced bread and salami and a bottle of flat Borzhomi.

The priest had been moody all morning. Finally he spoke in his leisurely French.

'Would you explain to me again this blasphemous thing you said about the virus of religion contracted in childhood? I wish to understand your theory.'

Burnell went through his argument again. In the end the priest said, 'What you say might apply to another form of belief – ideology. For most of the twentieth century, most of mankind was sick with one ideology or another. Maybe God has left this world . . .'

Khachi came and told them to get on their feet again. Ghvtismshobeli was no more than a stroll away. The approach might be dangerous. They should keep their silly traps shut.

Burnell nodded in agreement. 'From the mouths of babes and gunmen . . .'

10

'Time Had Run Out'

In Burnell's mind was a clear picture of Ghvtismshobeli, the Church of the Mother of God. In the WACH offices he had studied plans and old sepia photographs. He knew it for a monastic church, founded in the mid-sixteenth century by the strangely named King Zrze, and never completed.

He was unprepared, nevertheless, for their first sight of it. A brilliant scarlet in the western sky was flooding the cliffs about them with outrageous light. The going had become harder. They emerged through a thicket of stunted oaks on to a clearly defined path, where the priest and Burnell rested while Khachi reconnoitred ahead. There, partly visible, were the roofs of Ghvtismshobeli.

'"Childe Roland to the Dark Tower came" . . .' It was no time for quoting Browning, if there ever was one. Khachi returned to say in a whisper – Kadredin translated it into French – that the place was occupied. The occupants might well be dangerous.

This was bad news.

They moved forward cautiously. King Zrze had granted the church many hectares of land. The Communists had curtailed the land to a mere two hectares; the rest of the old church lands, cultivated for centuries by Christian and Muslim, had become wilderness.

Encircling the church and dormitory were walls of Communist razor wire to keep out intruders. It was for this reason that Jim Irving had given Burnell the wire-cutters, but they were not needed. A heavy vehicle, possibly a bulldozer, had been driven up and flattened the wire into the earth.

Here the approach was steep where a cliff had crumbled, taking stone steps with it in its fall. Inside the fenced-off area, a small house had stood. Shellfire had broken it open. As though in a wild token of self-destruction, the house had spewed out its miscellaneous contents to the elements.

The ruin spoke of lawlessness. The house had been built in part of breeze blocks. Perhaps a caretaker had lived here with his family, in the bygone days of Soviet power. Furniture spilled into brambles and rank grass from gaping mouths of rooms. Smashed beds, mattresses, a mirror, clothing, the entire clutter of domesticity, lay exposed to rot. Burnell wondered dully if there were corpses among the fallen rubbish. It was a gruesome introduction to Ghvtismshobeli.

As they negotiated this dismal site, music came to their ears. Wild and ragged, the sounds originated in another building, a corner of which came into view. The building stood foursquare between them and the church. It was a dormitory, intended for monks and holy men, pilgrims, and others, all of whom no longer existed. A cautious reconnaissance revealed figures on the upper colonnaded balcony which ran the length of the building. One man appeared to be armed.

Khachi signalled to Kadredin and Burnell to keep down. He crawled forward, clutching his gun. No sooner had he disappeared than shots rang out. Flocks of starlings, passing overhead through the dulling sky to roost, scattered with cries of alarm. Kadredin looked at Burnell with horror on his face. Burnell bit his lip and moved up to see what was happening. If the boy had been killed . . .

Khachi lay behind a bush. Without looking back, he gave the signal to lie flat. As he did so, more birds flew overhead. More shots rang out.

The lad and the two men scrambled back into better cover and consulted in whispers. The dormitory-dwellers were probably shooting at birds. Such random firing suggested a rough lot. Only four men, according to Khachi; of course, more might be in the building. Both Kadredin and his gunman were against Burnell's idea of simply appearing and hoping to be allowed to go to the church unmolested. At best, they would be beaten up and robbed.

While they were in this state of indecision, dusk came on and an almost full moon gained strength in the sky. They had retreated to the shattered house for better security. Burnell caught a movement and looked round hastily. It was only a reflection of Kadredin he had seen, caught in a cheval glass lying amid the debris.

That the mirror remained unclaimed, even though it was cracked, convinced him that they had met with ruffians. The ruffians had no women with them, who might have moderated their behaviour. Women would undoubtedly have claimed the mirror.

'Will these people be superstitious, do you think?' he asked Kadredin.

'Staying so near an empty church with its tombs? If they're ignorant men, they will be nervous.'

So it was that, a few minutes later, a spectral figure could be seen in the thick dusk. It paraded slowly in front of the dormitory, moving towards the church. This awesome figure was enveloped in white, in a sheet which also served as head-cover. In its arms it carried a babe in swaddling-clothes – or at least a bundle closely resembling a babe in swaddling-clothes.

The figure glowed with a ghostly aura, rendering it at once clear to the view and indistinct in detail.

When the spectre came into full view of the dormitory balcony, a cry went up from that quarter. Then shouts of alarm. 'The Mother of God! Preserve us! The Mother of God herself has arrived! See the infant Jesus in her arms! This dump is haunted!'

Burnell crouched behind a bush, directing the beams of the moon on Kadredin by means of the cheval glass. He listened with grim delight as the noise of alarm from the dormitory increased. He turned the mirror away: the Mother of God faded from view. Kadredin immediately ran back for cover, dragging the torn old sheet from his shoulders. He threw the filthy pillow he had cradled back into the destroyed house.

'You were very convincing,' Burnell whispered. By way of congratulation, he and the lad patted the priest. The latter mutely shook his head.

For simple minds, simple ruses. Of the success of this one they were soon aware. The stamp of boots, the noise of fighting, came from the dormitory. A pistol shot sounded. Screaming, shouting, then comparative quiet.

Minutes later, six men emerged, rushing into the courtyard. With all the haste they could muster, they harnessed up an old nag to a farm cart and set off, bumping down the trail by which the bulldozer had once entered the church grounds. They could be seen dimly in the moonlight, zigzagging downhill, shouting at each other to keep quiet.

Burnell, the priest, and the lad stayed where they were, crouched in concealment until dew and the evening chill got to them. The dormitory was approached with caution. A door stood open, from beyond which came a flickering light. Keen to show he was no coward, Burnell entered first. After a hall came a refectory. Refectory, kitchens – now in ruins – and a washroom occupied all the ground floor. The ruffians had started a fire in the refectory grate, burning logs dragged in from the woods.

Khachi went and stood by the fire, grinning and warming his hands. He seemed to want nothing more. He remained by the fire while Burnell and the priest searched the cubicles upstairs almost light-heartedly. Most of the cubicles were littered with excrement, and little else. On the balcony, where the ruffians had recently lounged, lay shells of cartridges, bottles, and a scatter of rubbish. A tin mug of coffee was still warm.

Their one great find was a quarter of roasted pig or boar, still smelling pleasant. This provided the basis for a meal, eaten with grapes, beside the refectory fire.

'So God has brought you safe to Ghvtismshobeli,' Kadredin said.

'*Kargi.*' Burnell was not going to argue tonight.

A discussion took place as to whether the gang might return. There was nothing in the dormitory to suggest that the ruffians were doing anything more than passing through the area. It seemed unlikely they would return. If they did so, it would be after daybreak, and their creaking cart would give warning. So Kadredin and Burnell sought to reassure each other while the young gunman cleaned his gun. How, Burnell wondered, does Khachi differ from Larry Foot? Here, no one greatly minds a little shooting.

Before turning in, Burnell went on his own to look at the church. He could not but wish Stephanie was with him. The moon was lower, lending a slanting light to the scene. He put his hand to the aged fabric, feeling the warmth coming from it.

Beneath his palm were brick, mortar, moss. He read them as if they were the firm flank of a horse. Whereupon, feelings of reverence conducted him back to the days of his boyhood when he used to ride with his mother, and to the Christmas when she and his father had given him Lollipop. Again he stood by the mare, patting her, overcome by gratitude. Then he swung himself up into the saddle, and he and his mother on Blaze had set off at a canter, towards Elmham Rise.

Many years later, when his father had remarried, Lollipop had been put out to grass in the upper pasture, where she could see horses on Farmer Hitchens's farm. But what had ultimately happened to his beloved mare . . . that part of the story had been stolen from him, along with much else.

Now he stood alone. His sensibilities were extended towards the building he had come to examine. It was as though the masonry had a kind of moral force or, at least, in the intentions of its builders, a powerful influence on the moral considerations of men, reminding them at once of morality and mortality; and he was sure such reflections had visited him before, at the site of other ancient structures now forgotten. Although he had studied the plans and knew the dimensions as figures, here in its presence he found the Church of Ghvtismshobeli larger than he had pictured it in imagination. Now the dark bulk of it loomed above him, continuing its centuries-long wait. This, he thought, this moment was worth everything.

On the far side of the venerable building the waters of Lake Tskavani glinted. Strange whisperings came from the reeds, while owls hooted about the church tower. Supposing one encountered the real Mother of God, as seemed not impossible, what could one say?

It was a creepy old place, no mistake about it. He was not sorry to return to the dormitory after a while.

By morning, all was different. The church was merely a monument to the past; it seemed smaller than in its moonlit avatar, perhaps a reminder of how much of the universe was subjective. Burnell was merely a representative of WACH with a covert interest in the fate of an ikon.

Ghvtismshobeli's tiled cupola reared above its pantiled roofing. Its walls, once richly carved, had been defaced at some period. They were now fairly covered with ivy. Walking round the exterior before venturing in, Burnell reflected on what he knew of the church's history. Old Douglas Freshfield had visited this spot in the eighteen-sixties, and had even included a steel engraving of the church in his book. But churches had not excited him greatly and he had made no mention of ikons.

The church, Burnell saw, had no grand claim to architectural merit. A casual viewer would regard it as Byzantine. In fact, it had been built over a century after the fall of Constantinople in a Caucasian style, and hastily built at that. It remained unfinished: a modest memorial to impossible dreams, set in a commanding position at an unfavourable time.

The structure was built of a local porous tuff or travertine and brick, arranged in patterns. The brick remained in good condition, mellow and pleasant; the tuff had weathered badly and had been inexpertly restored in places. Little here to start hearts a-beating at WACH. Burnell made a few notes and strolled about, enjoying the day and the destination.

He was alone. Father Kadredin was morose this morning, and out of sympathy with Burnell. He resented having been made to impersonate the Mother of God, and so to commit blasphemy. So he remained in the dormitory, for penance helping Khachi clear human excrement from the rooms.

For Burnell, solitude was welcome. He regretted only that he had been foolish enough to allow his cameras to be stolen. He reproached himself for his incurable gullibility. Monty Broadwell-Smith had deceived him all too easily.

Stephanie – had she been here – might have asked why the

church of Ghvtismshobeli was set in such a remote place. But churches were occasionally built to demarcate the frontiers of a king's domain. Ghvtismshobeli was designed to serve that function in the sixteenth century. King Zrze, ruler of what later became the Adjara Autonomous Region, was a sworn enemy of the Turk. Zrze commissioned the church to be erected to mark the extreme south-western point of his small kingdom. On one side of it, the northern, lay Lake Tskavani; to the south lay the expanding empires of the Mohammedan faith.

As Georgians never tired of telling their visitors, Georgia was surrounded by enemies. This was certainly true in the sixteenth century. The Safavids, moving in from Persia, captured Tbilisi – Tiflis as it was then – on two occasions. In 1555, the Ottomans and the Safavids divided what would become Georgia into two spheres of influence, the Ottomans taking the western half. Ten years after that, Zrze built his church. It became a monument to the triumph of hope over experience – and of experience over hope, for the Ottomans came notwithstanding.

Zrze left in a hurry. The decoration of his church was never finished, the interior decoration scarcely started, before the masons had to down tools and flee for their lives.

The Ottomans did not destroy Ghvtismshobeli. There it still stood, facing down the valley of the Tskavani, symbol of vanity and courage as well as holiness.

Father Kadredin appeared at mid-morning, his tall thin figure slightly stooped. Burnell looked at him enquiringly.

'So our fellowship is ended, sir,' said the priest in his fluent French, holding out a hand on which dirty fingernails predominated. 'I must now return immediately to Bogdanakhi, my duties completed, and take the lad with me. I only pray that you will not be murdered, as is undoubtedly likely when you are left here alone.'

'What's that? We've only just arrived. I'm not prepared to go yet. We haven't been inside the church yet. What are you talking about?'

'I am speaking of a task fulfilled, sir. As I am sure you know, I was paid only to guide you here. Not to guide you back.'

'It's blackmail, is it? Let me tell you straight, that won't work with me. You know very well you were well paid for both journeys.

You know it, I know it. Now then, just remind me of something King Zrze –'

Kadredin shook his head until his large eyes trembled. 'It's disgraceful when a Western man, rich, well placed, takes advantage of a poor Georgian priest. Disgraceful, yes. What else can one expect from an atheist? And I'm only asking for five hundred . . .'

'A deal's a deal, Kadredin. Stick to your side of the bargain.'

'I can stay only if you pay me. But you could obtain more money from your organization without harm to your own pocket.'

'Oh, you're prepared to come to Frankfurt for it, are you?'

More head-shaking. 'You are humorous at my expense. I shall go home.' He turned away.

'Two hundred,' Burnell called.

'Three hundred.'

'Two hundred and fifty.'

'Done.' The priest turned back.

'Payment when we are back in Bogdanakhi, OK?'

'As you will. Beggars can't be churlish, isn't that what you say? That's two hundred and fifty for me and two hundred and fifty for the lad, Khachi.' This was said in a forceful, man-of-the-world style, very unfitting for a man of any religious order.

'No, it's not. He gets part of your share.'

'Aren't you ashamed to talk that way, even if you are an atheist? Khachi risked his life for you last evening.'

'He risked it for you too, so you share with him.'

'Atheist!' The word pronounced with precision, as if newminted.

'Swindler!'

'That a priest of the church should be spoken to in such terms . . . Aren't you ashamed?'

'You said you weren't a priest. You said you'd lost your faith. You're behaving like a beggar. What are you?'

The question was effective in stopping Kadredin in his tracks. His protuberant eyes became glazed as he stared at Burnell, perhaps hoping to find the answer where the question had come from.

Finally he came out with the admission that he was nothing. He did not know what he was. He asked himself the question:

143

what was he? This time, he admitted he was a beggar, just as Burnell had intimated: a beggar in a nation of beggars. That was what he and the nation had been reduced to. He could only say in his own defence, for what it was worth — and it was probably worth nothing — that he supported someone he preferred not to name in Bogdanakhi whom he wished to get out of the cursed country. When the heads of mayors could be kicked about in their own public square, what hope was there for decent men? Without awaiting a reply, he begged Burnell to forgive him for behaving in such a despicable way over money, he being an honourable German gentleman.

Burnell said he was English, having no idea what else to say to this man of such changeable moods.

Correcting his own error, Kadredin explained he had been overwhelmed by the thought of his own wretched behaviour. He was appalled to reflect how he had been forced to beg a few rotten miserable dollars from a rich man. How right Burnell had been to refuse him.

'I didn't refuse, damn it! I offered you two hundred and fifty.'

Kadredin spat into a ribes bush. 'What's two hundred and fifty to you? It's nothing. Worse than nothing — an insult.'

'You refuse the offer, do you?'

'No, no, I didn't say that. Poor defrocked wretch that I am, a Georgian shunned by all decent humanity, what right have I to refuse your pittance? I accept with gratitude.'

'All right, change the subject. Tell me what I want to know about King Zrze. When did he die?'

During this uncomfortable dialogue, Kadredin's brow had by turns darkened and lightened like a cloudy day. Now it brightened once again, and he tossed back his lank hair with a haughty gesture.

'Huh! The lowest Abkhazian peasant could tell you that. For the moment, I forget the date myself. I do recall that Zrze inherited the throne at the age of twenty-two. That he did by strangling his father — a conventional medieval way of becoming king. Perhaps this Church of the Mother of God —' the priest crossed himself '— served in part as an act of atonement.'

'So he was a bit of a character, was Zrze.'

Kadredin said defensively, 'He was widely loved by his people, and also enjoyed support abroad.'

'Oh, yes, so I believe. Isn't it true he found an unlikely ally in Pope Pius IV? Pius IV's last act before he died was to make an unexpected gift from Catholicism to Orthodoxy. He despatched to King Zrze something for his newly built church: an ikon which had reached the Vatican from a pillaged church in Borzhomi. Isn't that so, Father? An ikon generally known as "The Madonna of Futurity"?'

Kadredin's long face assumed a weary expression. 'I've never heard of such an ikon,' he said.

'You've never heard of Pius IV's gift? The lowest Abkhazian peasant could tell you about it.'

'I don't mix with peasants,' Kadredin said, as the clouds came again.

It was time to enter the church. Burnell led the way to the wooden door in the narthex. Kadredin and Khachi followed behind. The door was locked. Two planks had been carelessly nailed across it.

Kadredin came smartly forward. To one side of the door, the stone of the pillar had been carved to represent two peasants entangled in vines. Taking firm hold of one of the peasants' heads, the priest pulled out a small section of the stone, cut about a sinew of the vine. From the aperture behind the block he removed a large iron key.

Once the door was unlocked, they could wrench off the planks. During the long disease of Communism, the church had been forbidden territory, on the grounds that it might, in this remote place, provide a focal point for a reviving Church. Nevertheless, the building had been preserved. Even in the years of oppression, Ghvtismshobeli had remained a symbol of nationalist pride, which the Soviets had not dared tamper with.

The church, with its blind arches and few windows, preserved a grim interior appearance. Burnell and the priest stepped inside, to be met by cold and dark. The Eastern Orthodox religions had always preferred to create darkness within their places of worship.

Here, the darkness, unrelieved by candles for many a year, had been allowed to accumulate. It bit to the bone.

Although Ghvtismshobeli was an empty shell, a sense of something waiting there had gathered, as in all deserted places. Emptiness is next to godliness, Burnell thought. They halted in the midst of the gloomy space.

The narthex door by which they had entered was set in an archway decorated with reliefs of various animals, sheep, wolves, a sportive deer. But the stonecarvers of the Tskavani area had had no time in which to finish their delicate work. Khachi, toting his inseparable gun, loitered in the doorway, a silhouette against the daylight behind him.

As if suddenly making up his mind to withstand the chill – or perhaps the chill of his own uncertain faith – Kadredin strode across the stone flags to where the iconostasis had once stood, separating sanctuary from nave. Taking up his stance, he began to sing. His deep bass voice flowed out, filling the bowl of the building with its resonance, a well-deep sensation of sorrow.

Kadredin's voice died away. In a little while, pitching his voice quietly across the space between them, Burnell asked, 'What were you singing?'

The tall thin figure remained silent for a moment. Perhaps Kadredin was praying to have his faith restored. Then he said, in his normal voice, '"*Theotokion*" . . . It's a hymn to the Mother of God. From the Russian Orthodox . . .'

The narthex shared a roof with the single nave. Sturdy columns supported the dome. The carving round doors and high windows was of a familiar toothed pattern. Kadredin wandered about, saying absently, 'Of course we hate Russia. It brings with it wherever it goes oppression, totalitarianism, injustice, criminality. Lazar Kaginovich is believed to be half-Russian. Yet there is another Russia. It brings with it Dostoevsky, Tolstoi, the gentle Chekhov, Borodin, and Tchaikovsky, and the blessings of the liturgical chants. That Russia we love.'

'You speak in the plural. What of yourself, Kadredin? Your singular self?'

'My French teacher was an eccentric woman. She taught me

146

plurals before singulars. So they come more easily to me.' His voice died away. To change the subject, he asked if Burnell was intending to take photographs.

'My cameras and the camcorder were stolen that night in Bogdanakhi.'

'You should be more particular where you sleep.'

The interior had been plastered and whitewashed, perhaps to cover hasty workmanship in those threatened last days of King Zrze's reign. The one mural to be completed stood above the lintel of the door by which they had entered. Slipping his pack from his shoulder, Burnell took out his black notebook and began to sketch. He was furious with himself for having lost his cameras; the priest's jibe had gone home.

Three personages stood against a dark blue background decorated with symbols. One was a grand man, bearded and clad in golden robes. Beside him was a small female whose head came up to the level of his hip. She too was dressed in gold, and wore a wimple. The man had on a golden crown, spired like a holy city, perhaps deliberately made too large for him. The third figure was of the Virgin Mary, in a light blue gown.

The positioning of the figures and their mannered gestures conformed to the iconography of a civilization, the heart of which had died a century before Ghvtismshobeli's foundations were laid. The artists entrusted with the task, scarcely begun, of covering the whole interior of the church with Biblical scenes had perforce to look back to the golden days of Byzantium, before Constantinople fell to the Ottomans.

As Burnell began to sketch, Kadredin came and stood at his right shoulder, purveying his familiar odour of sheep. He related how Zrze had defended his kingdom against the cruel House of Osman. It was a familiar tale of the clash of faiths, shedding of blood, courage and betrayal. There was generally a Judas in these histories – in this case, Zrze's brother, who sided with the invaders, and later converted to Islam.

The fresco, spotted with mould, showed Zrze holding a model of his new church. The model was being offered, with what some might interpret as a 'take it or leave it' gesture, to a behaloed

Virgin Mary. Clutching as she was an infant Jesus, she was placed in some difficulty as regards acceptance of the gift. Above her, stern but kindly, hovered an angel, dressed in the traditional cerecloths of angelhood.

Not only gestures but the composition and colours employed had been formulated in an earlier age. Burnell was moved by the fresco, by its naivety and sophistication. He had long admired the endeavours of the Eastern Church to portray what it regarded as the Infinite, while at the same time giving local potentates their worldly due.

And this local potentate, Zrze, struggling to retain control of his tiny state, had been gobbled up by the vaster forces of the House of Osman. Few recalled the name of Zrze; the world still spoke the name of his adversary, Suleyman I, the Magnificent.

'Some ikons were here, sir, some sent from distant lands. All were stolen, like your cameras.'

'Including the Madonna of Futurity?'

'Whatever that may be. Yet one precious thing remains. The documents of the religious foundation. I'll show you.'

He shuffled off to a wormy old table standing in one of the side chapels. Although a few stone jars stood against the walls – once possibly the receptacles for flowers – the table formed the only furnishing in the entire church. From its drawer Kadredin brought vellum documents covered with the looped Georgian script. He rustled the waxy sheets before Burnell. A large seal, the seal of King Zrze, hung from one of the documents.

'Go carefully! These must be valuable.'

'Ha! They'd fetch something on the open market in Germany, wouldn't they?' Burnell was offended by the crudity of this remark, though the same thought had occurred to him. It also occurred to him that Kadredin knew the church well.

'You'd better preserve them, then. Put them back in the drawer.' He went on with his sketch, nodding towards the small female accompanying the king. 'What of her, the woman? Queen Simonis?'

Sniffing, Kadredin went and returned the documents to the table. He pushed them into the drawer and closed it. For a moment he stood there, his prominent eyes turned up towards the roof as if he was in contemplation.

Bringing his sheep smell back to Burnell's side, he remarked that where theft was concerned, the Communists in their turn had been worse than the Turks. In particular they had stripped the church of an elaborate iconostasis. He believed the iconostasis now reposed in a museum in Moscow, if it hadn't been chopped up for firewood before getting that far. The Communists in Tbilisi had murdered a bishop on the steps of Ghvtismshobeli when he tried to deny them access. Kadredin chuckled as he told this story in dramatic detail, perhaps thinking that it would confirm the Englishman's opinion of the Georgians as barbarians.

'I asked about the woman, Father. Simonis. What do you know about her?'

'Ah. A tragic figure, Queen Simonis.'

'Queens usually are.'

'You see she's the small figure beside Zrze? You've drawn her too big.' He pointed up to the fresco. 'She's also in gold. Notice her wimple. It indicates her married status.'

The priest went on to explain that Simonis was the visible sign of a dynastic treaty – what he called 'a Byzantine package deal', and part of Zrze's scheme to form alliances with outside parties for the protection of his kingdom. Simonis made the difficult journey to Zrze's capital with a small entourage from Kiev in the Ukraine. This took place before she was eleven years old, before her menarche. It was King Zrze's intention that Ghvtismshobeli should later form Simonis's mausoleum.

What had been the girl's inward nature? Burnell wondered, looking up at the blank oval of her face. Damp had given it a patina of acne. She had been a pawn in a cold-hearted dynastic deal, deflowered to lend flesh and blood to a treaty. Had she been happy? How had the fearsome Zrze, beset by troubles, tolerated her? Come to that, how had *he* treated Stephanie?

'Strange how churches memorialize bloodshed, one way or another, from the Crucifixion onwards. Ever think of that, Kadredin? Bloodshed's rather a prominent feature of Christianity. Buddhism is entirely different. I never heard of Buddha strung up on a Cross. Most statues of the Buddha show him looking relaxed in a decidedly post-coital manner . . . Christians prefer blood to semen. Perhaps it's safer on the whole.' He laughed at the thought. 'So was Simonis interred here when she died?'

They walked by the lake, keeping a watchful eye for the possible approach of strangers. The whole great tumbled countryside was bereft of humanity. It could not have looked greatly different five centuries earlier.

On the northern side of the church, the landscape changed, becoming more bland and watery. Willow-fringed Lake Tskavani was dull and still, like a large wet fingerprint. Burnell stood there, enjoying the melancholy, with the old church at his back.

'It must have been easy to feel religious in such a situation.'

'And still is, sir.'

Poor Ghvtismshobeli! Nowhere so remote that WACH didn't want a piece of it. Along with the desire for knowledge, and a laudable determination to preserve whatever was of artistic merit, went an undercurrent of greed.

Perhaps it was inevitable that the technological culture of the West had spread to claim other cultures. Everything in the world was grist to the hungry mills of the West, of Europe and the United States of America. Ikons, *haikus*, *reistaffels*, saris, Kama Sutra, Tutankhamen, pandas, pineapples, idols, precious stones, ivory, agabati, Kabuki, opium, origami, Buddhism, bagels, *gastarbeiten*, algebra, the Elgin Marbles, squid, Bokhara carpets, jacarandas, geraniums, tobacco, turquoise, Turkish baths, Ming vases, Arabian Nights, nutmegs, netsuké, saffron, lapis lazuli, potatoes, poppies, roses, rhododendrons, turmeric, tomatoes, tangerines, yoga, yoghurt, Icelandic sagas, silk, bamboo furniture, baboons, *kung fu*, coffee, parrots, and many other items, all poured into the West. The world was hard up. The West was an acquisitive society.

It was a curiosity of history that no Arab *dhow*, no Chinese junk, no *daharbiya*, had ever sailed up Thames or Tagus. Yet little cockleshell galleons had slipped out of London and Lisbon on the tide and sailed round the world. Why could the Portuguese navigate and the Papuans, say, not? What was it that had agitated

European races and not others? Part of that particular dynamism had brought Burnell to the edge of Lake Tskavani, listening to a priest tell an ancient tale.

'Queen Simonis died,' Kadredin said. 'The Ottoman incursions were not the only problem. Plague returned in virulent form, ravaging the country. Rich and poor alike were overwhelmed. It was a judgement from on high. The ladies of Zrze's court became stricken. Some fled, some died in bed. There was no escape from death. When Simonis died, she was pregnant with her lord's child.'

'How did the king feel about that?'

Kadredin shrugged. 'King Zrze made all arrangements for her funeral. It was to be held here, in the uncompleted church. Such ceremonies as could be managed were performed. Despite the fear of pestilence, the court assembled. Nobody from the Kiev court would visit, for fear. History relates that the masons bowed their heads and wept as the body of the child-bride was brought forth.

'*Mais il n'avait plus temps.* Time had run out. It was the end of everything. We speak of the year of 1565, *m'sieu*. Even as this bell above us began to toll in the belfry – a newly forged bell, also stolen since – the Turkish army arrived in Tskavani. Picture if you will the scene. A hot day like today. The court in its finery, the little coffin heavy with lilies. And suddenly cannonballs arrive . . . The Muslim invader was at the very door.'

The priest squeezed his eyes tight shut. Deep feelings made him pause; or he was merely being dramatic. After his splendid singing, Burnell felt warmth towards Kadredin; he sympathized too with the way the man did not know his own mind. It was a malaise Burnell recognized.

'So what happened? Was Zrze killed?' It was all so long ago – though apparently not to the priest. Through his eyes, Burnell could see that perilous afternoon four and a half centuries earlier, the sun leaden in the sky, the royal party in their stiff Byzantine finery, the body of the young queen half buried under flowers, priests in the church resonant with the epicedium, scents of incense and ribes drifting in the air, the Turks like a sour breath of history emerging from the throat of the valley. Perhaps there was truth in Croce's epigram that 'all history is contemporary history'.

'Ah, how bravely the royal guard fought! They stood their ground while the king and his party beat a gallant retreat. Thirty warriors fell beneath the scimitar that afternoon. They stood firm against an army.

'King Zrze and his company escaped northwards with the coffin across the lake. They fled in two boats owned by Tskavani fishermen. It is said by local people that the lake trout assisted the progress of the boats, and helped speed them on their way.'

'They were Christian trout then, not Muslim trout?'

'It was a miracle, sir. We must assume the fish had no option but to help. Country people still speak of it. Unhappily, in all the confusion, the body of Queen Simonis – then fifteen and large with child – tumbled from the boat into the water. Burdened down with her jewels and finery, not to mention a large iron cross, she sank at once. The king jumped in the lake to recapture the body, but he too got into trouble. Imagine the tragic scene, sir – for he could not swim.'

'Didn't the fish help him?'

'The funeral party pulled the king into the other boat and rowed strongly for the northern shore. So they escaped certain death. The body of Queen Simonis was never recovered. It is said that her ghost still haunts these waters.' He gestured expansively towards the lake, looking blandly innocent of anything supernatural.

How was it these events of so long ago had been passed down in story through the generations, to remain obstinately in mind? Burnell asked himself whom he had known in his ten missing years. Who had been his friends of whom he recalled nothing? What tragedies, what comedies, had there been? Who had died that he should be missing?

'OK, so the church fell into Ottoman hands. What became of its contents? What became of this famous ikon, the Madonna of Futurity?'

Kadredin fixed his bulbous gaze on Burnell and rubbed a long pale cheek. 'As I told you, *m'sieu*, the curtains all, and the trappings, and the few ikons the church possessed, were looted. Many precious things. Perhaps you understand how this region has always been oppressed and poor and in bad health. Much has been robbed from us by foreigners. What last remained, the Russians took.'

'I'm asking you about one particular ikon, Father.'

Sighing, the priest turned to gaze across the lake, where a solitary cormorant was working. 'No doubt your Madonna of Futurity reposes in a museum in Moscow or Sergeyev Posad, once known as Zagorsk.'

'We understand otherwise. In Frankfurt WACH has a fairly comprehensive inventory of misappropriated works of art still held in Moscow or thereabouts. Records show that the Madonna of Futurity was last seen here in this church a couple of decades or so ago, in the time of the late President Gorbachev of the Soviet Union, as it then was. An Italian traveller was permitted to inspect the church. A man of probity, by name Carlo Morabito. He stated that the ikon was still here in Ghvtismshobeli.'

'Yes, yes. It's possible. If the Italian was connected with the Vatican, maybe he stole the ikon back. Almost certainly.'

Burnell laughed. 'Come on, Father. We've been frank with each other and even argued on religious matters, about which we disagree, without falling out. Why are you being evasive now about the trifle of an ikon?'

'We could fish if you desired, this evening when the fish are rising. Unless you wish to return to Bogdanakhi immediately.'

'Father Kadredin. The ikon. Come on, you know everything, don't you?'

Kadredin looked here and there on the ground, as if for a missing coin. 'It was told me that Englishmen are suspicious . . . Sir, I will confess it to you, then. I was once appointed resident priest of the Church of the Mother of God. I lived here almost alone in the dormitory for two years.' He glanced up to judge the effect of his statement.

'Well, the air is good. When was this?'

The priest heaved a deep sigh and tugged at his hair. He said that there had been a time when all Georgia had been under a

President Gamsakhurdia, an elected president. Ghvtismshobeli had been reconsecrated then, and Kadredin appointed its priest. For a short while, after he had cleaned out the church, services had been held in the ancient Orthodox style, with fine singing, led by Kadredin himself.

Those days, Kadredin declared, had been happy ones. He had tended the church and buildings with pride, restoring them as best he could. Woodworking was one of his skills. One day, pulling out some worm-eaten panelling in a cupboard in the dormitory, he had found a place of concealment.

He had fetched a candle. Reaching into the recess, he had laid hands on an ikon, wrapped in paper. Unwrapping it, he immediately recognized the missing Madonna of Futurity.

Interrupting, Burnell said, 'So you've actually handled this work of art? Where is it, then?'

'Who knows?'

'But you must know!'

'With what reverence I held it! Painted by Master Evtihije in the twelfth century and unharmed! I can describe it, if you wish.'

'I've seen reproductions of it. Very beautiful. So the Turks didn't get it? You found it. Where is it?'

'It was preserved by a miracle.'

'Another miracle? You mean to say one of Zrze's brighter priests was smart enough to conceal the item before the Turks topped him? So you found it? Where is it? What did you do? Break the news to the world's press that the famous Madonna was back?'

But Kadredin, simple priest, had simply reinstated the ikon – so he claimed – as the chief glory of the church, to attract larger congregations from the scattered peasantry.

Kadredin represented himself as being reluctant to let the outside world know the ikon still existed. As far as he was concerned, the outside world meant Tbilisi. And in Tbilisi, President Gamsakhurdia was in trouble and civil war had broken out.

As for the ikon itself . . . It was more than a mere work of art. Its significance was that it marked a link between the Vatican and Eastern Orthodoxy at a time when the Popes had officially interdicted the Eastern religions. This reinforced the local value of the Madonna ikon; for the conversion of Georgians to Christianity, generally dated from the fourth century AD, marked their turning away from Islam and towards Europe. The ikon was a blessed sign, arriving at a time when Islam was about to draw its veil across the region.

One day when Kadredin was pottering about his church, Muslim guerrillas from the province of Abkhazia had arrived from the north in an Antonev biplane and landed close to the lake. Kadredin went innocently to meet them. He had been tied up. The guerrillas had entered the church and stolen anything of value they could lay their hands on – some plate, and the Madonna of Futurity.

'Did they nick the iconostasis and put that on the plane?'

Kadredin looked pained. 'As I told you, the iconostasis was taken by the Russians. How can I speak if you do not believe what I say?'

Gullible though Burnell was, he could not believe in the flying guerrillas. He could see only marshy ground in the direction Kadredin had vaguely indicated: nowhere was there what looked like a suitable landing-strip. He made a note in his notebook; he was puzzled as to why Kadredin was so reluctant to tell this story.

'Did anyone else see these Abkhazian guerrillas?'

'I was alone at that time, as it happened. And it was dusk. You understand I mainly looked after myself in this remote spot. I had no protection.'

'So they took you off in the dark, did they? And you freed yourself, I suppose?'

Kadredin said he had freed himself and remained in the dormitory overnight. He was shaken. The experience convinced him that his life was in danger and that after this incident no congregation would make its way to his church. Of course he regretted the loss of the precious ikon. So he locked up the church and returned on his donkey to Bogdanakhi to report the situation to his bishop. He hoped the bishop would offer reinforcements so that the church could remain open. But then there had been political difficulties connected with the civil war. The account rambled here. The upshot of the matter was that the civil war ignited other uprisings. Gamsakhurdia had been thrown out of office and fled. There had been a riot in Bogdanakhi, and so on and so on. The bishop had done this and that. On his orders, the authorities had barricaded the church and surrounded it with wire, and Kadredin had never been able to return. Until now.

The cormorant was still fishing. Arms folded, Burnell stood gazing across the lake.

'So you volunteered to escort me here. Why was that?'

Kadredin paused before replying. 'You saw the trouble in Bogdanakhi.'

'Yes, but why did you want to come back here?'

'Sir, I am a sentimental man. I wished to be here once more before I died.'

After a pause, Burnell asked why Muslims should steal a Christian ikon.

The priest looked crafty. He tapped his high forehead. 'Just think for yourself. It has market value, that Madonna. The Abkhazian rebels can sell her for money for arms, of course. Today, she would be worth . . . ah, well, let's say you could take her to the auctions in München or Frankfurt. At today's prices I estimate she would be worth approximately eleven point six million euros . . . if she could be found.'

'So the Abkhazians didn't sell her? Is that it?'

The hands widespread, the crafty look. 'How can I say, sir, a poor dishonoured priest?'

'So what do you believe? That the Russians took the Madonna, or the Abkhazians, or maybe a wandering Italian? It can't have been all three parties! I don't understand your story.'

'Not my story, sir. Other people say this or that. Many blame me. Who can tell where truth lies? I am sad in my heart, please believe me, for only in Truth is there any value.'

Burnell smiled. 'But maybe even truth isn't worth – what was it exactly, now? Eleven point six million euros in the salerooms of München? You seem to have done your calculations, Father.'

11
'The Madonna of Futurity'

The dormitory was clean. The three men chose separate cells in which to sleep. Inspecting the ruined building, Burnell found there was indeed a cupboard downstairs, stacked with newspapers now yellow and crisp, at the back of which planks had recently been screwed into place. Doubtless there was room to conceal something behind them. That much of Kadredin's story could have been true.

Khachi cooked them up a meal of beans and a duck he had trapped in the marshes. Afterwards, he retired to sit in a corner of the courtyard, his radio pressed against his ear. Burnell sketched the exterior of the church, enjoying its increasing puissance as evening drew near.

Unexpectedly, the sober-faced youth began to laugh. After a while, he came over to Kadredin, talking excitedly. Kadredin had no responding laughter. Burnell caught the name 'Kuzloduy . . .' and began to worry.

Tuning in to Radio Tbilisi, Khachi had caught a news flash concerning the old Bulgarian nuclear power station at Kuzloduy. Kuzloduy had been taken off-line some while ago and was being closed down. A caretaker technician had noticed something wrong. He had tapped a dial and wandered off to his bunk. By morning, nothing could be done to stop the reactor going critical. The alarmist newsreader stated that the first unit was now burning its way down towards the Earth's core. However, a government spokesman had said there was no cause for alarm.

The priest shook his head at the folly of mankind. 'We are

happy and safe here,' he said dismally. 'Why should we be, when our brothers elsewhere are dying?'

'Even in the Nazi ghettos, men composed and played music – quartets, even an opera,' Burnell said cheerfully. 'Thank your God that human perceptions are at least in part blind . . .'

The sun as it set surrounded itself with a brutal iron halo the colour of liver. The celestial ember died, leaving a darkling sky in its wake.

'Don't stand around,' General 'Gus' Stalinbrass told his aide when he heard the news from Kuzloduy. 'Break out the anti-radiation suits. Get on the phone and find what interests the US has around – what's the name of this fucking place? Kluzzy? Speak to our ambassador in the Bulgarian capital. No, I'll speak to him. Let's have some action. We must be able to take advantage of the crisis some way. Levels of US, UN, EU, support to Bulgaria. Who's in charge? Do we have any forces there? Where the hell is this fucking country anyway?'

'The US Sixty-Ninth Fleet has units in the Black Sea,' said the aide. 'That's down where the Crimea is, if you remember. Crimea's in the north of the Black Sea, Bulgaria's west.'

'When I need a geography lesson I'll ask for it.'

'Sir. There's a Bulgarian port called Varna. Units of the Tenth Fleet are within fifty miles of Varna.'

'Is Varna on the coast?'

'Yessir. It's a port.'

'How soon could we get our Crimean missiles realigned on Bulgaria if we had to? Find out if we should bomb this Kluzzy dump and stop all the nuclear nonsense. Speak to Beagleberger and don't let the Air Force know what we're doing.'

'Yessir. But the Bulgarians are our allies.'

'Shit, Harry, you heard of Friendly Fire, didn't you?'

The aide was a rock-solid colonel from Shippensburg, Penn. He had been around, looking immutable or something, on the one occasion Burnell had come face to face with Stalinbrass. General Stalinbrass had been poring over an immense video map of the secret city under Moscow, preserved since before Brezhnev's day in the previous century and now being taken over as the UN Army HQ in Europasia.

'"World Cultural Heritage", my ass,' said the general, smiling at Burnell to show his flawless teeth. 'What in hell do you guys think war is all about? So a few fucking churches get blown up? So what? You a religious nut or something?'

'No, I'm not religious, General. My work is simply to catalogue sacred edifices and other buildings.'

'So you are a religious nut.'

'The case for preserving anything surviving from the distant past, sir, is that it represents the better side of mankind's nature – the creative side that aspires not to be barbarous. If all the world's art treasures were destroyed –'

Laughing, Stalinbrass interrupted. 'Come on, Professor. Don't give me that crap. Save it for the classroom. We're talking a handful of crummy Byzantine churches, right? What good ever came out of Georgia?'

He did not wait for Burnell's answer.

'You wanna go there for WACH, OK, good for you. Washington wants you to go with my blessing, so go. Fine and dandy. Harry's arranging a contact for you in – Harry, what's the place down there rhymes with "syphilis"?'

Switching off the video map, Stalinbrass strode across the expanse of his office while his aide consulted a Europasia map on the wall. In order to perch a ham on the edge of his desk, the general swept aside a photograph of his wife dressed as Marie Antoinette framed in gilt and one of Nicolae Ceausescu framed in silver. Perforce, Burnell followed him across the room.

'Tbilisi.'

'Feller called . . . shit – Irving. A good man, Jim Irving, bit past it.' He leaned closer, raising a hefty finger like a courgette to stop Burnell saying anything. 'Washington wants to improve its image. Understood. I want to improve mine. Do me a favour, Burnell – bring me back something I can use. Harry here will give you details of what we've turned up. What are those things, Harry? Ikons. OK. Something anyone can understand. An ikon with a pretty face on it. It would be good publicity for me, show I care.

159

Instead of having my ass chewed off in the world media all the time, *entiende*?

'You're a Brit, Burnell. Brits have a natural grasp of these things. Pull off this little deal and I'll see you OK. OK? Good man.'

The paw he extended was bigger than a pawpaw.

So Burnell had learnt of the existence of the so-called Madonna of Futurity. Before he left Stalinbrass's tremendous presence, he was given a folder of aged cuttings and photocopies of cuttings from various sources in various languages.

Most of these cuttings referred to a travelling art exhibition of the 1970s. At that time, much of the world was locked into an ideological confrontation between Communism and Capitalism. As part of the propaganda struggle, the Soviet Union had mounted an impressive exhibition of ikons which had toured the capitals of Western Europe, New York, LA, and Washington. Ikons from Armenia and Georgia were included, among them the celebrated Madonna of Futurity. Experts ascribed this work to an itinerant artist called Evtihije, of whom – in the manner of these things – nothing was known, except that he had died in some vague Armenian ditch after a lifetime of exemplary piety.

A TV documentary item related the chequered history of the ikon: that it had travelled to the Vatican and, more surprisingly, back. But many ikons had a history of travel. It was the quality of the painting, the luminous rendering of the Mother of God and her Child, and the positioning of the figures, which attracted attention.

Burnell's folder included an official report, dated later than the faded cuttings, from his own department in the WACH. It affirmed that the ikon had been returned to Georgia after the exhibition. Finally, a form from Tbilisi stated that the ikon had been reinstated in the historic church of Ghvtismshobeli; the form originated in the period before the Soviet Union broke up – in fact, when Kadredin had been in charge of the church.

Why had Kadredin volunteered to accompany him to Ghvtismshobeli? The reason he had given hardly seemed adequate.

Burnell's duty was performed with little more than a gesture towards those who employed him; he took every advantage of the bureaucratic inefficiency in which the offices in FAM were cocooned. In that respect, he embodied in himself the lack of enthusiasm characterizing a governmental-type department. There remained, however, General Stalinbrass's commission. That had certainly, in its crass way, caught Burnell's interest.

Now Burnell stood in the church for which the missing ikon had been named. He was certain that Father Kadredin was involved in the ikon's disappearance. Why else his evasiveness, the unlikely tale of the Abkhazi guerrillas, his setting a precise contemporary value on the ikon? Of course, much had vanished from the past; he was well aware of that. And yet . . .

He waited until the priest and the young gunman were asleep in their cells before moving. Going stealthily into the courtyard between the dormitory and the church, he was confronted by the beauty of the night. The moon shone in a clear sky, almost full. This was the moon Irving's beggar in Bogdanakhi would not see. Nothing stirred. He crossed to the church and was encompassed by its ancient stone.

The cold inside the building had intensified: it seeped like mist from the walls. Lunar window patterns were stencilled on the floor. As Burnell's eyes adjusted, the interior seemed to glow with its own luminance. He looked about him, listening, telling himself he was not superstitious.

There was nothing, only an immense susurrus from the fabric of the building. He concentrated on a search.

He circled the entire wall area, fingertips light on the plaster, looking for hidden doors or alcoves. Nothing untoward there. He crossed to the apse, where the altar once stood. It was reached by a single step from the nave. Above Burnell's head, three windows let in starlight. No scent of incense here, only cold and mould, where once darkly garbed divines had intoned for the sins of their congregation.

Close by the step was a square trapdoor Burnell had observed earlier. He knelt and attempted to lift it. The countersunk iron handle had rusted, and broke in his hand.

He went across to the main door and took up one of the planks which had previously barred entry to the church. With this he managed to lever up the trapdoor. It was heavy and without hinges. He set it down beside him and peered into the opening, regretting that his torch had been stolen along with the cameras.

Moonlight spilled over the lip of the hole. It enabled Burnell to see into a small crypt. Something rustled in the depths. There was a ladder, but Burnell felt no great inclination to descend. It looked as if a man could scarcely stand erect in the crypt. He shifted his position, hanging over the edge. Rubbish, leaves, perhaps bones . . .

As he hung there, sniffing the stale air, he heard a footstep behind him. Kadredin was standing a short distance away, his contourless figure mainly in shadow. Burnell stood up, clutching the shattered plank. They confronted each other.

'You are going underground, *m'sieu*?'

'You're an insomniac too, then?'

'The guilty cannot sleep. You wish to go down into the crypt? Go then, and I will remain here. You will find nothing, whatever you might be looking for. It is told that the crypt was designed to hold possessions of the young Queen Simonis, perhaps even the ornamentation adorning her poor little body. Matters fell out differently, as I related. Nothing remained to conceal.'

'No ikons, of course, Kadredin.'

'The empty crypt resembles an empty stomach, to my mind, sir. This entire edifice is the product of poor but religious men, the masons, the artists, the priests . . . Built in a poor age in a poor country. Such uncomplicated reverence is hard to understand in our day.'

'Maybe the money wasted on yet another church should have gone on a welfare system. Georgia's not poor, just ill managed.'

Kadredin came forward rather warily. He lifted the wooden trapdoor and snuggled it gently into place. As he straightened, he embarked on another monologue concerning the problems Georgia faced, and the oppression threatening from north and south. It was a land of great heroes and poets, yet alone in the world.

'Bedtime, I think, Kadredin.'

The priest came close with his rotten smell and adopted a more manly tone, advising Burnell to forget his own comfort for once. He understood poverty in a way Burnell could not. 'You come from a rich country, so you must help me.'

'I'm cold and I'm going to bed.'

They traversed together the moonlit distance back to the dormitory building. Far in the distance, a dog was howling and being answered by another dog.

Once in the hall, Kadredin caught hold of Burnell's arm. 'Don't yet go to bed. There's life still in the embers of the fire. Let's warm up, *n'est-ce pas?*'

Burnell allowed himself to be escorted to the refectory, where the priest kicked another log on to the remains of the fire. They had eaten here earlier; their crusts lay on the table, food for rats. Since moonlight did not reach into the room, they could barely distinguish each other's face; neither made any attempt to light a candle, as if they knew something dark was about to occur which demanded surrounding darkness. Burnell dragged up a bench which squealed along the floor, and stretched out his hand to a growing flame. He waited, not too dissatisfied with the unpleasantness of the situation. A snort would have been welcome.

Kadredin took his time before speaking. When he did speak, his voice was deep and mournful. He reminded Burnell of their whereabouts, far from anything that might be called civilization. 'Far even from the nearest brothel.'

Burnell said nothing.

'Does it occur to you, Dr Burnell, that you might be in danger? Khachi obeys me as a dog his master. Just suppose for instance we decided to shoot you, because it suited us. Who would know? Ruffians, wandering bands, guerrillas – anyone would be blamed when your body was found.'

Peering through the shadows at the pallid face near him, Burnell said, 'That terrible American general, Stalinbrass, would soon find out who dared kill me. Is this where your piety has brought you, to thoughts of murder?'

The silence which ensued was made no more enjoyable by

lack of any denial of the charge on Kadredin's part. While Burnell had seated himself, Kadredin remained standing, his tall shapeless body part of the cold shades, a plank of the place, his eyes gleaming red as they reflected the hot sparks in the grate. The fire was bringing out the stench of his sheepskin. When he spoke, it was to observe that the world was full of criminals. He paused, to add that many of them deserved no better than death. He merely wished to explain the situation, so that Burnell was clear in his own mind about it.

When Burnell said emphatically that he was clear, Kadredin affected not to hear. He declared he was unhappy. Another pause, during which the room began to fill with smoke. All being well, the two of them and the boy would return to Bogdanakhi on the morrow. He repeated, 'All being well . . .' Again he paused. His monologue consisted of silences stitched together with words; it was a spider's web of a conversation. This ikon . . .

Here again, he became silent. Into this silence, and out of the smoke, as it were, popped the head of Mayor Tenguiz Sigua, looking bloody and ghastly. Without saying a word, it reminded Burnell he was alone in a bloodthirsty country. Sluggishly, Kadredin started up on another tack. From Bogdanakhi, Burnell would fly to Tbilisi and thence to Germany. Pause. To Frankfurt. To the rich world. All being well.

'Exactly,' said Burnell. 'So we'd better turn in. Long trek ahead of us tomorrow . . .' He rose and, under pretext of stoking the fire, which was smoking furiously, grasped a stick that had served as a poker. His disquiet at the tone of the conversation was hardly soothed by observing that in the doorway, barring the way, stood Khachi; little of the youth could be seen through the smoke and darkness beyond the glint of firelight on the barrel of his gun.

Kadredin was not to be deterred from his slothful recitation. There was something he had to get off his mind – by force if necessary. He repeated, 'To the rich world . . .' For him there would be no such escape. He was trapped by a state of war he regarded as human sinfulness, in which he could feel no sympathy for either side. Pause. The peace and also the wealth of his beloved country was being destroyed by the greed of men seeking power.

That greed made everyone poorer. Pause. He sorrowed to realize that he would live in poverty until the day he died.

Kadredin's manner of speech became more animated. He told Burnell he supposed that if he happened – just happened – to discover the ikon in which he was so interested, the ikon showing the Mother of God with the Holy Child . . . then in that case, he would take it with him to the rich world; was that not so?

It was the turn of Burnell to pause. Assuming carelessness, he said, 'This precious ikon's not here, is it? Maybe it's in – who knows? Moscow? Kiev? Washington? Maybe the Vatican got it back . . . Maybe the old lame woman we stayed with has – the *Babo* has it in her kitchen, propped up by a pot of goat lard . . .'

In a low voice, the priest said, 'Many many men have visited the Church of Ghvtismshobeli over the centuries. They came and went in haste, like criminals. They have been after reliquaries, crosses, tapestries, anything that could be stolen. All the treasures are gone. The world is full of criminals – persons without religion.'

This time it seemed from his pause he was waiting for the fire to die. Then he said with great effort, 'Suppose I told you where the ikon was . . .'

Immediately, Burnell perceived that the priest had had to goad himself to this crucial point. The night, the solitude, the silence, the strange surroundings, had led him to see menace where none was intended. Simple ineptitude, rather than murderous inclination, accounted for his halting delivery. With this realization, Burnell's attitude changed. Keeping hold of the stick, he became brisk, he frowned commandingly.

He said he would go out and stand by the lake. There he would wait for two minutes. Two minutes only. Unless the priest came and made a concrete statement, Burnell would have nothing more to do with the whole business, would hear no further word about the ikon – or about Georgian poverty, or indeed about the corpse of any teenage queens. He would retire to bed and that would be the end of the matter.

He marched briskly away, pushing past Khachi, happy to feel he had reasserted himself. The moment the priest announced that he had some knowledge of the ikon's whereabouts, Burnell became convinced he was going to try to pass off a fake on his visitor. No doubt the real Madonna was long since in Japan or Saudi Arabia or Rio, adorning an office or a palace or a brothel, along with other stolen works of art of which WACH had cognizance.

The lake was phantasmal by night and, moreover, relatively smoke-free. He breathed in the fresh air with gratitude. A fish plupped, disrupting the silver sheen of the water. In the stillness, a waterfall could be heard. The waters of the lake poured on their devious way to the Caspian. Burnell thought of the Byzantine princess, tumbled in death into these chill depths. No doubt the trout had been pleased to receive Simonis.

Kadredin appeared. With him, walking by his side, was Khachi, toting his armoury, his radio jammed to one ear. This, thought Burnell sardonically, marks the end of my assertion of myself. Perhaps my fears were not liars and they have decided their lives would be simpler if they shot me. I shall die to the tinny music of Radio Tbilisi.

Coming up to him without preamble, Kadredin said, '*M'sieu*, the Mother of God ikon remains in the church.'

He burst into tears. He covered his great eyes with his papery hands. His body shook with sobs. He fell to his knees on the stony ground.

Thought Burnell, 'This is one better than being shot. Well, three-quarters.'

The moon was setting but the lad produced a torch. The three of them went into the church.

Kadredin, afflicted by one of his sudden mood changes, was now shouting and laughing. Oh yes, they could have an agreement. He would trust Burnell rather than his bishop. The bishop had cheated him over his living. The bishop didn't trust him or he the bishop. He clapped his hands – the bishop would see!

Khachi tugged at Kadredin's cassock, speaking urgently. Still suspicious, Burnell asked what the lad said.

'Oh, he wants to go to bed. Ignore him!'

He went on to declare his relief. Now all would be fine.

Burnell would take the ikon back to Germany. As an expert, he would see that it reached a maximum price at auction. The Alte Pinakothek in München would purchase it. They would share the profit, sixty for him, forty for Burnell – OK, fifty-fifty, why not? And he would be able to live out the rest of his miserable life in decency. God was good. At last he had some hope for the future.

But then again – he clasped Burnell's hands. How could he trust anyone? Even an Englishman? Everyone stole from Georgians, and from priests most of all. Once Burnell was away with the precious article, he would forget his poor friend Father Nolin Kadredin.

As soon as daylight came, he would draw up an agreement. Both would sign it. He would keep it. If Burnell tried to cheat, then Kadredin would send the document to WACH and ruin the thief's career. The world would denounce Burnell and God would strike him down for a thief.

'But you stole it, you fraud. Isn't that the situation?'

'Long ago, *m'sieu*, when I was young and wicked. Before I had God in my heart.' He spoke loudly, perhaps in the hope that God would be listening, and the words echoed nobly round the church.

'How long ago is that?'

'Many years . . . When I was in charge here, of course, in Gamsakhurdia's day. When do you think? When I was alone and subject to temptation. What do you know about such things, being an atheist? It's on my conscience, very heavy.' The long face in its large-eyed innocence could have adorned a fresco: Burnell could almost see something in the style of El Greco, with the dimpled feet of angels fluttering within an ace of his ears.

'Come on. You'll keep your sin and get rid of your Madonna, and profit from both . . . Where is this damned article?'

'Please understand, Dr Burnell. We must be straight with each other. Oh, I could kill myself – throw myself to drown in the lake, if it wasn't for respect for Queen Simonis . . . When you send me my sixty per cent share from Frankfurt, I can live decently with my son Khachi, not in Bogdanakhi but somewhere peaceful.'

'Oh, so Khachi's your son, is he?'

'I fondly believe so, sir. With that sixty-five per cent, I can take him to Athens, fair and beautiful Athena! There I'll have a room of my own, where I may think of God and gaze out at the Adriatic.'

'The Aegean.'

'That also.' He started to whine again. Having wrung Burnell's hands, he commenced on his own. In all his miserable days, he said, Burnell represented his first chance to deal with someone professionally connected with the Western world of art. That was why he trusted him implicitly. Burnell was famous, having written a book no one understood. So he could ruin Burnell's career if he did not honour their agreement.

All this while, Khachi stood by, playing his fingers along his machine gun as if it were a keyboard, in time to the music.

'So where is this work of art? Let's see it.'

Again the stern priest, stern and just, yet agonized. 'I've changed my mind. I can't trust anyone. My whole life depends on this one gamble. You will see the ikon in the morning, when you have signed the agreement.'

They passed out through the narthex door, above which King Zrze still offered up his model church to the Virgin.

The morning appeared surprisingly bright and unnatural. He suspected angels. Khachi was at work in the courtyard. A fire was blazing there, where a Land Rover was parked. The youth had killed a deer and was busy cutting it up with a huge knife. His movements were stylized. The knife went over his head and down, over and down. The process smothered him with blood, until he was red from head to foot. Burnell was haunted by a feeling of premonition.

'I'm glad you're not after my blood,' he said, approaching the youth.

For answer, Khachi showed him a face as savage as Lazar Kaginovich's. It was Lazar Kaginovich's. He rushed up to the cupola on the church and aimed his gun. Burnell was staring down its black muzzle when he woke, startled.

There was comfort to find himself still alive in his improvised bed, yet he experienced disappointment. He was reminded of Greek plays where all the violence took place off-stage. Daylight was filling the small cell, revealing the crumbling plaster. It was time for Act V. He got up, semi-eager to play his role through, more eager to examine the ikon, if it really existed.

Kadredin and his gunman son were by the lake. In an echo of the unpleasant dream, Khachi had a fire going. Kadredin was playing an open-air role against a background of lake and trees. Approaching Burnell with his arms full of sticks, he said proudly, 'Fish for our breakfast to celebrate, *m'sieu*. Then the agreement, then the famous Madonna. You see that clever Khachi has caught trout by tickling?'

Dropping the sticks, he demonstrated the art of tickling with his hands. 'Patience and cunning – that's how trout are caught. They will come to your hand under the bank to enjoy a little tickle. And when you have them entranced, when you hear them purr like cats, then – whoosh! – you hurl them quickly from the water on to dry land. And there's your meal.'

Having no wish to become Kadredin's meal, Burnell made a neutral comment. But the fish, roasted over the fire, were certainly tasty. Afterwards, they went into the refectory where an agreement was drawn up.

Now the priest was a lawyer, very business-like with his phraseology. The agreement, which both men signed, bound Burnell to get the best market price for the celebrated twelfth-century ikon known as the Madonna of Futurity. It should be sold within a year. Fifty per cent of the receipts would be despatched within seven days to Father Kadredin, by registered post, to a specific address in Bogdanakhi. Kadredin, for his part, would maintain silence until after the sale. He agreed to send Burnell a receipt for the money by registered post. This agreement was drawn up on a page torn from Burnell's black notebook.

Both men agreed that their signatures should be renewed before a lawyer when they returned to Bogdanakhi, and a copy of the document deposited with him.

Kadredin tucked the paper away in his smelly sheep garment. Once the ikon was in Burnell's hands and he in Bogdanakhi, a helicopter would take him off to Tbilisi, as prearranged. In Tbilisi, a military plane would return him to FAM, as he had come. At this juncture, Kadredin was inclined to delay, to discuss many minor points. Burnell interrupted.

'Enough. Show me the ikon.'

The priest led the way to the church, his skirts flapping about his thin legs. The lad trailed behind them, toting as ever his armoury. Inside, Kadredin paused as if sunk in thought, looking under his eyebrows at Burnell. Burnell maintained an aloof stance, as heraldic as that of King Zrze above his head. Sighing, the priest went over to the apse. He knelt, and tried to lift the trapdoor. This he succeeded in doing only with Burnell's assistance and broken fingernails.

Burnell stared down into the bones and dirt, assuming they were about to descend.

But the ikon was concealed elsewhere. In his time as resident priest, Kadredin had hollowed out the timbers of the trapdoor. The ikon, wrapped in cloth, had been inserted into the hollow and wired securely in place. Oak laths had then been nailed over it, concealing the insertion, and the whole stained.

Burnell pulled out his wire-cutters and prised up the nails, while reflecting on the good sense of the hiding-place; no one would look at the trapdoor while venturing down into the cellar. He repeated this observation to himself, noting its sexual implications.

Elbowing Kadredin aside, he lifted the cloth-covered bundle from its place of concealment and unwrapped it. In a moment, he held in his hands the Madonna of Futurity.

He carried the trophy to the door of the church to study it under a better light.

The ikon was painted on a wooden panel measuring, he estimated, only twenty-eight centimetres by twenty-one. Yet it possessed grandeur; he was unprepared for its impact.

Master Evtihije had painted one of the great standard subjects of the Christian Church, the Holy Mother and Child, symbols of unity and pure love. The Mother of God, dressed in a rubiginous hooded garment, held the Child tenderly in her arms, clutching one of His hands. About the Child she had wrapped a flimsy golden robe, partly covering His blue garment.

The Son rested His face against His Mother's cheek, regarding her lovingly. She, however, gazed beyond Him, out of the picture.

The Virgin Mary was long-nosed and dark of countenance, with fine arched eyebrows. Her tall figure was depicted with a kind of monastic simplicity and set against an infinite golden background. The curve of her halo intersected the smaller orbit of her Babe's halo, to emphasize their unity.

Burnell turned the painting over in his hands, testing the wood with a fingernail. He had no doubt that this was the genuine article, eight and a half centuries old, lost for many years. It was unstained by age, except in one corner. The loving closeness of the couple had softened the stiff lines of their draperies. The Virgin's tenderness of expression was reinforced by delicate brushwork, still as clear as if it had been painted that very day. The composition was a statement of a deep love, both divine and human. And yet . . . It also held a mystery. The Mother of God's eyes as she gazed from the picture were sorrowful, her mouth pursed. Tears came to his eyes, knowing he had once been held as Jesus was held.

'Oh, it's beautiful . . . Just beautiful . . .' He felt the inadequacy of words. 'It radiates light.'

'You can probably get twelve million euros for it. Twelve and a half.' Kadredin rubbed his hands. He had hardly given the ikon a glance. 'Wrap it up, wrap it up carefully. Stick it in your pack. Let's get back to town. Put it in auction as soon as you can. Ah, how I need that money! Escape! Athens!' He slapped Khachi on the back.

'So art's no longer to be appreciated. It has merely to appreciate.'

'Don't cheat me, now. We're friends, isn't that right? What real good is that thing to me? I've had enough. I'm sick of poverty, sick of anarchy, sick of the living disaster of this country of mine. I want to get out. Let's move on, eh?'

'All right,' Burnell said to himself, 'so that's all you care about this miraculous painting? – A meal ticket? I'll fix you.'

He told himself he owed General Stalinbrass nothing either. No matter what the ikon might be worth on the money market, he could perhaps keep it for himself. How it would transform his living-room in the apartment in Soss City. He could look at that beautiful worried loving mother every day. Just to possess such a rare object — one he had himself discovered — would bring him more fame than anything a shoddy auction could do.

'Yes,' he said. 'Let's go back to Bogdanakhi.'

He found it difficult to speak. Nothing to do with religion, he told himself. But the love of a mother for her child . . . that's different, fuck it.

12
A Crowded Stage

They came on the approaches to Bogdanakhi late in the morning of the following day. Even from a distance, the sound of Beethoven rolled out from the public address system.

Khachi had been acting as scout. Burnell and Kadredin made their way round the corner of a meat-processing plant. Ahead was Khachi, disarmed and held by soldiers. Others had their weapons trained on Burnell and the priest.

'Holy Mother and all angels!' Kadredin exclaimed, as West Georgian soldiers rushed forward and seized the pair of them. They were hastily searched for guns before being marched to an APC. More soldiers dragged them into the vehicle. As it roared away, Khachi called frantically, struggling in the grip of his captors. His voice was lost in blue haze and noise.

The crackle of rifle fire sounded as the APC headed for the city centre. Heavily armed men jostled in the streets, which appeared more tumbledown than ever.

'This means the Dead One's still in town,' Burnell said to the priest. He received a blow across the face from the nearest soldier.

Before reaching the main square, the vehicle swerved left and entered a narrow side street filled with people, most of them in uniform. This mob set up a hullabaloo as Burnell and Kadredin were off-loaded and made to stand on the pavement. 'Death to the Nazi German swine!' called a voice.

'I'm English, you fool,' Burnell shouted.

'Death to the Nazi English swine!'

They were pushed through the stage door into a small theatre, the Oktober Tenth Revolutionary Theatre. Playbills showed that *The Night of Epiphany* by William Shakspere had recently been enacted. Now something more serious was in production. The stage on to which the two were pushed and kicked was crowded with two dozen performers who, judging from their dazed expressions, were awaiting their final curtain.

Guards stood over them, their faces set as grim as critics.

Down in the auditorium, from which all seats had been removed, a sell-out gathering of soldiery was assembled.

'This is your fault, Burnell,' Kadredin said. 'You got me into this. These madmen will shoot us.'

'It can but make the groundlings cheer.'

The response did little to cheer the priest, who began shouting to those round him in Georgian, protesting his innocence. The other prisoners hung their heads. When one of the guards struck Kadredin across the shoulders with his rifle, he subsided, hiding his face in his hands.

So the situation remained for a half-hour, with the prison quota on stage being occasionally added to. 'The big crowd scene,' thought Burnell, pulling a gloomy face to himself. Above him loomed the sea coast of Illyria; very rocky; not a place in which to holiday. In the auditorium and the boxes above was much coming and going.

A whistle blew in the street. Two men marched forward from the wings, to seize hold of a grey-haired man. He looked up at them, smiling weakly, shaking his head, denying something, denying everything. As they dragged him away, his hands fluttered like the wings of a broken seabird. Nobody made a move to save him. He was forced out through the stage door.

Once in the street, the man began to scream – presumably at what he saw there. A shot rang out. There was no more screaming.

Burnell saw red. In those weak fluttering hands had been nothing but innocence and helplessness. He turned and struck the nearest guard full in the mouth. The man reeled backwards under the unexpected blow and fell from the stage into the orchestra pit with a crash.

A great commotion broke out. The sea coast of Illyria underwent an unscripted earthquake. Immediately other guards were on Burnell. He was borne to the ground, to writhe under a shock assault of heavy boots. His life was possibly saved by his victim's dive into the pit: the noise of it attracted an officer's attention. He came forward. After ordering the guards to stand away from Burnell, he addressed the latter in German, telling him to get up. Shaken, Burnell replied that he felt safer lying where he was until he was released.

'You'll be up for trial soon. You can protest your innocence then. For now, stand up and remain silent.'

'You couldn't tell me what's happening, could you?'

'Stand up and remain silent.'

Kadredin pressed forward, beginning incoherently to protest his own innocence. The officer turned away. Kadredin's face had gone the colour of fine volcanic ash. He said to Burnell, 'You'll get free because you're European. You'll get all the money. I'll be shot.' He crossed himself.

'Nonsense, we've done nothing. It's OK. You're halfway to Athens.' He could hardly stand upright for pain, pain in his back, his side, his legs. Reality came and went in a system of stabbing attacks.

Kadredin raised a fist. 'Don't you understand? There's been some kind of revolution since Mayor Sigua was killed. It's clear Kaginovich has taken over the city. These are his soldiers. At such dreadful times you get shot for nothing, nothing at all. I've seen it before.'

'Oh, shut up. I think I'm going to throw up.'

'They won't shoot me. This remains a Christian country. They don't shoot priests.' This rapid change of mind did not make him look noticeably happier. He tugged at his long hair in desperation.

Another hour passed. Burnell could not recollect the Georgian word for coffee. Or hospitalization. Several more prisoners were dragged from the stage by the firing-squad, taken outside, and shot. The process of elimination was counterpointed by a supplement of more prisoners, some in decidedly bedraggled condition.

The crowding on the stage never grew less. The stench of fear and breaking wind accumulated.

A smartly dressed young lieutenant pushed through the auditorium crowd and climbed on to the stage. It was two-thirty-five. Pointing a finger at Burnell, he ordered him to come along. As they went down into the auditorium, Kadredin called out, 'My dear friend, tell them I am innocent. Take care of what you have. But life first, remember. Life first.'

Groaning, Burnell could believe only that the priest had his priorities right.

The officer escorted him upstairs and along a corridor to one of the theatre boxes. The box had been converted into a room by boarding off the view of the auditorium. Burnell's entrance was hastened by a fist in his backbone, just where pain had already located a soft spot. His officer entered behind him, closed the door, and stood alertly with his back to it.

'Jim!' Burnell exclaimed. Immense relief filled him to see James Irving again. However, Irving's friendly face was altered for the worse by a ripe dark bruise which had closed his right eye.

Irving gave Burnell a kind of smile. 'Little misunderstanding here, Roy, as you Britishers would say.' His arms were bound behind his back. He groaned. 'You OK?'

'So far so good.'

Burnell also recognized the other occupant of the improvised room. Wedged behind the small table was Ziviad Orpishurda, his back to the auditorium. His large hands rested on the table. Under one of his hands was a service revolver, its black muzzle pointing towards his captives. He smoked a cigarette without removing it from his lips even when he spoke. As usual he was wearing a black SAS jacket, on which insignia showed that he had been promoted to the rank of captain.

Orpishurda accorded the new arrival no recognition. Speaking formally, he said, 'Roy Burnell, you are arrested for acts of espionage, carried out against the people of the West Georgian Republic. The penalty for such acts is death.'

The milling about of prisoners in the auditorium sounded through the thin boarding at his back.

'I told you this is all crap,' Irving said. 'You know it's crap. Can we stop this farce? Burnell is completely innocent.' Orpishurda rose. So small was the room, he could hit Irving across the face without coming round the table.

'I am no spy,' Burnell said. 'My credentials were thoroughly checked before I was allowed anywhere near your country. And I intend to leave as soon as possible.'

Sighing, Orpishurda indicated a piece of paper on his table and said, 'You have sent a cable to the American General, Augustus Stalinbrass. Do you deny it is so?'

'Is that the action of a spy?'

'We believe it is. And we hold other evidence of your subversive activities. Quite sufficient to have you shot. You understand that you are now on trial. I am appointed your judge, by authority of the officer commanding this city, General Kaginovich. Do you understand?'

'This is lunacy. I demand a phone call to the British Embassy in Tbilisi.' He was struck from behind by the guarding officer.

Orpishurda ground out his cigarette underfoot, as if to show how greatly he respected the spark of life. 'You have no rights here. I am afraid you can demand nothings. You have only a chance to view the evidences we hold against you. Do you wish to take it?'

'What evidence?'

Orpishurda rested his elbow on the table and his forehead in his hand. He gave another sigh. Without looking up, he waved his free hand at the lieutenant by the door. The officer snapped into action and lifted a plastic box from the floor, to place it in front of Orpishurda. Sighing again, Orpishurda turned the box upside down. Photographs slid out across the table. Negligently, he pushed them about with one finger until five were arranged in a row, like playing cards.

The photographs were immediately recognizable. Burnell saw that they were the shots he had taken of the mosque where he and Irving had first met Lazar Kaginovich, and of the surroundings nearby, and of a group of West Georgian officers taken outside the mosque, including Ziviad Orpishurda.

'You took these?' As he asked the question, Orpishurda shuffled a cigarette out of a packet and applied it to his mouth without lighting it. 'Our agent appropriated your cameras from a certain notorious house where you visited since a few nights. As you see, Mr Burnell, the films are developed. So I ask, what do you see here?'

'Shit, you know what these are. What's the problem, for God's sake?'

'Yes, it's rather a heavy problem, in fact.' He laughed. 'The photographs are evidence that you have photographed our military installations. A military headquarters. Some of our officers. And the grounds in which we see one of our camouflaged field mortars.' He flicked his fingers at the pictures.

'Mortars? I saw no mortars . . .' He remembered he had seen a mortar, and continued hastily, 'I've no interest in your mortars. I photographed the mosque simply because it was a mosque.'

'You lie. It has not served as a mosque many years. These photographs provide true evidence of your spying activities. This man Irving is your accomplice. The penalty for spying is death.' Then he lit his cigarette.

Irving said, this time without force, 'I tell you, that's all a load of crap.'

'I'm sorry. This is a Christian country but the penalty for espionage is everywhere the same. Burnell, do you deny you took these photographs?'

Burnell put both clenched fists against his forehead, protesting at the madness of the whole thing. 'Of course I took the photographs, I don't deny it. You saw me. You posed for the camera. Look at this picture. You and your pals grinning at the lens . . . Besides, I have written permission to photograph for World Antiquities and Cultural Heritage.'

'Only is to photograph religious structure. No military installations.' Shaking his head, he repeated, 'No military installations. You are guilty. I formally declare you guilty. You foreigners should stay in your own countries. That's the end of your trial.' He banged an open palm on the table.

Raising a hand, he snapped his fingers at the lieutenant by the door. 'Now you will be taken to a cell. You'll get a meal. I'll see to it. You will be executed by a firing-squad some time soon.'

Irving exploded with rage, shouting that international law was being defied. To Burnell he said, 'There was an uprising against Kaginovich by the town garrison. The Dead One put it down. That's why they are all still in Bogdanakhi. They don't quite know how to proceed. But Captain Ziviad Orpishurda is an honourable man. He understands that the outside world will give no aid to the West Georgian Republic while madmen like Kaginovich are in charge.'

More severely, Orpishurda repeated that foreigners should stay in their own country, minding their own business.

Taking a deep breath, Burnell gained control of himself. Although he had never particularly wished to be sentenced to death, he had wanted to be a warrior, brave in battle. Here at last was his chance to be brave in a theatre.

Throughout the hours of his imprisonment, he had kept his pack slung over one shoulder; it had become a part of him. Drawing himself up, he said, 'Captain Orpishurda, I have one request. That you will let the innocent man, Father Nolin Kadredin, go free immediately. He is a priest pure and simple, ignorant of military or political matters.'

When Orpishurda said nothing, and did nothing beyond staring fixedly at a point ahead of him, Burnell continued. 'Furthermore, I request you to hand over this pack to Father Kadredin, since it contains items belonging to him. Will you do this?'

With equal gravity, Orpishurda replied that he could grant nothing. Since they were at war, he must obey orders as well as give them. He added in a low voice, with a guilty look, 'I regret this situation has developed . . .'

His tone encouraged Irving to speak again, glaring through his good eye. 'Listen, Captain, you know we are both here for the good of your country. Before dusk, a helicopter will arrive from Tbilisi to take Burnell away. It's all fixed. Let him go. Keep these harmless photos, if you must, but –'

Orpishurda lifted a hand, scowling at Irving, but the latter continued, shouting, 'Be positive, man. Why try to frame Burnell? Why give your new republic a bad name? If you shoot either of us, you'll have the whole EU against you. What's more –'

The captain stood up. He swelled until he appeared to burst from his black jacket. His bristling presence seemed to fill the little makeshift room. He spat out the stub of his cigarette, seizing up his revolver. 'One more word, I will shoot you dead, Moonman! I do only my job. I'm a soldier, no bloody politician.'

As he lifted the gun, Irving stiffened. He moved back a pace, but the lieutenant pushed him forward. The space suddenly boiled with frustration, fear, hatred. Seeing Orpishurda's face, purple with fury, the lieutenant also drew his revolver.

The door opened and Lazar Kaginovich entered.

Kaginovich moved not hastily: almost at a funeral pace, in the manner that Nemesis arrives to mortals, in full confidence that resistance is in vain.

Two husky brutes accompanied Kaginovich. They were ordered to remain outside the box, and to see that nobody intruded.

The Dead One was transformed since last Burnell had seen him. His uniform was heavy with medals. He bore the rank of general, with a crimson flash on his epaulettes. His large sheepskin hat still crowned his narrow head.

Orpishurda immediately stood to attention and saluted, executing these movements with such vigour that his papers went flying.

Burnell saw Kaginovich's face in profile. It was almost fleshless. Tension had drawn back the skin as if it were a sheet, leaving tight white lines of strain. Little cups of yellow had formed under the eyes, where a nerve throbbed. His eyes were black, staring. They were never still – such life as there was in the face was in them, an independent darting life.

Taking in the situation, glaring from one to another, the Dead One drew back his narrow lips. He showed his teeth as if about to bite. Every movement was under rigid control. Orpishurda was drained of colour, at sight of his superior.

Kaginovich let the tension build before speaking. He held out a hand. 'Captain Orpishurda, surrender your revolver. You are under arrest for propagating subversive opinions during the mutiny.'

The captain obeyed without a word of protest, lowering his head in submission to his general. Without another word, Kaginovich accepted Orpishurda's revolver. His head turned from one side to the other as he surveyed Irving and Burnell.

'Captain Orpishurda, you were interrogating two foreigners known to be spies. Why is only one of them bound? Has this other man been searched for weapons? Why has he been permitted to retain a pack?'

In a low voice, Orpishurda said, 'He was searched below. So I was given to understand. He is unarmed. Sir.'

'You "were given to understand . . ." What kind of an officer are you?' He turned his glare on Burnell. Again the hand came out, demanding. Burnell did not understand Kaginovich's order, but its meaning was clear.

Yet for a second he hesitated to slip the pack from his shoulder. The little lieutenant rushed forward, eager to curry favour with his superior. He snatched Burnell's pack, unzipped it, and spilled its contents on the table. The ikon fell out, still wrapped in its cloth.

Kaginovich turned the bundle over with the muzzle of the revolver. At his order, the lieutenant unwrapped the cloth. The ikon lay revealed under the light.

In an even tone, Kaginovich said, 'You are a thief as well as a spy, Burnell.' Irving translated the remark. 'You will be shot at once.'

Deepening his voice to keep it from shaking, Burnell said, 'This is the lost Virgin and Child, ascribed to Evtihije and known as the Madonna of Futurity. Far from being a thief, I am the discoverer of a precious cultural item of Old Georgia. Acting on behalf of WACH, I intend to remove it for safe-keeping, away from the present conflict.'

He knew from Irving's tone of voice as this was translated that he had said something unlikely to be well received by the madman who stood nearby. He felt icy, despite the heat in the box of a room.

The eyes of the Dead One remained fixed on the ikon. He did not move as he spoke. 'You are aware why this ikon bears the name it does. The Mother of God looks away from her Child. She appears to stare gloomily into the future. There she sees the fate destined to befall her Son.

'Maybe she foresees also the fate of Georgia – to be over-run by enemies of Christ, by Muslims, and by foreign thieves and spies like you.'

The melancholy calm of the Madonna's face gave Burnell courage.

'Perhaps more than that, General. The Holy Mother may indeed look towards the future. Maybe she sees the bloodshed that will blemish the religion to bear Christ's name. And the bloodshed still being committed in the name of religion.'

The Dead One fell into a rage at Burnell's words – or else he feigned a rage. Foam and spittle burst from his mouth. He seized up the ikon from the table, to raise it above his head.

Grasping his superior officer's intentions, Orpishurda – who had been standing motionless at attention – cried in a loud voice, 'No!'

With a ghastly grimace, Kaginovich brought the ikon down and smashed it over the edge of the table. He tossed the shattered pieces away into a corner of the room.

While the fragments were clattering to the ground, he flung himself at Burnell. As he did so, he pulled his own revolver from its holster. His free arm went about Burnell's neck, so that face was pulled against ghastly face. He thrust the muzzle of the gun hard up under Burnell's ribs.

Burnell emitted a shriek of pain and anger. Momentarily, he was bereft of conscious thought.

13
Richard and Blanche

The light was a dove, soft and grey, filling the dining-hall with inaudible music. All along one side of the room were locked windows reaching to the floor. They gave a pleasant illusion of freedom, looking out on parkland and a line of beeches almost too near the walls of the institution for comfort.

The trees were supervising the long glissade from summer into autumn. While most of their leaves remained green, the more forward-looking had already slipped into a less demanding yellow, while the really venturesome were trying out a scarlet-tipped approach to September.

In the dining-hall, much the same applied to the patients, male and female: the lees of summer were clearly read on their countenances. Some resembled anybody one might meet outside the institution, except maybe that their gaze was duller, their pace slower. Less forward-looking ones had slipped into a more valetudinarian mode, forgetting to shave or apply make-up. And the least venturesome were bundled into grey dressing-gowns and slippers, shuffling in their blank-eyed approach towards a kind of mental September.

One of the last patients to enter the dining-hall and queue at the cafeteria for his *wiener schnitzel* defied these gradations. He had been delayed by a nurse after his daily session with one of the resident psychoanalysts. Younger than the other occupants of one of the tables at which he now dutifully sat, he walked at a proper pace, wore a grey dressing-gown, and had forgotten to shave. He ate his meat and potato with properly controlled movements of knife and fork, but without appetite, pausing every now and again to stare out at the parkland in which the Institute was set. His gaze was alert for the sparrows flitting about the boles of the trees.

On the tray beside his main plate was a dish containing yoghurt, muesli, and honey. He ignored this when he had finished his *schnitzel*, put his knife and fork together, and rose to leave the table.

A woman sitting opposite his place reached out a detaining hand, calling his name. He smiled, but did not pause in his retreat. Leaving the hall, he walked a short way down the corridor, ascended the curving stair, and entered his ward on the first floor. The ward was decorated in cheerful colours and partitioned, so that each of its six beds enjoyed some privacy. He went to his bed by the window. To his partition was affixed his name: ROY EDWARD BURNELL, together with a series of graphs designed to show at a glance the state of his health and mind.

In the bed next to Burnell, hidden by the partition, lay a man who whispered to himself in a language one of the nurses had informed him was Finnish. He had been an operative for Behavioural Dynamics SA until he blew a transponder. It was difficult to keep the slight noise of his whispering at bay. Sometimes in the night, meaningless words seemed to Burnell's tired brain to writhe into fragments of sentences in German or English. '. . . nothing before her but the tiresome inexorable . . .' '. . . speaks considerably with a smile . . .' 'the mischievous château leans to the right . . .' Once, he thought he heard, perfectly enunciated, 'creeps in this petty pace . . .' Such was the effect of random Finnish phonemes, Burnell lay in dreadful anticipation of hearing an entire *Macbeth* recited by accident.

Burnell picked up his edition of Montaigne's *Essays* but did not read. He stared out of the window, one finger tucked snug among the pages to mark his place in the 'Essay on Experience' ('A man must do wrong in detail if he wishes to do right on the whole . . .'). He waited, with a convalescent's listless patience. Eventually, his sparrow – well, be honest, Richard's sparrow – came and sat on the window sill. He could distinguish it from all the other sparrows. It perched on the sill only for a minute. In that time, it opened its beak and chirped. Then it was gone, lost among the leafy branches of the beech. The thickness of the glass was such that Burnell could not hear its note. But he knew the bird always came and cried 'Richard! Richard!' at this particular window.

A patient called Richard had once occupied the bed on which he now sprawled. Richard had been one of the world's victims, too good, too kind, too gentle, for the workaday struggle. And so he had ended up here in the institution. All the attempts to befit him for what passed as normality had failed, and indeed were exquisite torture for the unfortunate youth.

Richard had had no human friends. The other inmates feared his innocence. Like St Francis of Assisi, he had made friends with the birds, or rather with one bird: the visiting sparrow. That sparrow had learned to come to Richard's hand. Its small avian aorta had expanded with love of him. It was the only creature in the world to recognize the true beauty of Richard's soul. So ran Burnell's sick fancy, part amused, part disgusted.

Endless sessions of heavy Freudian psychoanalysis had finally proved too much for Richard. He passed away one night without a struggle, and a male nurse – probably from Lithuania – wheeled his body away at 2.25 a.m. Next morning at sunrise his faithful little sparrow fluttered up to the sill to be with his friend, only to find him gone. Now every morning still, back the sparrow flew, his avian aorta breaking, calling for ever, 'Richard! Richard!'

Determinedly though Burnell tried to banish this ludicrous piece of sentimentality from his head, he could not forget it. It rolled before his inward vision like a detached retina. The sparrow frequently perched on his sill to remind him of its tragic story. As often as it came, he would thump on the window to drive it off.

'You might have been Richard's friend, you little sod, but you're not mine!' Then he would mourn his own callousness and wish to make up his quarrel with the bird. Perhaps if he were kind enough, patient enough, it would grow to love him as well. Then when he left this place, if he ever did, it would fly about calling 'Burnell! Burnell!' He wasn't going to have a lousy sparrow using his Christian name.

185

Sparrows were smart. Though this one was pretty dim if it hadn't gathered by now that Richard had handed in his *schnitzel* ticket. Perhaps the other sparrows would learn his name from this one. It would pass from one bird to another. They would even find his name easier to pronounce than 'Chirp! Chirp!' Mother sparrows would teach it to children sparrows. 'You want another worm? OK, let's hear you say it, duckie . . .'

Soon the whole park would be full of birds – not sparrows only, but thrushes and starlings and robins – all calling in chorus, 'Burnell! Burnell!' On balmy nights the barn owls would shriek the syllables. He watched an old black crow one day. In its harsh voice it appeared to caw his name. A skylark high above the rooftops cried it with delight, 'Burnell! Burnell! Dear Burnell!'

Shit, he said to himself, I really am going round the ruddy twist . . . Is that all that's left? Personality gone, just my name remaining.

But what if migratory birds got hold of it? There'd be an international incident . . . Geese on their way across Canada, heard honking 'Burnell! Burnell!' over Lake Winnipegosis . . .

He covered his ears, cringing on the bed.

'Mr Burnell. Mr Burnell!' God, the fucking condors in the Andes . . . He looked up. The male nurse from Lithuania was standing by his bedside, professionally obsequious in his outsize trainers. 'Are you orkay, Mr Burnell?' He hated the way this chap lengthened the 'o' in words. Presumably all Lithuanians did it. Yet another reason not to go to Vilnius.

'What do you want?'

'A visitor dornstairs to see you.'

'I said I didn't wish to see any visitors.'

'Or well, there's a nort frrom this orne.'

Burnell opened the envelope. The note was brief.

Mon cher ami,

Please can we see each other. I know something of your problems and realize you may not be able to remember me. However, we are old and indecent friends. Truly. Maybe you need me as much as I need you.

Moi, with my knowledge of Spanish and other tricks,
   Your French friend,
   Blanche Bretesche

He repeated her name to himself. It carried no resonance; or did some faint fragrance drift back to him?

She rose from a chair under a long window as he entered the visitors' room in which she was waiting. The light entering the room was green, filtered through the trees outside.

Her eyes were also green. She wore a grey suit. Her dark hair was swept across her forehead. She smiled rather uncertainly. Neither of them knew exactly what to do. Through her awkwardness he perceived her grace.

Then Blanche moved determinedly forward and kissed Burnell's cheek. He held her body to his. 'Hello, Roy. I'm your French friend, Blanche. It's only six weeks since we were last together. You seem to have been in warm water since then. A busy six weeks.'

He was frustrated. Although he certainly liked the whole appearance of this lady, he hated to ask about what he could not recall. During his time in both hospital and institution, he had fought shy of seeing anyone, in case complete strangers should impose themselves on him in the guise of friends he had forgotten. In that respect, life in Georgia had been easier: everyone was a stranger, and no pretence.

They attempted to chat inconsequentially. She told him of a strange dream she had had, in which Burnell sailed off for distant shores in a giant shoe.

When Blanche reminded him that they had last met in Budapest shortly before his ten years were stolen, he saw she was, despite herself, pained that he had no memory of their meeting.

'We were close then . . . Blanche?' He offered up her name tentatively.

'Yes, we were close.'

The reticence in her answer told him something of her strength of character; he immensely liked the considered warmth of her expression. But finding no way to overcome the abyss in his own mind, he was forced to retreat from her unspoken invitation to ask further; or at least he postponed that moment by asking if she would like coffee, assuring her it was good Bolivian blend. When she assented, he rang for service.

She too had her difficulties, trying not to feel affronted that the long pleasant history between them had been destroyed. When she asked if he knew he was at present in an institution in Soss City on the edge of the Niederwald, his laughing assent brought a smile from her.

'I'm not mad, just lacking . . . There's much I want to ask you, of course.' He paused hopefully.

She replied that she could not face an interrogation. However, she explained who she was, that she lived in Madrid, being head of the Spanish Division of WACH. Karl Leberecht had been in touch with her concerning Burnell; once she could get free of work, she had flown to FAM to see him. She said that he had promised to stay with her in her apartment despite his lack of Spanish.

His hesitation in replying to this invitation stretched into silence.

He cast his gaze down, only too aware of the demons pursuing him: Larry Foot, the broken Madonna, Lazar Kaginovich – and behind those furies, the avenging vacuum, eating up relationships. Blanche rescued him by asking about what she called his adventures.

'I have to sort myself out. You know.'

'Is it awful?' she asked, adding swiftly, as if she flinched from a truthful answer, 'You look fine.'

'My ribs have all but healed. Seems that my kidney's OK.' He forced a laugh. 'I exercise every morning. It's now mainly a morale problem. You may have heard I was beaten up a bit in Georgia.'

She gave him one of her best smiles. 'Roy, honestly, you do let yourself in for these things! I know all about your scrapes in the Caucasus. Everyone knows. Did you know that? Everyone knows! You're a hero. Your story was carried in all the media. Do they allow you to watch TV in here?'

Before Burnell could answer, a knock came at the door and an attendant entered with a tray of coffee and biscuits which he set down on a side table. Burnell signed his slip. Blanche rose, moved the table nearer Burnell, and sat down beside him. She began opening her shoulder-bag, but on impulse he reached out and clutched her hand, thanking her in German, French, and English for coming to visit him. When, in response, she made the slightest gesture towards him, he seized her in his arms, clutching her to him, feeling her warmth, burying his face in her dark hair. They remained like that, feeling the life in each other's bodies.

'Oh yes, Roy, we were quite close . . . Hasn't your father been to see you?'

He reminded her that his father was confined to a wheelchair. No, his step-mother had not come, but she had phoned. His sister Clem had written. So had Aunt Sheila.

From her bag Blanche produced a copy of *Le Monde*, folded to the international news page. As she passed it over, he saw it was dated some days previously. The headlines read: 'TEN KILLED IN LIVERPOOL RIOT'; 'MORE NICE MURDERS'; 'PATAGONIA PAEDOPHILE RING REVEALED'; 'BULGARIA EVACUATED'. The usual kind of thing. Further down the page was Burnell's photograph, with the headings: 'KAGINOVICH KILLED. Architect Praised'. Burnell could read no further.

As he returned the paper, he told Blanche that Leberecht came to see him every day. His kindness was greatly appreciated, although WACH had not been pleased by the Georgian incident, since their charter forbade operatives to interfere in political matters. A discreet member of the government had also interviewed him.

Blanche's expression grew more anxious, as she tried to determine what kind of trouble he might be in. Her presence had seemed to light up the rather sombre room; now she drew back into herself when confronting the problem of violence, which had erupted in a man she had seen at his most tender.

She asked, 'But you had to kill him? He was threatening you?'

They had remained touching. At her question, he stood up, busying himself with pouring coffee, his back to her to conceal his anger. 'Look . . . Blanche . . . I'm undergoing – well, you know, psychotherapy, about all that. I don't want to go into it. Sorry.' With an effort, he spoke more calmly. 'Kaginovich was going to kill me. That's a puzzle too. I mean, why exactly.'

He broke off, struggling to contain his emotions. 'Blanche – he smashed an irreplaceable twelfth-century ikon. Smashed it to bits! How can anyone understand . . .' He tried to bury his face in his left hand before speaking more calmly. 'He was a violent man. He lived by violence. It would have meant nothing to him to shoot me down . . .'

'But he didn't shoot you . . .'

He passed her a cup which rattled slightly in its saucer. 'You don't think at such moments. Your mind goes blank. You act. I don't really remember acting. I know now I . . . See, I had a pair of wire-cutters in my hip pocket. I had forgotten they were there. But in the moment of crisis . . . The levels of the mind . . . We sometimes do things without knowing why.'

Blanche clutched her cup.

After a pause, during which she looked into his face as if searching for his next words there, he forced himself to go on. 'I stabbed Kaginovich in the throat with the wire-cutters. At first . . . that I certainly remember, he didn't even seem to notice. I kept stabbing. Hit an artery. We were both covered with – well, you can imagine. I kept stabbing till he fell backwards into Jim Irving's arms.' He laughed. A dry little noise.

Rising, Blanche clutched him and stroked the back of his head, muttering words of comfort.

As if she hadn't spoken, he said, 'It was an absolute nightmare. You see – you see, a part of me *liked* doing it, didn't mind the blood, didn't want it to stop. That's the reason I'm still in here.'

Blanche returned on the following day. Burnell had shaved and dressed with better care than usual.

They met in the visitors' room as before, kissing, holding each other briefly, scrutinizing each other. It was a bright morning: sunlight filtered in through the trees, gleaming as if in a TV shampoo commercial, putting a little colour in the cheeks of the sober room. For a while they talked generally but, lacking roots, the talk died. He said he was reading Montaigne. She suggested a stroll in the park.

At the entrance desk, Burnell had to be signed out. A breeze stirred as they went down the steps, suggesting danger to him; it was the first time he had been outside for a while. Seeing his hesitation, Blanche took his arm. He looked about for Richard's sparrow, but it was nowhere to be seen. He had offended it. The sun warmed him. Before she had arrived, he had taken a snort of slap and felt buoyant.

She wore the same grey outfit as before. Catching his glance at it, she explained that it was her FAM outfit; in Madrid she was more outgoing. As she hoped he would soon see. When he asked gratefully why she wanted him in Madrid, she fluttered her eyes, pulled a comic young-girl-dotty-romantic face, and said it was because he was tormented and she just *lerved* Dostoevskian characters.

Because it is always difficult to talk to patients without touching on their diseases, he was soon prompted to tell her about his last hours in Bogdanakhi. When the wire-cutters had been prised from his grasp, Ziviad Orpishurda and Jim Irving had driven him in a car to the helicopter pad. Orpishurda had guaranteed to release Father Kadredin and his son from arrest, and had then driven off furiously to break the news of Kaginovich's death. Irving had seen Burnell on to the helicopter. Burnell was in shock. In Tbilisi, where crowds who had just heard the news of the Dead One's death waited to cheer him, Burnell was sedated to await the flight back to FAM.

Blanche said that she had seen on the Madrid news that Orpishurda had taken over the West Georgian army and was suing for peace. She had glimpsed him saying something about restoring democracy.

'It's good news. I took him for a decent man – a Christian. So benefit's come of . . . my crime.'

They sat down on a seat commanding a view of the grounds, with the grand grey bulk of the institution at a distance. The low roar of traffic along the Wiesbadener came to them like a technological lullaby, but he was uneasy. The distant building had too many eyes. They found another seat in a small knot of birches – she called it a 'designer copse' – where laurustinus bushes were prematurely in flower, and they could not be seen.

She humours me, he thought, she's patient with me. That proves I'm an invalid. I can't put up with this for long. But the glow of the slap was wearing off. Even her beauty made him despair of himself.

After a while, she asked – not without an edge to her voice – if he had heard from Stephanie. He had to say not. He had not even been able to send her a card from Bogdanakhi. Blanche reminded him that Stephanie would have seen reports of him on TV, and know he was a hero. She sat back and listened, gazing at the bushes, as he became animated, swearing he would retrieve his ten years and discover how he went wrong with his wife.

She let the outburst die before saying, 'I see it may hardly be in my own interest, but I've had some enquiries made on your behalf. That *étron* Antonescu has been arrested in Budapest. The extent of his illegal EMV work is still being investigated, but it seems he shipped all stolen memory bullets eastwards, through a dealer, probably in Istanbul – a Russian who sells to the old Islamic Soviet republics, Uzbekistan and the rest. To be honest, Roy, there's not much chance that you will ever . . .'

She let her voice fade. When he charged her sullenly that she could not understand his feelings, she told him his best plan was to start over again and forget the past.

'I have forgotten the past! You mean forget Stephanie, don't you?'

'So you would have done, so you had, until she popped up in Swindon. Taking a break from that fellow she lives with. I hear he beats her.'

'I've got to get this problem sorted out before you and I can have a good straightforward relationship.' He admitted that Stephanie had told him she would never go back to him. But he had to know what had happened between them. Perhaps mistakes could be remedied. She herself had said they had enjoyed some happy years.

Blanche stood up, tucking a thumb under the strap of her

shoulder-bag. She looked down at him angrily, knees almost touching his.

'If you are going to spend the rest of your days trying to cling to something you've lost, then I can't help you. I'm not made that way. It's a dead end. I'm off. It is necessary I catch a flight back to Madrid this evening for a meeting in Toledo tomorrow. I need to attend it. So we may as well say goodbye now.'

The rumble of the fast nearby traffic sounded more loudly now, as if it would carry them both away. He jumped to his feet, protesting, ignoring the bandages round his ribs, begging her not to go. He was caught at a disadvantage: wasn't the essence of memory that it provided a guide to a way ahead? He would not describe the pain of not remembering how well he knew her, and asked her humbly to tell him – were they, had they been, lovers?

Late-summer sunlight played on Blanche's face with its expression halfway between exasperation and laughter. She came forward and wrapped her arms about him.

'Darling, doesn't your body tell you? You old loony, we have been lovers for years. Whenever we meet, we're between the sheets. Whenever possible. Surely your blood remembers? Mine certainly does.'

Then they were embracing, bodies against the papery bark of a silver birch. As he took in the warmth of her kisses, he knew that afterwards, back in the ward beside the muttering Finn, he would retrace the footsteps of this scene and the imprint of her words over and over, as if he were an infatuated adolescent again. She was reminding him of things that transformed and excited him, making him forget his convalescence. Much happened in which body was more involved than mind.

They were walking the grounds again. He told Blanche what he had strongly resisted speaking of in his daily sessions with the psychoanalyst.

He said he felt a need to explain to himself what went on in that foul little room just before he killed Kaginovich.

He had tried to forge his own character. Between the old arguments about nature versus nurture was a possible third way: one might be able to mould oneself, to follow, at least to some extent, one's own directives. Having no religious belief forced a man to construct his own morality. His idea of being 'good' consisted in trying to ameliorate the suffering of others, even at one's own expense, and in not giving anyone pain.

'Do you live up to that?' Blanche asked, though hardly in a questioning tone, as if she thought he was being pretentious.

'No, but you can keep trying,' was his response. And he had most singularly failed not to give pain in the Kaginovich case.

'But why look for mysterious explanations? The bastard was going to kill you.'

Then you had to ask why he was a bastard, why he had smashed the ikon, and so on. So Burnell said, and was promptly told not to feel guilty about reacting to save his own life. He had, after all, made the world a slightly better place as a result, and eudemonism was the creed to live by.

Ignoring Blanche's remark, which he well understood was designed more for his consolation than truth, he said, 'If only I had all my past behind me, I'd be a better judge. But what strikes me is this. It was not danger or evil which caused his attack on me. It was in some way the ikon itself.'

'You mean, his smashing it up? Rubbish! Roy, you're hanging about here thinking yourself into a maze. Forget it. Catch the evening flight to Madrid with me and we'll invent some cunning methods of therapy to nurse you back to sanity.'

Although he grinned, he shook his head and raised his eyes as if he would have them disappear into his eyebrows. 'Why did he smash it? That's what I ask myself. Sometimes I get an answer. You've seen reproductions of the Madonna of Futurity? In so many Byzantine ikons, the infant Jesus is held more or less at arm's length by His mother; both figures are stiff, symbolic rather than actual. In Evtihije's painting, that's not the case. Mother and Child are portrayed unusually close. She holds Him affectionately to her breast.'

Halting, he folded his arms and stood frowning.

'You know how Kaginovich was born? From a dead mother. So the story goes.' Untrue, like so many good stories, but . . . 'You don't have to believe the textbooks slavishly to understand he would carry that loss within him to the grave.

'No mother. Isn't that supposed to be one of the worst disasters that can befall a child? *No mother.* There's no guidance; you have to forge your own character, for better or worse, to become gentleman or Genghis Khan. It makes you internally into a sort of Frankenstein's monster, an anomic personality, which Kaginovich certainly was.' He checked himself, then continued, 'That ikon – that powerful depiction of mother love – threw him into a fit of jealous rage. All he'd lost, for all his conquests, suddenly it was out! He smashed the picture that reminded him of his unassuageable wound.'

Blanche was listening with half-open mouth, frowning in concentration.

'And you, Roy? Supposing all that was so?'

'Cod psychology? It might be true, all the same. I spend my days trying to make sense of everything.'

But she perceived that the remark hid something more he wished to say.

'Did you also hate the picture? Your mother died when you were a boy, didn't she?'

He was shaking his head, looking up as if for succour at the branches over their head. The sun was hidden behind cloud.

Asking her why they had joined WACH, he said it must be because what they sought to preserve had its taproots in the past, like a wisdom tooth in a jaw.

'I loved the ikon as soon as I saw it. Not hate, like Kaginovich, but love. Longed to possess it.'

The other thing she said had to be answered. He would hardly call himself a boy when his mother died. It was summer and he was away at school, scarcely realizing even that his mother's illness was serious, although he knew she had been having treatment. He was fifteen and a half, and a fast bowler in the first eleven. His mother died of cancer a fortnight before the end of that term.

By common consent, Burnell and Blanche sat down on a bench dedicated, a plaque informed them, to a dead doctor.

What had really hurt was that Tarquin, his father – he was sure from the best of motives – did not tell him his mother was dead until the school broke up and he arrived home to find her gone. To his agonized cry, 'Why didn't you phone me?', Tarquin had replied that he didn't wish to upset his son's cricket fixtures. Although he was aware that his father also grieved, from then onwards they had never again spoken to each other of Vanessa.

Burnell gave no indication he noticed that tears fell from his eyes, dropping straight down like winter sleet. Blanche bravely held her ground and let him speak.

But what had really hurt, he said, perhaps addressing no living listener, was that by the time Tarquin broke the news to him, his mother was already buried, the funeral was over, and he had never said his last farewells to her. That had really hurt. It still did. He had never said goodbye to her. That memory remained clear.

Blanche did no more than put an arm round him, saying nothing.

'Oh, well,' he said, and, 'Bugger. Emotion got the better of me! I suppose what I saw immediately in the Madonna of Futurity was myself in my mother's arms, secure and content. The mother was her, looking into the future with a premonition of the illness that would take her away from me.

'So, to see the ikon smashed, that beautiful image smashed . . . well . . . That's why I went ape.'

They sat and looked at each other, she from France, he from England, while German traffic roared behind distant trees.

She said that she sometimes thought that most of the great hoard of the world's evil, and particularly the violence of men, could be swept away in one generation, if only all today's children could feel loved and secure; perhaps the secret of all virtue lay hidden in a tit, a parental lap. 'Why do you wish to withhold all this from your psychoanalyst?'

'Because,' he said. 'Because I don't know if it's true. How is it that our most vital thoughts can be hidden from us?'

She had shared the tears; now she shared his laughter. 'You are the most maddeningly honest dishonest man I've ever met.'

'Oh, what the hell! Blanche, I don't know why I'm lingering in this madhouse. I'll have to get back to work. Take another trip somewhere. Somewhere where the population aren't all at each other's throats.'

'Fine. I've an even better idea. First of all, come back to Madrid with me. This very evening.'

'Come and learn Spanish?'

She clapped her hands. 'You do remember something! It's in the blood. That was our joke – that you wouldn't join me because you couldn't speak Spanish.'

'Lady, it was a fib. It's beyond telling how much your visits have meant to me. I can see clearly why and how we were – may I say are? – lovers. But I can't join you until I've got . . .'

She finished the sentence for him: '. . . that bloody Steff out of your system.'

14

In the Korean Fast Foot

The evening flight from FAM to Madrid's Barajas Airport was going to be full, as usual. Blanche Bretesche sat in her club-class seat, which the airline liked to refer to as an 'armchair', sipping champagne and staring out of the cabin window. She worried about Burnell and about herself.

She was well aware she might be mistaken by investing so much emotion in Burnell and could save herself hurt by making a break with him. 'Beware of Pity', she quoted to herself; yet pity was not her predominant feeling. Nor, even, was lust. She and he were compatible. Even his atheism − perhaps a more uncertain quality than he realized − held an appeal, although Blanche regarded herself as a Catholic. She tried to tot up the pros and cons of their relationship. This business about the death of his mother: Blanche thought she understood all the ramifications of that. He had faced up to the loss long ago; it surfaced only occasionally, like a wrecked vessel during phenomenally low tides.

And yet . . . The thought occurred to her that Roy's sorrow at having been unable to pay a formal adieu to his dead mother had left its scar across his character. It possibly accounted for Burnell's reluctance to say a final farewell to Stephanie, although Stephanie seemed long ago to have said goodbye to him.

But was that a valid insight? Or was it just a line of reasoning to which the generations since the turn of last century and the emergence of psychoanalysis had become indoctrinated? The Freudian Neural Highway. No one liked farewells.

Blanche smiled to herself. He shared her mistrust of received opinions. That was another reason for loving him.

But to look for reasons for love was a hopeless quest, *au fond*. Love still held its formidable attractions in an age in which a whole stewpot of beliefs simmered – rationality, romanticism, economic factors, faith, crass commercialism, asceticism, a thousand -isms. Love was unequivocally barmy. She liked that English word, barmy.

Love was also a pain in the neck.

How had it ever come about that humans *loved*? Wolves formed families; male and female wolves stayed monogamously together; they protected and reared their cubs. Blanche had a deep admiration for wolves, as for all wild things. She had never heard of anyone claiming that wolves *loved*. Wolves were the most clear-sighted of animals. Love occluded human vision, was a kind of tipsiness. Humanity thirsted for love like vampires for blood. Love is blind drunk – not a way to go through life. Or even through European airspace. Leaving him meant leaving something of herself behind.

A late-boarding passenger came and sat in the armchair next to Blanche. It was Doctor Maria-Luisa Cervera, helped into her seat by a steward. The learned doctor panted slightly before turning to survey her neighbour over her horn-rimmed spectacles. They recognized each other.

Dr Cervera, a well-known anthropologist, was in her eighty-first year, still indefatigably travelling. She was in charge of excavations at a recently discovered site in the north of Spain.

A stewardess came and poured both ladies champagne.

'I'm pleased to see you, Blanche. It saves me approaching you formally. We hope World Cultural Heritage might support our dig at San Pineda in the Sierra de la Demanda.' She sipped her drink, coughed, apologized. 'It's very worthwhile. Culturally important.'

The de la Demanda site was in the news. In a cave in the mountains, long covered by landslides, a grave had been found containing human-type remains. Dr Cervera had been called in. Her team of archaeologists and anthropologists were slowly uncovering the first articulated skeleton of an eolithic woman ever found. The skeleton was dated as between 300,000 and 350,000 years old. It thus predated Neanderthals, Cro-Magnon, and what was self-inflatingly called *homo sapiens* sub-species. Excavation was proceeding with caution. Dr Cervera was fighting to keep the entire operation in Spain, despite Japanese and German interests involved.

Blanche was curious if nothing more. Though even by calling the San Pineda cave a prehistoric cathedral she doubted whether WACH would provide financial support. Prehistory lay outside WACH's range. 'Bodies aren't in the charter.'

'One cannot over-estimate the importance of this discovery. And the rest of the cave has yet to be investigated. We hope for other revelations.'

'I could probably lay on a WACH observer. Might come myself.'

The two women fell into deep conversation as the airbus took off. It was hoped that further excavation might even reveal other skeletons. The findings would transform understanding of human evolution. The San Pineda woman had probably possessed a brain of 1,400cc, quite comparable in size to a modern human's brain. Artefacts and plants found beside her suggested religious rites.

'So the likelihood is that religion preceded humanity,' the old lady said. 'But we can hardly expect that La Pineda was a Catholic.' Her smiles did little more than rearrange a few wrinkles about her mouth; her eyes remained disinterested.

'From the photographs, I saw your ancient lady is bent double. Is that due to disease? Not natural posture?'

'La Pineda would have walked upright when young. We'll know better when we can get her out from the cave, but preliminary evidence indicates osteo-arthritis, and osteo-phytosis, such as you find among Neanderthals, in the lumbar regions. You've seen the Untouchable sweeping women in India, who spend most of their lives bent double at their trade? Or their *fate*, one might say. That may – just may – have been La Pineda's fate. We all get stuck in life attitudes, you know.' She muttered irritably to herself, putting a hand up to her temple as if to confirm a headache. Blanche did not like to speak. She could not help recalling how, as a child, she had believed that the old were another species. Dr Cervera said, almost in an undertone, 'In the world of prehistory, old age was practically unknown. It's a modern innovation.'

Blanche deflected her attention from the notion that everyone became stuck in their life attitudes; it made her uncomfortable.

'I've often wondered how largely illness acts as *agent provocateur* for religious faith. It is the incapacitated, isn't it, who turn first to God? Just as it's the sick who preserve the renown of Lourdes.'

The old lady punctuated one of her long silences with a sip from her glass. 'The sick. The incapacitated. The threatened. The aged. What a sacrilegious thought you have there, my dear. Religious people – I'm not one of them – would surely claim that God was an invention of the *healthy*, rather than the sick. It was the Son, down here on Earth, who got himself involved with the sick . . . "Take up thy bed and walk . . ." His father was busy healthily inventing galaxies.'

Another silence, then a postscript, delivered mischievously. 'Whether it was Jehovah who interested himself in our pre-Neanderthals, the Gospels do not relate.'

Blanche chuckled. 'So would you suppose that the Pineda People, if we can use that expression, were surprisingly advanced?'

Dr Cervera gave one of her cold old mysterious smiles. 'Do you regard us as surprisingly advanced?'

'Well, we're flying at nine and a half thousand metres, and here comes the champagne again.' They laughed together.

Blanche said, 'I suppose that if the Pineda People – you don't jump down my throat when I use that expression – had religions, worshipped gods or goddesses, they also loved each other as we do?'

Since she received no immediate reply, since Dr Cervera seemed intent on watching the bubbles dance as her champagne glass filled, she had time to reflect that her question was preposterous. It was easy to sound absurd when addressing such a learned elderly woman; she found elderly people in general difficult to converse with.

She decided to obliterate her rather embarrassing question about love – Roy, you wretch, make up your complex little mind, will you? – with another question the old girl might find more palatable.

'Do you think the human race will evolve out of some of its ancient inheritances? – Which could become recognized as fully as outmoded as granny's old tablecloths tucked away in the family chest? Would it make for a more reasonable, more peaceable, society, if eventually we all grew out of such emotional quicksands as religion and . . . well, passionate love?'

That was no better a question. Even while Blanche was posing it, she recalled that this illustrious dame had enjoyed a scandalous youth. Once on a time, her name had been linked with a Spanish film director, Luis Buñuel. She had then, by all accounts, been a turbulent lover. But that was in another century; besides, the wencher was dead.

Again the younger woman was challenged by one of those chill smiles. In the tallowy and wrinkled face were eyes as searching as needles. 'At my advanced age,' Dr Cervera said, 'I have outgrown both religion and love. Whether that's better, who can say? But you do, in a sense, miss what you once enjoyed . . .'

Karl Leberecht was Burnell's other visitor. He entered the great grey institution punctually every day at three o'clock, never staying long.

The institution was its usual self, as dignified as it could be, and perhaps not less hospitable than is the general nature of such places. Its grounds and pleasant flower beds still proclaimed summer, and one of its sparrows still bothered Burnell, up in his room, next to the muttering Finn.

Burnell entertained his friend in one of the downstairs visitors' rooms where he had received Blanche. Leberecht was an altogether more serious kind of visitor, who liked to discuss artistic matters.

He also informed Burnell that the loss of ten years of academic learning was in general regarded as an impediment to advancement.

Burnell said that, being without ambition, he could live without advancement. All he wanted was to be on the road again.

Although his Georgian commission had not been too successful, the civil war had made the whole operation difficult; at least he had located a valuable ikon regarded as lost. That ikon was now being expertly restored in Munich.

That, his superior agreed, was certainly something. But, he asked, looking with some compassion into Burnell's face, could he say he was really feeling his old self?

'Yes,' said Burnell.

'No,' said Burnell, when Leberecht visited him on the following day. 'I lied to you yesterday. The truth is – I tell you this as a friend – I don't feel like myself. I keep thinking . . .' He paused before being able to come out with it. '. . . I keep thinking I'm something lying in a hospital bed in a coma. No, worse than that – Karl, I keep thinking I'm just the interior monologue of someone lying in bed in a coma. What do you make of that?'

Leberecht said he would look into it. He became very serious. On the following day he was back at the institution, still serious, but relieved. As they sipped the institution's Bolivian coffee, he asked Burnell if he recalled the name of Peter Remenyi. Burnell certainly did; the name had come up on the electronic diary in his Soss City apartment.

'He was a good friend of yours, Roy. He was also a Hungarian champion ski-jumper. You took vacations with Remenyi.'

'Don't remember.'

'Then you don't remember being in a car crash with him. You escaped unhurt. Remenyi, who was driving, suffered a brain injury. He's in a coma in a Budapest hospital. Prognostications are not hopeful.'

Burnell's immediate impulse was to say he would fly to Budapest. That was not advisable, Leberecht told him; it would be a wasted journey. Remenyi responded to no external stimuli, and was thought to be slowly deteriorating. In short, a PVS case.

After much thought, they decided there had been a psychic linkage between the two damaged brains, Burnell's and Remenyi's. Burnell was relieved to know what had been worrying him.

'You must tell all this to your psychoanalyst,' Leberecht urged.

    'God, no, Karl, I want to get out of here. Send me somewhere easier than Ghvtismshobeli. I'll be fine.'

    Leberecht relented.

    'We've got just the place.'

The air was full of traffic. A few days after Blanche Bretesche flew westwards from Frankfurt, Roy Burnell was flying eastwards. WACH booked him on flights which took him first to Istanbul and then, with a change of plane, almost due east along the Black Sea coast. While Burnell snoozed, he was transported across the polluted wastes of the Caspian Sea, towards the uneasy nations which had only a generation earlier emerged from Soviet domination, Kazakhstan, Uzbekistan, and Turkmenistan. From Istanbul onwards, Burnell was seated among *hadjis*, and no more alcohol was served.

    They landed in the capital of Turkmenistan after dark. Burnell took a taxi to his hotel, where the bar was closed and a deal of unfavourable yawning went on at the reception desk.

    There were in Central Asia numerous venerable structures to be entered into the files of WACH and, if possible, preserved for future generations. The cities of Tashkent, Samarkand, and Bukhara were covered. To Burnell had fallen Ashkhabad, capital of Turkmenistan. Following Burnell's recommendations, a team of photographers would arrive to ensure that pictorial images of favoured buildings and art works remained in the world's memory banks even when the originals fell victim to time and turbulence. The process was analogous to the way in which the larger carnivores, now extinct, existed only on film or in gene banks.

    As he unpacked his bags in his sparse hotel room, Burnell had a light-hearted feeling that he was on holiday. How fortunate he was, he reflected, to hold such a pleasant job. The mental institution in FAM had consumed his days with activity. He had swum in the fine indoor pool every morning; had attended eurythmy classes in judiciously gauged light levels after breakfast; had tussled with his psychoanalyst before lunch; and had painted, undergone physiotherapy, and even tried anthroposophical and homoeopathic medicines in the afternoon. In the evening, he had avoided TV and

EMV and the totality sessions where everyone sat about cuddling each other, confessing or inventing their sins. He had read in the library, creeping up on the conclusion that he was still unprepared for Immanuel Kant's *Critique of Pure Reason*. And intermittently throughout the day he had worried about Blanche Bretesche.

By contrast, his brief visit to Ashkhabad and thereabouts would seem like a rest cure. Only one slight difficulty had arisen so far. Burnell had not been met at the airport, as arranged. There was no sign of a Dr Haydar, the WACH contact.

Well, all would become clearer on the morrow. He took a sleeping-pill and got into bed.

The usual terrible dreams attended him, their force orchestrated by an irregular drip from a leaky showerhead in the bathroom. He woke early and went out into the street to breathe fresh air before the sun became powerful.

Although it was September, summer reigned supreme, if blowsily, over the capital. He walked along Prospekt Svobody among the crowds. On the road, svelte limousines crawled between horse-drawn carts. On the sidewalks, men in smart business suits with pens and bleepers attached jostled beggars and down-and-outs. He turned into Shaumyana, and sought out the British Embassy.

The embassy building was closely guarded. Burnell had to hand his passport over and wait for twenty minutes before he was permitted entry. The British shared the building with the Portuguese. The Portuguese Embassy occupied the two lower floors, the British the two upper ones.

'What's all the security about, for God's sake?' Burnell enquired of the Turkmeni receptionist.

'Oh, you must have just arrive. We had British football team come here last week.' She led him down a corridor to where, in a small partitioned office, a freckled man with a shock of tousled hair sat. He was hemmed in by computer screens, files, boxes, an empty coffee carton, and a desk-tidy stuffed with expended Biros.

This laconic individual rose and introduced himself as Robert Murray-Roberts. 'The ambassador's away. I'm holding the fort. Some fort – more like a fart. Sorry there's a blip in the air-cond.

We're proud to have you here in Turkmenistan, Dr Burnell. Saw your face on the AshTV – Ash by name, Ash by nature – but there you were, for all of ten seconds. Tyrant-killer! Splendid stuff! Anything we can do to help, we will. Unfortunately we're a bit stretched at present. Just arranging a big exhibition here for next week.'

'Paintings?'

'Paintings?' He tousled his hair more thoroughly. 'Good God, no. They aren't too mad about representational art here, or Picasso, portraits or all that, and of course the Fezzes don't under-stand abstract stuff. No, we're going to be promoting the new Anglo-Malaysian car, the Protean. Six of them being shipped over for the show. Come and sit down, if you don't mind squeezing in, and have a chat. Move that old squash racquet. Got some whisky here, if you fancy a tot. My office is the nearest you'll get to a pub for many a mile. Glad to see a fellow-Brit.'

Burnell was cheered up by all this and enjoyed a plastic cup half-full of whisky. Despite his claims to be a bit stretched, Murray-Roberts appeared not to be too busy to chat. Not that Burnell was able to supply a great deal of British gossip.

'Mother wrote from Inverness to say a Swiss company is buying up a very old-established firm, Scott's Porage Oats. Terrible, isn't it?' Murray-Roberts said. 'The country's going to the rottweilers. Anyhow, you had a tough time in Georgia, I gather. Rough wee lot of buggers, aren't they? What happened to that ikon you were after, the Madonna of Futility, or whatever it was called?'

'Futurity. There was a good man with me, Jim Irving. He'd been an astronaut, and actually walked on the Moon last century. He got me away in a helicopter. I was in a terrible state of shock. This monster, Kaginovich, smashed up the ikon, but Jim gathered the pieces together and I took them to Frankfurt with me.'

'He walked on the Moon, you say? Some trick, eh?'

'The ikon was broken into four, plus a few splinters. It's all now in the hands of restorers in Munich. Too bad lives can't be repaired as easily. Of course most lives aren't as valuable as a twelfth-century ikon . . .'

Murray-Roberts stirred the contents of his desk-tidy with a

finger in a meditative way, and began a long speculative ramble about how rich you would be if you were born in the twelfth century and lived till the present day, provided of course you had invested wisely. Burnell said nothing. The whisky was making him feel unpleasantly drunk. It seemed that Murray-Roberts was throwing in a few tips about where to eat locally without catching hepatitis, and then reverting to a fantasy regarding the worth of a mile of London's West End, if picked up in the twelfth century for a song.

'Yes, quite,' Burnell said, apropos of very little. 'Apart from my WACH commission, I have a private reason for being here. I'm trying to trace a particular EMV bullet, copies of which were sold to this part of the world. Is there an EMV stockist in town, would you know?'

Looking serious, Murray-Roberts said he could be of no help in that respect. 'No way. The Fezzes are pretty hot on EMV. It's totally banned. They're not hot on much, but they're hot on EMV. Entering into other people's memories goes against some obscure passage or other in the Koran, I'm told. Ever read the Koran? Dull book.' He leant forward. 'Ashkhabad is a rum place. Really best to keep your nose clean. And not only your nose, ha ha! Stay away from the women – or boys, if you're that way inclined. It's not a peaceful place.'

'It looks fairly prosperous.'

'Och, it could be worse, considering where it is, in the middle of a bloody desert, I'm not denying that. They are bravely trying to live down a lot of bad history. The president they've got at the moment, Diyanizov, is not too bad a guy. He's for the development of Turkmenistan as a modern secular state, with plenty of foreign investment from the EU and aid from everywhere. We're hoping to sell him a Protean. This Protean exhibition only goes ahead next week with Diyanizov's direct say-so. For all that, foreigners aren't popular. Quite rightly, they fear foreigners will exploit them.'

'How secure is Diyanizov?'

Murray-Roberts re-tousled his hair. 'You see, you might describe Turkmenistan the way someone described the old USSR at the beginning of their revolution, way back when: "A modern state without a modern idea". There's no infrastructure. The banking system is all to cock. Tribalism is rife. Every now and then, whoever's in charge has to have a little war with the neighbours, just to unite the country against a common external enemy. That comes expensive. So the foreign debt mounts up. Chiefly to the Japanese. The Japs are clever little buggers. One day they'll own the whole country. Then maybe they'll even turn the deserts to profit. You'll know the name of Hengist Embry, famous American professor? He predicted all this. He predicted how one disaster simply encouraged another.'

'Is there much British investment locally?'

'One thing I should warn you about, Burnell. Lay off the British bit. We're not at all popular. Better to deal with the Germans. Pretend you're a Kraut. They're quite well liked. When their football team played in Ashkhabad, it lost five goals to six. A tremendous diplomatic coup. This bloody English team came out here last week and walloped the Fezzes eighteen to three.

'Bannockburn was come again! This embassy was under siege for three days and nights. Local staff stopped coming. The Fezzes set fire to a bungalow owned by some poor bloody Welsh building contractor who'd never seen a goalpost in his natural . . . I suspect that stupid football match is the reason why my six new bloody Proteans are still waiting to be unloaded from the docks in Krasnovodsk, so just watch your step, laddie . . . Maybe you'd give a speech at the university about the local antiquities or something. That might help the cause.'

Before they parted company, Murray-Roberts warned Burnell to stay away from Dr Haydar, describing him as a petty criminal drug-smuggler. However, Burnell had formed an opinion that Murray-Roberts was slightly paranoid, and probably had been even before the 18–3 English victory. In any case, it was easy to avoid Dr Haydar, since Dr Haydar was clearly avoiding Burnell.

When he had recovered from Murray-Roberts's whisky, Burnell hired a guide at the tourist centre and took a tour of the city. His first impression was of greyness: the capital was fighting to live down a sad and chequered inheritance. He had hoped naively for more mystery. One indicator of the confused state of the political mind was the variety of alphabets used on signs and elsewhere, each carrying its freight of different cultures and traditions. He could not but take a Western view of this diversity: even while relishing the *hors d'oeuvres* of cultures in all their picturesque discomfort, he saw them as standing in the way of an advance towards orderliness and development.

Burnell's view might be summarized as Progressive. Progress was a word long in disfavour, yet not entirely banished from court. Progress had conceived of countries with mixed ethnicity as 'melting pots'; and precious little melting had actually been achieved; the pots had all too often boiled over. As had happened in the United States of America. Yet to progress on an individual level continued as an inspiration.

The climate of Ashkhabad scarcely aided constructive thought. Although perched on the edge of winter (for it was said that Ashkhabad lacked the intermediate seasons of spring and autumn), the late summer was still achieving day temperatures of over thirty degrees Centigrade. Burnell had no complaints there; his boyhood holiday in Iceland had confirmed a fondness for high mercury readings.

He found few antiquities worth more than a condescending glance from WACH. The city had been levelled by earthquakes as well as totalitarianism. A major quake in 1948 had erased a gentler Ashkhabad – once just a Russian garrison town in a thirsty land. Only the little whitewashed houses, set in regular squared-off streets with their backs turned to an uncertain world, had anything to offer an aesthetic taste.

Burnell sought out a world-weary UNESCO man who drove him to a site beyond the city. Here the Parthians had once gloried and drunk deep in the pantheistic heart of their empire. Little remained to be seen among a general prospect of sand. The Parthians had, not to put too fine a point on it, gone. It was, as the world-weary man put it, 'an Ozymandias situation'.

Yet here too the obsession to rescue the past was in evidence.

Excavation was in progress, sporadically supervised by the world-weary one. Only a year earlier, a pair of Zoroastrian underpants dating from 200 BC had been found, well preserved in the sand. The underpants were made from the hide of a *caracul* or Persian sheep. This discovery provoked general rejoicing, as well as an article in *The Universal Journal of Archaeology*, wherein an expert who had examined the vestment announced that internal evidence proved its wearer had been red-haired.

After similar excursions, Burnell returned to the environs of the Hotel Ashkhabad and lay on his bed to assuage a headache brought on by heat and whisky. He thought of Blanche, of her excellence and excitement. 'We've been lovers for years . . . surely your blood remembers . . .'

On his third morning, the sound of firing woke him from a horrifying dream. Burnell sat on the side of the bed and tried to compose himself.

They'd been after him again, whoever 'they' were. A distant muezzin's cry, electric across the dawn sky, had transformed itself into a scream as his autonomous nervous system was extracted, struggling, from his body, out through his pineal eye. And then – centuries going by – he had had to remember to take every breath. All of consciousness was required for the task. At night, no sleep for him, for if he slept he would not breathe. Giant machines, devised to do his breathing for him, crackled and snapped. So he was thrown up on the shores of consciousness.

When the shots and a sound of running feet ceased, he went slowly over to the window. Outside lay the avenue, lined with acacias and bathed in the acidic light of another cloudless Central Asian day. He saw no bodies.

He showered and climbed into an ill-fitting suit which a Sunni tailor had run up for him in forty-eight hours. The suit made him look a little less foreign to curious eyes. Before leaving the room, he locked his suitcase. On the back of the room door, a fire notice urged: 'PLEASE EVACUATE YOURSELF ALONG THE STAIRCASES'.

The elevator of the Hotel Ashkhabad had ceased working, either during a recent war with Uzbekistan or since the visit of the triumphant English football team.

A pencilled note on the elevator gates said 'PLEASE DESCEND TOMORROW.' Burnell took the marble staircase and evacuated himself down it to the foyer. A number of men, some with guns at their hips, stood about smoking seriously, as if hoping by that activity alone to bring down the government.

Since the dining-room did not open until 2 p.m., owing to what was announced as 'ALITERATIONS AND REFURNITMINTS', Burnell went out into the street and headed for what he already regarded as his favourite restaurant. Heat was beginning to bite and smog to thicken. But the tree-lined streets were pleasant; he had been in worse places – some of which, doubtless, he did not remember.

A Korean company had established a fast-food restaurant, which proclaimed itself to be 'Tony's Fast Foot Café' in neon lettering. Entering, Burnell found himself a seat by the window on the first floor, where he could comfortably overlook the busy street. He ordered an omelette, coffee, and yoghurt. By local standards, the Fast Foot was clean and elegant. At eight in the morning, it was already full of customers – all male – most of whom appeared to have settled in for the day. Some played chess. Others argued and smoked. Some just smoked. The chamber reeked like a bonfire.

A small ragged newsboy, struggling through the customers, brought Burnell a German newspaper. He had learnt fast, and knew Burnell paid well. The *Berliner Zeitung* was only two days old.

The most venerable reactor in Bulgaria's Kuzloduy nuclear power station was melting down through the Earth's crust, it was reported. Officials from the IAEA in Vienna said there was no cause for alarm. They remained confident that rate of progress was slowing. When the escaping fuel reached the Moho, thirty-two kilometres below the surface, the increased density of material, they predicted, would halt its progress. Danger would arise only if the radioactive material penetrated to the greater temperatures of the mantle below the Moho. Meanwhile, the evacuation of urban Bulgaria and the lower Danube basin was proceeding according to plan. Units of the *Grossdeutschmacht* were in control. The US Sixty-Ninth Fleet was standing by off the port of Varna.

Turning the page, Burnell caught the name of Ziviad Orpishurda. A one-paragraph news item announced that Amnesty

International was condemning a General Orpishurda for a series of atrocities. Over five hundred men, women, and children had been massacred in the town of Poti on Orpishurda's orders. So, Burnell thought, the West Georgian army had made it safely to the sea, and to Orpishurda's home town . . .

The yoghurt was excellent. Unsmiling but polite, the Koreans moved among the tables. Josef Stalin had exiled their grandfathers and great-grandfathers here in the 1950s. Stubbornly uninte-grated, they still spoke Korean among themselves.

Scraping the yoghurt bowl, he thought of the Poti disaster. Its reality broke through his protective cynicism. Newspaper reports, TV coverage: they never revealed what was in the hearts and minds of people. Just as well perhaps . . . He was puzzled by his own pity for Foot and Orpishurda. 'Of man's first disobedience and the fruit of that forbidden tree . . .' Yep, sure had been a fuck-up somewhere, in limbic brain and legacy.

Through the smoke-shrouded throng, a broad-built man bore down on Burnell's table. His powerful face, assembled round a large nose, was working itself up to a smile. Announcing himself as Hikmat Haydar, he bowed, snatched a spare chair from another table, and sat himself down next to Burnell. He offered a large hand, a good percentage of which Burnell shook.

Burnell was sparely built. He felt himself fragile beside this mountainous man, whose head sat like a boulder on his frame, reminding Burnell of either Pelion or Ossa. Haydar was wearing an immaculate suit over a bright orange silk shirt open at a hairy throat.

From his breast pocket, he produced a crumpled business card, smoothing it with a fist before he laid it in front of Burnell for the latter's inspection. It read

DR HIKMAT HAYDAR
Curator-in-Chef
Archaeological Intensities Museum
1 Makhtumkuli Street
Ashkhabad
Turkmenistan

Smiling, Haydar explained, 'Is my old card. You see a misprint there. Not "Intensities" but "Antiquities". Also, I am no longer Curator-in-Chief, unfortunately.'

Burnell pulled the face of one horribly unimpressed. He said that he had been let down. Dr Haydar had not met him at the airport as had been arranged via WACH in Frankfurt. His hotel room had not been booked. He had had to make his own arrangements, assisted to some extent by Murray-Roberts of the British Embassy staff. He had been in the city for three days and was preparing to leave. His mission was accomplished, and only now had Dr Haydar appeared. Why was that?

Haydar nodded, evidently in full agreement. 'It's typical, wholly. All tourists come here in Ashkhabad and only complain. The city is filled with tourists, each with various demands, impossible to deal.'

He retrieved his card and reinserted it in the breast pocket of his suit, still nodding in agreement.

'But did you receive the WACH letter, Dr Haydar? That's what I'm asking.'

'Of course you are.' Nodding his great head again, he closed his eyes, as if forgiving Burnell for asking. 'Feel free to ask, please.' As he spoke, the large man was turning away to seize one of the Korean waiters by the coat. He ordered wine. He suggested cake, which Burnell refused, maintaining his disapproval.

Haydar tut-tutted a great deal, making a juicy noise of it. 'Cake here's good, never stale as elsewhere. But maybe too sweet for your British taste, possibly? I go to the aeroport for you but you must come another day. Frankfurt is one place and Ashkhabad another, you understand?'

'Yes, I'm pretty clear on that point, thanks. I'm also pretty clear that an arrangement is an arrangement.'

'So what you like to arrange today, for example? Perhaps today we take a drive to Merv.'

But Burnell had driven with Murray-Roberts to Merv the previous day. The site near the frontier with Iran had much to offer. Burnell had inspected the remains of five ancient cities, dating from several centuries BC, in one of which Scheherazade had spun her tales. Greek Merv, lost in heat haze, was being reconstructed with part-funding from WACH. It seemed as if for once WACH money was being well spent, with a sensible young German manager in charge of the site.

With a non-committal shrug, Haydar said, 'I know Mr Murray-Roberts, naturally. Maybe he can understand the problems of Turkmenistan, maybe can not. We have like a democracy, but still are problems. We have problems with the army, making wrong decisions. And a trouble in trade nobody understands. Also untrained referees for football matches, similarly.'

Being unamused was a bore. Burnell decided he must shed, or at least shelve, his annoyance with Haydar. One could hardly resent him, with his great face shining across the table, any more than one could effectively resent Everest.

'I'm told the same men are in power under President Diyanizov as were in power before the coup.'

Sweeping this remark away with a broad gesture, Haydar nearly swept away the creamy cake which was being placed in front of him. He fell on it, saying in low tones, scowling at Burnell under heavy brows, 'Careful what names you mention . . . Get to know about immense changes convulsing Central Asia and the republics such as this, and Kazakhstan, Kirghizstan, and the rest.' He gave a quick résumé of the civil wars which had been waged in Tajikistan and elsewhere. Such demographic upheavals threatened stability everywhere in the vast region, from Azerbaijan in the west to the Chinese frontier and beyond. 'Here we are peaceful.

'Also get to know me better, Dr Burnell. You will find a good man in a sea of imbeciles, unhappily. Take no offence of me. New avenues are hard to open. I'm your man. Not saint exactly, but yet a man.' He wagged not a finger but a whole hand to impress his point. The table shook. 'Much liberty has closed down since war with Uzbekistan. I tell you confidentially. Because we have inflation, Archaeological Antiquities Museum is closed down. Now is a museum no longer, but –' he rested his great chest over the table in order to lower his voice further – 'instead is a school for sons of *mullahs*, you understand? So I am out from my job, though I still practise it as best I can. Otherwise, I am also in trade to support myself and my wife, intermittently.'

When the waiter brought two glasses of a yellow liquid, he drained his glass immediately. Flapping his hand, he told Burnell to do the same: the wine was to seal their friendship.

Burnell took his glass slowly.

'Maybe is too sweet for British taste, *nein*?'

'So who is in charge of local antiquities? Murray-Roberts thought that was rather a grey area just at present.'

'Murray-Roberts! What that man thinks! The government, Dr Burnell, the government is in charge of local antiquities. It pulls down buildings for roads. We must be modern in Turkmenistan and have motorways for camels to travel! Yet we get no money from World Bank, only the excuses of the rich. Of course nothing comes from Moscow . . . Maybe we walk in the park where we can speak freely? Is not too hot for you?'

'Not too hot for British taste, no,' said Burnell.

Haydar smiled as he handed a wad of folding money to the waiter. 'Humour is good, eh? There's quite a lot, *nein*?' He rose.

They clattered down the tiled stair, through the swing doors and out into the avenue, where heat awaited them like a dozing watchdog. Haydar said, 'You mention the president's name in there at the table. So I am made nervous. Listeners or spies could consider we plot against him.'

'That would be ridiculous.'

'What you think is ridiculous and what I think is ridiculous – different things. For one instance, we speak in a foreign languages, *nein*? The mentality of Central Asia, let me tell you . . .' They picked their way between units of slow-moving traffic. Haydar's voice faded back into audibility. '. . . like a large palace. The hall anyone can enter. Then are various rooms where various people may go. Beyond are more private rooms, allowed to very few. And beyond them, some doors where the handle is never yet turned.'

'Are you talking about this country or about women?' Burnell asked, but his voice too was drowned out by hooting, and he never received an answer. In any case, he thought, you could apply Haydar's metaphor to almost anything. Perhaps that was what metaphors were for.

The park was a pleasant place, abutting an immense building

which had once upon a time been KGB Headquarters. A burnt-out gun-carrier stood among splintered trees, reminder of the most recent coup. Small boys played over it, shooting each other in friendly fashion.

'Soon will be winter,' Haydar said. 'One day, heat and summer.' He raised the fingers of his right hand above his head in order to snap them with maximum effect. 'Next day, snow and winter. No moderation here, in climate, in politics.' He looked smaller in the open air, his complexion less robust. Old men, bent and solitary, walked among clumps of birches, husbanding their secrets. In their pace was a slack-kneed deliberation, as if they carried too much history on their backs to hurry. Their woollen clothes were greenish with age. Their hands – unless they used a stick – were clutched behind their razor-edged backs. Knowing the direction in which they were bound, they watched the ground rather than the sky.

'People listen always in cafés. Diyanizov of course pays many to listen. Every chair that fills informs. Not many people speak English here. They are suspicious people, unavoidably. The war against Uzbekistan leaves men suspicious. And tribalism. Every day of the week bristles with its perils. It's new nations here, Dr Burnell. Always storms brewing. Old storms in new bottles.' He went into a lengthy discourse about the way in which the evil of listening had been propagated by technological devices; before radio, people did not seriously adopt the habit of listening.

'Your English is good, Dr Haydar.'

'I read English very much. You see, I am not Turkmeni. I come from Syria, at a long distance from here, frankly.'

A melon-seller with a small stall stood under the shade of an oak. He was dark, and wore loose white clothes and a telpek, a large shaggy hat. He tinkled a soft bell to attract attention as Burnell and Haydar went by. Haydar bought two slices of water melon, passing one to Burnell.

'We eat not from greed but to be kind to the poor vendor. We get dysentery as reward, probably. We're among savages. The vendors pump in pond water to the melons to enlarge them, just as politicians do to their speeches. So we're poisoned. The Turkmeni tribes really are nice peaceful people, but when money runs out, then they start to kill each other. Only in summer. In summer, easy to die. Winter comes – then it's too cold to die.

'Half the year, the winds from the high mountains chill the brain into sanity. But for the other half, the hot dead breath of the Karakum drives us insane. It is in that exhalation, Dr Burnell, our politics are forged, continually.

'There's no justice. Rhetoric, religion, yes – justice, no. There's criminality laws can't stop. Currency – mainly forged. Water – mainly bad. No free press. E-mnemonicvision banned – suppose you got an idea of reality from someone else's old dream, *nein*? A dream imported from the West? Ha! Maybe you'd die – or even worse, became a *giaur*, a German, a Christian. TV government controlled. Nothing bad must be said against Iran, Iraq, Afghanistan, Kazakhstan, Indonesia, Lebanon, or Argentina.' He was ticking off the items on his list with a digit aimed in Burnell's direction.

'Why Argentina?'

'Take a guess where the president's latest lady friend comes from . . . Yes, it's Argentina. Medicines – lacking. Poverty, yes – gross. Drug addiction – major. Illiteracy – growing. Population – ditto. Epidemics – rising. And nowhere can I find *The Hand of Ethelberta*.'

'Sorry. Who's Ethelberta?' Burnell had listened with scepticism to Haydar's diatribe, the hallmark of a bitter man. He relished a break.

Haydar looked pained and spat melon pips vigorously into a bush. 'You know *The Hand of Ethelberta*, naturally? By your great ancient novelist, Thomas Hardy. It is one of his best novels, I learn. Here, it cannot be found. Publishers in London and Paris are distant. Not to be discovered in all the stalls of the grand bazaar. Maybe the *mullahs* pronounce it blasphemous. For over three years I search it. I am homesick for Syria and Ethelberta. Still I say – welcome to Ashkhabad, Dr Burnell, heartily. At least we're better than Uzbekistan. It must be a misfortune to find yourself here.'

They threw the rind of their melons in the direction of an overflowing waste bin.

'I'm glad to be here. To travel. The horizon's my home straight.' He'd used the line before. Why, there was even a hope that here he might fill up the well of ten missing years with new experience.

Three young men and a girl passed by, pushing bicycles and laughing as they went. Their carefree expressions, the happiness they radiated, seemed to give a lie to Haydar's lugubrious account of the country and people. One of the youths, seeing the older men standing there, called out in a musical voice, at which the others chuckled and threw sympathetic looks at Haydar.

When Burnell asked what had been said, Haydar told him the boy had been quoting the national poet: 'Twenty years of my life have passed. O world, I have not enjoyed you.' He added that it was hard for young people to understand the old might also enjoy life.

'It's hard to appreciate another country if you suffer from homesickness, Dr Haydar. That has never been my trouble.' The claim unexpectedly conjured to his mind a troubling picture of his father's home in Diddisham and of his own rooms there – and of Laura, his stepmother, the beautiful Laura. Oh, those memories remained.

He stared down at the parched ground, perplexed at . . . well, there was everything at which to be perplexed, when you thought about it.

'You have written to me you need to see the mosque of Mostapha Pasha.' This was Haydar's first admission he had received any communication from FAM. He went on hastily. 'That's correct. It's of great interest, historically. The beautiful dome of azure rises on parapets. The mosque is well built of worked sandstone – a rarity hereabouts – and also of bricks in double rows. The date is from the end of the fifteenth century and is famous in all architecture. I shall drive you to it. We will use my elder brother's car, since he owes me a favour.'

The offer had come too late. Burnell had visited the Mostapha Pasha mosque. It had been much decayed and was hideously restored, following which decay had set in again. Having removed his shoes, Burnell had entered. The interior was as dispiriting as the exterior. The old *mihrab*, from which the Koran was read, proved to be a shoddy modern construction built of concrete. Most of the original tilework was missing. Nothing remained worth recording.

Irked by Haydar's praise, Burnell said, 'It wasn't to my British taste, Dr Haydar. Frankly, it's not worth a prayer, never mind a visit.'

'Ah ha, your English humour! "Not worth a prayer, never mind a visit . . ." I will remember it. In any respect, I agree with you. An ugly structure entirely. Built by a Jew.'

Always alert for anti-Semitism, Burnell bridled at this. He rattled off a lecture about the enlightened Rabbi Moshe Gourits who, celebrating his cordial relationship with his Muslim neighbours, had financed the building of the mosque in 1491.

Haydar rattled back. 'The Jew built in 1498, excuse a correction, not 1491, by the Christian calendar. A year of bad omens. Torquemada died and Savonarola was burnt.'

'The matter of the mosque is not that it was built by a Jew but that it was restored by Communists and incompetents.'

A melancholy look was his response. It descended over the great shining face like a shadow. 'I am a Syrian by birth, as I said you, although many years pass since I see my native land. Forgive my simplicity. Jews and Syrians . . .' He drew a fingernail across his throat so deeply that a weal appeared, and hung out his tongue. This performance he followed with a smile of untrustworthy charm.

Fearing he had been unjust, feeling, as he often did on his travels – it was another reason for travelling – that he would never understand other people, Burnell said, 'Excuse me. I suffer from the heat.'

'In maybe only a few days, the switch will turn and heat will be gone.' He paused under a large oak. They had strolled a long way from Svobodny. Seating himself, he invited Burnell to sit beside him. From the recesses of his orange shirt, he produced a leather pouch and revealed its contents. Burnell's own stash was running low. His eyes gleamed. 'This flight powder is the consolation for the terrors of the world, Dr Burnell. It is what in Turkmenistan makes politics in Turkmenistan endurable. Please be generous to yourself.'

As he inhaled, Burnell arrived at a complete understanding of the learned doctor's position. A breathing exercise came to mind. Chuckling, he tried to teach it to Haydar. They lay prone side by side, in the Corpse position under the spreading branches of the oak.

'You breathe in, counting four; hold for eight; breathe out for eight; empty for four. Then again: breathe in for four; hold for eight; breathe out for eight; still for four. Use your heartbeat to count. It'll slow as we increase the in-hold. OK, here we go: breathe in for four, not too deep; hold for twelve; breathe out for eight; empty for four. Quite still. We're building to sixteen. More twelves; breathe in for four; hold for twelve; out for eight; empty for four. Again . . .'

As the carbon-dioxide built in his blood, and apnoea came, he floated upwards. The figure of Haydar was a giant balloon beside him. It was immensely tranquil a metre or two above the ground. Along the branches of the oak, ginger ants toiled, as they had been toiling since the days of the dinosaurs. He realized he was wearing a *bourkas*, the all-enveloping cloak of the Caucasus, which greatly assisted his flight. Scarcely breathing, he and Haydar rose higher yet. The trees below were tawny with late summer, the ground was cinnamon, with lines of little white houses like sugared almonds awaiting the lick of a child.

The wind was taking them, howling like a wolf at the doors of their hearing, oddly musical, various as fever. They flew. Haydar was galloping and tumbling through the air like a black circus horse. The sky above them, a confection of barley sugar from the smoke of factories, enclosed them like amber. In them both was the glorious knowledge that blinkers had fallen from their eyes: they saw the globe as it was, in all its true beauty, pure as mountain sunlight, yet tantalizingly corrupt, filled with the good, the meek, the unmoneyed, and all who would inherit – and had already inherited, did they but dare to realize it – the world.

He found it difficult at first to disgorge himself from himself: consciousness was life's large intestine. Release was always something that had to be learned, over and over. So he clutched one corner of the great dark *bourkas*. The horselike person clutched another corner. With enormous uproar, exhilarating and slightly metaphysical, the magic cloak flapped and flew between them. Its independent existence – as it headed who knows where to some perhaps hidden *aoul* somewhere in the toothed Caucasian mountains – felt vibrant and touchingly real. Though to speak truth Burnell was experiencing anything real through a pair of spectacular question marks.

He said as much to the cloak, which had assumed the form of a woman, her mane of dark dark hair streaming back in the wind as if to rival nightfall. She had hold of his and the horse-person's hands. Smaragd eyes smiled from her suede face. Her magnificent breasts hung down, engine nacelles powering their flight. 'It'll take centuries,' she said. 'Love your lewd remarks . . .'

But who spoke? She was herself a serenade, eerie without being a Valkyrie.

As they swept along, racing the atoms of the air, wider vistas presented themselves below. Far distant, Ashkhabad was revealed like an orc's egg, cracked open to spill out its citizens, enabling them to rejoice in the glory of the day, the chiaroscuro of the smog. He heard the tinkle of the melon bell, and insane laughter.

But who laughed?

Then the city became still smaller, a pearl strung on the silver thread of its railway line, set in the faded sienna of the desert as if stitched to a great garment, the hem of which was the blue Caspian, trimmed with its sandbanks, distant and evocative as a glimpse of undergarment.

But whose undergarment? Who asked all the unanswered questions?

Who if not he was riding the bewitching flier now?

And there were no politics, just as the dark horse had said. No thefts. No lies. No assaults on the person. No violence or domination. No misery – misery had swollen and popped like a boil, and was still sending a foam of pus through the universe. No war between men and women. No debt or insecurity. No ignorance. Nor were there even Truth and Lies.

Only Wholeness. A wholeness which embraced Everything in its secret embrace.

A little unnerving at first! But its immensity soon became custom. As he himself was now absorbed into that great impersonal . . .

Adoration? All of Central Asia spun below, answerer of its own questions, the great grand hub the peripheries never knew. Bronze it was, bronze it sounded, bronze it smelt. Yet it was only the buckle glued to the belt of the corpulent globe, that little dowdy middle-parts-of-fortune globe rattling about in the sticks of the sky.

He was so accustomed to transformations – *transformations!?* – what else was all life, for God's ache, but Transformations? – that he scarcely did more than nose dive when he saw on the buckle the etching of an opening rose. Swooping nearer . . . nearer . . . even that took till infinity o'clock! – really, *really*, time was such an inadequate fluid to stage this whole shebang in – he saw the rose was not a rose but the genitals of his female friend, friendly female friend, half open in homely welcome, abud with its welcome and the dew of it.

Even as he stooped to kiss it, the pattern became just a pattern in the sand, the eternity of sand. 'It's a silly con,' he said, but who spoke? There again went the bells. And he was laughing at or with the Great Illusionist in the sky . . . Sand . . . Silly con . . . Silicon . . . he – or perhaps she – had been diddled . . .

Of course, laughter was at the heart of everything. He thought, waking (or did someone say it was the other way round?), it had to be laughter. In the Beginning was the belly laugh. The Big Belly Laugh.

'I've never been taken in by its pretensions . . .'

'Don't be taken in by its lack of pretensions either . . .'

But who spoke?

And in the general rejoicing, every wonderfully formed leaf on the oak above them sang. But who really sang?

And the ants still marched. But who really marched?

They snoozed first. Then they rolled about and groaned. 'Blimey!' Burnell said, surprising himself. Then they both sat up and picked the acorns out of their hair.

'Christ, what was that stuff?'

'Ask not Christ but Allah the Merciful.'

Already it was growing late. The flying woman was gone, the vision incorporating her shrivelled. The sunlight lay smoky and aslant across the baked park. The old men were tottering homeward, hands still locked arthritically behind backs, to be bullied by their sons and to gulp down the leftovers of family meals. They'd been in wars, and so knew little of general interest. Their thin voices called farewell to each other – until tomorrow, Ali – until tomorrow – until we meet here . . . or in Hades . . .

The day was gone.

'Wonderful wonderful stuff,' Burnell said, on an exhalation of four, wondering what exactly it was he couldn't remember. He had a raging thirst, and wanted to get back to his hotel. His aching bones craved a bed to lie on, or a bier. Yet he had wit enough to ask Hikmat Haydar if he knew of any other memorable Ashkhabad structure he should inspect, somewhere not logged in the WACH computers.

'Remember this, my friend. There are many many possibilities. We do not always see them but they are always there. It's only sometimes they're not there. So don't be deceived. One way or the other, in fact.'

Burnell repeated his question, with stumbling variations.

The melon-seller was wheeling his stall away. As he went, his soft bell tinkled. The sound, growing fainter and fainter, reminded Burnell pleasantly of Aleksandr Borodin's 'Steppes of Central Asia', with the bells of the caravanserai dying away into the all-encompassing distance.

Dr Haydar held aloft a celebratory finger, perhaps as a token that at last he had triumphed and could pour assistance like cement over this stiff Englishman.

'Yes, positively. Something memorably structure to your English taste. Tomorrow I arrive to your hotel early. I come in my brother's car and I take you to inspect a great Turkmen memorial, the Friendship Bridge.

'It's just as you would say it, demotically, "worth a prayer, never mind a vision".'

15
Makhtumkuli Day

The railway station was not far from Burnell's hotel. The station fascinated him. He walked to it while awaiting Dr Haydar in his brother's car. From a kiosk there he bought a postcard of the station itself and wrote on it a few lines to Stephanie.

'Dearest Stephanie, Ashkhabad is a pleasant modern city, situated on the world's longest irrigation canal. Isn't the news from Bulgaria awful. Still, the description of that hot thing boring down to the Earth's core is sexy in its way. Enjoying myself, hope you are. Love.'

Would Stephanie keep the card, as she had the one from Budapest, supposing it arrived safely? Ashkhabad was farther from Moscow than Moscow was from London. It had hardly been considered by the outside world until the disintegration of the Soviet Union. Burnell could see it was still remote and marginal, viewed from Santa Barbara and Humbert Stuckmann's fabric-filled lair. Did he believe that the future of the world was being shaped in these half-dozen new Islamic nations, or was that just a thought designed to make his own life less marginal?

These cards he sent from the distant places to which profession and inclination led him had once been mute pleas to Stephanie to think of, and possibly love, him again. Hope – rather like the view of Ashkhabad railway station – had faded with the years. Now the coloured cards were little more than boasts, irritants even. Dearest Stephanie, Look where your neglect has got me: bloody Central Asia . . .

Of course, there was that other reason for his being here, that other faint hope. This he explained to Dr Haydar.

The traffic in the main avenues of Ashkhabad was unusually thick, as Haydar complained when he arrived, an hour late, wedged in the driving-seat of his elder brother's Volkswagen Golf.

After the trip the previous day, they were friends. Shedding his usual reserve, Burnell said, having climbed into the little wheeled oven, that he needed Haydar's help. Some of his most private moments had been stolen from him, to be sold round the world on the black market to EMV addicts. Once he started on the subject, he found it hard to stop. 'My most private and precious moments. Not only my learning, my academic skills and experience, also – you'll understand this, Dr Haydar, as a married man – my most intimate moments with my wife, now my ex-wife. Years of our life together. Happy times, sacred times, successes, failures. Nobody's business but ours . . . Stolen, for others to – to gloat over. If privacy goes, what's left? In England and Germany there are laws against such things, with heavy penalties . . .'

'Shut up, will you?' yelled Haydar, shaking a fist out of the window. They were crawling in thick traffic. His anger was directed at a man hooting continuously in the car behind. 'Camel-driver!' he shouted. But the road was choked with vehicles, all hooting. 'Sorry, Roy, what did you say?'

'It's the latest form of vandalism. Mental vandalism. In England, when a man's private erotic moments were stolen and sold as pornography – as mine have been, alas – lawyers laid down that this was, among other things, defamation of character, since –'

'Hang up a moment. Curses! You dung beetle!' He halted the car abruptly, avoiding a bump into the car ahead. People were jostling past and between vehicles. They swarmed to where armed police were manning a barricade across the road.

'*Scheiss*,' said Haydar, with a sigh. He hit his huge forehead with the heel of one hand. 'I am forgotten. You know what today it is? It is Makhtumkuli Day. General Makhkamov will speak in the square as a tribute. We're trapped. No Friendship Bridge today. Very sorry.'

'What's Makhtumkuli Day?'

'You heard of Makhtumkuli? Of course you do. *Schweinhund!*'

'Bloody hell!' The camel-driver behind had rammed into them. They were jerked a metre forward, bumping into the car in front. The driver of this car immediately jumped out, full of rage, and ran back, fists in air. On seeing the immensity of Haydar, a quarter of whom was hanging out of the Golf window, he shouted an apology for carelessness and returned quietly to his vehicle.

'Makhtumkuli,' said Haydar with impressive calm, 'is great national poet of Turkmenistan. Poet, humanist, folklorist, truly great man, son of a poet, Azadi, who is still read in this region.'

Crowds were jostling by, cheerfully on the whole. A middle-aged man in a business suit came up, clapped Haydar on the shoulder, and fell into conversation with him. Burnell stood by, content to watch what was happening. Many of the younger men drifting past were talking into mobile phones. Who could say if they were conversing with each other?

Turning back to Burnell, Haydar said, 'This is a good man, Seydi, who would like to shake your hand and welcome you to Ashkhabad. He would like to invite you to a meal some time, but I said the food was not to your English taste. He is related to my wife, and is also a silversmith.'

While shaking Burnell's hand, Seydi also clutched his arm as if to draw him closer, smiling in a companionable way and nodding his head to express approval of all foreigners. He spoke rapidly. Haydar translated.

'The dear man deplores your ignorance of Makhtumkuli, of which I informed him. He says the poet was another silversmith, so he particularly admires him. He says the words of the poet are known and sung all over Central Asia. He wishes to recite a verse to you which he hopes will express the forthcoming unity of the world, when Turkmen and British shall join hands.'

'Very optimistic of him,' murmured Burnell.

'The verse expresses the unity of Turkmenistan nowadays, as the country itself becomes unified.'

Seydi struck a recitational pose, raising a hand above his head.

226

> *'Turkmenler bir yereh Baaghlasa beeli,*
> *Ghoorudar Ghulzumi, deryayi Neeli.*
> *Tekeh, Yomut, Gookleng, Yaazir, Aleeli,*
> *Bir dowleteh ghulluk etsek baasheemiz.'*

People passing had stopped to listen. Some nodded their appreciation. Concluding his short oration, Seydi again shook Burnell's hand, gave a bow and moved off.

'Well, you see what my friend said about is the various tribes of this country, Gokleng and so on. If all the Turkmens will serve as a single state, and gird on the Belt of Determination, they will make the Nile run dry and also drain the Red Sea. It's an aspiration.'

Recalling how the Aral Sea had already been drained, with disastrous effect, Burnell was not greatly taken by the aspiration, but was too polite to say anything. Perhaps sensing his response, Haydar said, in a disgruntled tone, 'These things are metaphors, allowed to such poets. Everyone wishes for unity. For this they prize Makhtumkuli. The poetry is not to your taste?'

It seemed to Burnell a good moment to change the subject.

'OK, so what are we going to do? I'd say we were stuck here, and likely to cook.'

'I should have droven the other route. I forget the day. Now we are jammed, obviously. No escape. If we escape, it looks hostile. Rejoicing is compulsory on Makhtumkuli day. So we park the car and go to listen to General Makhkamov's speech.'

'Is that — er, safe?'

'For us? For my brother's car? Come. We park here during the speech. Men must listen to lies occasionally. It's a duty when a poet dies, *nein*?'

Before they left the Golf under a tree, Haydar removed the spark plugs from the engine and locked all doors. They joined a gathering crowd, among which camels were numbered.

A considerable crowd had already assembled outside the main mosque, where a railed platform had been constructed. Above the platform hung two large portraits, one of Makhtumkuli, one of Diyanizov. Both men, the poet and the president, wearing square beards and telpeks, appeared rather similar, except that the poet looked left, the president right.

The crowd consisted of men and boys, mostly wearing suits, with *keffiyehs* slung loosely round their heads. The sun shone down on them, the greatest of Allah's gifts. People were silent, except for the vendors who moved among them. On the outskirts of the crowd stood a more rural kind of men, dark of visage, turbanned, some with dogs or even small hairy goats on leashes. Behind them, and lining the square, were APCs and American-built tanks, drawn up with their guns pointing into the square. The tank crews lounged beside them, smoking.

All of which was pleasant to the inner Burnell. That mysterious compartment had registered long ago a saying he read in the pages of the *Upanishads*; there, the wisdom and insanity of the East had been encapsulated in a parable – which in fact he had completely misunderstood in practical Western fashion – concerning two birds. These two birds, according to Burnell's understanding, lived in the fruit tree of life. One of the birds ate the fruit. The other watched the fruit being eaten.

Burnell regarded this as a representation of his own inner life. He wandered, yet something within him was always still. This was, to his mind, a healthful state of affairs. Yet the division – that was more questionable. There certainly was division in the mind. He saw it embodied before him.

In the increasing crowd, there were no women among all the men. True, a small number of women stood unobtrusively apart, to one side, not laughing as African women would have been, not chattering as English women would have been: rather, conversing sidelong, if at all. Many were veiled, some went in *chadors*, covered from head to foot. The fashion for the veil had returned at the time of the war with Uzbekistan, when men were away at the front, following these same tanks now aimed at them. Most of the women were observing the word of the Prophet to 'draw their veils close round them'.

After gaining independence, Turkmenistan had been a relatively secular state. The women went unveiled. There were no mosques to be found. Visitors from round the world had been welcome, even the greedy oil-seekers, who came from as far away as the Argentine, the prospecting Japanese and Koreans. None of these exploitive nations had anything to offer in the way of spirituality. But the neighbours, the cousins in Turkey, had Islam to sell: gradually profit stood aside for the Prophet.

The seclusion of women Burnell found most dispiriting. He missed their bright presence in restaurants and shops and, to some extent, on the main streets. He had visited a brothel but felt little more than compassion for the girls imprisoned there.

Yesterday, a woman driving an open tourer had waved a greeting. He had been too surprised to return the wave, had missed the instant, and she had driven by. She was probably on the staff of a European embassy, possibly Italian. He still carried an impression of her smile, her hair blowing free in the breeze, her naked wrist, unbraceleted.

And what did these people think, as they struggled for cohesion? Were the poet and the president like the two birds?

The previous evening, still slightly decayed from his 'flight powder' trip, he had walked into the lounge of his hotel. There he found a huge crowd assembled – men again, all men. He had expected it to be a political meeting. No. They watched television. They watched an old American soap opera, 'Dallas', dating back to the eighties of the previous century.

The immensely rich, immensely immoral characters of the teleplay swaggered across the screen in their fine clothes. Blonde women flaunted their figures, lounged by swimming-pools. The men lied and cheated their brothers. Everyone drank and fornicated and murdered. But they possessed what the watching Turkmen wished for, a generation later: success and wealth. And in the background was something else, oil, promoter of the Dallas greed, which also excited the audience.

Here was the Satan of which the Koran warned. Here was the universal tug-of-war between materialism and spirituality. The gross pleasures of the West tempted these sons of Allah. They probably, Burnell thought, looked up to J.R. Ewing and the dreadful 'Dallas' family as something to aspire to. With all its faults, wasn't the path of Islam a better way? Which of those two fearsome birds would eventually come home to roost unaccompanied in Turkmenistan?

Parallel with his thoughts, interwoven with them, went the mellifluous voice of Dr Haydar, keeping him informed of the situation in the square.

'You see, this President Diyanizov stands for the development of Turkmenistan as a modern secular state. Could be it's the influence of his Argentinian wife, as some say. This General Makhkamov who comes to address this crowd supports the president. They're both of the same ethnic group. But the *mullahs* wish to follow a much more traditionalist pattern of life. That would mean many restrictions – also many difficulties for us Unbelievers.

'So we hope perhaps to hear something interesting from the general. Perhaps about which way the struggle goes.'

'But you said Makhkamov was a liar.'

'All politicians lie, *nein*? Luckily, truth is also cunning, and escapes men's lips by accident.'

The sun continued to shine. Allah remained merciful, if watchful. A band played, its notes bleached in the fierce sunlight. Then the general appeared, marching purposefully to the platform. A guard of honour saluted.

Makhkamov was a small thickset man, with a pair of dark piercing eyes which searched the crowd as he ascended the platform, accompanied by two lieutenants. He was clean-shaven and moustached, with a row of medals on his khaki chest. He moved with the military strut of soldiers everywhere who strove to appear more like robots than human beings. Burnell had seen such men before. In his experience they did not last long. But there was an unending supply of them. Like the endless supply of people who admired men who strove to appear more like robots than human beings.

Haydar translated parts of the general's long speech into Burnell's right ear.

'First he quotes from the poet Makhtumkuli. "I said unto my Beloved, 'Offer to me such gifts as you have: I'll not ask for more.'" That's nice. He gives the words heroic interpretation. Now of course from the Koran about enemies: "Fight against them until idolatry is no more and Allah's religion reigns supreme."'

'Family squabbles? "Dallas"?' thought Burnell. 'Maybe this strutting general watches old soaps too.'

'Now he says, "Those who fought in the war against a cruel enemy – he means Uzbekistan – you will be rewarded. Those cowards who stayed at home, you will receive not a crust when the time comes." Um, the Koran again. Looks bad. Speaks of ancient enmities. Quotes, "Did you suppose that you would go to Paradise untouched by the suffering which was endured by those before you?"

'He's cheering up his army by berating the others. He says, well . . . It's like "our brave heroes, all who took up arms, all who prepared to die for our great nation, all who stood fast against an evil foe – et cetera . . . they're all going to – well, come into high office, he says . . ." We'll see . . .

'Now he speaks more largely. Foreign policy. "We shall become a great nation in world affairs, guarding our independence under a just God." Nothing about economics. More about God. He's on good terms with – Oh, he says, "Your scars will gain you power. We shall be ruled by brave and honourable men." It's what the poet expected. "That's why we still celebrate his birth on this day" . . .'

At last it was all over. The crowd cheered with more diligence than fervour, the gun barrels of the tanks dipped in salute. The band struck up what is generally termed 'a lively air', presumably to awaken hypnotized intellects: in this case, lively airs from *The Merry Widow*.

As they elbowed their way through the crowd, Haydar remarked, 'Oh, to live in a country where cowards are allowed to rule . . .'

Burnell said, 'People always rant after a war. Perhaps it's a necessary part of the build-down from the excess of adrenaline swilling about in national veins. Generally, though, nothing gets done. So what emerged from the general's speech? Is the secular state or the Islamic one to prevail?'

'Nothing's clear . . . Maybe that's best for a while . . .'

231

'Diyanizov himself made no appearance. Why's that?'

'I warn you, have care in what you say.'

Remarking that the crowd didn't exactly go wild, Burnell said that a speech and its reception were like a novel. A sort of blind deal is struck. He elaborated on this fanciful idea as they elbowed their way back to the Volkswagen. A writer may be clear in what he wishes to say, though the ends of the book may be obscure – what it will earn in the way of fame and approval. You might say the same about a speech-maker and his speech: his listeners also have a blind date, like readers. They expect to be entertained and informed, and maybe . . . well, moved to get on with their lives. From what Haydar translated, it seemed that both sides today were disappointed. The novel, in other words, would not sell. It had nothing new to offer.

Baffled by this, Haydar said that Makhtumkuli never wrote novels.

At the car Haydar restored the spark plugs. He merely remarked that some people liked to hear what they had heard before; it was like reading and rereading an automobile maintenance manual; it reassured them in times of transition.

This time, Burnell was baffled and remained silent. He had never read a maintenance manual, which listed facts: whereas novels – even when they got some facts wrong – strove to present a record of the complexities of human existence.

Flinging his brother's car into gear, Haydar backed through the slowly dispersing crowds, hooting vigorously. 'Could be it's always transition time. Muddles, Dr Burnell. Countries with arbitrary frontiers – here as in Africa created with a ruler on a map by an imperial power. Rulers create sorrow. It's not just a religious question solely, no. Tribes here – "ethnic groups", we learn to say – they must compete against one another. Two varieties of Tekkes form a large group in Central Turkmenistan. There are also Ersaris, Yomuds, Goklans . . .' He sighed. 'Not bad people, pretty easy-going. But with needs.'

He added that those needs were constantly frustrated by the peculiar climatic, geological and geographic situation of Central

Asia. All things conspired against the aspirations of the people – as Burnell would see when they reached the Friendship Bridge.

They moved into a main avenue where progress became easier. Haydar ceased to interrupt himself with shouts at other drivers.

'But don't you really like the Turkmen?'

'Let me say you of one incident when I liked them so much. I could kiss all of them. We have bomb outrages in town, occasionally. A few months since, a café "Faraghi" was blown up. Customers liked that place. So immediately the fire was put out, they came back. With them they brought chairs, tables. They set them up outside the "Faraghi". Then others fetched what drinks could be saved, or other lemonades they fetched from home. The customers all came every day, to eat and drink there, outside, until the owner could get his services going again, properly. They would not allow to die a place they loved. Then I knew these were good people at heart.'

'Mind this fool! . . . Phew! So you don't intend to return to Syria or the West?'

'The West I hate, honestly. Not her literature, which I find enlightened, Tommy Hardy especially. But the rude behaviour, the ambitions. They cause many troubles. That's how Russia always makes mistakes, looking to the West, not to the South. Maybe it's envy, maybe admiration. I grow to hate Russia more and more. And maybe nationalism most!'

He raised his large hands off the tiny wheel to laugh at his own folly. 'You see, all men here believe wanderer's blood to run in their veins. Also, my wife is a local lady of the Goklan tribe. Maybe I introduce you one day, if you will stay long enough. Being Goklan, she wishes never to eat the bread of any other nation. Let me ask, Dr Burnell, do you like your own nation?'

'Umm, yes, I suppose so. Yes. How far is it to this Friendship Bridge?' He and Haydar were friendly, but Burnell's feelings were private.

At last they were moving through the suburbs, amid light traffic, mainly lorries. Pleasant trees shaded the streets. It was a while before Haydar spoke again.

'Then why you wish to come to such a place as this?'

'I tried to explain to you. I know my stolen memories were exported as EMV bullets from Hungary into this region. Murray-Roberts informs me that President Diyanizov and his wife have a large library of Western so-called pornographic bullets. Mine may be among them. I want them restored to me. I need them.

'Unfortunately, after this idiotic football match, the British Embassy is at rather a stand-off with the government. Can you arrange for me to secure an audience with Diyanizov, or some senior government representative?'

Haydar made a deep noise in his throat, something between a growl and a sigh. In moralizing tones, he declared that memory was a curse. In his opinion it only made trouble. They had just been forced to listen to what he described as 'that fine little General Makhkamov, who never met a live enemy on the battlefield'. Makhkamov had been about the old business of stirring up memory in the people for his own purposes – to remain in power. Leaders always needed enemies; people didn't. The general had reminded his audience of thousand-year-old grudges against other peoples, Uzbeks and so on. Such tactics led to further disruption, victimization, war, and madness. Memory was the curse of nations. Better, he said, overtaking a line of camels, to live without memory.

One of the hazards of travel was to hear other points of view; Burnell was always impressed by the firmness with which people clung to their own ideas – and by how much people talked, as if talking were a major pleasure like eating and fornicating.

'Dr Haydar, it's memory that gives us identity as individuals. Without my memory I can have no future. Let me ask you again. Is it possible to have audience with Diyanizov?'

Again the growl. 'Don't be in a hurry. It's a fault. Maybe tomorrow. I see. Old Goklan saying is, "Sit tight on your horse and watch the grass grow." Today it's we visit the bridge.'

Although he hated to ask favours, Burnell persisted. 'Murray-Roberts is trying to trace the chain of dealers. Even though EMV is illegal here, he says there are EMV dealers in Ashkhabad. Maybe one of them sells to the president. The section of my memory that was stolen was reproduced maybe five hundred times, so I am informed. I need one of those bullets to restore my memory. It covers a crucial period of my life, missing years. I could have the memory reinserted. I'm incomplete without it, can't live, can't go forward, can't develop, can't –'

'What if you were a thief or swindler in those years . . . You should be glad it's forgotten.' Haydar smiled at the thought. 'Maybe you lived in Australia or committed murders . . .'

'How far is it to this bloody bridge of yours?'

They were approaching a roundabout. To one side stood small boxlike houses, white-painted, to the other a large boxlike factory, grey-painted. In the distance, a luminous line of mountains.

Haydar slowed the car, muttering to himself. There was a road block ahead. A camouflaged tank was manoeuvring into position near it. Armed guards were unbaling razor wire across the road, directed by an officer. The scene was dusty and dead, except for a woman dragging a child into the safety of a house.

'Trouble.' Haydar switched off the engine. They sat waiting. A lorry drew up behind them as an officer on a motorcycle approached.

The officer dismounted. He thrust his face into the car on the driver's side and looked about the interior suspiciously. Without speaking, he opened the rear door and pulled away a rug lying on the back seat. Finding nothing under it, he threw it back, slamming the door. He demanded Haydar's and Burnell's identifications. They handed over their documents. Haydar made mild soothing remarks, smiling at the officer in a mollifying way. The officer's face remained frozen. A radiophone crackled information at his shoulder.

The officer scrutinized Burnell's EU passport and his WACH credentials before returning them with a few courteous-sounding remarks. His stiff manner had suddenly changed.

'He says you need not look worried,' Haydar translated. 'As a visitor from the West, you are welcome to be here. He also wishes to announce you he is a football expert, and thinks that the English team deserved their 18–3 victory over Ashkhabad United.'

'Please thank him and say I hope that next year the victory will go to the home team.'

More conversation passed between Haydar and the officer, with much nodding towards Burnell and emphatic smiling. The officer shook Burnell's hand before instructing Haydar to turn the car round and head back to town. Before moving to the waiting lorry, the officer gave them a salute and a smile in farewell.

'He's one of the Orazov family,' announced Haydar as they headed back into Ashkhabad. 'I happen to know them, since once I made a deal with them for some valuable carpets, which he remembers. He regrets we cannot leave the city today.'

As tonelessly as possible, Burnell asked why they could not leave the city.

Captain Orazov had explained that there had been trouble in the main square as everyone was dispersing after the speeches. As General Makhkamov was entering the mosque, some bad guys had fired at him from close range. Fortunately they had missed. It was believed they were members of PRICC.

'"Prick"? Is that a rapist group?'

Haydar said the acronym stood for the Party of Renaissant Islamic Counter-Culture. The army was now hunting these terrorists and had ordered all exits to the city to be closed, so that the villains could not escape.

'It's what happens, I fear, Dr Burnell. So we visit tomorrow the Friendship Bridge. It will still be there, doubtlessly.'

To hide a certain degree of frustration, Burnell remarked on the courtesy of the officer.

Haydar agreed. 'Ali Orazov is a good man, and all Turkmeni are hospitable. We are invited to take dinner with him this evening, to compensate for the disappointment to our foreign guest. I hope that will be to your British taste.'

Evening brought a measure of coolness to Ashkhabad; the streets were crowded with people. The rendezvous with Captain Ali Orazov was held in the restaurant 'Faraghi' which Haydar had previously praised. It transpired that he was a part-owner. It was luxuriously carpeted and fully patronized. Western music issued at tolerable levels from the loudspeakers.

Despite his reservations about Dr Hikmat Haydar, Murray-Roberts had agreed to come along with Burnell. On his arm was a bony and rugged Mrs Murray-Roberts, who looked about her with either displeasure or myopia, saying nothing. When Burnell greeted her, she informed him she disliked Fezzes; consequently, he took against her blue English dress, which revealed the pale hollows behind her collar-bones.

Two other women were present.

Haydar was not escorting his wife, who, he said, preferred to remain at home; but Orazov and another male friend, a cousin Orazov – 'enlightened people', said Haydar – brought along their wives. These ladies, corpulent and grand, dressed for the occasion and wore sari-like garments of gold and crimson. They said little during the meal and ate plentifully. The service was excellent, the manager fawning on Haydar. Wine was brought, with lemonade for the ladies.

The meal was half over before Burnell managed to catch Mrs Murray-Roberts's attention, although she sat on his left side. When, by way of opening a conversation, he asked her if she enjoyed the local food, she replied one had to accept whatever was one's lot. To which Burnell said, raising an eyebrow, 'How fortunate then, that one's lot contains such a tasty *pilau*.'

She said, in a low voice, so that her husband on the opposite side of the table could not hear, that Burnell was only in Ashkhabad for a few days, for pleasure. Emphasis was laid on this last word.

'You have no taste for the exotic, then, Mrs Murray-Roberts?'

In a tone even lower and more pointed, she said, sighting him with her nearer eye, 'I suppose you've had intercourse with the local whores.'

'Not yet, ma'am. Do you happen to know a good address?'

She had stopped eating. Her whole face did a sort of shiver. 'Your father was a lecher, too. And a breaker of homes.'

He was surprised they had become so intimate so quickly. 'You are acquainted with my father on both counts?' He poured himself more wine.

Murray-Roberts, seeing a situation was developing, shot his

wife a warning glance across the table. She picked up her fork, only to wag it and say, 'I'm disgusted to have to sit next to you . . .' After a pause, receiving no reply, she began a catalogue of woes. Her first husband, Reggie, had been employed in a chemicals company in the south of England; he had worked his way up to managerial level at an early age. In the early nineties, Tarquin Burnell, Burnell's father, had come along. As a management broker, he had advised the directors and shareholders to divide the company into two. Tarquin, she asserted, made a rich living in industrial advisement. Her first husband had been moved to the struggling paints division and relocated in the north-east. Within a year, this new company was bankrupt, though the other half in the south prospered. Her husband became unemployed; within months he had to sell up everything to pay the mortgage on their new house. That too had had to go, and the marriage broke up.

'You left him for someone in a safe job, eh?' said Burnell. He realized that the industrial tale was vaguely familiar; he had heard a less prejudicial version of his father's activities. Much of Tarquin's income derived from his industrial advisement services; the division of an ailing chemicals company, stricken by recession, had been hailed as a triumph of foresight at the time.

Mrs Murray-Roberts said, 'I blame your father for Reggie's suicide. I always have. Everything was fine till he came along.'

'Still, your present husband seems a splendid chap.'

When it appeared she was not intending to answer, Burnell continued with his meal. He was about to enter the conversation on his other side, when she nudged him in the ribs and said, 'Reggie's sisters took care of the kids. They never speak to me. That's what your father did. Do you wonder I'm bitter?'

'I don't suppose he meant it personally.' They were distracted when the manager of the 'Faraghi' brought the men complimentary brandies and joints of strong grass.

Leaning across the table, Murray-Roberts said, addressing Burnell, 'Good smoke, eh, my friend?'

His wife replied. 'Drugs are ruining this country, ruining it. Not that it was much before.'

238

Her husband responded temperately. 'It is a fine country, considering its geographical and historical handicaps. Much to admire here. But there's no doubt that heroin is a big problem. It comes in over the mountains from Afghanistan, y'know, Burnell. If there's anything to rival its spread, then that's probably EMV.

'But some things have improved since the early post-communist days. Like they grow more of their own food. I could tell you some tales about that . . .' This he proceeded to do. After the collapse of the Soviet system, the UN had stepped in with massive food supplies. Most of it came from the USA. The USA grew enough food to feed a second planet.

'Which planet do you suggest?' Burnell asked. 'Mars? Are they hungry on Mars?'

'They're hungry everywhere,' said the lady.

'I'm just telling you what a Foreign Office chap, Howard Parker-Smith, told me. Deep-frozen chicken was sent out to Central Asia by the megaton. Breasts to Uzbekistan, drumsticks to Turkmenistan. Assholes to Tajikistan. Could have started another war.' Murray-Roberts laughed and drew deep on his joint, leaning back, sighing with pleasure.

With delicate gestures of apology, a spread hand, a drooping right shoulder, a smile like a minor abdominal operation, Mrs Murray-Roberts said, 'It is not easy to be spiritual in Ashkhabad.'

'Ever tried it in Birmingham?' Burnell asked. The smoke was getting to him. He downed his brandy in one. It turned everything radioactive as it burned its way down.

Orazov's cousin, who spoke a little German, drew the company's attention to six Russians who were sitting at a table near by, concentrating on getting noisily drunk.

The cousin explained that many Russians had remained in Central Asia when the Soviet Union collapsed. They had never integrated and were unpopular. Fortunately, the 'Faraghi' was enlightened, and allowed in foreigners, even Russians. But you could smell that Russian smell from here, couldn't you?

'Och, they're OK. They get the work done,' Murray-Roberts said. 'They make pretty good mechanics.'

The argument spread. Everyone began to talk at once, excitedly, laughing and gesticulating. Only the two Turkmeni women ate on, unmoved by controversy. Mrs Murray-Roberts, too, sat tight, looking disapprovingly from speaker to speaker, as if awaiting the moment when someone asked her, as final arbiter, for a definitive opinion on the matter. Ali Orazov issued more anti-Russian sentiments, looking to Haydar for support. Haydar blew out a gust of smoke and said that Russians brought criminal habits with them wherever they went. But ah, what music! Russia was a musical nation with a musical soul which Turkmens lacked. Mother Russia reverenced music more than any other nation on earth.

Burnell remembered hearing similar received opinions from Father Kadredin in Ghvtismshobeli. Mellowed though he was by this time, he said, 'That isn't strictly the case, Hikmat. When the Russians invaded Poland in 1831, they burned down Chopin's house and threw his grand piano out into the street.'

'Well, *Chopin*!' said Haydar crushingly, appealing to the company with a wide gesture. 'What do you expect? Chopin was Polish, *nein*?'

16
Burnell Speaks!

Black sand and red piled up against the window panes, found no purchase, slipped to the concrete sill. The next blast of wind, which was felt throughout the building, cleared the sill, only to add fresh sand. The process was hypnotic. It was like being inside an egg-timer, constantly turned this way and that.

The contents of one of the largest sand deserts in the world, the Karakum, were attempting to pour themselves into the city and make of Ashkhabad one more of the buried cities of the region. But the wind was uncertain of itself, blowing mainly from the north-west, then veering to north. The colour changed, tending towards a red like rust.

And indeed it carried rust within its mighty breath; and not only rust but insecticides, pesticides, fertilizers and defoliants. For to the north, over the frontier in Uzbekistan, lay the remains of the Aral Sea, poisoned lakes formed from what had once been the world's fourth largest inland ocean.

Local people blamed the great wind on many things, on the war, on the Uzbeks, on the catastrophe in Bulgaria, on global warming, on the season, on EMV, on the government, and of course on the Wrath of God.

But blame for the death of the Aral Sea rested squarely on the bleak ignorant centralizing science-fiction brains in 1960s Moscow, which longed for a gigantic project, in order to show off the superiority of Soviet engineering. Accordingly, these dinosaurian brains decided to deflect the great rivers flowing into the Aral in order to irrigate the so-called 'Virgin Lands'. Cotton crops would thrive where the Aral died.

The terrible Minvodkhoz, the Ministry of Water Resources, had struck. Great canals were built by slave labour. The Aral began to withdraw from its beaches. Its waters grew more saline as they evaporated. Its fish were poisoned, so that its fisheries one by one shut up shop. Boats ceased to ply for either work or pleasure, for both land and sea were ruined; the very air became poisoned. Thirty million people found their lives devastated, their modest coastal townships rotting stumps in receding gums. As the dust blew about from the exposed chemistries of the sea bed, diseases arose which civilized nations had forgotten long ago.

The death of the Aral Sea, drying out the climate, was an affliction experienced hundreds of miles away; the sands throwing themselves against Burnell's window announced the fact. They died when the wind died, as suddenly as it had arisen, itself plagued by the illnesses it carried. But cotton grew.

Burnell went to stare out of his window. A new earthquake appeared to have struck Ashkhabad. Low buildings were half buried in sand. Yet within a couple of minutes, huge machines, yellow in colour, crawled from their hiding-places and began to scoop the bitter dusts into their maw.

He filed his notes in the morning. Shortly after two in the afternoon, he pulled on his shoes and, after a moment's consideration, put on a tie. He went down the dusty staircase into the foyer, where he was met after a while by Robert Murray-Roberts, who trudged in from the street looking glum.

'Weather's on the change,' he said. 'Come next week, we'll be freezing our arses off.' He shook hands with Burnell. 'Very good of you to agree to talk to the university at such short notice. We should have quite a decent crowd. They can't pay you, by the way, Roy, the buggers, but the embassy will cough up something for your expenses.'

They dodged a man with a broom, brushing sand from the foyer with long melancholy strokes, possibly inventing a way to paint a really modern abstract.

'Who am I talking to?'

'It's sure to be the Humanities Department – students and student teachers with a grasp of English. Run by a Russian cove, a Professor Ivan Nastiklov. A wee emotional type, you'd say. I had to give them a title for your lecture, by the way, so I chose the title of your book, *Archetype and Architrave*. Hope that's OK. I expect you're used to this kind of thing back home.'

'Moderately. It's *Architrave and Archetype*, by the way.'

'Fine. Fine, just as you like.' They were getting into his car. It started after several attempts, Murray-Roberts swearing in a resigned way – the curses might have been prayers – about sand in the engine.

As they moved slowly through the city, they could not but observe that most of the population was involved with the extraction of grit from one place or another. Men, women, children, dogs, were all at it, scratching, cleaning houses, clearing paths, beating animals, polishing, blowing, brushing, besoming or shaking. The whole place looked like an Asian pastiche of a Bruegel canvas: crowded with little figures engaged in activities intended to illustrate rather gormless proverbs.

Better a sandstorm by day than a cold bed by night
A blocked carburettor is worth a whole philosophy
When deserts move, shift your tent
Respect a dusty wife: she will not provoke lust
A door to a dirty wind is like a leaf to Muhammad's ass
Only Uzbeks enjoy bad weather
Men sleep but a good broom is a watchful eye
Souls in Heaven delight in the smell of a well-groomed camel
Beat your rug towards your neighbour
God has sovereignty over all things; curse not when his grit enters your eye, for you are being blessed.

The University of Ashkhabad was an extensive concrete building, surrounded by lesser temporary-looking structures, much like universities all round the world. It was situated on sloping ground; on various levels and terraces some attempt had been made at landscaping, but the phenomenal wind had drowned the place in sand. Burnell and Murray-Roberts passed an outdoor canteen where students sat about drinking glasses of tea, looking as idle as only students can.

They entered an unlighted hallway, dominated by a large photograph of President Diyanizov and characterized by an institutional smell, at once hygienic and unpleasant. Nobody came forward to meet them. By this time, Burnell was feeling uneasy. He had agreed to give this impromptu lecture merely to keep in with the embassy; now he was beginning to regret it.

Professor Nastiklov appeared before them. He made no apology for failing to greet them on arrival, offering Burnell instead a hand which brought to his mind a picture of two frogs attempting to grasp each other in copulatory embrace within the shallows of the River Yukon.

Nastiklov was small and bounderish, with no bridge to his nose and up-swept black and grey striped side-whiskers. The upper half of his body was dressed in a shirt with unfastened cuffs and a black waistcoat which acted as a dandruff trap. Squinting up at Burnell, he said, 'So you're Herr Roy Burnell. You're older than I thought. Do you believe in God, may I enquire? The Godhead?'

'Not greatly, I wouldn't say.'

'"Not greatly, I wouldn't say" . . . I suppose God's not to Western taste these days?' said Nastiklov, unwittingly using one of Haydar's lines. Glancing over his left shoulder, he said, 'How about the devil, then? You believe in him, don't you?'

'God gave us the brains to doubt his existence. I suppose that takes care of the devil, too.' Burnell made to move forward but Nastiklov stopped him.

'Well, I know you're brave. After all, in Georgia, eh?' Chuckling, he made wicked little stabbing motions to indicate obliquely the death of Lazar Kaginovich. 'Don't worry, I would not want to get on the wrong side of you, Roy Burnell.' His dyed black hair, plastered to his skull, rose in a small horn or ear on either side of his head. He resembled, all in all, a distraught cat.

'Hadn't we better get on with it?' Murray-Roberts asked.

'Oh, I don't mind if my routine's interrupted.' With this comment, Nastiklov scurried down the dim corridor. They followed, to a crowded office – 'My bunker,' said Nastiklov, sniggering, 'like Adolf Hitler's' – where a diminutive Muslim secretary poured each of them a sweet lemonade of strychnine flavour.

'But I won't say anything against Adolf, in case you like him. You see, we Russians – well, as the Professor of Psychology here, I can see into people's souls, but I've learnt not to speak my mind, no. As they say in Odessa, "To make friends, keep your trap shut" . . . Amusing, isn't it? Just bear that in mind, Herr Roy Burnell . . .'

'I'm here to speak,' said Burnell. 'My piece if not my mind.'

'Ha!' Nastiklov repeated Burnell's remark several times, trying to make sense of it, sometimes changing the word order as if the sentence were Latin.

Taking tiny sips at his glass, licking his lips frequently, Nastiklov's feline aspect grew more apparent. The way he flicked his head from side to side, eyes half closed, to scrutinize first one of his guests then the other, made Burnell think, 'Ah, Balaam's Cat!'

'Say nothing controversial,' he warned Burnell. 'Comprehensible, OK – but remember you're talking to Muslim students. No politics. No religion. As a *giaur*, you're not even supposed to mention Allah. In fact the duller you can be, the better.' Half under his breath, half into his glass, he added, 'Shouldn't be too difficult . . . Nothing controversial . . . You can't trust them . . .'

After a second glass of lemonade, and no immediate ill-effects, Nastiklov led them into a well-equipped lecture room, the raked seats of which were filled by silent students. They rose as one on the entry of their professor and his guests.

Having led Burnell on to the podium, Nastiklov began to introduce him at length, first in Russian, then in ornate English.

The introduction took peculiar form, being in the main a discourse on the rise of Germany following the Congress of Berlin in 1878, which Bismarck had mediated as honest broker. Of this, Nastiklov gave a full account. When he mentioned that Russia had been apportioned Bessarabia, the audience, silent until that point, gave a loud cheer.

Used to all kinds of madness when in a lecture room, Burnell nevertheless found this lengthy preamble hard to swallow. Nastiklov spoke for twenty minutes before sitting down. With a merry self-satisfied gesture, he motioned to Burnell to rise and do his worst.

'Good afternoon. After that introduction, anything I may say will surely sound irrelevant. Nevertheless, I was invited to speak to you on the subject of "Architrave and Archetype", so that I propose to do.

'For those of you who are not architectural students, I should explain that an architrave is, in a general sense, a moulded frame surrounding a door or window. I use it in my book in a metaphorical sense, being interested in the way in which styles of architecture permit us insight into the human psyche and human ambitions.

'I assume you are all familiar with archetypes. I'd define an archetype as follows – and I rely heavily on the original work in this area by Carl Jung. There are certain innate psychic and behavioural predispositions universally present in all human beings of whatever race. These predispositions may find unique expression in each individual, yet they underlie and guide human existence. We're all the same, in other words; national differences count for nothing in these psychic regions. Such entities have been inherited from the mammals which preceded us, evolving slowly through the immensity of time.'

He noticed a rumble of discontent at this statement, but pressed on without pause.

'What are these archetypes which are of such importance and such ancient vintage? To give you an example. Just recently, remains of a pre-human species have been excavated in mountain caves in the Sierra de la Demanda, in the north of Spain near Burgos.'

At this juncture, the audience came alive, and gave a loud cheer. Could it be that news of the archaeological discovery in Spain so delighted them? Or could it be that a secret sign had been given them, in order to encourage the speaker?

Mystified, Burnell continued. 'Thank you. The Spanish discoveries are good news, since they will further our understanding of our own species. There are strong indications that these pre-humans, who died half a million years ago, conducted religious ceremonials. So we may say that the religious impulse is an extremely old archetype, influencing our behaviour whether we are Christian or Muslim. Other –'

At this moment, up popped Professor Nastiklov from his chair next to Burnell. Fists first on hips, then right arm raised to wag an angry ill-manicured finger at Burnell.

'I'm sorry, sir. I have to interrupt you. You are a welcome guest to our university, coming all the way from Germany to speak to us, but we cannot permit intellectuals to insult this audience as if we were rug-sellers. We look to you for enlightenment, not racial abuse. To dare to suggest that there is any resemblance between the enlightened worship of the All-Highest and some pre-human mumbo-jumbo is to defile our hospitality – you who have partaken of our refreshment and our best attentions.'

At this, Burnell was somewhat taken aback.

'I'm suggesting no such thing! You totally misunderstand something which could not have been put more clearly. If you expect me to continue, sit down, sir.' But the audience was in an uproar, most of the students jumping up and standing on their chairs, angrily waving papers or their *keffiyehs*. Some were shouting incoherently. Burnell was reminded of England's House of Commons.

To Nastiklov he said, 'You've ruined my speech and insulted my intelligence. I'd bloody well insult yours if I thought you had any.'

'No, no, no, no, no. Let us be friends, *mein herr*! Russians and Germans have traditional friendships.' The little professor lowered his voice, so as scarcely to be heard above the uproar. 'I didn't mean a word I said. My position as a Russian here is insecure. I'm a frog on stilts in this Muslim University, a rudder without a boat. I said what I did only to curry favour with the audience so that they will think better of me. Please understand.'

'You worm, Nastikof, you little worm!'

Nastiklov violently nodded his head, so that the two horns of hair fell flat on his skull. 'I know, I know. True, alas. A worm of blue blood. But you will soon leave this place. My fate is to stay.

You are fortunate. I must cling to my career, such as it is, like a rat to a sinking ship.'

'So you're willing to make a fool of me to do it.'

'I'll silence these imbeciles, you see. Then you carry on. Afterwards, we have a huge meal in recompense. I buy it for you.'

Before Burnell could argue, Nastiklov turned to the audience and made waving signs with his hands. Gradually, the row subsided. All this while, Burnell was conscious of Murray-Roberts in the front row, red of face, vainly trying to suppress convulsive laughter. Only this sign of normal human behaviour saved Burnell's sanity.

'He apologizes! The *giaur* apologizes!' yelled Nastiklov. 'Our dear guest says it was a story, a joke, without meaning. Be seated and Professor Burnell will proceed.'

Still furious, Burnell could not find it in himself to quit the platform. He began to speak again in a shout as the audience subsided into their seats.

'What we have just witnessed is a perfect example of the folly of human behaviour. On a small scale, maybe, but still utterly contemptible! Let me deal with an archetype which provokes folly on a much larger scale. I refer to an archetypal imperative unfortunately of great phylogenetic antiquity, the aggressive archetype. It is that which triggers wars.

'We are, however, no mere helpless victims of our impulses. We can to some extent control them, as I now control my anger. That is what is meant by civilization. By conscious consideration of these hidden archetypes, we may be able to prevent orgies of destruction.

'What I'm saying is that the light of consciousness – that architrave we have ourselves built into our souls – may be strong enough to overpower those archetypes which, once of assistance to humanity, now threaten to overturn the delicate fabric on which civilization is built.

'For example. Can we suppose that the recent war between Turkmenistan and Uzbekistan could have been avoided? Imagine a situation where the leaders of both countries had met calmly and judiciously and –'

He was made aware that Nastiklov had jumped up again, scarlet of countenance. The Russian began screaming at the audience. 'He now insults our brave people! He insults our leaders! He pours scorn on our beloved President Diyanizov! We know who started the war. Who started the war, my friends?'

The audience, scrambling up again, yelled as one man, 'The enemy! Uzbeks! Uzbeks! Uzbeks!' They rushed to climb on the platform, like revolutionaries storming the barricades.

'You see, you idiots!' shouted Burnell at the top of his voice. 'Siddown, will you? It's that damned stupid archetype popping its rocks again!'

'Quick,' said Nastiklov, grabbing hold of Burnell. 'Out the back or the bastards will lynch you!'

He led the way through a door at the back of the platform.

They found themselves in a dim-lit corridor. As Nastiklov turned and locked the door, hammering started on the other side.

'The herrings! The sprats! They'll never get to you. I defy them. I protect you with my useless life. Come with me.' He was perfectly calm now, though a little out of breath. Burnell would have preferred a faster pace down the corridor as they crunched their way over the sandy floor.

'You're a creep of the most vile order, Nastikof. I detest you.'

'Hush, I have to win their respect, damn them. We get a vodka in my office. I save your life, didn't I?'

'You nearly caused my death, you slime. And what about Murray-Roberts?'

Nastiklov winked. 'He's a big boy, Murray-Roberts. And probably Jewish.'

It was a relief to be locked into Nastiklov's office. The last thing Burnell wished to do was drink with this repulsive little man, but a slug of Stolichnaya was irresistible. He quickly took a second glass. It was a delight to feel his head spin in a sly anticlockwise fashion, like a gyroscope defying gravity.

'By the bloody way, Nastikof, I'm not a German. I'm English. Murray-Roberts is Scottish. I'd just like to point that out. And to hell with Bismarck.'

'Why don't you like the Krauts?'

'I like them very well. I'm just telling you I'm English.'

'The Krauts kill many people.'

'Meaning what? Meaning the Russians don't?'

'So you like the Krauts to kill people? Millions, perhaps?'

'Are you referring to the war last century, World War II, when the Nazis exterminated six million Jews?'

'Pah, everyone kills Jews. Did English kill Jews? No? Now England is no longer an important country and Germany is.'

Burnell made a move towards him. 'You insult me or the Jews once more and you are going to suffer. I'll flatten you, so be warned.'

Putting his hands up to his face, Nastiklov squeezed it until saliva ran from his mouth. His lips took the shape of an orange Möbius strip. 'I'm sincerely as terrified as a molehill. I forget momentarily you are none other than the assassin of President Lazar Kaginovich of the West Georgian Republic and will kill without compunction. You were seen on the local television. I'm sincerely afraid of you. What am I? As you say, a worm on a sinking ship. You – you, on the other hand, you are a hero or a villain, depending on point of view. Inhabitant of a once-great country, rich, able to travel, friend of Jew-slayers. Also, I believe someone stole your memory.'

Burnell hit him in the face. It was rather a squashy business.

Nastiklov fell back against his desk, accidentally planting one hand in a plate of congealed half-finished *pilau*. No doubt for safety's sake he took his meals alone in his office. Bringing his hand up to his bleeding mouth, he covered it with grains of rice, which he blew at Burnell.

'I respect – I really respect a strong man. Help yourself to more vodka. Please forget the expense.'

As he began to weep, there came a banging at the door. 'The knocking at the door in *Macbeth*,' he said, and started to shout for help.

It was Murray-Roberts, of dishevelled appearance. Burnell let him in, passing over the vodka bottle without speaking.

Announcing that the students had gone, Murray-Roberts, whose hair and clothes were more than unusually distraught, took a deep swig from the bottle. Surveying the scene, he said, 'Christ

Almighty, Burnell, man, you've beaten up the Professor of Psychology!'

'Is that what the little fucker is? But yes – what else could he be? I'll give him another punch if he provokes me again. As for you. You got me into this madhouse, you Scots git!'

'Stay your Sassenach hand.'

'I think you should give me another punch,' said Nastiklov, between sobs. 'Not only would it serve me right, it would probably make you feel less insecure.'

Passed the bottle, Burnell also took an immense swig and suddenly began to snivel. 'He's probably right. I probably do feel insecure. You'd feel insecure if you'd lost ten years' worth of memory.' He pulled his tie off. 'It's hotter than a witch's twat in this office.'

He sniffed, swigged more vodka, blew his nose on his tie.

'Och, man, for fuck's sake . . . I bloody wish I couldna' remember a thing of my mankey past.' Under the benign influence of the Stolichnaya, a Glasgow accent was emerging.

'We none of us wish to remember,' Nastiklov said. 'Oblivion! Pass the bottle! In particular, I'd like to forget my nationality, which has caused me nothing but trouble since the days of that scum Gorbachev. I do forget it, but in this racist hole people keep reminding me I'm just an old Red.

'I know you hate and despise me, but underneath my nationality is quite a decent person. Hardly a man – I accept that, yes – a wimp, perhaps, but nevertheless a decent God-fearing man. Of course I fear God.' He crossed himself. 'Of course I fear God. The stinker has it in for me.' He shed more tears.

Burnell put his arm round the Russian's shoulders. 'Shh, don't cry, Ivan. There's no God. It's just that religious archetype I was trying to tell you about. It's all a hangover from old times. The Spanish mountains. Sierra de la Demanda – they were nuts about religion even then. There's no God. Honest. No God – only us. Take my word.'

'Who then am I to blame? Who's to take the blame?' Through his tears he said, 'Roy, there's another bottle in that cupboard.'

★

'What I can't understand – what I can't understand is why someone like you should want to come to scruffy places like Turkmenistan.'

'Ivan, you see it's like this. It's like this, I just happen to like scruffy places . . .'

It was such a funny answer they both roared with laughter. The current scruffy place Burnell and Nastiklov were in was a small upstairs room in a private Russian bar-café. Robert Murray-Roberts was also present. He had collected his bony wife, Madge, who was urging sobriety on him and pointedly ignoring Burnell. Burnell and the Professor of Psychology were unrestrained.

A balalaika group played while they ate. A young woman occasionally sang a song in a minor key. A couple danced smoochily in one corner, locked close together, gazing into each other's eyes. Ivan Nastiklov had been as good as his word, and was standing them a meal after their escape from the university. The four of them sat at one end of a table covered with a floral table-cloth.

It was just past five o'clock and Burnell was beginning to forgive the Russian for being a worm.

After a raft of *zakuski*, there followed a meat-peppers-and-potato grill, plus salad, something called *porosyonok*, which turned out to be sucking pig, with herb sausages, followed by ruinous chocolate cakes. Burnell and Nastiklov washed this lot down with beer, while Murray-Roberts and wife stuck to mineral water.

'You like scruffy places, yet you live decently in Europe, a civilized place to which Ashkhabad is like a minnow to a . . . a wash basin. You must know so much, Roy – in your head, know much.' Nastiklov tapped his own head to confirm the point, perhaps checking for a hollow ring.

'Now that's where you're wrong, Ivan, that's exactly where you're wrong. I'm ignorant, an ignorant man. What do I know about – well, Goethe, super-conductors, Scandinavia, Singapore, where Whirling Dervishes live, economics, Sibelius, Mrs Sibelius, nuclear physics, lantern fish, how you cook *ratatouille*, Fibonacci sequences – no, I do know a bit about them – croquet, Walter Crane, change-ringing, Rigel, Goethe . . . Hang on, I said

Goethe. The Black Sea. I don't even know how deep the Black Sea is at its deepest point. And I bet you don't either.'

Nastiklov laughed. 'I want to tell you something. Come here.' He beckoned, though they had drawn their chairs close and were almost leaning on each other. 'I can tell you this. I know how shallow it is at its shallowest point. One centimetre. *One centimetre!*' They almost collapsed with laughter. Still chuckling, Nastiklov said, 'You perhaps knew these things – I bet you knew these things – before your memory was stolen. Before that, I bet you knew all these things.'

'How do you know my memory was stolen?'

'Because I'm psychic. I can read the mind. Read any mind . . . You're famous, that's how. I've had to deal with a man who sold a part of his memory, yes, went to Istanbul, went to Istanbul and sold his particularly emotic remory –' he struck the table so that all the glasses jingled '– erotic memory of his first love.'

Burnell tried to interrupt, but Nastiklov forged on gesturing dramatically if randomly.

'He was paid a lot of money from the EMV studio. Came back here, built himself a big house, couldn't bear not to have that precious memory, memory of his first love. Couldn't bear to be parted from it. Mentally ill, became mentally ill, like a shadow. Shadow on the wall. Needed treatment. In the end, had to buy a copy back, have it reinserted. Then it wasn't how he remembered the memory had been. Deep depression followed as night follows summer. Had to be locked up in a mental institution.

'Of course, we Russians, we have a melancholy streak. You know that, Roy? A melancholy streak. It's heretidy. Heretidy. Heredity. In the genes, you know? Slav melancholy. All that space, the long winters, the long spaces, the balalaikas, the peasants, the Cyrillic alphabet. That contributes to melancholy, you know, the Cyrillic alphabet. Those shapes, implanted as children . . . I'm Ukrainian, but it's easier . . .'

He started to draw some characters on the cloth.

'For heaven's sake, do behave,' Madge Murray-Roberts said. 'Rob, make them behave. I'm bored out of my gourd with this company. Let's go.'

'Why should I behave, lady?' Nastiklov asked, shooting her a look of hatred. 'I it is who pays to be here, behaving as customary, and arch-friend of the poropitor. Owner.'

Leaning across the table, Nastiklov beckoned Murray-Roberts to bring his ear closer, and then closer still. When due proximity had been achieved, the Russian fixed his cold eye on Madge Murray-Roberts and described how unpopular people used to be given tarantula schnapps. It was a drink in old Turkestan, to be given to those you wanted to get rid of. This remark was accompanied by a knowing wink.

The desert just outside Ashkhabad, he said, was full of deadly scorpions and tarantulas. You caught a number of tarantulas and put them in a pot. After them, you threw in slices of dried apple and apricot. The horrible brutes flung themselves in a fury at the fruit, biting it and injecting their poison into it. This fruit was then mixed with newly fermented wine. About thirty spiders were needed to a litre of the deadly wine, one small glass of which was enough to drive a man insane: he became first paralysed then raving mad, and died crying for more of the liquor.

While delivering details of this recipe, Nastiklov kept his gaze fixed wickedly on Mrs Murray-Roberts.

'What if you use scorpions instead of tarantulas?' asked Murray-Roberts. 'What like is scorpion schnapps?'

'Phuh, not even a Scotsman would drink that much,' Nastiklov said.

Burnell's attention had been caught by a slender woman who was singing to the balalaika accompaniment. She wore a long green gown which emphasized her sinuous figure. Her gestures were minimal and a lock of dark hair had fallen over her brow. The song, whatever it was, signified something tragic. He saw it in her lovely eyes, the delicious downcast look she gave, so languorous, so seductive.

The song ended. Murray-Roberts clapped, as did some of the other diners. Burnell rose. Moving smartly forward, he caught the singer's hand before she disappeared behind the curtain. The band struck up 'Days of Wine and Roses' with tremolo effect. He put his arm about the singer and danced with her. She made no protest, possibly being accustomed to drunken male behaviour, which might account for her languor.

He closed his eyes, inhaling her perfume, all perspiration and Persian violets. 'God, you're so lovely, you sing so beautifully. That song went to my heart. I know I'm a bit pissed but I'm really smitten. Come with me to my hotel, stay with me all night. Please, I need you, I want you. We're surely made for each other, you foreign beauty.'

She didn't understand. Perhaps she was Turkish. They drifted in the tiny space. He savoured the warmth of her body against his. The balalaikas twangled like a bamboo grove in autumn breezes, with an exoticism that called to mind a thousand vague desirable sensations − all of them associated with the female anatomy moving within the circle of his arms.

'I want to lead a better life, darling. With you.'

The music stopped. The leader of the balalaika group was a heavy man, gaudily decked out in long moustache and short waistcoat. He came forward with an unpleasant look on his face, intent to part or maim them.

He said in German to Burnell, 'Get back to your seat, you drunken *scheiss*, or else sing a song. Or else I throw you downstairs.'

''S a good idea. I don't mean the stair. The song.' Burnell raised a lordly hand. 'I sing for her. Stand back, man. Preferably return to your banjo.' He raised a hand to attract Nastiklov's attention at the other end of the room. 'Ivan, Ivan, I'm going to sing a song.'

He had a good tenor voice. He sang 'I Know Where I'm Going', dripping with Russian melancholy, to which drink as well as the Cyrillic alphabet contributed. Softly, a balalaika joined in, picking like a small bird at the tune. The whole group entered the melody, soft as snowfall. Burnell was carried away with pleasure. The audience clapped. Someone threw a congratulatory bread roll. He sang the song again. '. . . shoes of bright green leather . . .' The singer in the green dress, who was kind, kissed his cheek.

Smiling modestly, he returned to his seat at the table, amid a scattering of applause.

'That was disgusting,' said Madge. 'Rob, skates on. Let's go.' Burnell gravely presented her with the congratulatory bread roll, which he had caught.

Nastiklov threw his arms about Burnell and hugged him. 'Bravo, my friend. You show much true spirit. Let me tell you this, I'll tell you this. What I believe in my professional percacity. Percacity. Pocacional professity. See, I don't agree with Sigmund Freud, don't agree with him at all. Or Adler. Neither Freud nor Adler. They're responsible for those doctrines which unlashed – unleashed a wave of hedonism right across the twennieth century, right across it. Mistake. Cause of much misery. Hedonism. Worse than Stalinism. Other side of the same coin, see? These empty doctrines made the century a living hell for everyone.

'See, the quest for pleasure, the quest for power – that's what they believed in. As vatimotion. As motimotion, motivation – ha, I have that word by its tool! Stalin and Freud were wrong about basic human motivation. All wrong. You know what the real need is for human life?'

'A pee. I need a pee,' said Burnell.

'No, no, no. I mean something spiritual. The human need is really deeply to find a meaning to life. A true meaning. Only then can a life be said to be fulfilling, to find a true meaning. You see what I mean? The light at the end of the tunnel. It's awful to die and not to know, like a – like a calf in a pigsty . . .'

Burnell agreed, sipping a little mineral water. One had to go in search of significance. 'When I lost my memory –'

'There you are,' said Nastiklov excitedly. Sweat poured from his striped side-whiskers. He thumped his little fists on the table. 'Your memory. What stole it? New technology. The culminating technology of the twennieth century. Holy Jesus! First nuclear power bombs threatened life in general. Then EMV process – the refinement of power – homes right in, destroys the human mind, the very centre of . . .'

'Look, forget the twennieth century, Ivan. It's the twenny-first that is killing me.'

Swaying, Nastiklov rose and loomed over Burnell, as far as that was possible. Flattening his whiskers against his face with his left hand in an attempt at seriousness, he said, 'I'll give you some advice, my son. Real good advice. You're a celebrity, aren't you? A celebrity of the first rank. You murdered a head of state – Laser What's-his-name. Tell me if I'm wrong, but you murdered him. The world wants news, the world wants drama. It wants to look deep into the human psyche, it wants the drama of the . . . Anyhow, you have a saleable coddomity. You could sell that memory of that Georgian drama to a good EMV studio. It would be bought all round the world. You could make a fortune of money.'

'Forget it! That's a horrible suggestion. Makes me sick.' In fact, Burnell was beginning to feel so inclined.

'Make a fortune, seize the ottopunity when it's there. Then you can afford to buy a really good ten-year memory to fill in your own vacuum. See? A rich wealthy memory of some happy guy living I don't know where. Not Turkmenistan, certainly. Not Russia. Bavaria, maybe. Sarawak, let's say. Have ten years of bliss inserted, be happy every after. I'd do it! I'd do it – my life's been nothing but a long fismortune . . . Wouldn't you?'

He addressed this question to Murray-Roberts across the table but, before the latter could respond, Nastiklov grabbed himself by his genitals. 'Holy Jesus, I need a pee too.'

As he fled from the table, Murray-Roberts leaned over to Burnell. 'Let's go. Madge is bored. So am I.'

'I must see that lovely singer again,' Burnell said, standing up. 'She fancies me. You know that, Rob Roy? Fancies me. And I fancy her.'

Murray-Roberts jumped up and grabbed him. 'She just happens to be married to the sodding bandleader, laddie, so forget it, *versteh*? You've had enough booze to last a week. We're getting out of here.'

'But my friend Ivan. Telling about the quest for the meaning of an indiffiz – an individual life.'

'Don't be silly, Mr Burnell,' said Madge. 'He's a perfectly horrid little man as you'd realize if you were sober. Even other Russians avoid him.' She evidently spoke through a mouthful of ice cubes.

'That's a racist remark if ever I heard one.'

'Then you never heard one. So let's go, or we leave you to make your own way home and get yourself robbed in some smelly alley.'

Subdued, Burnell followed them across the room and downstairs, singing as he went, '. . . the de'il knows who I'll marry . . .'

At the bottom of the stairs, he swerved adroitly away from the Murray-Robertses and burst into the men's room.

Ivan Nastiklov was there, hanging over a basin, vying with its pallor, muttering to himself and disliking what he heard.

'Can't stop. Got to pee,' said Burnell, pushing past him. And proceeded to do so.

Nastiklov had gone from his manic into his depressive phase. The change had altered him physically, so that he seemed to have shrunk inside his clothes. He pointed with trembling finger to a cupboard which stood beside the solitary wash basin, almost blocking the entrance. 'There's the devil himself, Roy. See him squatting up there? He's after me. He's coming to get me.'

Burnell was groaning with pleasure and relief. 'Nonsense.' He did not even bother to look round.

'You must be able to see him. Holy Jesus, stop pissing for a minute, will you? He's up there – fat little bloater in a funny yellow check jacket and tight trousers.'

'Nonsense. You're drunk. Besides, the devil doesn't pee. What would he be doing in here?'

'It's no joke, you intensitive English bun. He's not after a piss, he's after me. Just my rotten Russian luck. To think I'm going to die in a lousy Turkmeni urinal . . . Oh God, pray for me, Roy. You're a civilized man, the devil may listen to you.'

'Ahhhhh . . . Sorry, I'm not the praying sort. You won't die. Forget it. Go upstairs and have another drink. Give my love to the singer.'

'What a miserable life I've had. I should have left here when most of the other Russians left. Look, look, it's true, he has got goat feet . . . Why is life dominated by death?'

'That's nonsense, Ivan. Cheer up. The fact is, life dominates death, at least while we're alive – which after all is all we know. Life wins hands down all the time. I speak as one with my cock in my hand. Death's nothing. It plays no part in our actual lives. The rest's imagination. There must be a Russian proverb about that.'

'Oh, there is, there is. "When things are blackest, try arsenic."'

Burnell was finished, and tired of this conversation now that he was feeling more sober. He dashed cold water over his face to improve matters further. His intention was to be a little sympathetic towards the sad Professor of Psychology but, catching a glimpse of that bizarrely haggard face, its whiskers drooping, he said as he left the room, 'Shit, you're right, Ivan, he is up on the cupboard. Nice jacket, though.'

The slamming door cut off Nastiklov's scream.

17

Glimpse of Airing Cupboard

The air was sweet with a scent of tear gas. A helicopter clattered just above roof level, trawling the streets with its search light. General Makhkamov had let the sun go down on his wrath.

Murray-Roberts drove to his modest bungalow in the foreign quarter of Ashkhabad and waited while his wife got out.

'Good night,' Madge Murray-Roberts said crisply to Burnell, and to her husband, 'Don't be late, Rob, darling, will you?'

They watched her retreating figure until she entered the front door and switched on a hall light.

The back seat of the Fiat was cluttered with tennis racquets and various items of sports gear. Burnell squeezed out and sat in the front with Murray-Roberts. They wove their way into less salubrious areas of the city, where the effects of the day's sandstorm were still apparent.

'You're sure you want to do this?' Murray-Roberts asked. 'I shouldn't be on this kick if the ambassador was here. You know EMV's illegal in this country.'

'It's a must,' Burnell said, fighting an internal fight to become more sober.

'Your pal Dr Haydar phoned after leaving you, just before the phone lines went down. I'd steer clear of him if I were you. He's a known drug-runner across frontiers. We don't have anything to do with him officially, but we have stretched points in his favour.'

'So he gave you a name?'

'Syria's rather popular with Britain just now, can't think why. Seems Britain's popular with Syria too – again, can't think why.'

'They read Thomas Hardy.'

'Bugger it, should have taken that last turning.'

They stuck in a traffic jam at a crossroads Burnell now recognized; he was becoming familiar with the geography of the city. A camel harnessed to a flat truck was being cantankerous and blocking the road. Burnell was glad of the momentary halt, having many things on his mind and not knowing which should take precedence.

'Is your wife a teetotaller?'

'Madge is a Cumbrian lass. She doesn't get on with Russian food.' This remark was followed by a ruminative pause. 'You were playing with fire, grabbing that girl singer the way you did. You're not in Europe now, you must remember.' Another pause. 'I've a rooted objection to having my tool sucked.'

'You're an unusual man, Robby,' Burnell murmured.

Murray-Roberts was following his own obscure line of thought. He said nothing more until the traffic was moving again.

As he steered through the evening rush, tooting with the best of them, past the camel-coloured Iraqi tour buses rife outside the Hotel Jubilienaya, the first secretary explained that no one – not the embassy, not Dr Haydar – could engineer an audience with the president, certainly not on matters as personal as a stolen memory; a stolen memory, he added, rolling out the words, 'with considerable erotic element . . .'

'Suppose Diyanizov had a copy of your memory, he'd not be likely to admit it. Maybe not even to his nearest and dearest, if he has any of that ilk. The exception being the Argentinian wife, of course.'

'Your wife dislikes me.'

'She's a bit shy.'

Chinese-built trams rattled along the centre of the avenue as they eased their way down the long Ulitza Engleska. The name was a reminder that the British had once been here, in the dog days of Empire. A contingent of the British army had defeated the Red Army near Ashkhabad in 1918, and briefly occupied the area.

Remaining of brooding appearance, Murray-Roberts condescended to say that because of the British occupation, almost a century past, one still saw fair-haired chaps about – not all Russian. Some owed their existence to the fruits of British loins from Glasgow and Liverpool, several generations ago.

'What was the place like then, do you think?'

Murray-Roberts gave a snort. 'Prosperous.'

After they passed a busy market, its fruit stalls illuminated by kerosene lamps, the street grew drabber, the pedestrians less willing to move out of the way of vehicles. The car slowed to a crawl.

'It's about here . . . Dog's Piss Alley. My wife was married previously, you know.'

'You've been here before, Rob?' Burnell stared hopelessly at the chaotic street scene.

Murray-Roberts was deliberately non-committal. 'I know the area. Bastard called Reggie. Went bust.'

He turned down a side street where the Tarmacadam gave out. The street appeared to be barricaded with posters and advertising signs for everything from athlete's foot ointment and condoms to hair tonics, as little shop jostled with little shop. A clump of bamboo arched over the road. Men in turbans sat relaxedly in front of their stalls.

The Fiat pulled up next to a *chaykhana* from which music tinkled. The night was as purple as a bruise. As the two men climbed out of the car, Burnell stared restlessly about, looking for he knew not what. The theatricality of the scene almost persuaded him it had all been staged for his benefit.

Smells of sweetness and dirt encompassed the people drifting arm in arm down the middle of the street, the stallholders, and the idlers who waited in doorways. Sometimes those doorways with their peeling paint sheltered sleepers wrapped in sheets like corpses. This appeared to be a foreign quarter; to Burnell's ill-informed eye, most of the people he saw were Afghan or Pakistani. A woman looked down on the scene from her balcony, to which a flowering creeper aspired. What, he wondered idly, was her life like; to read her memory via EMV would be instructive.

'What a dump, eh?' remarked Murray-Roberts.

Burnell intimated that he recollected Iceland as being worse.

A cart creaked by, bearing empty oil drums, with a musical

note at every revolution of its wheels. Barefoot urchins ceased throwing sand at each other in order to throw it at the cart. Cicadas chirruped endlessly, out of tune with the cart wheels. The great noble hump of a mosque could be seen through trees. In the tight-packed street, an enviable sense of continuity with the past prevailed.

Clearer-headed now, Burnell breathed in scents of cooking. Apart from the cables trailing like lianas along the line of shops, apart from the naked electric light bulbs which, woven among the stands of bamboo, cast bars across the pavements, this scene could belong to any date in the past – how many centuries? He lingered, enjoying both the durability of the scene and something responsive in himself which was not transient.

'Let's go,' said Murray-Roberts.

Why did he like what Nastiklov had called 'these scruffy places'? A Georgian in Tbilisi had talked about the poet Lermontov, and of Lermontov's love of nature and the Caucasus. He had quoted a Russian writer's verdict on the poet, that Lermontov had *l'amour extra-terrestre pour la terre*. Perhaps Burnell had that same crazed love – though less for nature itself than for nature where it became frayed round the edges. The scruffy places.

He wanted to linger, despite his friend's call. A woman sang in a high register from the *chaykhana*, while bats fluttered round an overhead lamp. Burnell experienced once more the melancholy romanticism of the East, that bottomless sense of joy and hopelessness, the drug so hard to cure once it had entered the system. People passing by were slow and courteous in their movements. Which one among them had ever thought of painting his house or insuring his car or engaging a gardener or buying a dog licence?

Perhaps he was still far from sober. This was a land of nightingales, sewers, and roses. Soon winter would fall. Everyone would freeze in their inadequate housing. He loved the place.

It had been a good day, so full, so unexpected. And now an EMV shop. And who could say what might happen on the morrow, when he visited the Friendship Bridge. The lecture with that madman Nastiklov had been a lot of fun, at least in retrospect. Just as well, really, that the Russian had stopped his talk. At the mere mention of archetypes, the eyes of the students had started to glaze over: the closing of their minds had been almost audible. Funny how many people found the most important things in the world either boring or just beyond their compass. So much for their shagging compasses . . .

And with that reflection went a familiar ground bass, the mixture of awe and contempt in which he held most things, himself included.

He turned and followed Murray-Roberts down a narrow alleyway beside the teahouse. An animal slunk into the shadows.

From the rear of the teahouse came normal culinary sounds, a rattle of metal utensils, knives being sharpened, plates being stacked, a waiter being yelled at. Taking a short break, a cook leaned against a side door. He was singing to himself and took no notice of two passing Europeans.

At the end of the alley was a muddle of huts. Men could be discerned by the huts, waiting in the darkness for the millennium. To one side stood a large building constructed of breeze blocks. Fruit bats poured startlingly from an enormous quercus tree overshadowing the building. Murray-Roberts banged at a metal door.

'This is it.' He had instinctively lowered his voice.

'Although it's illegal.'

'Where is he?'

'Although it's illegal?'

'It's not difficult to buy off a magistrate or two . . . Where is he?'

The metal door opened a fraction. Murray-Roberts said something in Turkic. The door closed again, and then was reopened. They entered.

A beefy man with every indication of being a chucker-out, including the beetling brows, the steroid muscles, the statutory earring in his left ear, bowed to them and held out his right hand. Murray-Roberts deposited folding money – a wad of new-printed manats – in it.

They had entered a large store, lit by flickering tubes of yellow neon. This was a shoddy plastic supermarket of dreamtime, a new Aladdin's cave, rendered claustrophobic by head-high lines of racks

264

dividing the space into narrow aisles, like the runs in a rat maze. Every rack was filled with the multi-coloured plastic cases of e-mnemonicvision bullets. The bullets were arranged into categories and paraded in their thousands, their hundreds of thousands. They contained real memories, however acquired, from men, women, and children of all races and creeds. It would have been possible for an alien visitor from another galaxy, had it sufficient idle curiosity for the task, to patch together, from this shed alone, a history of the multitudinous human race: a history bizarre but possibly not bizarre enough to hold anyone's attention for more than, say, a million years, Earth-time.

Murray-Roberts moved down one of the narrow aisles without hesitation. Burnell followed like a faithful hound.

At the far end of the building, near an emergency exit, was a glass-fronted office, the picture of untidiness. Ranked VDUs exhibited minuscule fragmentary replicas of the whole shop, implying theft was a popular sport here. Perched on a high stool sat a small wizened man in a yellow silk jacket. He climbed stiffly from his stool and greeted Murray-Roberts with courtesy, his Oriental face creasing in a smile of recognition. Murray-Roberts introduced him as Mr Khan.

Mr Khan put aside a cigarette, coughed, and shook Burnell's hand.

Burnell explained his problem. Khan looked sad, and resumed his cigarette. Slowly, he indicated with his left hand, raising it to head level and drawing it through one hundred and eighty degrees, his immense stock. He spoke in hesitant German. Evidently the phrase 'a needle in a haystack' had not occurred to him; but he spoke sorrowfully of the trade in which he engaged merely in order to support a numerous family.

It was, he admitted, not the most honest of trades. To add to all his other problems, e-mnemonicvision had been banned through-out Central Asia because of a high pornographic content. Were the years of memory stolen from Burnell of high pornographic content?

'I'm given to understand,' said Burnell, with a degree of reserve, 'that what was saved from my stolen ten years for the entertainment of voyeurs was, firstly, my academic knowledge, and, secondly, my courtship and marriage.'

Khan nodded. 'High pornographic content.'

He went on to say that memory-theft occurred all over the world, but mainly in a few centres where the technical skill existed; Hong Kong, San Diego, Buenos Aires, London, Budapest, Johannesburg, Djakarta, Copenhagen, etc. 'Mainly the places you would expect.' He intimated that Burnell was fortunate; in inexperienced hands, the actual operation could prove fatal, leading to total amnesia or, in a number of cases, to permanent coma. 'Called PVS,' Mr Khan murmured, turning his eyes apotropaically to the ceiling.

Some of the memories in his store had been legitimately obtained and properly produced. They issued, in the main, from the big EMV studios in Los Angeles, Tokyo, Munich, Paris, Bombay, and Singapore. Many people were ready to sell exceptional periods of their life memories for handsome sums. Thousands of memories, some renowned, represented fragments of real lives, happy, melancholy, crazy. Sad memories – deaths, suicides, maltreated pets and children – had enjoyed a great vogue with voyeurs in West and East a year or two previously.

Many EMV voyeurs drove themselves mad, piling false memory on false memory before the previous ones had faded.

No, he said, he had no facilities here to fix a memory permanently. His was just a store with voy facilities. Any memory you viewed here soon faded, like a headache.

Khan shuffled over to the nearest rack. He gestured towards his stock, pointing here and there, explaining in his accented German. While legitimate bullets were labelled correctly, stolen memories were often deliberately mis-labelled, to foil detection. Stolen memory bullets generally contained a muddle of unedited material from various sources. It was impossible for any voyeur to know whose memory he was experiencing.

Seeing Burnell's expression, Khan raised a knowing finger and conducted him to a side table.

Following instructions from their mutual friend, Dr Haydar, Khan had set to one side six recently acquired EMV bullets from his stock. He showed them to Burnell. Burnell picked them up with reverence. The bullets resembled tubes of acrylic or oil paint, having a blade end and a blunt end. Their cases bore the legend '*Fabriqué en San Marino*'. This, Khan said, meant almost certainly that the bullets originated from an illegal EMV studio in Budapest; it was the studio's way of covering its tracks. The registration number was very likely fake. No, the name of Antonescu meant nothing to him.

'Do you buy for President Diyanizov?' Burnell asked.

Half closing his rheumy eyes, Khan gave him a sidelong glance. '*Mein Herr*, I am merely a poor store-owner. Ask me no such question. "*Die Welt zerfallt in Tatsachen.*" But there are no facts in my store, only illusions.'

'What's he on about?' Murray-Roberts asked.

'Believe it or not, he's quoting Wittgenstein: "The world divides into facts." Rob, I'm going to have to voy these bullets.'

Murray-Roberts scratched his head. 'You're not likely to find your stolen years. You know that? Also, keep the intensity low, take my tip. I've known poor wee buggers who've blown their brains out on EMV.'

Burnell pulled a cheerful face. 'Don't worry. People are always blowing their private lives apart. It's all a matter of lifestyle.'

'Go ahead and good luck. Hope you will find your memory. I can always amuse myself in here.'

His heart beating rapidly, Burnell sorted through the cases. Their titles, in Turkic, German, and English, suggested a slightly tangential acquaintance with at least the latter tongue. 'Animals Sequestered with a Green'. 'Not in My House Ran Any Rivers'. 'In the Hat Warfare Jumper'. Other titles were equally informative.

A row of e-mnemonicvision cubicles stood against one wall. Burnell hurried into the nearest. He seated himself in the chair, adjusting the projector over his head. He switched on according to instructions. A small panel with LCDs lit. He inserted the first bullet into the system unit and touched a couple of keys.

His eyes closed. Almost immediately he lost any clear perception of his surroundings – an instance of how quickly short-term memory could decay. In what felt like the very marrow of his being, electric current stimulated the amacrine cells of his brain. It tickled. Next moment, the synaptic transfer was made, and the memory data digitally stored in the bullet flooded his cortex with mnemons.

The vehicle was bumping across a scrub-filled plain. Every now and then, trees remained, deformed not only from drought. Their lower branches had been hacked away for fuel. The lone occupant of this desolate scene was a heavy bird which scuttled from their path and flew off.

Burnell – or his substitute – was in the cab, driving. His hands were on the wheel, black, sinewy, holding tight as the brown country jarred past. Sitting beside him was another black, wrapped in a worn green cloak. His face was not remembered. Discomfort was remembered: discomfort and the dusty trail through a denuded land.

The interior of the hut was dim. Dry heat and light outside, where the vehicle baked, then shadow as he stepped inside. Its details were too familiar to register. A greeting, a sense of relief, a sip of water. Flies buzzing – the very note of frustration.

The world of memory was not like the real world. Nor was it like a movie shown in cinemas (though movies now tended to imitate the complexity and vagueness/*pointillisme*/sharpness of memory). Nor was it like scenes in novels or in paintings. It was its own art form, more curious than could have been anticipated: often a patchwork of association.

If the impossible were achieved, and Burnell had been able to travel back to the early nineteenth century in his home country – say to the year 1834, when the Houses of Parliament burned down – he would have found it disorienting. He would have understood the speech of the people, but not their underlying assumptions, not many of their concerns. The taste of the food would have been strange. The very sound of musical instruments would be foreign to his ears. The look of everywhere and everything would have presented challenges.

The present knew of the 1830s, just before the invention of the camera, only through old prints and paintings and the raft of the printed word – contemporary and more recent records. The past had become tidied, translated, reinterpreted for a different sensibility. The image of 1834 was familiar enough: the reality would have been vastly more preposterous and alarming. Of memory, the same could be said: the storage system was incomplete and self-editing.

The shock of the old was one of the attractions of e-mnemonicvision. And yet – and yet – who would be naive enough to expect Leonardo Da Vinci's painting of 'The Last Supper' to be an accurate representation of that hasty snack which Jesus took with his disciples? Everything must undergo transformation: and to that process which a human body must submit, human memory must also conform.

So any memory-set, gathered from various stores in the brain, presented startling inexactitudes: lay revelations, mystic hiatuses. Burnell knew he was driving a vehicle across a tropical land and entering a dismal hut. He did not know who he was. Only that he was not Burnell.

He was speaking a tongue unfamiliar to his everyday palate. He approached a woman who crouched by a bed, uttering words of consolation. She did not look up on his arrival. He moved nearer to her, hesitantly, to set a gnarled hand on her shoulder. Vision smudged hand and shoulder within the distortions of a tear.

As she did, he too looked down at an emaciated child lying on a blanket. The blanket was red, black, mustard-yellow, and soiled. The child, a boy, was dead. He knew it had died of a variety of ills, mainly pneumonia, brought about by near-starvation. He had come from a township as fast as he could.

The boy's lips were drawn back, revealing pallid gums in a horrifying grimace. The teeth looked too large for the shrunken face. Ex-Burnell reached out and closed with his dark hand pale mouth and eyes. At this, the woman rose to her feet. She began to shriek, beating her head with clenched fists to allay mental pain with physical. She was wrapped in a material of bold design: strong blue flowers bursting from among green leaves. The flowers covered her from neck to ankle. Her broad handsome face was distorted with grief.

269

Feeling his own weakness, Burnell stooped, tenderly lifting the dead child from the bed. He looked about him, uncertain whether or not a third party was with them in the hut. Flies kept up a menacing note. The boy's body was appallingly light. Probably Burnell was the father of the weeping woman; probably she was the mother of the boy. Thought entered the captive memory or faded, like an uncertain radio signal. He had other people in mind, dark, concerned, slow-moving, some driving cattle before them.

Slow-moving himself, he carried the boy from the hut into the eye of the sun. The veldt, the rough track, a dozen more huts, his vehicle – nothing else. The woman remained behind in the hut, standing against a wall, letting her grief pour from her. The blue flowers on her dress were drooping, drooping.

The sun at zenith laid its weight on his shoulders. The world appeared dung-coloured. Other people were arriving, all of them thin, the women thin as rakes, some carrying children, walking as if against a fog. Although they spoke the incomprehensible language, yet Burnell understood it, and replied. Each laid hands on his shoulders, where the deep hollows were, and on his face. Grief was shared by all means of communication in their power.

All suffered alike. Sense of community was strong.

He settled himself down under a dying tree – little more than its whiskered trunk remained, and one lopsided branch – easing himself down, still clutching the dead boy. Cross-legged in the stick of shade, he wrapped the body in the rug, hugged it, rocked it, cried for it and the promise of life which had fled. Other old men squatted by him, prodding grey fingers abstractedly in the dust.

Burnell said to them, 'We have not long before we follow the dear lad . . .'

Heat dried the tears as fast as they formed.

A last leaf fell from the one branch remaining above him. It floated down, to settle on the forehead of the dead boy. All the world was lost in contemplation of the leaf, as if it was a miraculous sign.

It settled green on the wrinkled grey forehead. It turned yellow as he stared, altering its living form as it did so. Within minutes, it had withered and turned brown. It became nothing, and blew away on the lightest breeze. The cheek too was beginning to wither . . .

'It's not my child, not mine . . .' He was still speaking in the strange tongue even as the machine switched off.

Sitting up in the plastic chair, Burnell focused on the scene round him. He was imprisoned in his glass booth; in the neighbouring booth he saw Murray-Roberts, eyes closed as he lay back in his EMV chair. The store was still there, its shelves packed with imprisoned memories. He pushed up the headset and went to walk about, the sense of bereavement still heavy on him. He leaned against a fixture and took a snort of slap up both nostrils.

Khan grinned at him, waving a lighted cigarette in friendly greeting. Burnell managed a feeble response.

He paced up and down, arms folded across his chest. Almost as if the bullet continued to unravel in his head, he imagined the old black man, whom he had briefly been, going to the nearest city, Harare or wherever it might be, to sell his memories to raise cash. The EMV agent would have paid him almost nothing. Perhaps a dollar or two would be forthcoming for him to give to the mother of the dead boy.

And the old man, being made free of all memory, would no longer carry a burden of grief. Wasn't that the most immoral aspect of e-mnemonicvision?

If I had my memory of Stephanie back, thought Burnell, would I not be retrieving an old grief of which at present I know nothing?

Yet he forced himself back into the booth, to go on seeking through the illegal bullets, '*Fabriqué en San Marino*'. He tried the next one. It contained four sequences of memory from different sources, some longer than others, all less harrowing than the previous scene of death.

He lived through a six-day voyage over a great reef, where he scuba-dived. The voyage ended with a huge party on a small island. Here he took part in a moonlit orgy.

Then he was a witless brute of a man, living in an apartment in a bleak township where snow lay thick. Among horrendous drunken bouts and fights came an exhilarating drive over tundra to shoot reindeer. In the dim mind was no compassion for the slaughtered beauties sprawling dead in the snow.

He was a woman, successful and high-spirited. She ran a popular clothing store in a Patagonian town, with occasional buying and partying sprees in Buenos Aires. Her cherished memory was of winning a prize in a downtown dance hall, which brought her an interview on an evening television programme.

He spent a tense but uneventful week in a small picturesque village in the Alps, where a married couple lived in fear of their mentally deficient son. The couple once discussed selling their memories to EMV in order to raise money to send the son to a good safe institution.

While they lasted, these memory episodes were as real to Burnell as memories of his own life. They filled his brain. He came out of them exhausted. In some of the episodes, he had gained a clear picture of what he looked like; the cheerful Patagonian lady spent many minutes every day scrutinizing herself in the mirror; in other episodes, he knew little of resemblances – the drunken reindeer-hunter saw no one clearly. Lying in the plastic chair, he wondered about the rigours of human existence, and about the people he had been. The wish was strong to learn what had happened to them after their memory had been stolen, for he briefly knew them better than he knew his friends.

Yet their joys, their sorrows, their unresolved problems, grew faint fairly quickly; no transference was made in Khan's EMV projector from short-term to long-term memory. Already the poor old man with his dead grandson was beginning to sink from mind. Only a falling leaf of sadness remained.

Burnell turned to the next bullet, labelled 'Shirts in a Cupboard of Linen'. At the touch of the Go button he was transformed.

He was aware of his new mnemonic person as little more than a pair of boots, a hard body, a pair of arms with sleeves rolled up. In one of his hands he was clutching a sickle. Heat made his arms glisten with sweat. He felt himself to be young and lusty as he inhaled the warmth of an early summer afternoon. It was England, and the cuckoo called distantly across the fields. Peace was like the flavour of fresh-picked mint in his mind. His sickle moved in practised sweeps. He was cutting down cow parsley and goose-grass.

Whoever he was, he worked his way along steadily, avoiding some camellias which had finished flowering. His curved blade whispered its way through the severing stalks. Every now and again, straightening his back, he caught glimpses of the garden and a smoothly mowed lawn. Of the house, only a peak of roof was visible.

He saw a woman walking beside an ornamental pool, tall and fair. Tantalizingly, her back was to him. When he wiped the sweat from his brow, she was gone. He bent his back and continued with the work, enjoying the rhythms of it, the swing of his strong right arm.

The strip of bank was finished. He raked into a heap what had fallen and wiped the sickle blade on his jeans before laying it on an oak bench. By now, the mild sun was lower, slanting towards an avenue of lime trees, and the day at its most perfect. He walked slowly across a courtyard cut diagonally by shadow and into the house by a rear door.

Sunlight soaking his retina painted the interior in reds and greens until his vision cleared, as he climbed a narrow back stair. It was dark on the stairway and on the upper landing which led to a bathroom. The framed and glazed pictures on the passage wall yielded only reflections, not the prints themselves but ghosts of light, back-gleams of distant doors and windows.

The small bathroom was wood-panelled, its panels painted white, with tiles above the basin. Yellow soap lay by the chrome taps. Tree tops were visible through the small high window. He pulled off his damp shirt and washed his face and torso, drying them on a thick blue towel.

In so doing, he caught a glimpse of his face in the mirror to one side of the basin. Sharp-featured, red-faced, fair – was it fair? – hair.

Leaving the shirt on the floor, he trod over it and went across to an airing-cupboard to find a clean one. Opening the door, he was met by a crisp fresh smell as of newly baked biscuits.

Inside the cupboard, neatly laundered and set on shelves, clothes lay in immaculate array. Ironed sheets were stored on a low shelf, with duvet covers on a shelf above. Shirts hung on a rack in orderly fashion. There were piles of clean handkerchiefs and stocks of women's garments. Dresses hung crisp and creaseless.

Burnell reached forward towards the shirts and –

– without pause was running down the right wing of a football pitch with the ball at his feet. Green field, blur of crowd in a stadium. Cheering. The Italian Luigi Raniero, charging towards him. The roar of spectators went unheeded in his heightened state. In his determination, he knew nothing would stop him. He swerved in the split second Raniero was at him, tapping the ball neatly round to the left of his opponent's boots, instantly recapturing it. Ahead lay the goalmouth and –

He squeezed the Off button on the zapper he held in his fist. The memory died. He was back in his chair, gasping with shock. Bootleg memory bullets often switched in this fashion from one fragment to another fragment, completely unrelated. The bullets contained no credits or fade-ins, no editorial matter. Most – like this one – were not edited at all. In a composite bullet, snatches of various memories were thrown together, often lopped from longer memory sequences.

Leaning back, shutting his eyes, Burnell let his pulse rate sink to a more normal level. Damn the footballer! He concentrated his thought on the earlier episode. Had he stumbled on a fragment of his own memory or not? Had he once been the young man with the sickle in the pleasant garden? Had that been his more youthful face glimpsed in the mirror?

How to be certain? Although he believed for an instant he had caught a moment of his own past life, he recognized how greatly that belief was prompted by hope. The mystery of the EMV medium was how often vital things – like personal identity – failed to come through; personal identity was so integral it took second place to such matters as the sweep of the sickle, the details of the bathroom. Memory – it was an old saying – 'played strange tricks'.

And. A trivial hour in a summer's afternoon . . . the passage of possibly nine or ten years . . . youth's happy habit of inattention . . .

Who was the woman? Whose the house?

His shrink in the Frankfurt institution had told him that one fragment of retrieved memory, implanted in the brain, could reanimate others. Awakened dialogue between hippocampus and cortex was such that messages would leap synapses and propagate adjacent neurons, until what was lost would be recovered, to a limited extent.

What the shrink had not touched on was the question now facing Burnell. Where did memory shade into imagination? The Budapest theft had left him as disadvantaged as an old man, unsure whether what came to mind was what he thought he remembered or what he remembered he thought.

In the early days of his association with Stephanie, he had – hadn't he? – bought a derelict country house, with the aid of a loan from his father. She and he – hadn't they? – had worked on restoring the place. As rooms and lawns were re-created, and the light let in, they had been wildly happy – hadn't they? But – had those rooms, those lawns, been the ones he experienced in 'Shirts in a Cupboard of Linen'?

He had felt no undeniable stab of recognition. The fragment, visually lucid, proved unclear. Perhaps the past was always unclear, crumbling even as it travelled through the processing plant of the present.

He had managed no close look at the woman walking by the ornamental fish pool. But the courtyard, the side of the building, the house itself, the stairs, the upper landing, the bathroom . . . They had not seemed distinctive, were indeed common to thousands of English homes. The identical brand of yellow soap reposed in identical basins in thousands of houses. And of course the original owner of the memory had taken no specific notice of that with which he was already familiar.

But the airing-cupboard. The owner of the memory had

looked into the cupboard merely to find a clean shirt. Its orderliness he had taken for granted.

What lingered with Burnell was that orderliness.

Supposing he had come on a fragment of his own memory, had just seen himself, had almost been himself, as he was possibly five or six years earlier. Then the woman by the pool could have been – most likely was – Stephanie, that dear young tender Stephanie when they were first in love, when magic still enfolded their relationship, when one emblem of their love had been the resurrection of a mansion and the flinging open of its windows. The time of enchantment.

If all that were so, then the orderliness of the airing-cupboard might provide a clue as to why they had parted. Perhaps Stephanie had found him too untidy in his habits. Perhaps he had found her too pernickety . . . . How trivial such shortcomings seemed in retrospect, viewed from a shabby plastic chair in Central Asia. This was where his questing nature, and a blindness to domestic virtues, had brought him.

That small room, just large enough to walk into, was almost a secret compartment. It was part of Stephanie's domain in the old house, remaining in darkness for most of the time. Stephanie stocked it with the clothes she had washed and ironed, no one but Stephanie. Not so much as a sock there but knew her caring touch.

And had he for some reason thrown it all away?

His shoulder was being shaken. Murray-Roberts was saying, 'Wake up, old stick.'

18
The Friendship Bridge

On the following morning, a member of the Hotel Ashkhabad's staff pushed a letter under the door of Burnell's room. It arrived in a blue envelope with a Spanish stamp on it.

Burnell stared at it from his bed, eyes half open. It was without meaning. His dreams as usual had been bad. He rose shakily and went into the shower.

As the chlorinated water trickled over him, he thought of the EMV bullet he had bought expensively from Mr Khan. He still could not decide whether or not he had actually stumbled across a fragment of his own memory. Back in Frankfurt, he could have an expert reinsert it into his brain and lock it into the declarative memory. In that way, he would reclaim at least something of what had passed.

Uncertainty held him back. An ascetic side to his nature disdained the idea of having false memories inserted, as many people did, to supplement their impoverished lives with transplants of other days they had never experienced.

He lived out of his suitcase. Samsonite was his home. His clothes, both laundered and soiled, lay about in the room. Forgetting to lock his case when leaving the hotel on the previous day, he had left papers and books strewn everywhere. A half-eaten melon attracted small dung-coloured flies on the window sill. His alarm clock lay face down on the bed. As he sought about for a clean shirt, he perceived the general disorder. So this was the kind of man he was . . .

His mind returned obsessively to his ex-wife. Perhaps the clue to the break between them lay within that glimpsed airing-cupboard, among those sweet-smelling ledges. In that hot little closet of hers, where all was stowed neatly away, awaiting inspection, the tidiness of her mind was revealed. Everything ready to wear, pristine, tended . . . Had he tended their relationship? Surely he had been tender. Perhaps his mind had been too much on his career. He could not believe he had been unfaithful to her.

'Stephanie.' He spoke her name aloud, trying it out on his lips. The airing-cupboard served as a revelation. Yet he could in no way be certain it had ever been theirs. All that had been theirs had been stolen.

Again he found himself up against the brick wall of a question: how does a man manage to get through his life? What is there that helps him to swim through a sea of circumstance? He had been the first-born of his parents; traditional wisdom had it that first-borns always made the most difficult passage through life.

Half clothed, he went over to the door and picked up the Spanish letter. Without thought, he ripped open the blue envelope.

Roy,

Will this reach you? Have I ever entrusted a letter to the mails of Tartary before? And other enthralling questions.

Most enthralling of all, how is my unremembering lover faring? I imagine you searching for samovars in Samarkand and suchlike.

I'm just back in Madrid from the mountains, having persuaded our WACH Director – not the most lovable of women – to part-finance the dig progressing in the Sierra de la Demanda. This project is so important, worth sacrificing just one mouldering baroque church for. They're building a new road up to San Pineda as more experts are called to the site. And – this is the hot news – a pictograph has been found on one of the rocks. Well, we now know it to be a painting though it much resembles a big squashed insect. Imagine! The earliest ever representation of a human. We're getting in experts in AMS radiocarbon dating who will give an exact date. That will take a while.

When I visited, I was permitted to enter the inner part of the cave. Imagine a vaginal passage opening into a womb – as you easily can! That's how it is, narrow then opening out. You crawl over plastic matting, laid over the deep rotting vegetation.

They keep the lights dim as possible. It's difficult working conditions. There lie the skeletons. Yes, plural. A second skeleton is being uncovered. Maybe complete. How about that? Which is more astonishing, the bones or the pictograph?

Of course the archaeologists and the rest have good living accommodations, but I slept under the stars for two nights. The proximity of alien galaxies and those alien creatures lying reposefully (is that an English word? – French *reposant*) only metres away was enlightening and elevating to the mind.

Your friend Stalinbrass is still wrecking the Crimea. We have a report his forces have partially destroyed the Livadia Palace, where once the Romanovs gloried and drank deep. *Eheu!*

When you are done with those samovars, please come and visit. You would also love the mountains. We can learn together some prehistory – and much else besides. I love you so I quote Valéry to you, '*Le temps scintille et le songe est savoir . . .*'

I'm so impatient to know so much,
    Blanche

Sighing, Burnell folded the letter, slid it back into its envelope, and put it in his suitcase. Blanche's presence returned to him with great clarity, and the sound of her voice, and the concerned look on her face when she had visited him in the FAM institution. Her physicality and her intellect were things to cherish – but – but to consider another emotional involvement was beyond him just at present. The airing-cupboard held more revelation than the cave.

But Blanche's letter served to remind him that his official work in Ashkhabad was over. He would test out the remainder of Mr

Khan's Budapest EMV bullets and then get back to the West. Suddenly, the mere phrase 'the West', glowed with promise. After he and Haydar had visited the Friendship Bridge, he would phone through to the airport – no mean feat in itself, he was aware – and book a flight via Istanbul for home.

He went back to the bed, sat on it, and took a snort of his favourite reviver. Then he reread Blanche's letter.

Dr Haydar was to have arrived with his brother's car at noon. It was after three when he strolled into the hotel. When Burnell asked him what had delayed him, Haydar said merely that the car would not start – 'but the bridge will wait for us'.

It was hot in the car, even with the air-conditioning working. Yesterday the transport had been small and green. Today, Haydar drove an imposing black Russian Chaika, an up-to-date model. When Burnell commented on this, Haydar said merely, 'I borrow it from another of my brothers. This one a rich brother-in-law.' The vehicle gave a noisy ride. Silence fell between the two men.

'Is not too many miles into the desert,' Haydar said, reassuringly, as Burnell mopped under his collar. He was himself dressed in a beige linen suit, under which was a matching shirt and – incongruously, it seemed – a tie. To top up the image of prosperity, Haydar wore a red carnation in his buttonhole. His ample body loomed over the steering-wheel. The car snorted on its way.

They came to the roundabout where, on the previous day, Ali Orazov had been setting up a road block. Today, the place was deserted, the road ahead empty. A family of beggars sat under one of a line of wingnut trees. A wind was blowing, whipping leaves from the trees where ragged children played.

'Soon the weather changes,' said Haydar. 'My wife has a family saying, "Better the wind to blow in the air; if it blew under the ground, the dead would refuse to be buried."'

The asphalt gave out. They were travelling over a dirt road with open country ahead. The city lay behind them under a tattered amber smog. Dust, the droppings of the desert, stirred about their wheels. Mountains became visible, their crusty ridges a blue outline in a slatey black sky. It was as if they delineated a country without material substance.

'Iran,' said Haydar. He changed gear as they headed downhill. 'Where the dead refuse to be buried . . .' He gave a curt laugh.

The River Garakhs was shallow, fast, and icy. It flowed between sandy banks, racing to escape from the desert. Burnell and Haydar stood looking at it, heads full of the kind of non-thoughts rivers evoke.

For a short distance, this insignificant river acquired importance, as it marked a division between two distinct worlds: Turkmenistan to the north, Iran to the south. Here, for over half the previous century, the great iron world of the Soviet Union had expired and the more enduring world of the mosque commenced. Here, God, Marx and Lenin had surrendered in the face of the mountains and minarets of Muhammad.

The main barrier between these worlds was the extended fortress of the Kopet Dagh mountain range, which ran for many kilometres in either direction. The monotonous flanks of the range loomed on the far side of the Garakhs, extending as distantly as eye could see, eroded, practically treeless, without habitation.

On the Iranian side of the river, a settlement of mud-coloured huts had established itself. A road led back from this settlement into the mountains, towards a pass, somewhere beyond which lay distant Teheran. Nothing moved on the far bank. The sky above the pass was black.

On the northern side of the Garakhs, Turkmenistan presented no more enlivening a spectacle. The land was desert. As soon as they had left the capital, habitation petered out. It was as a hotel porter had told Burnell, in tones of contempt: Ashkhabad was thoroughly modern – beyond it, in the country, all was as it had ever been.

Burnell took in the desolation with interest, letting the wind whip his hair.

At one point on the way they had sighted derricks, where a Japanese oil company was prospecting. Once, by the roadside, they had passed a cluster of *yurts*, weather-beaten tents by which

Akhal-tekke horses were tethered. And, only a few miles from their destination, Burnell had watched a group of people trudging along beside loaded camels and mules – an archaic frieze soon left behind in the dust. Dust was an increasing problem as the wind fretted the land.

The road from Ashkhabad, potholes and all, gave out as it reached the River Garakhs. There stood Friendship Bridge.

'In the spring, after the seasonal rain, flowers come,' said Dr Haydar, with a majestic sweep of his hand. 'Then wild tulips are blooming here, plenteously. All the land is a patchwork of flowers, very colourful.' He leaned back against the bonnet of the Chaika, drumming with thick fingers on the enamel. 'I remember it being so. Now – nothing; for the cold winter comes. You can feel it in the wind, undeniably.'

Together, they walked towards the bridge.

The Friendship Bridge was unfinished. Indeed, scarcely begun.

The stub of it resembled some great failed animal from an earlier epoch of Earth's history. It stuck its snout out a short way over the flood, blindly quizzing the Iranian shore.

Its design was primitive. It had been constructed much as a child's bridge might be constructed from wooden blocks. One stump of supporting pillar stood on the bank, a second in the river. Nothing more of it had been built. Over the stumps had been laid intimations of road in giant concrete slabs: an embryo road, no more than nine metres of it, already crumbling, the snout of the monster in decay.

Burnell walked below the land end of the bridge. It jutted some metres above him, dislocated from the road below, with reinforcing rods trailing wormlike from the body of concrete. He struggled with the anger filling him. He saw no purpose in their visiting this abortive hulk of masonry. It had certainly not been worth two hours of travel over a bumpy road.

'Let's get back to town, Dr Haydar. I have things I wish to do.'

'Yes, yes, immediately. I see it's not to your English taste. But first we must climb up on to the bridge. Then you will understand better, surely.'

He led the way, heaving himself up an iron ladder, the rungs of which were stapled into the near pillar. For a large man he was very agile. Burnell felt obliged to follow. It was possible to swing up, grasp a girder, and heave oneself on to the flat part of the bridge. Clouds of dust met them. Lizards scuttled into hiding.

They stood together, some metres above the ground. The height made them more aware of the wind. Shielding his eyes with a hand, Burnell said, 'Look, we'd better be getting back.'

A withered orange of sun cast gloom over the land. Temperatures were falling. It looked and felt like the end of the world.

Haydar, however, was jaunty. 'I know there are things in your mind, Dr Burnell. We all of us have them. Once we are past our youth, all men have things in their minds. For women it is different, possibly. But we do not know what women think.' Walking to the end of the concrete structure, he gazed down into the grey waters below. Wind whipped open his jacket. His tie fluttered over one shoulder.

'This bridge is called Friendship Bridge for some obvious reasons. The Turkmeni say for a joke the name is because, like friendship, it should never have been started but now will never finish . . . Huh. Not too humorous for your English taste, eh?'

'I've lost my sense of humour . . . It'll be dark in another hour.'

'The founding stone of the bridge was laid by the late President of Turkmenistan, the predecessor of Diyanizov. He was a devout Sunni Muslim, an ayatollah. But the war swept him out of power. He died of a disease soon afterwards, as people do when swept from power. When the war with Uzbekistan started, President Diyanizov ordered work here to stop.

'Of course it will never be resumed. We no longer wish to be so friendly to Iran since their recent changes in Teheran. Some here recall an old Goklani saying, "Iranian ponies have only three and a half legs".'

Some of his words were lost in the wind. Burnell turned his back on the gale. He spoke formally. 'Dr Haydar, a storm is brewing. Best to get back to Ashkhabad.'

Haydar's large face was powdered with dust. He shook his head sadly, disappointed at Burnell's lack of perception. Turning his back to Iran and the river, he clutched his lapels preparatory to making a speech.

'I think we are friends, although I know Mr Murray-Roberts is not my friend. Or his excellent wife. So I do not bring you to this remote spot for an idle amusement. This place is what you must carry back with you in memory to England. The bridge is not a bridge but a memorial, you see. So it stands in my mind. I could say, it stands even for a victory for the West!' He tapped his broad forehead with the heel of his palm while speaking, for added solemnity.

'Yes, a monument to the magnetic attraction of Western culture. That magnetism felt even in this poor tragic country, where no copy of *The Hand of Ethelberta* is to be had, for money or love.' Smiling to himself, perhaps in irony, he stared down at the pattern of wooden planking embedded like fossil imprints in the slab of road.

'When the Soviet Union fell apart, many men wished to embrace Islam, but the pull of the West was even stronger. Happily, some men want not to abase towards Mecca five times in every day . . .'

A battery of winds sprang up. Stinging sands were dashed against their faces and they were blown some way across the bridge. They crouched for shelter under a low parapet while the wind roared overhead.

'When it is stopped, then we go back to my brother's car,' Haydar said, his face close to Burnell's. 'These storms do not last a long time.'

'It was madness to come out here with the weather changing.'

Haydar laughed. 'And maybe we are both mad to leave our own countries. Few will do it. To escape memories or to find them. *Que sera sera*, isn't that what Italians say? You must try to appreciate what has befallen in this place, at a crucial moment in history, why I bring you here.

'When Soviet Union collapsed, was a great day all over the world. Of course, for the Muslim republics, some difficulties came. Turkmenistan needs to trade, and trade became disrupted.

But, frontiers were open, suddenly. Never before had they been open, except for some very old people. Freedom! – A strange word. Who among us is really free?

'So. On that day of first freedom, a procession of ordinary people came here from Ashkhabad. My wife was among them, with some of her friends. They came along the road we have taken, to this very point, to look across at Iran. In previous times, you see, the frontier was forbidden – I mean, with patrols, who could shoot people who tried to cross it. And yet, in Iran, many people had relations.'

From his crouched position, resting an elbow on the concrete, he imitated the action of someone firing a rifle.

'It was a wonderful occasion on that day. You can imagine. Across the other side of the Garakhs, there appeared Iranian people. They came out from the mountains. They cheered to this side. This side cheered to them. Can you imagine? On that day were two thousand Turkmeni here, of all tribes, and maybe two hundred Irani over there. After all, same families are on both sides of the frontier. They were divided long since by that monster among men, Josef Stalin.

'Prayers were said in rejoicing. Some of the youths from Ashkhabad, they strip off their clothes and swim across the river at this point. One young boy, no more than ten, he drowns and no one sees it till is too late. Otherwise, is all rejoicing. You can imagine. The people embrace, each to each, warmly. It was an occasion for many tears, Dr Burnell, tears and kisses. Here, my wife stood. She waved to an older sister across the river. You can imagine.'

He fell silent, letting the sand scour their ears. The lizards had disappeared, taking shelter in the cracks of the stonework.

'One man among the Iranians brought a – loud-shouter? Yes, a loud-hailer. He calls out to this side some news. He calls names, telephone numbers, radio wavelengths. Names of lost relations are called across this very river on that day. Many people cried, cried because lives were so broken. You can imagine.

'All that is spoken on each bank is – what do you call it? – reconciling words, quite private. No words of politics, because the

285

people who came here were poor. No great ones with political interests, *nein*?'

As he talked on, Burnell saw how deeply mixed the feelings of the man were towards the country which was now his home. Did he hate or love Ashkhabad? Perhaps he would be unable to say.

'The poor people congregated on both sides of the river, rejoicing. They stayed till the sun set. The date was the Thirteenth of Azar by the Muslim calendar.

'At dusk, the young men swam back to this bank here. Some carried gifts from the Iranians, such as prayer beads and sweet-meats. The newspapers described the day as a day of seething emotions. There came demands that a bridge should be built to link the two countries, so that Muslim could speak to Muslim. A bridge of friendship!

'So such a bridge was begun at last, under the old ayatollah president. What a fuss was made. Then some clever person observed that the Iranians did not build a road towards the bridge on their side, unfortunately. Instead, they became busy waging a war with the Muslims in their other neighbour, Iraq.

'At that time, too, Turkmenistan had trouble with guerrillas invading from Afghanistan. So work on the bridge ceased. After the war with Uzbekistan, the new president came in. That's Diyanizov, born in the same street as the old president, of the same Tekke tribe, but now looking towards the West, and for instance inviting in your World Cultural Heritage.'

'And Western pornography,' said Burnell with feeling.

'He has a wife from Argentina, don't forget. So Diyanizov declared that the bridge was a political mistake. That is why I rejoice. I rejoice it's never to be completed. The bridges to be built must not be southwards to Islam, or that means looking to the past. Instead, they must be built to the westwards – to Turkey and Hungary and Paris and England, where sin is more of a pri-vate thing and where judges are not *mullahs*. A look to the future.'

To emphasize his meaning, he patted Burnell on the shoulder as if he were an old dog. They still crouched under the parapet, and the wind still blew. The sky grew darker. As he rambled on, his voice was sometimes drowned by the roar and whistle of the wind as it burst among the interstices of the bridge.

This monstrous song of nature caused Burnell's thoughts to wander. Gloom filled him. The bridge to him represented no great cause for rejoicing. He saw it as one more blighted crop in the tangled field of human relationships. To accept the bridge as a stone metaphor for his own present situation was beyond his conscious compass. But it bore down mutely on his awareness.

In his work, he was accustomed to monuments that endured, structures whose venerable and refined qualities inspired reverence. This abortion of a bridge inspired only disgust. He could never rejoice in it, as he did in the buildings it was his duty to catalogue.

Because there was melancholy as well as honour in his duties, his favourite reading had long included Edward Gibbon's *Decline and Fall of the Roman Empire*. Able to recite whole passages of the old unbeliever by heart, particularly when slightly drunk, Burnell recalled now, crouching against the concrete, Gibbon's reflections on transience. 'The art of man is able to construct', Gibbon had said, 'monuments far more permanent than the narrow span of his own existence: yet these monuments, like himself, are perishable and frail; and in the boundless annals of time his life and his labours must equally be measured as a fleeting moment.'

And if that labour should be to stock, without fuss, an airing-cupboard with fresh sweet clothes . . . It was important, surely, to remember that monument to a past love. Even if it was not his . . .

Nothing of this could be explained to another person. Not to Haydar. Perhaps to Blanche.

He saw his own life as no more than a worm cast in a vast tract of history. And his family? His grandfather had lived through the dissolution, peaceful on the whole – as on the whole the institution had been – of the British Empire. His father had lived through the collapse of the Communist Empire. He was himself passing his life in the years following those momentous events, during the expansionist phase of the EU superstate.

The Turkmeni were seeking a political stability which so far eluded them and their neighbours. No models of stable government existed in their past from which they might gain strength:

there were instead memories of oppression, massive abuses of morality (and agriculture), and, more distantly, the legend of that Golden Horde which had once laid waste in its path all the cities of Asia. In fact, the Friendship Bridge represented an aborted hope, a hand stretched towards the outside world, but not stretched far enough.

He sensed something of the complexity of emotions Dr Haydar felt, whose wife's sister must remain on the other side of the torrent. That was part of an historical necessity.

And how had he, Roy Burnell, come here? Certainly, he had managed to obtain no introduction to President Diyanizov from the authorities in Frankfurt or London. Fearful of the paid assassin, Diyanizov saw no visitors. Had Burnell ever really hoped that he might retrieve that vital missing part of his memory? Or had he already come across a fragment of it in Mr Khan's emporium, and found it inconclusive?

Burnell had drifted because he was, essentially, a drifter. Despite the best of educations, he had refused to join the family's various business enterprises. He had dedicated himself to . . . Well, dedication was hardly a word he cared to apply to himself.

Tarquin Burnell, his father, was now confined to a motorized chair. An old embittered man who trundled slowly about his estate, bullying gardeners, harassing his second wife. Soon he would inevitably pass away. The estate would be broken up. And the avenue of lime trees planted by his grandfather . . .? Already Burnell could feel latent regret, awaiting the release of his father's death.

His father had liked, had loved, Stephanie. Of course Burnell had no more chance of getting her back than there was of standing and demanding, successfully, that the sandstorm cease.

Those vital scenes remained to be retrieved, to be reinstated in his memory. He needed better evidence than a cupboard full of shirts he failed to recognize. Oh, Stephanie, how did our relationship go so badly wrong? You were the most precious thing in my life. Had there been someone more precious to you than I? If only I knew, if only I could remember . . .

But would things then be different? Could he rectify a past

fault? Could that broken bridge ever be reconstructed to cross the chilly river of separation?

Tears filled his eyes, to be instantly dried by the heat.

He felt his own identity fading into the abrasive world about him. Never was it more clear to him why, and how fatally, he clung to the memorials of the past. And the time would come, not today, perhaps not tomorrow, when he would join the dead, and the broken estates, when he would succumb to the same processes of mutability which had transformed the bridge from design to ruin. Yes, the time would come.

Well, it was no great matter . . .

The sand was gathering about the two figures, who crouched as if imploring Allah for his mercy. It lay thickly drifted under the parapet.

Roy Burnell yielded up his thoughts to let the sand take over. He heard it howling through Turkmenistan, through the universe, covering everything, the living and the dead.

19

A Toe and a Tow

'The headlights work well,' Dr Haydar called.

Burnell made no reply. He sat on a block of stone by the unfinished bridge, deliberately not watching Haydar's ineffectual attempts to start his brother-in-law's car. Though Haydar and the recalcitrant vehicle were only a few metres away, he could scarcely see them through the advancing gloom.

The sandstorm had died. It left behind disgruntled noises of thunder muttering in the Iranian range. The vast bleak theology of landscape about them was working up to a sermon on the Ultimate Darkness. It suited Burnell's mood that grains of sand had penetrated the carburettor, or jammed the fanbelt, or clogged up the air intake, or whichever of a line of explanations Haydar offered up to the desert to explain why the car had – definitively, it seemed – broken down. Had he now started the engine, disappointment would have been Burnell's main response. He nursed a perverse wish that things would become worse.

So he sat or crouched uncomfortably, awaiting fresh admissions of incompetence and humiliation.

Haydar stopped struggling. He had the bonnet of the Chaika propped up, and leaned exhaustedly over the engine, gasping. His carnation had wilted in his buttonhole and he tossed it away. He had already ripped off his tie and stuffed it in his jacket pocket.

At last, in a mild voice, he said, 'Speak, please, my friend.'

'"Here one can neither stand nor lie nor sit
There is not even silence in the mountains
But dry sterile thunder without rain . . ."'

'Yes, yes, I hear it. But what shall we do, my friend? I cannot make my brother's car to go.'

'Brother-in-law, you said. Then we stay here or we walk back to the city. I cannot think of a third alternative. I don't imagine we can swim back.'

Closing down the bonnet, Haydar went and sat in the car, turning off its lights. Burnell crouched where he was, listening to the thunder and the repetitive noise of the river.

Many minutes passed. Haydar came over and stood by Burnell. 'I am sorry for this difficulty, my friend. Perhaps you are annoyed. If you will push the car, I will throw in the gear and then she may start up.'

'Where can we push it? I can't push it through the sand.'

'No, no. We push her downhill towards the river bank.'

Burnell wearily agreed to give it a try. Between them, they managed to turn the car in the right direction. Between them, they persuaded it to roll. When Haydar jumped into the driving-seat, Burnell, with an effort, heels digging into the sand, kept it moving.

As it met the incline, the black Chaika gathered momentum. Burnell shouted, Haydar threw the car into third gear. The engine spluttered and caught.

'Look out!' yelled Burnell as the car surged forward. It had suddenly remembered the excitements of power. Haydar shouted too. But the car rushed down the bank, bounced, and plunged its nose into the River Garakhs. The engine died with scarcely a bubble of protest.

The phrase 'Now you've done it' sprang to Burnell's mind; he wondered if he had ever used it, perhaps in those stolen years. Conquering the impulse to use it now, he said coldly, 'We shall have difficulty in pushing your brother-in-law's car out of there.'

Climbing from the driving-seat, Haydar had to wade up to his knees to get ashore.

'The brake failed.'

This was said rather as an aside, an excuse he knew would never work. Standing looking helplessly at Burnell, he said, 'My brother will be distressed.' He then smote his forehead with moderate force.

'Brother-in-law.'

It seemed best to Burnell to show his anger by saying nothing more; he husbanded his resources in case Haydar said something like, You pushed too hard. Haydar, however, was perfectly resigned to the situation. He declared they must wait by the bridge for the night. Someone would be by in the morning to help them, undoubtedly. And he had in the back of the car a picnic, which meant they could eat. Also rugs, under which they could sleep. 'No "flight powder"?' asked Burnell, using the term Haydar had used for the drug which had proved so effective a day or two earlier. 'Now? In our hour of need?'

'I have some. But it is better not to take it. We must stay alert in case robbers chance to come on us during the night.'

'Is that at all likely?'

'Iranians may be only a hundred metres away.'

There was nothing for it but to accept the inevitable. Since the picnic and the rugs were above the waterline, they were easily retrieved from the back seat of the car. The men sat with their spines against the blocks of the Friendship Bridge and ate. Haydar unwrapped cold kebabs, pitta bread, and a peppery sausage, together with apricots and persimmons. He also produced a flask of hot Russian tea. They ate by torchlight, in silence, engulfed by the warm dark.

'If the wind blew underground, the dead would refuse to be buried,' said Burnell.

They both laughed.

Thunder still rumbled across the river. Phantasmal sheet lightning occasionally revealed a distant hump of mountain. A night bird called, with a cry that seemed to say, 'Everyone's gone. Everyone's gone.' The thought of the sparrow that used to call 'Richard' came to Burnell's mind, making him feel sad on its behalf.

When they settled down to sleep in the sand and gravel in the shelter of the bridge, Haydar said, 'I feel much to blame for your discomfort.'

'It's pleasant to sleep outside occasionally.'

He lay under his rug, looking up at the stars, thinking of Blanche, lovely Blanche, under the Spanish stars. Close to her, according to her letter, had been the two pre-human skeletons. Perhaps that was safer than sleeping near Dr Haydar: Burnell was beginning to regret he had not heeded a phone call from Murray-Roberts early in the day, announcing that the British Ambassador had returned to Ashkhabad, and it was time Burnell stopped associating with Haydar, who was heavily into an unspecified crime.

With such uncomfortable thoughts, he fell asleep.

He slept for two hours when a pain in his right foot roused him. One moment he was asleep, the next in mortal straits. He sat up suddenly and began to shriek with agony. When settling himself down under the blanket, he had kicked off his shoes and socks for comfort. His immediate thought was that a snake had bitten him. His cries roused Haydar, who lumbered over and shone his torch. An angry red spot had formed on Burnell's big toe.

Exclaiming, Haydar dropped the torch on the ground. He whipped his tie from his jacket pocket and bound it tightly round Burnell's foot, clamping it still with two massive hands round the ankle. Throwing himself down full-length, he began to suck lustily at Burnell's toe.

Crazed with pain, Burnell writhed and threw back his head, arching his spine as if under tetanus attack. So forceful were Haydar's powers of suction, he felt the blood being drawn out through his whole body, from throat to toe. Every so often, Haydar spat into the sand and took a deep breath, before sucking again with renewed vigour.

'What is it? What is happening?'

'Allah have mercy on you. It's a scorpion bite.' He resumed his powerful suction. Loosening the tourniquet, he sucked again.

The fire of the poison mounted to Burnell's brain, shooting up the right side of his body and burning its way down his left. In a delirium, he broke from Haydar's hold and flung himself against the bridge, banging his head as if determined to split it open and end everything.

He was scarcely aware when he was seized by powerful arms and pinioned. With a tow-rope taken from the half-drowned car, Haydar proceeded to bind him to the ladder set in the concrete. The knots went tight: he could do himself no further damage. He crammed a handkerchief into Burnell's mouth, so as to stifle his cries, in case ill-intentioned persons were attracted to the spot. With a tender palm, he soothed Burnell's forehead.

'My friend, you may survive. The scorpions hereabouts are known for the potency of their venom. I have done all that I can for you. The rest is in the hands of chance. It is my blame that I forget and permit us to sleep so near to a piece of building, where these little animals live . . . By the dawn, you will be recovered or you will be beyond further harm.'

'Mmmmmmgh,' Burnell replied. His eyes rolled deliriously.

With Haydar sitting by his feet, he remained in a fainting condition for hours. His body convulsed as the fires of the remaining poison circulated. Sweat stood hot on his forehead and rolled down cold inside his shirt. He shivered and blazed. For a while he was unconscious.

When he roused, he tilted his head about, looking for Nastiklov's Devil. The Devil remained out of sight. He gazed sickly up at the stars. Possibly there was a lightening in the sky behind him. Or it was the torch still burning. Or it was a false dawn. Or he imagined it. Carried along with the grand revolution of the sky, the Pleiades were moving towards the West. Ah, the West, he thought . . . How he longed to be back in the West, under the tender care of Dr Kepepwe for preference. When he attempted to pray, the words would not come. When he tried to think of death, which he was sure was imminent, he could recall only a Road Safety jingle, 'Poor Overtakers Make Rich Undertakers', which played endlessly through his tormented brain. Sleep swooped in like a kitehawk on its prey.

Nightmarish dreams culminated in the vision of a group of Arabs praying and chanting. Opening his eyelids was like heaving up gravestones. Dawn had arrived, sick and haggard. A group of dark-faced men were praying and chanting.

Haydar came from the river with a dripping cloth and applied it to Burnell's forehead.

'Haydar, I saw the eyes of God,' gasped Burnell, and straight away fainted again.

God was still about, a burly decent enough fellow, with a cordial nod of the head to Burnell. He was accompanied by all the other gods humanity had ever dreamed up – a swarthy and malodorous lot, and no mistake. Beards and horns in plenty, robes, loincloths, jewels in forehead, belching smoke, flaming swords, turbans, haloes, armour, multiple arms, multiple skulls, elephant heads, purple skins, immense phalluses – all that and more, as they swarmed towards Burnell, but hardly a one that a man in his right mind might think of praying to.

And a dictatorial lot they were! 'Thou shalt not this', 'Thou shalt not that' . . . What you had to sacrifice to them, how to serve a burnt offering, when and where and what to kill or copulate with, when you should work, who you should torture lingeringly, whether you should wear a veil or a top hat, what to sing, and whether pork was good for you. They had a line on everything. With holy book, thunder, thumbscrews, and instruments of circumcision they pressed forward.

The goddesses looked to be of rather better class. Most of them wore white gowns, down to the floor, carting their moons and mystic union cards with them. Some were more snazzily dressed, some weren't dressed at all, one had snakes messing about in her hair. The eccentrics among them had multiple eyes, breasts, or sharp knives, and looked as unappetizing as the male holinesses.

They were all advancing on Burnell, who was covered for the purposes of delirium with teddy-bear fuzz. Behind Burnell was Nastiklov's Devil, laughing and saying in a sneering tone, 'That's it, Roy, you tell 'em!'

Struggling with indecision – uncertain what exactly to tell 'em – Burnell swam back to something like consciousness. The dark-faced nomads of the desert were still present at the scene. They had abandoned their prayer routine and were busy harnessing their camels to the Chaika, still half-submerged in the River Garakhs. He was surprised to see what appeared to be whales, sporting in the waters.

Haydar came to him, full of concern, and asked him why he was crying. Burnell told him how God had spoken to him in his dream, telling Burnell that he (God) and Shakespeare were alike in being no one, and Burnell resembled them both. 'Imagine,' he said, as Haydar, now wearing a nun's habit, took him gently up in his arms, 'Imagine having to be Shakespeare – without Shakespeare's genius . . .'

'Don't fret, dear.' (He had been mistaken: it was his mother, back at last, as he had always hoped.) 'Because I have a curious story to tell you about that. At the railway station in Ashkhabad, there's a nice bookstall which sells the *Guardian* and a few English books. I found one with your name on. It's all about your travels. And in the book – isn't this a coincidence?! – you actually buy something at that very station bookstall. I forget what.'

'Do I meet you in the book, Mummy?'

'Yes, dear, you do. On page 296. I thought it was so sweet that I had a little part in it, considering how long I've been – you know, um, *dead* . . . You'd better wake up.'

This last remark was uttered in such a deep voice Burnell was startled. Staring hard, he realized Haydar was near by, still in his bedraggled suit and looking concerned. 'I'll untie you,' he said. 'We'll get you back to the hotel as soon as possible.'

Limp though Burnell felt, he found he could stand. The Chaika was nearby, dripping, salvaged from the river. The nomads were standing with their camels, the animals looking as expectant as their owners.

'You'd better pay them with some flight powder,' said Burnell. He treated it all as a joke. The gods and his mother still lingered nearby. Haydar might be massaging life back into his limbs, but that did not mean to say he was not another hallucination.

'They'll tow my brother's car for us.'

'Brother-in-law.'

'Yes. That's what I meant to say. How you feel now?'

'Funny.'

'Good. You will be OK.'

'Look, I'm grateful. You didn't see my mother just now, I suppose?'

'I'll get you into the car.'

'Oh, piss off, Haydar. I know you're just another hallucination.'

Tenderly as possible the hallucination stowed him away in the back of the car. In a few minutes, they were heading back towards Ashkhabad.

Slowly.

20
PRICC Strikes

Among the consolations for being stung by a scorpion at the Friendship Bridge was this: that it made one feel like a reasonably demented character in an old Russian novel. Burnell lay propped on thin pillows, listening to the non-tune of his dripping shower-head in the bathroom, wondering if he was sinful enough to have been vouchsafed a glimpse of teeming godheads; that is to say, he knew he had merely been delirious, yet the illusion that he had not been delirious kept returning from outer space, persuading him he must now be delirious.

And then the visitation from his mother, telling her curious story . . . He was more reluctant to dismiss that as an hallucination.

Owing to intellectual shortcomings, he was unable to determine whether it was flagrantly impossible that one might hold a kind of telepathic communication with those near and dead to one.

He half woke, half dreamed. Outside, a muezzin told Allah's day away.

Although he was imprisoned in the seedy little hotel room, his mind wandered. Memory was elusive; it did not keep to one department. Despite what had been stolen, impressions might remain. He might remember a generalized affection for someone he had forgotten. Stephanie, for instance. And Blanche, it seemed. And other women, other friends. Perhaps his longing to be reunited with Steff was really a residual longing to be reunited with his mother. Or with Blanche.

Such thoughts became as tangled and untidy as an old neglected hedge. He emerged from a thicket of them only when

Robert Murray-Roberts looked in on him to say a hasty farewell. Burnell found Murray-Roberts's fixed notion that he was laid up in bed after too much alcohol and other substances rather offensive, and closed his eyes on his guest.

Murray-Roberts said impatiently that a car was waiting outside the hotel to take him to the airport. The ambassador had returned overnight and ordered Murray-Roberts to fly immediately to Krasnovodsk to find out why the consignment of Protean cars was being held up at the docks. Both he and the ambassador were convinced that the delay was deliberate, the by-product of England's unfortunate 18–3 victory over the Turkmen team.

He seriously advised Burnell to drink no more foreign piss, as he called it.

Replying as curtly as feebleness permitted, Burnell explained how he had been stung by a scorpion.

'There are some strange creatures in the Karakum. I could have told you that. And I don't just mean the Fezzes. You were lucky it wasn't a sand viper, or you'd be underground by now. I warned you about Hikmat Haydar, didn't I? What in hell's name was he thinking of, taking you out there?'

Defensively, Burnell said it was absurd to come to Ashkhabad and not gain some knowledge of the desert.

'I don't know what Madge will say. Anyhow, the desert's been coming to Ashkhabad. These freak sandstorms are all because the ecology's buggered up, after they buggered up the Aral Sea. It'll probably be winter here by the time I'm back from Krasnovodsk, and we'll all be freezing our arses off. You're lucky, man, you're away. I hope you've your flight booked.'

Burnell said he was leaving on the Istanbul flight on the afternoon of the following day.

Sitting himself down firmly on the side of the bed, Murray-Roberts brought a silver flask from his hip pocket and proffered it. Burnell refused. Shrugging, Murray-Roberts took a swig himself. He said, as if by way of excuse, 'I hate flying Turkmenistan Airways.'

Leaning closer to the invalid, he said, 'Let me give you a tip, OK? Stay clear of the embassy now I'm away. Someone, I won't say who, put in a report about your behaviour with a woman in a restaurant. They don't like these things, you know. And you've made yourself *persona non grata* by your association with Haydar. I'm going to speak out of turn so keep this under your bonnet. Haydar's a drug baron on a large scale, and the law's closing in on him. There's also a tax matter with carpets sold to a company in California. Stay clear of him, that's what I'm saying. We don't need any more slurs on the character of the British after the football match disaster. He's gone into gun-running, which is what has got Diyanizov and Makhkamov off their arses. He won't easily buy himself out of this spot of trouble.'

'I don't believe this, Rob. Haydar's almost penniless. I happen to know that. He had to borrow his brother-in-law's car, the Chaika, for the trip to the Friendship Bridge.'

'Och, away with you, Roy, you're more of a fool than I took you for! That black Chaika? That's his, that's Haydar's own. He's a dozen cars or more. You know Mr Khan's shop where we were the other evening? Khan's only the manager. Haydar owns it. Haydar's probably the very guy who imported your bootleg memories here from Budapest. He's no friend of yours, let me tell you.'

'He bloody well saved my life.'

'He bloody put you in danger. He deals large-scale with Western connections in Hungary. That's why he's been tolerated — the poor old country needs a thriving black-market economy. Now he's turned munitions dealer, that's too much for the government. He's selling to the rebel party, the PRICC. So he'll have to be stopped.'

Burnell's response was one of flat disbelief. The two men parted coldly. Murray-Roberts pocketed his hip flask and went off to the airport.

Doubt sat uneasily on Burnell's shoulders. Montaigne had claimed that mixing with the world had a clarifying effect on the judgement. In this case, the opposite was true.

In all his travels, Burnell had yet to visit a country where he had not been told tales of massive corruption and pending arrests: Zimbabwe, Morocco, Brazil, Chile, Hungary, Poland, Ireland, the countries of the Mediterranean: all had similar stirring modern legends. Generally a member of the ruling regime was involved.

Well founded or not, the stories lent a certain glamour to life – and to the teller.

Sighing, he rose and showered. That there was no room service made him want coffee all the more. He began to gather up his scattered belongings and pack. His apartment in Soss City became increasingly attractive in prospect. He would be due for leave in November; perhaps he would visit Blanche Bretesche in Madrid; he lingered over a vivid image of her parted thighs.

His thoughts drifted to the discovery of the skeletons in the Sierra de la Demanda; strange how taboos regarding the dead did not apply to the long dead. It was strange, too, how real the appearance of his mother had seemed during his poisoned delirium. Even more curious how she had specifically mentioned a bookstall at the railway station . . . He had not been to the railway station and was not likely to now: in twenty-four hours he would be in the air, heading westwards.

Of course it was not *really* the apparition of his mother. The delirium brought on by the scorpion poison had spawned strange illusions; it didn't take much to tip the human brain into unreliability. Just supposing she had returned briefly from some unlikely limbo – of course he did not believe that for a moment . . . Then surely she would have had something of more general interest to tell him, something blatantly less false. Were there liars in limbo? The Gospel story of Lazarus returning from the dead did not relate what he had found there.

He looked about him rather helplessly, and spotted a pair of dirty socks in a dusty corner.

Among Burnell's reasons for a readiness to leave Ashkhabad was the hotel room.

Burnell thought of the hotel in Budapest, the Gellert, and how it differed from this one. This room was functional and he was glad to be here. Nevertheless, its shortcomings were many; it had been built in the dull imperial days of Soviet imposition, when hotel rooms in Turkmenistan were designed to be of precisely the dimension of hotel rooms in Tallinn, Lvov, and Ulan Bator, and formed from the same inferior concrete. So, in this phenomenally dry country, there was damp in the corners, the sound as of appa-ratchiks being throttled from the inadequate plumbing of the toilet, and the inconvenience of ill-fitting doors. The hotel food was tolerable when available.

The staff had not been trained. There was a pleasant manager, of a nationality Burnell had not yet fathomed, but he was a timid man who wandered aimlessly about his ground floor, never ven-turing upstairs. He was probably right to be timid: the previous manager had been a Norwegian, his name still execrated and mis-pronounced, who had introduced so many new rules in the name of efficiency, that one night aggrieved chefs, experts in halal and horsemanship, had threatened his life with his own knives. He had fled. Rumour had it he now cooked squid at a stall on the docks of Piraeus.

Over this much-travelled country, there had been no tradition of hostelry in the Western sense. Soviet Communism had dis-couraged travel; the old comfortably flea-ridden *hans* had decayed. Under a succession of nervous governments, they had yet to recover.

The Gellert in Budapest, on the other hand, had always been subject to the demands of travellers. Many of those travellers, who numbered among them bumptious dukes and demanding barons, were people of influence – that class of persons who made a point at least once in their lives of visiting the great cities of Europe, often accompanied by their reluctant families or mistresses. Even under the imposition of Communism in the twentieth century, such tra-ditions had not entirely died; it had never been impossible to secure an omelette at midnight, or a bottle of Tokay at six in the morn-ing from a Gellert porter. This tenacity of hospitality had much to do with the Hungarian character, and as much to do with the sumptuous marbled ambience of the Gellert itself, the faded red carpets of which had always seemed to presage the august arrival of a British royal or the golden footfall of a Saudi prince.

These days in Ashkhabad, Saudi princes stayed in the Hilton, under Japanese–American management.

Burnell stuffed the socks into his bag.

★

His intention was to revisit Mr Khan's establishment that evening, his last evening, to inspect more stolen bullets. Somehow he never got there.

His confidence in recovering his memory had been sapped. Thanks to Haydar's prompt action, he was alive; but the poison in his system had the effect of weakening reality. Reality appeared to him paper-thin. With a vague idea of rethinking his life, he rang the Professor of Philosophy at the university.

It sounded as if Nastiklov happened to be fortifying his spirits with a bottle of something. 'Look here, Burnell, it's no good talking like that. If you really were stung by a scorpion, which I doubt, it was a mark of an anatomical displacement. Accidents don't just happen. All's explicable in terms of quantum mechanics. The very word "accident" is a misnomer. Humans have to fit into – well, be *crunched into* – an ongoing series of physical events, just as I'm supposed to fit in with the nonsense that goes on in this university, me, a professor, ex-member of the Soviet Academy . . . Events control everything. Write that down, my friend – "events control everything", not vice versa. It's hubris to imagine otherwise. Hubris is mankind's middle name. I'm trying to write a book about it – got interested a publisher in Palermo. We're biology, Burnell, biology through and through. Think what that means. We are fragile constructs in a hard inorganic universe whose events roll over us. It's a transitory thing being an organic being, unstable. That's the word, unstable. Every seven years, our whole systems are renewed, skin, blood, bone marrow, everything – seven years, that's not so much as an itch in time. OK, so what else is renewed, I ask you? No, not a vehicle licence, Burnell, I speak of what? – Why, of the *psyche*, the human psyche, that – that cul-de-sac of brain which developed in the last half-million years. Psyche has no place in the scheme of things, it just happened to materialize because of the increased complexity of the human brain. Similarly as electronics grew out of the complication of electric disciplines or hamburgers from ham, or Pavlova from Pavlov, or – or defecation from the deaf. So that's what we carry around with us, a psyche, unlike the cow or the cat. It does us no good, it's what in my book I call the Hubris Centre, it's a metaphysical growth, it merely allows us to question things like how the universe started and where's it going to end, and meanwhile should women have the vote or is it bad for us to eat butter or smoke or is there a God or similar rubbish. Wait, there's some fool at my door . . . GO AWAY, DAMN YOU! *I'm busy slitting my throat!*

'Sorry! As I was saying, the psyche is merely an extension of anatomy, including the anatomy of the brain, and has no practical function but to make us worry about this and that and another. Where we came from, where we're going to, when the answer in both cases is plainly nowhere. God knows, I worry how long I can hang on here in this lousy rotten job. But you see, the point is – dash, what is the point? Oh, yes, I remember. The point is, Burnell – you sang well in the restaurant, by the way – "I Know Where You're Going To" – that the psyche is renewable; like the cells of the anatomy, every seven years comes the cell-by date. Every seven years, we change. A new disc goes in. Your philosophy doesn't have to be consistent, can't be consistent, in fact. Didn't I tell you that the basic human drive is not for pleasure or power, as those old rotters Freud and Adler proclaimed. No, no, the basic drive is to try to find the meaning in life. So don't you see the answer to your question is it doesn't matter a toot – I never discovered, by the way, what is a toot – is it the owl's cry? – whether or not you were visited by your dead mother. The question can't reasonably be answered because it's not a reasonable question. She did speak to you; she didn't. In either case, what she said was all nonsense, and you yourself admit it. Why doesn't the answer matter? Because it's just one more ghost worry thrown up by this error in evolution, the psyche. Nothing the psyche devises is to the point, you understand? Because it has no relationship – no viable relationship – with the external world of event. To give an analogy, it's like my unpleasant situation stuck here in this university, its one real intellect, with idiotic students asking me ghost questions. Now you ring in the middle of the night and ask me another ghost question, you, *you*, a grown man from the West, with a pleasant singing voice. Mrs Murray-Roberts, by the way, is a considerable harpy. But of course it's ridiculous any more to expect philosophical sense from the West. Immanuel Kant saw to that. All I have to say to you is that your psyche simply changed as another seven years were up. It caused you a little pain, which you interpreted as physical and external – this absurd scorpion theory of yours! – and in a little kind of playback episode as discs were changed in the faulty internal computer, fantasy occurred. You thought you saw some gods and some defunct relations and all the rest of the caboodle, as if you had drunk of tarantula schnapps, yes? Such illusions every person plays out in their spatch-cocked brain-boxes in moments when so-called rationality is not all it should be. Not that it should *be anything*. As I think I explained, there's only externality, which happens to be so bizarre – so really bizarre, Burnell, damn you – that the tinpot little human brain – constructed basically from slime, let me remind you – has to make up stories in order to find itself a role of some importance in the scheme of things. Ridiculous! Can you imagine if I started to believe I actually owned this university? – which heaven forbid! – owned it lock, stock, and bottle. They'd put me away, wouldn't they? In some psychological ward, for having derisions of grandeur. Funny farms all over the known world are packed with loonies who think they're someone important . . . Fantasy! Well, old friend, you numskull, that's what the human race does with its precious time, forgetting it's just an animal. To use one of your silly English phrases, it's too big for its brutes.'

'Boots,' said Burnell, but the tide of talk continued to wash over him. He put down the phone as softly as possible and faded into sleep.

In the morning, Burnell was feeling his normal self. He rose, showered, and went down to eat an omelette and yoghurt at the 'Fast Foot'. His favourite newsboy appeared promptly and sold him the *Frankfurter Allgemeine*, together with a smudgy local newssheet designed for foreigners and called, with some ingenuity, *The Foreigner*. Printed in Russian, German, and Japanese, it bore the day's date.

The headlines announced 'AIRPORT PENETRATED, PRICC SUSPECTED'.

A ministerial statement was printed without comment. 'Police are about to apprehend three young men who made their escape after a dawn infiltration of security at Ashkhabad Airport. Slight damage was caused to the runway. A bomb is believed to be the cause. The men are believed to be members of the right-wing terrorist organization, PRICC, the Party of Renaissant Islamic Counter-Culture. The airport will be closed until further notice.'

Burnell gave an almost human cry of pain.

Abandoning his omelette, he dashed into the street and went to the travel office. The office was closed, guarded by two soldiers.

The air was growing colder. Recalling Murray-Roberts's warning to stay away from the British Embassy, he turned instead to the German Embassy. This embassy was a grand affair, built, as far as could be determined, of glass and ebony.

The consular waiting-rooms were already crowded with people nourishing an urgent desire to leave Ashkhabad: Germans mainly, but with a fair demographic sprinkling from the rest of the globe. Joining the queue, Burnell was enveloped in the camaraderie which springs up among those who face shared adversity – in this case having to speak in an hour or two's time to a desk clerk who was already observed, even at a distance of twenty metres, to be pronouncedly hostile.

The 'Three Young Men' of the official government bulletin had already become legend. Blowing up the airport runway was seen either as an act of barbarism or as a strike against an unpopular president. The consensus of opinion in the queue, however, was that the Three Young Men were Shi'ite fundamentalists of the PRICC persuasion, who saw the airport as a source of Western contamination. Paranoia lent strength to this theory. The airport stood for a point of contact between a pure Muslim state and the pollution of Capitalism, together with all that was unholy. This was the place where German, Japanese, and American jetplanes entered, and where the new Boeing 777 was due to make a maiden landing shortly. Since AIDS and atheism were Western inventions, why not blow up the airport?

The Turkish lady ahead of Burnell had other ideas. Speaking in a whisper and a sort of multilingual Germanic Esperanto, she told him the bomb was planted by President Diyanizov himself, in order to have a pretext to crack down on his political enemies. Rolling her eyes, she assured him that the city was about to undergo a reign of terror, or, as she put it, a 'regiment von terribilitism'.

'It's nothing,' said the clerk when, an hour later, Burnell reached the counter and began to speak to him. He was young and highly polished, with a bright colour, like an ornament won at a fair. He pushed General Stalinbrass's faded letter to Burnell back over the fake marble counter, using one immaculate finger-tip to do so. 'It's merely a minor disruption, Mr Burnell. Happens here with the exchange of the weather.'

He spoke perfect English. Producing from under the counter a brochure entitled 'Visit Exciting Ashkhabad!', he pushed it forward with the same fingertip he had previously used, saying, 'Return to your hotel and wait a few days, when the airport will reopen. Meanwhile, enjoy the colourful local scene. Have you visited the famous market, every Sunday? Have you visited the new mosque? Have you purchased a sheepskin hat yet?'

'You don't understand. I have been on business here which is now complete. I must report back immediately to World Cultural Heritage in FAM.'

'Have you visited the old Parthian fortress at Nisa?'

Burnell gave the official a black look. 'Nisa already comes under WACH jurisdiction. What I'm saying is that I need to return to Frankfurt immediately. Are there no other international flights available from anywhere in Turkmenistan?'

'May I suggest you take a train, Mr Burnell? The railway station still functions normally. A Trans-Caspian train transports you to Krasnovodsk, on the shores of the Caspian Sea. In Krasnovodsk is an international airport, from whence you may fly on to Frankfurt-am-Main. When we last received news from it, that air-port was in working order.'

Drumming his fingers indecisively on the counter, Burnell swore under his breath. 'Could you book me a seat on the train?'

'You may phone from your hotel. Train bookings do not form part of our service to the general public.'

'Thanks a lot . . . What sort of place is this Krasnovodsk?'

The clerk looked down his nose at Burnell; though young, he

was formidably tall, or else standing on a concealed box. 'You mean, compared with Ashkhabad? Is paradise . . . Next, please.'

All trains from Ashkhabad were crowded. Such was the conclusion Burnell reached, after an afternoon spent phoning the railway station booking-office. Though the station was close to the hotel, he could not face the obstacles of buying a ticket in the flesh, given his insufficient command of the Turkic language. He had heard from other travellers of the difficulty of discovering the right wicket at which to purchase the right ticket of the right class for the right train.

Finally, he managed to reserve a seat on an express departing for Krasnovodsk at five the following afternoon. He lay back on his bed, exhausted by the anxiety of hanging on to a phone, at the other end of which a clerk had pottered away, perhaps to check a timetable, perhaps to take his own mysterious journey to the ends of the earth. His success meant he had only twenty-four hours to wait before quitting Ashkhabad, provided nothing else went wrong.

With the evening opening before him, he put on a pullover and took a taxi to Mr Khan's EMV store.

It was not that he still retained any great expectations of recovering his memory of Stephanie, or his academic knowledge, or any of the other matters which had crowded into the stolen years: though the dregs of hope are always the most potent. A somewhat morbid interest attracted him towards all the imprisoned detritus of other past lives, furtive, intricate, no more indelible than snow, and, in their variety, both comic and alarming.

There was the *chaykhana*, and the crowded road, purple in the dusk. A great cummerbund of golden fire confining the western horizon put the scattered street lights to shame. He paid the taximan and made his way up the narrow alley, to knock on Mr Khan's door.

Khan showed him to the section euphemistically labelled 'Love'. For an hour, Burnell gorged on unedited sexual encounters. He fed with amazement on that basic human activity in all its beauty, haste, luxuriance, or squalor. He sprawled under the EMV helmet, flattened by the weight of lust, living other lifetimes – some mistily perceived, some sharp as winter frost. From infant erections to death-bed orgasms, on they came, panting for the mad mutual moment. But none of those moments had once been his and Stephanie's.

He emerged at the end of the hour, dazed and over-heated. He reflected on how frequently sexual satisfaction was the man's alone, so rarely did the man show any real interest in the woman herself. Having sampled female memories – those stolen delicacies – he saw how often women were dismayed by the selfishness of their male partners. Only the sapphists in their antic suctions saw to each other's gratification.

As he paid the storekeeper, weariness must have shown in his face. Khan said he was about to close.

'Perhaps you will favour me by drinking a glass of tea with me in the *chaykhana*, sir?'

Burnell assented cheerfully. Any company was better than none, as travellers had long since discovered. Nevertheless, he was too preoccupied to listen closely to the old man's chatter as the day's takings were locked away in a safe. His head was slowly disentangling itself from the bootleg memories. He needed to get outside for a few deep breaths.

Of all the torrid and fleeting love scenes which had passed through his head, he dwelt on one. Two lovers meeting somewhere outdoors in the dark. A clandestine encounter. She youthful and he seemingly no less so. They met by a waterfall. It must have been summer, since the flow of water was a mere trickle. But as to whereabouts this was, the memory gave no clue. Nor could the faces of the lovers be distinguished.

But the feel of the woman's body as she shed her light clothes had been real enough, and her perfume. And the male's intense feelings of love. Mingled with passionate desire had been genuine reverence for the shy spirit of the other. The affair had indeed seemed like a true reciprocal affection, as they clutched each other on the dry bank. Something in the scene caught more than Burnell's mere prurient interest. He wondered who the couple were, and what had happened to them; his compassion was aroused. But even as he wondered, the memory faded, dispersing like a dream. He was left in the stuffy shop with its garrulous owner.

Setting the security system, they emerged into the evening air. The shopkeeper locked his door. The two of them walked the few metres to the teahouse, where old men were already gathering. Some chatted, some played draughts or chess. Strings of coloured lights, draped across the façade, were already lit as night closed in.

The *chaykhana* was a two-storey affair, the verandah on the ground floor sheltered by a long sloping roof. A silk tree, with its finely textured leaves, grew to one side, giving its name to the place, 'The Silk Tree *Chaykhana*'. Rasping music played in the rear. Khan chose a table indoors by a window, where they could watch the traffic.

Burnell produced his stash, offering some to the other man, who refused with a smile and shake of the head. He began to talk in patchy German and English about his finances, his illnesses, local affairs, even how much the owner of the *chaykhana* over-charged. Burnell summed him up as a bore as he took his slap up both nostrils. His attention wandering, he thought of poor mad Ivan Nastiklov, who at least went mad about metaphysical things, in a traditional Russian way.

Tea in beaded glasses was set before them on the table, as Khan described how a customer had cheated him over a few coins the previous week.

'I'm not interested in all that,' Burnell said rudely, interrupting the monologue. 'Petty complaints, what are they? Signs of a petty mind! Look, you're stuck here, peddling your awful trade, what do you really know of the world? Can't you raise your sights a little and see what's happening? Not just the political stuff – the universal racism – all this wretched constant upheaval everywhere . . . Have you ever dared to think that human societies have had thousands of years in which to attain stability, and still haven't achieved it?' He talked rapidly, marginally preferring his own nonsense to Khan's. 'Why? Why the failure? Why the constant flux, constant struggle? The world is permanently criss-crossed by refugees, fleeing some form or other of persecution. Are we all mad? If you thought about these things, it would take your mind off your arthritis, your cheating customers. Have you ever considered the terrible psychic storms shaking humanity? We're an unstable species, the men worse than the women.'

'You want a woman? I know a good place we can go to.'

'Far from here?'

'No far.'

'I like a good drive to a brothel. Anticipation. A little excitement.'

'Drink your tea first. The women won't run away.'

'What did you say your name was?'

The storekeeper's name was Abden Hodja Khan. He lit a long brown marijuana cigarette and began to chatter again. His cheeks were cramped under high bones. Wrinkles at the corner of his eyes gave him a humorous appearance, belied by a mournful utterance. His narrow right hand lay on the table, playing with his plastic teaspoon. He watched the hand as he spoke, as if it were an animal with an independent life.

'What you claim about mankind is quite a possibility. Allah wills all things. I don't like to live in this city. Not in any city. Things are never settled in cities. The hopes, they come down. The prices, they go up. The houses, they pull down. The roads, they dig up. For me, open air is best thing, *versteh?*'

Khan declared that he was a Kazakh. He had come from the remotest eastern region of Kazakhstan. 'Far from here, far, far. In the snowy Tien Shan Mountains, near by the Chinese frontier.' As he spoke, his hand deserted the spoon, to point through the trellised walls of the *chaykhana* in the direction of a distant Cathay.

His ancestors had been wild and free, he said, with a melancholy glance under his brows at Burnell – wild and free. Caring nothing for cities, which they regarded as prisons. He was born during a howling storm in a small yellow-painted hut with two rooms and an iron stove. The hut was set on a shoulder of the lower slopes of a mountain they called Big Bear. His mother made much of little Abden, and taught him to read. They had sturdy horses; occasionally his father and uncles traded foals in exchange for supplies. Food and animal skins.

As a boy, Abden Hodja Khan rode with his father among the mountains.

'I loved to ride as a boy,' said Burnell, but was ignored.

'Snow and shine, snow and shine, always in the saddle! From early years I have my own pony – you'd say his name is "Blade". Just my father and me, only humans in any directions. We hunt, always hunting. Always in the saddle. Overhead, the open skies. On our shoulders, eagles.'

He patted his shoulder. Burnell sat listening remotely, sipping his green tea.

'We relied on our eagles, my father and me, relied always. My father he trained them. Big birds, sir, intelligent, on our shoulders. Then the flight. Very swift the eagle flies. Rabbits they catch for our food – anything what moves in the snow. Foxes also catching by our birds. The fox coat very valuable. When we don't hunt, we sleep, drink maybe *kumyss*. My father he know everything of the wild.'

'Tell me, did you get on with your father?'

Hodja had closed his eyes and bowed his head, the better to recall the time of which he spoke. Without opening his eyes, he said, 'Yes, I suppose. I try always to please my father.'

'My father took me to Iceland once.'

Khan ignored the interruption, sipping tea noisily.

After a pause, he continued. 'In the summertime came the geese, flying to our lake. Some said they had flown over the Himalayas from India, at immense heights. In one summertime, my father he taken me to a horses fair in a place called Lepkeli. Do you visit Lepkeli ever? Many people there, mainly Kazakh, very jolly. At night, the dancing, oh, all night the dancing . . . But I have a misfortune in Lepkeli.

'There in Lepkeli I see my first railways train.' He acted out this dramatic moment, placing a sheltering hand along his brow. 'The train he run on the lines from Urumqui in China to Alma-Ata, our Kazakh capital, Alma-Ata, and from Alma-Ata west, through Turkmenistan and in the end to Moscow. Moscow! Imagine. It was a name I heard, *Moscow*, like a jewel in a tiger's throat. And then I see that diesel haul those carriages along the iron lines. That strong diesel! I go so near I can felt the heat of its machine heart.'

312

He sighed. The right hand released the spoon, to lie open on the table. 'It's my imagination was like in a trap. *Versteh?* It's the idea, eh? Not the real thing – the imagining. What a curse, sir, is the power of imagining to a man! I know I had to ride on that great train. I must go. That one time I didn't pleased my father. He wept big tears. I never saw something like it. But still I left him. Being young, sir, I left him at Lepkeli, with our horses . . .

'So I end up captive of Ashkhabad. This far only I get, then I am throw from off the train. I have no ticket, no money. I have never been yet to Moscow. A prisoner of cities, like many men. Why is it, eh? Once I was free. Then I sacrifice it in a moment. What can I do?'

'You could phone home,' Burnell said, finishing his tea.

'What could I have to say?'

'Why do you sell so many bad memories in your store? Are men so perverse? Don't people long for happy memories?'

'Oh, people enjoy bad memories many reasons. Like seeing a strong video – you know, violence, killing. Maybe they feel heroic. At least EMV gives to people a choice of miseries.'

Beckoning the owner of the teahouse to show he was ready to pay, Khan said, 'Memories of other people stops you being your-self. That's a relief, eh? An escape.'

'Is your past in fact as you say? The eagles and all that? The remote mountains? The snow?'

A look of sorrow passed over the shopkeeper's face. 'Sir, I tell you this. Maybe I just was born here a bastard in Ashkhabad, and always stuck in this city. Why not? But if my days in the wild Alotau with my father are a substitute EMV memory, then I am made happy with them. I can't tell what is true. Why should I tell? It's not a matter.'

'Doesn't it matter to Allah whether things are true or not?'

Khan shrugged. 'I pay the bill.' He summoned a passing waiter.

Burnell put his money on the table. 'But what if those memo-ries of yours were miserable and not happy, as you claim they are?'

'Anything is better than to think I am a prisoner of Ashkhabad since boyhood. What kind of life would that be?' He rose. 'Now you like go and see those ladies.'

313

21
Subterfuge

The brothel was a two-storey private house behind a supermarket. Downstairs was the room where girls sat about at tables while coloured non-alcoholic drinks were served. Upstairs were cubicles and bidets. Khan referred to the place as either – Burnell could not be sure – 'the Casa' or 'the *khazi*'.

Burnell checked his watch. The AIDS light was still on green. He was safe.

He chose a young girl with a wide Tartar face and good teeth. Khan went with an older woman who knew him, and greeted him without especial delight.

No sooner had Burnell entered the girl than she began to writhe and moan in simulated orgasm. While appreciating the theory behind this subterfuge, Burnell was irritated by it, considering it a dishonest way of speeding customer input.

'Short Time' was what he paid for. He gave the girl *baksheesh*. After all, she derived less pleasure from the encounter than he.

22
A Brief Discourse on Justice

When they met downstairs, Abden Hodja Khan was disgruntled. He had apparently enjoyed little success.

'Age creeps up on me, sir,' he said, as they went into the night. He lit up one of his brown cigarettes. 'Life is unfair.'

'Not at all. Not at all, Khan. I'm always amazed at the way in which injustice is spread about with awesome equality.'

23

To the Krasnovodsk Station

On his last morning in Ashkhabad, Burnell took a little breakfast in a restaurant in Ulitsa Chekhova. He felt his hours dwindling down, shorter and shorter, like the chapters of a novel by an author who is running out of ideas.

A sturdy figure filled the doorway. It was the ex-Curator of the Archaeological Museum, Dr Hikmat Haydar. Burnell rose and clutched his immense right hand.

'I wished to say goodbye but did not know how to find you.'

'Well, I find you instead, my friend. But it is not yet goodbye, positively. I will accompany you on your journey this afternoon.'

Haydar sat down at the table, smiling, spreading himself. The chair creaked under his weight. He desired to leave Ashkhabad for some while, and so he would make the journey to Krasnovodsk on the shores of the Caspian with his friend. He would visit a kind old auntie who lived in what had once been called Lenina Prospekt in the sea port. Besides, the distance was not more than six or five hundred kilometres, and they could enjoy conversation on the way.

'Will your wife accompany us?'

'My wife does not travel,' said Haydar. 'She will not eat the bread of foreigners.'

Railway stations round the globe are more substantial than airports, less sinister, less brittle with tension. Their scale is less inhuman. They are places where people meet rather than depart.

In many regions of the world they have become more convivial than in their country of origin, England, where travel is still regarded as a test of national character.

The Ashkhabad station had been built to last a thousand years. Unlike the Third Reich – which had proclaimed a similar objective – it was well on its way to fulfilling its target. Though of a predominant style which Burnell thought of as Stalinist Criminal, its main archway and multiple turrets evoked something of Asia, with its follies and grandeurs, its longitudes and longueurs, to remind travellers that here was the Golden Railroad to Samarkand. Here was the Trans-Caspian.

Its thronging interior echoed with announcements in strange tongues. It was crammed with stalls mobile and otherwise, peddling ices, poisonous drinks, sherbets, sweetmeats, sheep-cheese puffs, steaming bowls of *lahgman*, suitcases, bird cages, kites, bright-coloured toys from distant Bombay, Beijing, and Chengdu – and paper books and magazines.

Many people in the immense crowds were wrapped against the change in the weather, wearing thick woolly leggings, or swathing their legs about with whatever material was handy. They made the atmosphere more exotic.

But Burnell was hardly conscious of them. He suddenly remembered his mother's words, spoken to him in his scorpion-inspired delirium. By a turn of fate, here he was at the station, as her ghost had predicted. Somewhere here on a bookstall, he would find a book, a travel book – was it by him or about him? Had she made that clear?

It could not be a book by him or he would know that much. No, that was not necessarily the case. Supposing he had visited this part of the world before, during the years of stolen memory . . . Supposing on that occasion he had done the identical things he had done this time. Supposing he had even been stung by a scorpion before. Supposing he had even met Murray-Roberts and Dr Haydar before – and they had just happened not to mention it this time. No: absurd. But they might not have been here in earlier years. Supposing he had travelled in Central Asia and written a book about it . . . If it had been published – well, let's say years

317

earlier: then not just he but the rest of the world have forgotten about it. Supposing . . . A word that embraced infinity.

As he was bumping his way over the cobbles of these speculations, he was pushing through the crowds looking for a bookstall carrying English-language books.

Of course it was preposterous to imagine he had written any such volume. But the alternative was even more alarming. The alternative would be a book featuring him in it as a character. In which case, he would be reduced to fiction, someone with no existence beyond the printed page. What if he came on that book, 'Burnell's Travels', or whatever it might be called, and found himself to be merely imaginary . . . And an imaginary subsidiary character at that . . .

What price reality then? 'Shit,' he thought, 'the universe is badly at fault. If I'd been in charge of creation I'd have found some less tacky medium than time to stage the whole performance in.'

He would have started to tremble had there been room to do so in the general crush. 'Well,' he said to himself, 'there is an argument which says our whole world is nothing but a dream.' Who was the Chinese idiot who dreamed he was a butterfly and woke to wonder whether he was not a butterfly dreaming it was a man, or words to that effect? Shortly following his mother's death, he had gone to a monastery in Nottinghamshire for a week of yogic transcendental meditation. On the wall of the Hall of Meditation (draughty in a rather Nottinghamshire way) hung a painted scroll which read, 'I prayed to my soul to keep on dreaming me and my soul said, Who's there?'

Recalling that scroll now, he wondered why his maternal hallucination by the Friendship Bridge bothered him so: he was a rational being. He toured all the stalls in the station foyer. No English books anywhere. Just to make sure, he toured them again. Still no English books. The hallucination had been joking. Was that good or bad? He could not decide, just as he had never decided whether he was into Bartók or Chaos theory.

The stall at which he was standing stocked foreign newspapers, most of them printed in Arabic script. Among them he saw a London paper, *The Independent*. It was only two days old.

Scanning its headlines, he was surprised or otherwise to find General 'Gus' Stalinbrass had been assassinated. Stalinbrass had stepped ashore at the port of Varna and had been hit by a sniper's bullet an hour after landing. Seventy people had been rounded up and arrested but nobody had been charged as yet. Stalinbrass had died in a naval hospital that evening.

Turning to the Obituary page to see what good could possibly be said about that ferocious soldier, Burnell saw at the bottom of the page another name he knew. The champion Hungarian skier, Peter Remenyi, had died after many days in a coma. He left behind a widow and two children.

Closing the paper abruptly, Burnell shoved it back on the rack and went to sit down on a nearby bench, nestling against a fat Turkmeni lady.

The world, no doubt about it, was more weirdly constructed than anyone could realize. Had his near-death by scorpion coincided with the hour of Remenyi's death? Had the vision of his mother led him to this one particular newsstand in order that he should pick up *The Independent* and read there of the death of his friend?

But of course Peter had ceased to be his friend. He had no memory at all of Peter: only his name in green lettering on the screen of his electronic diary.

Then there was the business of his being haunted by Remenyi's coma. Because that seemed insoluble, he had carefully put it to one side.

It must all be highly significant, or it meant nothing.

But as much could be said of an individual life.

He felt rather faint. Nastiklov was right. Man's main drive was a quest for meaning in life, bugger it. How much more straightforward would be drives for pleasure and power, as advocated by – to use Nastiklov's phrase – 'those rotters Freud and Adler'.

Behind the steamy windows of the station restaurant, meals were being served up at a great rate, mutton curries, pilaffs, kebabs, and a hundred dishes of exotic name. Doors swung to and fro, waiters bustled back and forth. Over everything genial disorder reigned. A bowl of chicken and paprika soup would be welcome, but Burnell had not the courage to enter the mêlée. He bought a hot dog at a stall instead, his spirits reviving as he chewed. Hot dogs were ideal antidotes to metaphysical scares.

His equanimity regained, Burnell, squeezed among the immense jostle of people, felt something he recognized as contentment: the scent of a great unknown Asian world with its own laws, tongues, and customs he could never learn. To a foreign eye the pressures of the twenty-first century seemed scarcely to impinge on this world. He had no knowledge of why such impressions made him happy. Was there a lost memory which might explain it? Had a woman – perhaps some idle unprofessional whore who had taken a fancy to him – once told him a secret, or even made a gesture, through which he had been able to enter, if vicariously, into the beckoning-forbidding universe of Muslim faiths?

The noticeboards announced trains due to make routine journeys eastwards to Bukhara, Samarkand, Alma-Ata, and even Kashgar in Sinkiang Province. A cheap ticket would carry you to the unknown.

But he and Hikmat Haydar were to be travelling westwards, heading away from the mysteries, the yellow distances, the irregular, towards a world of money markets and regulations, where airports never closed.

He climbed aboard the Krasnovodsk train. There was no point in staying where he was. There never had been, for as long as he could remember.

Haydar arrived dressed for the journey, a carnation in the lapel of his sand-coloured suit and an astrakhan coat draped over his shoulders. He appeared unusually anxious as he boarded, complaining about the numbers of armed police patrolling the platforms. 'They're looking out for the Three Young PRICCs, I suppose,' said Burnell, carelessly. Haydar continued to mutter, clutching more closely to his ample chest a heavy carrier bag.

The bag bore the legend 'Nieman Marcus, Dallas'. The sight of it, the sight of Haydar in his finery, filled Burnell with pleasure. Here was something of which he could be certain. He could be certain that Murray-Roberts had not lied to him. Haydar was a crook. Today in his immense suit he looked the part.

It was expedient for him to let things cool down in Ashkhabad. This was why he was on the train, and had somehow finagled himself a reservation in the same compartment as Burnell.

'At five do we leave?' Burnell asked, glancing at his watch, conscious that his grasp of syntax was disintegrating under a bombardment of home-made English. Beginning to get nervous, he rose and looked out of the window. Certainly there were police on the platform; one was licking an ice cream.

'I can tell you what I read on the timetable by the ticket office,' Haydar said. 'The notice says: "The times printed on this timetable are times before which trains will not leave." From that, you gather what you gather. This train will not leave definitely before five o'clock.'

The train pulled away from Ashkhabad station at five-twenty. Burnell considered this not bad at all. Hauled by an immense Czech diesel, the carriages clattered through suburbs and cotton mills, in the direction of the Caspian; before Ashkhabad fell away behind them, the heating was working, and they closed the window.

Watching with interest, Burnell saw the 'Nieman Marcus, Dallas' carrier bag go up on the luggage rack, to be pulled down again as Haydar had second thoughts. He settled himself with the bag on his knee, keeping tight hold of it.

On the luggage racks, numerous boxes of wood and cardboard were already stacked, all tied about by string. They belonged to the first occupants of the compartment, a grim-faced man and woman sitting close together by the door. Not a word escaped them. It was as though the clothes in which they were swathed ensured their silence. The couple eyed all newcomers suspiciously; the male did his best to envelop himself in cigarette smoke. In a muttered aside, Haydar told Burnell the two were Russians – something Burnell had already gathered for himself. Russians had been leaving the Central Asian republics for years, often to face poverty in what they regarded as their native land. From the labels on the boxes overhead, it could be gathered that this glum couple planned to take a ferry across the Caspian, from Krasnovodsk to Baku, the Azeri capital, and thence northwards by rail: the hazards of which prospective journey probably accounted for the unsmiling countenances.

A gipsyish woman with two boys aged about eight and ten moved into the compartment, to take up the remaining seats between them. After settling her children, the woman exchanged a few words with Haydar. The boys were either well behaved or cowed by the novelty of a train journey. They sat opposite Burnell and Haydar, to stare at them with expressions devoid of curiosity. The woman, who had shifted from another carriage, took some while to accommodate herself, nervously arranging luggage and clothes. She was swathed in white, in her late thirties, draped with cheap bazaar jewellery. Though pleasant-looking to Burnell's guarded scrutiny, she was running to embonpoint and corsetry.

When she finally became content, and had stuffed sweets into her sons' mouths, she leaned forward and showed her three rail tickets to Haydar. Haydar answered her questions with elaborate courtesy, speaking with gravity over the top of his carrier bag.

Ever curious about women, Burnell remained standing by the window, occasionally looking down at the woman and out at the disappearing city. He had achieved little, he reflected; but that was nothing new. At least Ashkhabad had sustained his interest. There was that familiar pang, always induced in him by train journeys, at the thought that he was leaving the present. Although there was no point in staying, the present was always a kind of paradise; being kicked into the future was never comfortable.

Perhaps the story of Adam and Eve could be understood as a journey from present to future, beyond the Eden of the moment into the bleak world of tomorrow. His Eve of the previous night had offered him little in the way of fruit. To start with, she had tried to fob him off with a hand job. Perhaps her vagina was sore: it must be an occupational hazard in her way of business. Her nipples had lain as flat as coins, her eyes had been dark and – he had not troubled to explain it to himself at the time – dim. Of her life he knew nothing; now that the train was carrying him out into the Karakum, he could never learn anything about her circumstances. He longed for her as he stood at the window looking back: not physically, much, but wanting to know what misfortune had trapped her in that place Mr Khan knew well. Had she enjoyed any years of happiness before her imprisonment?

What the original riper Eve had been like remained a mystery. Nothing was known of her except that she took an apple from the tree of knowledge and gave it to her lover. Gustave Doré depicted her as a well-built Victorian lass with ivory haunches. That stupid misunderstanding with the erotic apple tree – it must have been a Cox – and the snake, and God in a vile mood about what was merely a childish misdemeanour . . . The present so soon became the past, when the almond tree would flourish instead. Had Eve enjoyed any years of happiness before the unfortunate incident?

It came to Burnell that he had read a scholarly commentary on Genesis which discussed that very question. Some authorities believed that Adam and Eve had spent many pleasant years together before they were cast out of Eden, others that they had had only a few hours. That seemed a miserable swindle, rather like losing . . . well, not exactly, no.

Then there was the question of fornication. Apparently Adam and Eve had had none of that until they were kicked out into the wilderness. Genesis did not disclose if she even gave him a hand job. Once beyond the Garden, the sexual act became their consolation. Much misery followed for the first parents, with their two sons at odds with each other; at least Burnell's AIDS light remained on the green.

'Mother,' he muttered to himself, 'I know not why these questions bother me. It's so endlessly long since I tasted the fruit of the tree of knowledge. If you managed to appear to me before, please do so again. I'm going home to see Father now, at Diddisham Abbey, where you died.'

The train was rolling through cotton fields, which soon gave way to desert. Desolation stretched on either side. No human being could be seen, no bird or animal. The landscape appeared as it had been thousands of years ago, late-afternoon glow suspended above it like fossil light.

'We can pull the blind if you hate to see it,' said Haydar. Burnell took his seat. The vacant places of Earth held a fascination of their own. Maybe Adam preferred the wilderness to the garden. He began to tell his companion of an expedition to Iceland on which his father had taken him as a boy. Haydar interrupted, remarking that such places were what he called an English taste. Who would wish to go to Iceland unless they had urgent business there?

For reasons obscure even to himself, Burnell began a defence of Iceland. In fact, he had been uncomfortable and wet for most of that strenuous trip and had moreover been forced to read Burnt Njal's Saga. He was elaborating on the virtues of the hot springs when a commotion arose in the corridor of the train. Haydar was immediately alert and peered out. The gipsy woman also rose and started to question everyone in an anxious manner; where-upon the Russian man ordered her curtly to sit down.

She shrieked a little as she complied, and her boys, glad of a diversion, took up the cry.

Haydar patted her shoulder and told Burnell a random inspec-tion was in progress. He tut-tutted, saying that these inspections made life wretched for passengers, alarming – as he put it – 'women and horses'.

As he spoke, he pushed his heavy Nieman Marcus bag on to Burnell's lap. 'Keep hold of it, please, until the police have passed.' He tapped the side of his ample nose with a forefinger by way of caution.

Burnell protested he could do no such thing. Looking down into the bag, he saw only an old grey garment, tucked on top of a package. Haydar held it firmly in place on Burnell's knee, hush-ing him as if dealing with a child. The Russian, rolling his yellow eyes, puffed out smoke as if to provide a screen for anything unto-ward.

'Just hold my bag a moment only, dear Mr Burnell, a moment! You are English. Inspectors are often rough men, but they will not touch your belongings because you are from England and Western countries. The bag is innocent. It contains some delicacies for my old aunt in Krasnovodsk, merely.'

'What are the police looking for?'

'Oh, you know police – ignorant men wherever they are found. They look for contraband possibly. Nothing, nothing, really. Show them your English passport. They will disappear.' He gestured with wide arms and wicked expression, convinced that vampires would disintegrate at sight of a silver cross.

He had to raise his voice because the white-clad woman was shrieking at her boys, who clung together in fright.

Thought Burnell, the man may be a crook, and this bag may be full of heroin, but – what the hell, he sucked out my poison and saved my life. Would I have been willing to do the same for him? I owe him something.

Angry voices were raised in the corridor. The express ground to an unexpected halt. Wails of distress sounded from afar.

In the gathering dusk, desert could be seen on either side of the track, heaving up into dunes like dissembling shoulders. The vulnerability of a stationary train became apparent. Haydar raised his gaze to the ceiling, the Russian couple exchanged glances and shrugged, mutely remarking, What do you expect from this lot?

After a minute, two uniformed inspectors squeezed into the compartment. They were armed, and saw to it that their boots made a great clatter as they came in. Following them came the train's female conductor, a large woman in large boots, a blue serge skirt being her chief badge of gender. She wore a red handkerchief round her head and a peaked cap on top of that to increase her air of being intolerant of nonsense. She pulled a scary face at the two boys, who shrank into their corner, raising spread fingers to their eyes.

One of the inspectors stood by the sliding door while the other checked tickets. The latter was plainly nervous and inexperienced, despite his years. The boys' mother, being anxious, asked questions, to which she received grunts for answer. The boys were made to stand up. An inspector went through their pockets. Their mother was ordered to take her packages from the rack. She rattled all her bracelets in protest, but pulled them down, whereon the inspector, a grizzled man of dark complexion, poked through her modest possessions with business-like contempt.

When the inspector had discovered nothing there, and the

gipsyish woman had clucked a little, the turn came of the Russian couple. While the man smoked sullenly, arms folded across his chest, his wife rose and harangued the inspectors. She was a short dumpy woman with an upturned nose which turned up even further in her refusal to take her belongings down from the rack. The conductor, intervening, thrust her red face forward, vulture-fashion, to shout in her ear. Argument ensued, counterpointed with gesture.

The Russian woman's puffy face grew crimson. When she turned to her husband for support, he told her curtly to sit down. The conductor placed her hands on the woman's shoulders and forced her into her seat. The inspectors, muttering, seized down the various boxes from the rack, wrenched undone the securing strings, and examined their contents one by one.

With clumsy haste, the inspectors unloaded everything on to the floor. As the woman, still red-faced, set about restoring possessions to their boxes, she complained angrily. The conductor yelled at her to be quiet. This had some effect. The Russian's complaints became more guttural, more closely akin to the growls of a cornered tigress, but she continued them unabated.

During this procedure, Burnell sat clutching Haydar's carrier bag. He had turned it so that the legend 'Nieman Marcus, Dallas' was visible to the inspectors, in the hope it might instil respect in savage minds.

The threatening situation served to remind him he was far from the legalities of England. He experienced the melancholy sensation, which overwhelms all travellers at some time when in a country where they scarcely know a word of the spoken language, that they are trapped in a lift in a skyscraper, descending out of control from the ninety-ninth floor, with only a couple of uninhibited lunatics for company.

The Russian woman was made to open her last box. This contained kitchen utensils, each packed in newspaper, the Cyrillic on which seemed to aggravate the bearded inspector. He unwrapped everything, throwing the paper about the carriage, ignoring the woman's angry growling. The compartment filled with egg whisks and cauldrons.

The male Russian scarcely moved. He remained rooted to his seat, arms folded. As the last saucepan emerged from the folds of *Izvestia*, he cast down the butt of his cigarette and ground it into the floor with his heel. Catching Burnell's eye, he said in German, 'You see how these progeny of Genghis Khan hate us. They're swine, savages!'

The two inspectors stood contemplating with satisfaction the Russian woman's attempts to repack her possessions. Then the senior inspector turned to Burnell.

He extended a grimy hand for Burnell's ticket.

He scrutinized the ticket for a long while, holding it close to his eyes and then at arm's length, as if puzzled by the nature of the object. Turning it about one last time, he enquired of Burnell in rudimentary German, 'Where did you buy this ticket, *mein Herr*?'

Many wild and not necessarily amusing answers passed through Burnell's mind. He was too conscious of the incriminating bag on his knee to utter them, merely replying, 'On Ashkhabad station.'

'And you go to?'

Perhaps the man wished to be officious. Perhaps he could not read. Perhaps ticket inspectors on the Bukhara–Ashkhabad–Krasnovodsk line were selected after strict illiteracy tests.

'Krasnovodsk station.'

'*Deutsch*?'

'*Engländer*.'

Sniffing, the inspector clutched the ticket with both hands. 'Passport,' he said in English.

Burnell produced his passport. The inspector merely scratched his head with a corner of it. Without bothering to look at it, he returned it, together with the ticket which had so mystified him. At the same time, he nodded severely at Burnell, as if to make a point too profound for words.

He passed on to Haydar. Haydar was made to stand. The inspector patted his pockets with delicacy; he could have been hunting for butterflies. In the soothing tones of one accustomed to handling nervous hounds, Haydar encouraged him. The inspector looked up into the great face above him and gave a guilty smile. His inspection of the Syrian passport was cursory; evidently the

fact that Haydar was accompanying an English visitor was sufficient to bestow respectability. The inspectors pushed past the
stooped figure of the Russian woman, still scrabbling among her
belongings, and made for the corridor.

The senior of the inspectors paused at the door and looked
back at Burnell. 'Sagh bol,' he said. Goodbye. Possibly he felt that
his status was improved by having Westerners travelling on his
train. Burnell raised a relieved hand in return.

The conductor ceased to rub her bottom against the door jamb.
Inserting two fingers into the corners of her mouth, and two
more up her nostrils, she pulled one final frightening face at the
two lads and followed the men out, slamming the compartment
door behind her.

The Russian fished another cigarette from a sandalwood box
and lit it. As he breathed out smoke into the atmosphere, he said
calmly in English, 'You see – universal swine and murderers,
child-killers, cannibals, abusers of humble kitchenware.' He made
no move to assist his wife, who was now kneeling to repack their
belongings into their boxes.

Still feeling extremely uncomfortable, Burnell turned away
from the other passengers and took a snort of his slap. A movement outside the carriage caught his eye. A bird had alighted in
the sand with a flash of blue and white feather, to peck at something thrown from the train.

To Burnell's untutored eye, the bird resembled a jay. He could
not positively identify it. The bird had to live here – the humans
were only passing through. How many cared about the name of
the bird? He sighed to think how little he knew.

But the designer drug was taking hold. Feeling a warm glow, he
perceived the bird as a sign of survival in adversity. He had no
reason to feel melancholy. The scorpion poison had brought
depression in its wake – and thanks to Hikmat Haydar nothing
worse than depression. He was on his way home; he could put
behind him all the morbid philosophizing and the chimeric
appearance of his mother. True, he had not retrieved his memories, but he could live without them.

Haydar removed a large coloured handkerchief from his pocket

328

and wiped his brow with it. Retrieving his Nieman Marcus bag, he tucked it safely between Burnell and his own solid bulk.

'How do these officials enjoy to meddle,' he said. Excusing himself, he took a swig from a silver flask and rolled his eyes with a heavy undersea movement. The two lads, thinking this *moue* directed at them, shrank back further into their corner.

To cheer himself up still further, Burnell took out Blanche's letter and read it again.

The train had been stationary for some while. Distant uproar came from the end of the carriage; several voices could be heard, choral in dispute. The shouting became louder. It was terminated by the slamming of a door. The female conductor stomped along the corridor, testing wheel-strength with her tread. In a short while, the train began slowly to move forward.

The two boys peered out of the window and became excited, screaming at their mother. All except the two Russians looked out at the desert.

There, an old man of meagre appearance was picking himself up from the ground where he had been thrown or kicked. Beside him stood a lanky youth, dressed in tattered shirt and trousers, beating dust from his clothes. They called in desperation to someone on the train. The young man started to run alongside the train, waving and shouting.

Haydar laughed. 'These two were booted out from the train, doubtlessly, because they tried to ride without tickets.'

Burnell was staring out at the heavy grey sky, the colourless wastes of sand over which darkness gathered. 'What will happen to them?'

'They must walk.'

'We're kilometres from anywhere. They'll surely die.'

'It is undemocratic to steal a free ride on a Turkmen train, my friend.'

Burnell remained gazing at the bleak scene. As the train gathered speed, the thin youth ran forward determinedly, leaping for one of the doors, and clung to its handle. The old man stood helplessly by the track, arms by his side. Already he was dwindling with distance. In a moment, he was lost to view.

The mother called to her boys, but they had the window open – cold air poured in – to see if the young man fell off. Instead, he managed to scramble up on the roof of the express, which by now was travelling at speed through the thickening dusk. They cheered his bare feet.

Somewhere to the south of them, distantly, stretched the Karakum Canal. Burnell supposed to his companion that at least the old man could find water there to drink.

'The Karakum Canal is fed from the Amu Darya. That great mother of rivers is known classically as the Oxus,' Haydar explained. He was breathing deeply and nodding his head, regaining lost equanimity. He added, as postscript, 'The waters are poisoned nowadays by many chemicals.'

The fate of the old man who had been thrown off the train was no concern of his.

24

Singing in the Train

Night had embraced the speeding train.

The white-clad gipsy woman opened up a small basket and produced some food. She offered it about with a wide smile. One of her eye teeth was capped with gold, which either added to or detracted from her charm in Burnell's eyes. The passengers, with the exception of the Russian couple, gladly accepted her *samsas*. Burnell's pastry, filled with minced lamb and chick peas, was delicious. He in his turn passed round fresh apricots. Haydar countered with cans of Coke.

The comradeship which springs up between travellers everywhere enveloped them. Haydar fell into conversation with the white-clad woman. He had tucked his palms under his haunches. She gesticulated freely, rattling her bracelets. Burnell fell into a light doze, dreaming of fair women.

Haydar roused him saying that the woman's name was Elmira. He described her as an illiterate of the worst class, though posing as something else. She had been worried in case she had been defrauded and sold wrong tickets. Being illiterate, she suspected all men of trying swindle her. Holding wrong tickets, she would have been thrown off the train with her sons, like the two men, to freeze to death in the night. Now her mind was calmer, she had every intention of begging for money.

'From me?'

'From you because you ate her *samsa*. And because you are English. And from others on the train. She expects to earn her fare in that way and in other ways, probably.'

'Such as?'

Haydar plunged his face into a lopsided frown, as though to indicate that men of the world needed no explanations in such matters.

As if she understood what was being said, Elmira smiled at Burnell. Again the flash of gold. She nodded the dark curls on her head, encouraging him to say something to her.

'Money she wants,' Haydar said. 'Yet she claims to be a lawyer – and also a singer who sang in theatres and other such low places.'

Burnell asked if the woman would sing for them. When this request was grudgingly translated, Haydar frowned and said, 'You see, how like all illiterates! She cannot read, so something must be compensated. Thus she asks for money, typically. Only then and then only will she sing.'

'Tell her I will sing to her. She shall then sing to me. No money will change hands.'

After some discussion this arrangement was agreed upon. For politeness's sake, Burnell leaned over towards the Russian and asked if he would mind their singing.

'You may cut your throat for all I care,' replied the Russian, with grave courtesy, showing his little teeth in a smile.

Burnell rose and embarked on 'I Know Where I'm Going'. His voice filled the compartment. People from further along the express, hearing the strange song, clustered about the door to listen.

Everyone appeared moved, applauding heartily, the two lads rolling about in delight. Even the Russians felt themselves inspired to clap. Burnell was implored to sing again. But it was Elmira's turn.

The lady rose to her feet and bowed to the company, with a special flourish towards Burnell. She made many pretty protests before singing. Throbbing, throaty, the notes of a Russian song poured from her. They seemed to come not merely from her lips but from the rest of her, so wholehearted was her performance. The audience applauded wildly. Elmira threw them kisses. The men present were encouraged.

In response to Burnell's question, Haydar said the song was

tragi-comic, entitled '*Chto Mnie Corye*' – 'I'm going to be obedi-ent and accept what fate brings'.

The compartment was now under siege. First-comers were being forced in by pressure from behind. A small man with pock-marked countenance announced he would sing a traditional Uzbek song. It dated, he said, from the dawn of history. His Oriental cast of features was set off by a grey lounge suit. He said that the nation to which he was proud to belong had sung this song in the saddle.

The song required an amount of roaring and changes of tempo. Haydar endeavoured to interpret for Burnell's benefit.

> '"The day will dawn –
> The gallant hoof of horse will take
> Us galloping – galloping – from grass and steppe
> Westwards. We throw both men and animals
> Into the great grey animated wave
> To win the honours of sea, rain, beach's gold."

'So it continues, saying nothing about raping women and burn-ing down villages. Frankly, I hate Uzbeks as I hate illiterates.'

'You hate Jews too.'

Haydar made his throat-slitting gesture. Bottles of vodka were now circulating in the compartment. The Uzbek was applauded, though without conviction. He faded into the crowd.

The Russian arose, grandly unbuttoning his knee-length coat. He climbed on his seat and began to sing in a deep voice, gestur-ing occasionally, a smouldering cigarette gripped between his fingers. He sang, '*Ekh, Byla – Nie Byla*' – 'What use is this sad life of mine?' It was his wife's turn to sit impassively.

Elmira was excited by the growing audience. Displaying her pretty and plump arms, she motioned other people to enter the compartment, and announced she would sing again for their delight. Haydar shouted at her to sit down or he would call the conductor back.

'She can't read, but she can smell coins. Soon she will sing to earn money. We shall be awake with her yowling all night.'

'I wouldn't mind hearing another song from her.'

'Don't be insane. She will have the whole train crowding in here, bloody gipsy that she is.' Heaving himself up, Haydar began to shoo the intruders from the compartment. They left as though expecting no better treatment, to throw their own party in the corridor. There the Uzbek sang again. Others joined in, singing and dancing.

The occupants of the compartment fell silent, looking at one another.

Into that silence, the Russian spoke. 'Cannibals,' he said. 'Always rancour. Never some pleasantness.'

'A helping of pleasantness, I'd say,' said Burnell.

It must have seemed to Haydar that the Russian's comment was directed against his overbearing behaviour. After a minute, he said, turning to Burnell, 'You know my kind heart, but deep reasons exist why I don't trust illiterates, intolerably.'

As he spoke, he smiled ferociously at Elmira and her boys. So fierce was the smile that the boys shrank back in their corner and hugged each other. Launching into a reminiscence, Haydar's expression became fixed. The Russian fanned smoke away from his face, as though to hear more clearly.

My story is full of sorrow and horror (said Dr Haydar). It tells of happiness destroyed for ever. Yet it is set in one of the most beautiful parts of this world of ours. I speak of a certain valley in Kirghizstan, that remote state once called Kirghizia, in the days before the Soviet Empire fell apart.

The particular valley of which I speak was not so far from Bishkek, the capital city of Kirghizstan. It enjoyed solitude, and the peace that goes with solitude. The small town of Kegeti, hidden in that generous valley, did little to disturb the peace. Although some might judge our climate harsh, with the deep snow that fell every winter, we knew nothing else, and asked nothing else. We enjoyed each season in its turn. As in the primitive world, far from cities, every season brought its pleasures, and men and women lived within that embrace.

Surrounded by nature, and with serious employments to occupy us, we felt ourselves blessed.

If you've never been to Kirghizstan, I should add that our town, Kegeti, was — is — about one and a half thousand kilometres to the east of Ashkhabad, well on the way to China. Close to Kegeti Valley is a trail leading southwards which crosses the frontier into the mighty ever-slumbering continent of Cathay. The trail, known as the Kashgar Road, has been used by travellers from time immemorial.

Before I tell you of the tragedy which befell Kegeti, I must describe the place. In those times, the inhabitants numbered only about three thousand. A small town, you see. A dashing mountain stream runs through it, dividing the town into two parts. Wooden houses climb irregularly up the slopes on either side of the stream. From every verandah, under which the townsfolk store their pine logs for winter, mountains and forest can be seen.

Well, it's an alpine place, unspoilt, and, as I've said, quiet. I'm speaking now about the days when we were under Communist rule. But Moscow was far away. All we really needed was about us. The market stalls in the town square, where the statue of Lenin stood, sold fish, meat in abundance, bread, quinces, melons, lemons, grapes, apricots, and much else besides. We rarely needed to journey as far as Frunze, as Bishkek was called.

Despite its remoteness, Kegeti had a claim on the outside world's attention. In the tumbled terrains above the valley floor were past fortifications, towers, lost villages, even a palace, relics of past ages. In these monuments to forgotten nations, occasional treasures were found. Excavated items were installed in Kegeti's small museum, or else were taken to the grander museum in Frunze. Our museum was in intense rivalry with Frunze Museum, as you may imagine.

So intense was this rivalry that the directors of the two museums, the large but more distant museum and the small but accessible museum, hated each other. And I was the director of the Kegeti Museum.

Everywhere we look in the world, we see divisions. Even that stream of ours marked a division as it ran through the town. In the spring, when snows were melting, it was a torrent. In autumn it was tame; boys paddled in it and floated sticks. But at all times of year, it so happened that we Kirghiz families lived mainly on the east side of the stream. On the west side, it was mainly Uzbek families. Our museum was situated on the east side. My house was only a few metres from its door.

Why was I so happy, my friends, in those bygone days? It was largely because of my relationship with my wife.

My wife's name was Ranisa. How beautiful, how calm and enchanting, was Ranisa! About her features and character was something delicately Oriental. Her lips and her eyebrows were as fine as if drawn by an artist, while her eyes were as clear as if she had just been born. She wore her dark hair long, tying it up into a bun in the day. Ah, Ranisa, there are none like you today! Beauty attended her every glance and gesture.

I must tell you how I met this paragon among women. I was sent by the authorities to the ancient city of Osh, there to attend an historiographical symposium. Its organizing secretary was none other than Ranisa. I fell in love with her the very day the conference opened. So, I don't doubt, did many of the other speakers at the event. But somehow it was me she favoured. A miracle, you see!

Although I was Kirghiz and she Uzbek, at least in part, we hardly paid attention to such distinctions in those days. The great thing was to be good Communists, and work properly for the community. Ranisa liked the way my speech had been properly prepared and contained facts, not empty rhetoric.

Osh is a modern city now, I believe, but its history dates back to six or seven centuries before the birth of Christ. In Osh, with Ranisa, I ate the finest pomegranates I ever tasted. It had been an important city on the old Silk Road – which probably accounted for the lucid Chinese quality of my beloved's face and body.

So we were married in Kegeti. Ranisa was happy with the simple life of the mountains – a woman who sang at her work. I can say we were truly fulfilled in our lives. We slept together in a large wooden bed in which we could listen to the sound of the stream pouring down from the mountains and never drying – like a blessing, you might say.

Ranisa bore me three children, a boy – Rejep – and two

daughters, both of whom exhibited from babyhood their mother's good humour and intelligence. Also living with us was Ranisa's older sister, Evranileva. When still in Osh, Evranileva had married a Cossack husband. This man was a powerful political figure, but privately a cruel and drunken brute. One night he beat Evranileva so badly that she fled from his house. After some adventures, she came to live with us in our mountain retreat.

Because of this bad treatment, Evranileva was a haunted woman. She made no friends in Kegeti but at least she was kind to her nephew and nieces, and was a good cook into the bargain. And she adored her younger sister.

Well, little can be said about a contented life. It can't be recaptured in words, or even in the memory, so smoothly do years flow by. Besides, it's really sorrow the world's more interested in hearing about. Sorrow – well, that's inexhaustible . . .

Of course we had our excitements. Often I'd be away for days in the hills, investigating the archaeological sites. Rejep came with me when he was old enough, riding in front of me in the saddle. I tried always to make sure that the museum in Frunze did not hear of any new finds we made. It stole from us what it could, just as Moscow museums stole – I should say 'requisitioned' – from Frunze.

It was wonderful up in the hills – almost as wonderful as down at home with Ranisa, and game was plentiful. Existence in Kegeti was as good as it can be on Earth, I'd say.

At this juncture, Dr Haydar sighed and looked about as if awakening from a dream. He had been staring straight ahead as he talked, his right hand resting on his Nieman Marcus bag. Now he looked with heavy-lidded gaze down at the floor, as though disinclined to continue further with his narrative.

The singer Elmira had appeared to listen as raptly as Burnell, as if so addicted to story-telling that it held her even when in a language incomprehensible to her. Her two boys clutched each other and by so doing had turned themselves temporarily to stone. As for the Russian couple, they swathed themselves in cigarette smoke and kept their own counsel.

His hands clasped in his lap, Burnell looked about him as he listened to Haydar's tale. Studying the faces of the others making the journey to Krasnovodsk with him, he realized he was half lost in the story and half in his own musings.

The express fled on its way, passing indistinct Geok-Tepe. Lights had come on in the carriages, to cast a flickering illumination on the cold dead ground over which they sped.

Haydar took his silver flask from his pocket and swigged at it. He sighed, wiped his mouth slowly and thoroughly, and then began to speak again. As he talked he looked into the dark eyes of Elmira.

I said this was a story about an illiterate. So it is, and the worse for me that it should be so.

Ranisa and I ran the little Kegeti Museum between us. When I was on an expedition in the mountains, my wife was left in sole command. The only assistance we had was an Uzbek. The Uzbek's name was Pikuli. And Pikuli was an illiterate.

Now everyone in our town knew Pikuli. He was always about and I should explain that he was a kind of standing joke. A lumbering, ill-formed young man, very dark, and uncouth in his speech.

Children always teased Pikuli. The bigger ones threw stones. There was something about Pikuli. He was a Caliban, a thing apart. Yet surly as he looked, he was harmless. You might say that basically his nature was so mild that others took advantage of him; or you might say that he knew if he struck anyone the whole of Kegeti would have been angry. Fighting did not happen in Kegeti.

Pikuli was the odd job man at the museum. He was our sweeper. Any heavy work, any dirty work, any extra work – Pikuli did it. I realize I regarded him as a beast of burden. I took advantage of him. So did Ranisa. But we were never unkind. Indeed we felt sorry for him. Ranisa would often reward him with a mutton bone or a slice of apricot tart. Then he would look at her with such an intensity of gratitude she was sometimes frightened.

You can say only that Pikuli was one of society's victims. He was an orphan. His mother was a mountain woman of an Uzbek tribe, who had been violated and died shortly after giving birth to her son. He lived on the west of the town, in what had been a winter shed for goats. At the time of which I'm speaking, Pikuli would be maybe eighteen or nineteen.

Day after day, Pikuli did whatever work was given him to do, without complaint. If someone hit him with a stone, he would bark like a dog – but never attack.

As I have admitted, I took advantage of him, and was contemptuous of such an unschooled creature, who had never shown the slightest interest in learning anything. Yet – I admired Pikuli. Yes, for all his sullen looks, there was something saintly about him. He walked with a slouch, his black hair hung over his slant eyes, but there was innocence, I thought, in his rare smiles. He reminded me of one of Dostoevsky's holy fools. So I treated him decently, of that I'm sure, though I had to kick his ass a few times to get him moving. More than once I stopped Rejep throwing stones and mud at him. Ranisa seldom raised her voice to the fellow.

And so life went on its smooth course, until we heard new names in that world beyond Frunze, the names of Mikhail Gorbachev and then Boris Yeltsin. News came that Communism was worn out, that the great Stalin had been mistaken, and – most amazing – that the Soviet Union was collapsing. Imagine! It was like hearing that the sun had gone cold! I stood up in our local council and denied that such a thing could happen. It must be a propagandist lie. I had been educated – as had everyone in Kegeti – to believe that we would probably take over the whole world when Capitalism fell apart. Instead, somehow we had ourselves fallen apart. Our leaders had deceived us.

Now, we cannot understand how such foolish understandings filled our remote valley. But so it was. Everything we had been taught had been wrong. Every word we had read in our books at school had been a lie . . .

To this day, I have nostalgia for the old order. Like everything, it had its blemishes. But at least it had laws, under which we enjoyed peace. It is true that in President Leonid Brezhnev's day, when I was a boy, there were difficulties – the war with Afghanistan may be criticized in retrospect – but at least society was stable and everyone knew what was what. That's the secret in life, to know what's what. No sooner was President Yeltsin in power than troubles began everywhere and society became disrupted.

Still, you try to continue to live life as before. The kids must be brought up properly. You imagine that the troubles will pass . . .

Up in the mountains, close by the Kashgar road, excavations were taking place on the site of a twelfth-century bastion. The archaeologists were having problems getting their salaries paid, but still they kept working, being dedicated men. They had dug down into a cellar and brought up various buried objects, including a bronze instrument, which we identified as something used by Chinese camel-drivers to blow pills down the throats of sick camels. An inscription on the instrument had still to be translated.

When the archaeologists radioed me to announce that they had found a grave with a coffin which seemed to contain someone who had been of high rank in this world, I saddled up Scoundrel, my mare, and rode into the mountains. What happened while I was there, in the encampment under the ancient pines? Why a *riot* broke out in Kegeti!

A riot? I had always imagined that riots were things which happened in distant parts of the globe, Milan or Los Angeles or even Moscow or Osh. I had imagined that a riot needed at least a thousand people, or let's say five hundred. And there had to be an important building to besiege, a palace or a TV station or a police headquarters. In Kegeti – so I believed – we had not enough men to start a riot. And no important buildings . . .

Yet there was Ranisa on the short wave, telling me she was besieged in the museum, with a mob yelling outside.

I saddled up my mare at once, and started for home.

Night was falling by the time I arrived back in Kegeti. Mist was gathering. I approached warily from the south.

The town lay silent. The square was deserted. Although the street lights were shining, no other lights showed. Son-Kul, the main food store, was closed. The Korean café and the Naryn Restaurant had their shutters up. No cars moved. No one was about at all.

I reached the museum, my museum. The heavy glass door was shattered. A pool of blood lay on the marble steps leading up to the entrance.

This sight woke in me a great fear for my wife. Also a fierce anger at this violation of our legality.

Climbing into the museum through the broken door, I called to Ranisa. In the silence which followed I had an image of my elegant and demure spouse lying dead on the floor. I searched the place. She was nowhere there. The exhibits all remained undisturbed.

I left the museum and my horse and ran home. There was silence except for the burble of the stream. Then a few shots, distantly, in the woods. Rifle fire.

Happily, Ranisa was safe. She greeted me unharmed in the house. She was nursing my shotgun, and her sister and the children were huddled by her. She told me that when the rioters had broken the museum door, the leader had severed an artery on the falling glass. This accident had saved her. The mob leader had collapsed and had had to be rushed to the hospital in Frunze. A couple of his friends had driven him away. The rest of the rioters, subdued by the sight of blood, had simply dispersed.

'It was not serious,' Ranisa said. 'I should not have radioed you, but I was frightened at the time. The noise they made was so scaring. The mob gathered on the bridge and then came along the street.'

'But what did they want?'

Ranisa gave an uneasy laugh. 'They shouted that they wanted their independence.'

'Independence from what? For what? Who were these madmen?'

'Uzbeks.'

So that was the start of it. Of general disaster. The history of nations rushes on like a river, beyond individual control. Suddenly we were no longer Soviet citizens. That was all past. We became Kirghizi and Uzbeks. Ethnic distinctions opened up like terrible wounds coming unstitched – wounds of which we had scarcely been aware.

It's true, as I said, that Kirghizi lived on one side of our stream and Uzbeks on the other. But this arrangement had always been regarded more as a law of nature than any kind of political division. Now it became a political division.

There had been plenty of intermarriage between the two races. We also had some Russian businessmen in Kegeti, and possibly the odd KGB man. Also a handful of Koreans. Even they had intermarried.

All these marriages, like marriages elsewhere, had been happy or wretched in various degrees, the degree rarely depending on racial stock. Of course there had been jokes – but jokes without a sting in them. Now there was a sting. The time for jokes was finished.

I was a responsible member of our community. As a Kirghiz married to an Uzbek, I resolved to talk to the Uzbek community. The morning after the riot, Pikuli turned up for work as usual, looking no more dishevelled than he usually did. I set him to sweeping up the broken glass and repairing the museum door with some planking. He worked without comment or complaint. Leaving Ranisa in charge, I walked over the bridge to see my friend Turav Serov.

Turav Serov had the compact build of an Uzbek. He was a bright intelligent young man of my own age. His deep-set green eyes were generally alight with humour. We'd sat on the same bench at school together, and he often accompanied me into the hills.

He was sitting in the teashop with some companions, engaged in earnest conversation. Serov did not greet me in his usual amiable fashion. No humour showed on his face, while the others fastened their gaze on the table and did not look up at me. More abruptly than I had intended, I asked him what had happened on the previous day.

'What is it?' I asked. 'I see you're angry, Turav. Is it anything serious?'

To this day I can hardly credit Serov's reply.

'Serious, you ask? I'll say it's serious. At the end of the Afghan War, when bread went on ration for a year, you people, you Kirghizi – you got twice as large a ration as us Uzbeks.'

I could not believe I was hearing correctly. The Afghan War had ended years ago. As for the question of rationing . . . It was true there had been a famine elsewhere, man-made, because good Kirghizstan grain had been despatched to feed the soldiers returning from the war. At that time, a lorry had driven up from Frunze to Kegeti every day, loaded with loaves of bread which were fairly distributed. So I had been told, although I had been posted away from Kegeti at that period.

I said to Serov, 'Why are you talking about this bread rationing? What has it to do with the riot yesterday?'

He stood up and faced me. 'We were cheated over the bread ration. You think that's nothing, do you?'

'Look, bread was distributed daily during the time of shortages. No one starved, did they? Every family in Kegeti got its fair share.'

'How do you know? At night, a second lorry came, delivering bread only to you people, you Kirghizi.'

'That's a lie. Obviously a lie. In any case, why bring up this ancient rumour now? It's all past history, not at all important. What is important is that a mob – a mob, Turav – tried to break into the museum yesterday.'

Then the other men started shouting at me. They said the bread ration was just one of many ways in which the Uzbeks had been cheated throughout history. They were not prepared to stand for it any more. They demanded their independence. That was the word Ranisa had heard: *Independence*. Just to pronounce it seemed to drive them mad. They banged the table, spat in my face, bellowed the word in chorus. Independence, Independence!

In the end, I left the teashop in fury. To reason with them was impossible.

Next day, by the way, a notice appeared on the teashop door saying 'Uzbeks Only'.

Back in my house, I strode about and cursed until Ranisa calmed me. When we discussed the problem, we decided we should call an urgent meeting of our Kirghizi friends.

That very evening, seven close friends came. They were shouted at on the way by Serov's clique. A stone was thrown.

Nothing particularly serious, but the seven arrived in angry mood. Most of them were carrying their shotguns.

'We must talk about this calmly,' I said, as they crowded into our small living-space. 'Please leave your guns by the door. This is not a shooting matter. We need to talk and consider. We can't have trouble in Kegeti. It's always been peaceful and we must keep it that way. If our friends the Uzbeks have a grievance, then we must meet it honestly.'

Grinko was our schoolteacher, a tall man, tall as a bulrush and as mild, with a neat white beard. He spoke now in his piping voice which generations of children had imitated. 'We cannot discuss anything with your wife in the room. She's an Uzbek too.'

When he looked round for support, heads nodded in agreement.

'Don't be daft,' I said. 'You all know Ranisa. She's my wife and she's certainly not going to be sent out of her own living-room.'

'Oh, I'll go rather than be a thorn in anyone's flesh,' said Ranisa, looking embarrassed. 'I'll go and make some tea for you all.'

'No, you stay,' I told her. 'Principles are principles.'

'Yeah, and an Uzbek is always an Uzbek.' That was Penukidze, a man who worked in the Naryn Restaurant. 'I'm not stopping here. We don't owe the Uzbeks a thing, so it's no good you being weak with them. We've got to show them where they get off.'

Someone else said this, if you can believe it: 'And what about what happened in 1916? A million Kirghizi were slaughtered, by Russians and by these same Uzbeks.'

'That's a million years ago, you fool!' I shouted. But they shouted louder.

That was how it went. There was no rational way out of the cruel dilemma in which the history of the previous century placed us. It had to be war or peace. In a life-threatening situation, instincts from pre-human days revive. Most terribly, shadow projections make us see in those who oppose us all the dark things we suppress in ourselves. On either side of our little stream, enemy territories sprang up, in which Uzbeks saw us as cheats and oppressors and we saw them as murderers. No intellectual bridge could span that crude division. By the week's end, shooting started.

Of course the new enmity fed on past glories and defeats. Hate was a poison in the bloodstream. Old memories rose to choke us, and made men mad.

Where all the guns came from it is hard to say. I was told there were Belgians in Frunze who sold armaments to both sides, and gun-runners in the hills.

I never thought to see the rather weedy Grinko manning a machine gun. But so it was. Soon the whole town was armed. And Ranisa and I were not trusted by either side.

At this unhappy hour, news came from Osh reporting pitched battles in the streets. There too, Kirghizi and Uzbeks who had once been friends were fighting each other.

Frunze however remained peaceful. With a sad heart, I decided to move my small and vulnerable family from Kegeti, to find refuge in Frunze.

25

Snow in the Desert

The express train slowed and came to a halt again at this juncture in Haydar's narrative. Snow fell beyond its windows. The lights from the train revealed the desert with its huge limbs embalmed in white.

Burnell had risen to stare out of the window at curtains of snow against the fast-moving carriages while the unwinding narrative went on behind his back. He found himself seeking some unifying symbol for climate and story. Now that the last poisons had ebbed from his system and he was leaving this land in transition, he felt a necessity to make sense of what little he had learned. The white veils of storm outside were composed of individual snowflakes, each fashioned in unique complexity; they paralleled the wholesale displacement of individuals which followed the decline and fall of the Empire of the Soviets.

Unable adequately to bear witness to that disruption, he was going home, not much better or worse for the small tragedies on which his own life had impinged. And yet – the crooks at the Antonescu Clinic, the artful Romanian himself, who had burgled his brain, had set up a private enterprise following the collapse of state control; Burnell was himself an indirect victim of this particular human snowstorm. It affected everyone.

Fleetingly, as the train slowed and the lighting-system flickered, he grasped the interplay between historical processes, the pitfalls of national life, the variousness of human relationships, and the immutable laws of nature against which ambition constantly scraped elbows: all those elements which together drained into the sewers of human dreams.

Small wonder the Ghvtismshobeli Madonna had looked with apprehension into her future – or that she had been smashed when she reappeared in the hard world of men.

Elmira's small shriek brought him back to the present. He turned from the window.

Although Dr Haydar had paused in his story-telling, he continued to hold the stance he had adopted: legs apart, the better to rest his bulk, hands clasped under belly, head lowered, he stared at the floor of the compartment with an unmoving bullish stare.

In Haydar's attitude, stubborn yet perplexed, fixed enough to recall a minotaur pent, Burnell saw a problem related to the social turbulence and ethnic struggles in which Central Asia was embroiled: confusion and loss of identity. In the whorish arms of commercial technology, confusion was compounded.

All except Haydar were astir, rising to see what had caused the unexpected halt. Elmira and the Russian woman were talking together. Elmira's boys hammered excitedly on the window.

One of the inspectors was walking along the embankment outside, his coat collar turned up against the wind. Already his beard was glistening white with snow. It was the man who had earlier thrown the youth and his older companion off the train for having no ticket. Passengers called to him; their voices were puny against the whine of the storm and the crackle of cooling metal. The inspector made no response, but trudged along towards the rear of the train, flashing his torch back and forth as he went.

Despite the weather, men were spilling from the rear carriage, shouting, beckoning. Soon others were climbing out into the desert, leaving their tracks in the snow.

After a brief dispute with Elmira, her boys ran from the compartment, pushed along the crowded corridor and scrambled down to the embankment. They waved to Burnell and followed the inspector along the line. Elmira said something to Haydar in a complaining tone; he did not look up.

She stood close to Burnell to peer from the window. He inhaled her perfume, identifying it as patchouli, a scent favoured by whores. The heavy fragrance, so familiar to him, caused him to move an inch closer. Elmira moved away, giving a bracelet a rattle as she did so.

More people were pouring from the train, glad to take an opportunity to stretch their legs, even if it entailed turning white in the process. A German couple, a man with a younger woman by his side, saw Burnell's European face. They called up cheerfully that a young beggar had fallen off the roof of the train. They might have been announcing Christmas. Burnell responded in German.

Night wore on. Snow continued to swirl between heaven and earth. The Trans-Caspian was still, the constellations wheeled overhead, surreptitious behind cloud. Burnell and Elmira left the train and joined the crowd standing by the track. All round them was the great muffled world, and to one side the heavy blind wheels of the train. Elmira smoked a cigarette. She kept casting a glance up at the window of their compartment, perhaps anxious in case someone stole their belongings. Burnell spoke to her. She smiled but merely shrugged her shoulders, over which she had thrown a colourful shawl.

Talking to a English-speaking passenger, Burnell learnt that the young beggar – some said 'beggar', some 'terrorist' – had fallen off the roof a way back along the track. Maybe he was one of the Three Young Men who had tried to kill the general, in which case Allah's justice was done. His body was being collected. Another passenger was laughing: the fool must have frozen on the roof. It served him right. People had to pay their way in this life.

Out of the whirling dark came a group of men, staggering a little, carrying something between them. The inspector was there, carrying only his torch. Between them into the train lights came a stretcher, on which lay the broken body of the young man. It was passed up to hands on the train, whereupon the crowd began to scramble back aboard out of the snow, shaking themselves and their garments.

Everyone chattered excitedly. Despite the lateness of the hour, and the delay, everybody was put in good humour by the incident. The men in the rear coach, who had seen the youth fall past their windows, were regarded as heroes. All and sundry went to pat them on the back. The inspector too was congratulated, but he made a surly face and disappeared into his own cubbyhole.

With a blast of its klaxon, the express began to move, picking up speed. Burnell, Elmira and her boys settled themselves back in their places. The Russian couple shrank back from any chance contact with wet garments.

Haydar sat withdrawn in his seat. The carnation drooped in the buttonhole of his suit. To show her compassion, Elmira gave him a pastry with dates in. He ate it slowly, chewing each mouthful thoroughly while she watched, and then – without invitation – continued his story.

Both Ranisa and I were reluctant to leave Kegeti (Haydar said). But the decision was soon made for us. The Uzbeks obtained mortars, I can't say from where. In times of war, weapons always become available. A guerrilla group established mortar positions in the western hills above our town, from which they could bombard its eastern, Kirghizi, side. Before long, the museum was hit and a fire started.

When the mortar shell struck, I was in the basement of the museum. I was packing some of our more precious artefacts away for safety, working with the faithful Pikuli. You remember Pikuli, my illiterate odd job man? We ran upstairs, got the fire-fighting equipment, and managed to extinguish the blaze.

Pikuli was a clumsy creature. In the excitement, he fell over a large ammonite and burnt both his hands in the fire. He whined to go home, but I bandaged up his hands in my office and made him stay on. I was afraid the building might suffer another hit.

Later, in the afternoon, I did a foolish thing. Upset by the miserable turn of events, I still hoped that old bonds of friendship might reassert themselves and sanity return to our valley. I hoped that even our enemies would cease to be enemies if we treated them kindly and justly – turned the other cheek, you might say. For so it states in the Koran, 'Good and evil deeds are not alike. Requite evil with good, and he who is your enemy will become your dearest friend.' So before returning home to Ranisa, I wrote a note to Turav Serov.

Men like Turav Serov had been our friends for many years. I refused to think of them as enemies – that would only perpetuate the conflict, to my mind. Innocent fool that I was, I never understood bitterness. Not then. Now, yes, but not then. I held the view, quite apart from my Communist beliefs, that we must all suffer in life. The demon rat of death and decay always gnaws away in the foundations. There's also an old saying – Kazakh in origin, I believe – which states, 'Never trust the tussock of grass you sit down on: it does not understand you, you do not understand it.' Well, I didn't understand enmity at that time. Pikuli was the tussock I happened to sit down on.

I gave him my note to deliver to Serov. I have gone over that foolish well-meaning gesture every week of my life. I blame myself one day, I exonerate myself the next, only to curse myself again on the third day. Injustice is part of natural law. It's the way the universe is constructed. Holy books never tell you that.

Most of us have within us an ethical imperative to be and do good, but that's quite apart from any illusory God. And it is precisely this terrible natural injustice which should draw men together as brothers in understanding. Religion and ideology have brought terrible confusion to that basic situation, in which humans find themselves. OK, I accept that Communism had its faults, at least as practised. But at its core lay a belief that all men were brothers. Hypocrisy, maybe. But Christianity is no better. Christians believe in universal love – or so they say. But that certainly is not how they act. Same with all Muslim sects. What horrors are committed in the name of religious justice!

Anyhow . . . Where does philosophy get you? It never bought a single potato.

I wrote this damned note to Turav Serov saying I hoped that the Uzbeks would not continue to bear us hard feelings, as we bore them none. I said that I was leaving Kegeti with my family and hoped to come back when conditions returned to normal. And I wished him well.

And I gave the note into the hands of my illiterate, knowing he could not read what I wrote, and sent him off to Serov on the other side of the stream.

Then I went home with a strangely light heart. I used a back street in order to avoid sniper fire.

Ranisa and I had devised a plan the night before. Bless her, she was a well-organized lady. She had packed bags containing blankets and clothes. She had stored food, water, and necessities in saddlebags. She had made our three children ready. They sat about, playing with marbles, unusually well behaved: Rejep, the boy, and our two dear girls, Nadja and Gulija, the youngest.

My sister-in-law, Evranileva, argued against leaving. She feared the journey and clung to what we had. I was forced to tell her that we would leave without her if she would not come. Choking back her tears, she stuffed some items into a pack – the same pack with which she had fled from Osh and her swinish husband.

I reassured our little family. There was no danger. We would leave Kegeti when dusk fell and climb the mountains to the east, taking the pass into the next valley, which was virtually uninhabited. From there it would be quite easy to continue downhill to Frunze. Once we reached the road, it should not be difficult to stop a vehicle and get a lift into the town. In Frunze, we could stay with an old aunt of mine until we found better lodgings. We should be there on the following night, safe and sound.

To the rear of the house my mare Scoundrel was tethered. I loaded her up with the saddlebags and other baggage, ready to depart. The children could ride on her in turn. I foresaw no difficulties.

We also had a big brute of a dog, Sawdust. The children begged for Sawdust to come with us. No reason why not. Ranisa and I found ourselves treating this expedition as an adventure, and smiling at each other with childish excitement. Only Evranileva was downcast.

Directly the sun was lost behind the ridge of the mountains and our valley began to fill with shadow, I told the family to file quietly out through the back door. As I walked through the rooms we had known, their dimness filled my eyes like water. Now all the happiness we had known there was to be lost. I shivered. Perhaps I felt a presentiment of what was to come. I buttoned my coat and locked the house behind me.

They all stood outside, looking trustingly at me: the two sisters, the three children, even the animals. Behind them were the few vegetables we grew, never to be harvested. Beyond that was a wood fence and then the ascent into the pine forests – the way we had to go to safety.

I thrust my sporting-gun into the saddle holster and helped young Nadja up on the back of Scoundrel. We set off without a word. Only Rejep looked back at Kegeti and waved goodbye.

Already the town was growing faint in dusk and mist. Few lights showed.

Unfortunately, that mist rolled up towards us and soon enclosed us. Progress became unexpectedly difficult. Although I knew all the trails well, I became confused. The trees, pines mainly, hemmed in the fog. Not until the early hours of the next morning did we climb above the fog into clear air. We had missed the direct way to the pass.

The pale horns of a new moon rose to encourage us. By then we were all exhausted. We pressed on, not speaking above a whisper when necessary. I kept to myself the fact that I no longer knew exactly where we were. The only course was to keep on climbing.

Ranisa carried little Gulija for some hours without complaint. She had to rest at last. Evranileva was begging to stop. I left them among the trees, holding Scoundrel's rein, while I went to scout ahead with the dog.

Night birds cried about me. The forest was thick now. It was almost impossible to make any progress in the dark.

Sawdust found a deer track. Following him along it, I surmounted the ridge. The way lay downhill into the next valley. With some relief, I moved forward to an enormous rock, from the cracks of which ferns grew. I retraced my steps and brought my little party to the rock. There we settled down as best we could, to get what sleep we might. The two little girls nestled against their mother.

While I dreamed that I was still awake, Sawdust's growl awoke me. I seized the dog's damp muzzle and soothed him. We were snared in the moistures of a grey dawn. The trees dripped. Banked among their branches were patches of mist like snowdrifts slowly uncurling. Alarmed, I stood and listened. I could hear nothing but the constant seepage of water. We were probably no more than three miles from Kegeti.

These woods and slopes had always been friendly. The belated realization came that that might no longer be the case.

Sawdust was still growling softly. Scoundrel moved restlessly, snatching at tufts of grass. Kneeling, I shook Ranisa till she woke. What a look she gave me – an immediate recognition of the uncertainty of our situation. Detaching herself from the girls, she stood and stretched. We held each other, for love and warmth. We held each other, and kissed, little knowing it was for the last time.

I went a short way down the trail to peer ahead. Still I saw and heard nothing untoward, and returned to Ranisa. We roused Evranileva and the children, hushing the childish voices which carry such a long way. Nadja was asking to go home. A crust of bread each, a dried apricot, a sip of milk, and we moved on our way, of necessity walking in single file. I went first, leading the mare. Ranisa brought up the rear.

As we negotiated our way downhill, the day improved slightly, though dark cloud moved rapidly over the ridges above us. Nadja was sneezing with the first signs of a cold.

At length, the path, meeting another, became wider and levelled out. A stream trickled among bushes to the right hand. To the left rose a cliff of rock. Soon there was rock on both sides hemming us in. We waited here. Evranileva nervously said she heard voices. After a minute, we moved on.

The rock – part of a bygone avalanche – fell away. The pines thinned. We emerged into a clearing. Ahead lay more level ground, open pasturage.

And to one side stood Serov, armed, together with three other armed men I did not recognize. Their guns were aimed at us.

26

The Executioner

What happened next belongs to another order of existence (continued Haydar). Or perhaps I mean of perception, for the brain has a primitive corner which awakens in the presence of extreme danger. This must be so, because such occasions are experienced in a special sick light, and events seem to penetrate the skull on a slowed time-track. Perhaps this level of perception, in its strangeness, owes its inheritance to the Eolithic, when humans were learning to think: and of course – oh, of course – such mortal threats have occurred ever since, every day, somewhere or other, in some awful part of our world.

So it was that a tableau seemed to hold for uncountable minutes. Rejep recognized Serov and half made a move towards him. Only the stillness of his parents restrained the lad. Ranisa gave me one horrified look and grabbed hold of the two girls. In that same extended moment, I was moving towards Ranisa to protect her.

Even Serov seemed frozen, with a sick smile of triumph on his face. That smile told me I had betrayed my family as clearly as if he had waved my note before my eyes.

It was Evranileva who broke the evil spell. Dropping the pack she carried, she started to run for the shelter of a clump of trees standing in the open ahead. Step by step she went, heavy skirt flickering. I seemed to see her retreating figure in that same slow-motion and ghastly light. Step by step, flicker, flicker. The distance between her and the trees scarcely diminishing.

The report from Serov's gun sounded as if from a great way off.

One of his companions fired a second later. The smoke from their muzzles was clear on the heavy air. That I saw. Ranisa clutching the children to her – that I saw. Evranileva still running – that I saw. Her headscarf fluttering from her head to the ground – that I saw. Her steps going wilder, her body toppling out of balance. Birds rising in a dark flock from the grass ahead of her. All that I saw. We all saw. We could but watch.

Until Evranileva fell forward, plunging into the ground, her legs continuing to kick.

And as I saw it all in that sick light, I too was acting without volition. I was slipping my sporting-gun from its holster on the mare's saddle and raising it to aim at Serov's chest.

But Serov and the ruffians with him were also in movement. Much action was crowded into a moment, as if time had become elastic and was now contracting. Sawdust rushed forward at the men, teeth bared. He was clubbed down by a rifle butt which smashed his skull. My mare, alarmed by the firing, broke away from Rejep, who had had hold of the reins. She galloped off across the open ground. Momentarily, I felt anger, as if we had been deserted by someone with human feelings.

I fired. Serov fired first. My rifle perhaps saved my life. Serov's bullet hit it, sending it spinning, shattered. The barrel struck me across the right temple. I even saw myself, detachedly, falling down unconscious, nerveless.

Even before I recovered my senses, I was scratching at dirt, working at some unformed plan, dragging myself into a sitting position. Against my back was rough stone. Rushing noises filled my ears, while the pain in my head was so intense I feared to be sick. Opening my eyes was a major achievement.

The Uzbeks had dumped me into a small byre. It was a low-built hut, part of the wood-tiled roof of which had collapsed. From the smell of the place, no cattle had been kept here for some while. Nettles and thistles grew in one corner, where an old wine keg had been thrown.

With an effort of will, I got myself on to my feet, to stand panting with my hands against the stone wall for support.

The door of the hut consisted of five vertical planks, crudely joined together and eroded by weather and worm. It had been pegged shut from the outside. Although I wrenched at the thing, it did not move. It now entered my mind to listen. I heard the sound of shouting and drunken laughter, sharp and brutal. And another sound, faint but continuous. Rain was falling. I stood under a hole in the roof where water poured down over a broken tile and cooled my throbbing head.

I peered through the cracks in the door. Men were staggering about in the downpour, boots stomping and splashing in mud. Serov's three companions had been joined by other Uzbeks. Some were men from our town, from Kegeti. They were all drinking. The rougher men I did not recognize were wearing uniforms; they must have formed a guerrilla force, hiding in the mountains.

To these brutes, sloshing about with their bottles, I had betrayed my family. By writing my note to Serov, I had merely shown what I regarded as decent human feelings.

As I applied my eye anxiously from one door crack to the next – how can I speak what I saw? In the rain . . . In the mud . . . I will say only this – that my dear wife, and not only my wife – imagine, my son, my little pure daughters . . . they were being stripped and defiled by those swine Uzbeks. The monsters swaggered about, breeches down, at that filthy work. Only Serov was not drinking, although it was evident he too had taken part in the rapes.

I fell to the floor of the byre, vomiting. No one heard me for the rain and the cruel laughter.

When I forced myself to stand and look again, how I longed for any weapon to kill at least one of those beasts before they killed me! Serov was calling his animals to order and shouting for the executioner. I heard the word in disbelief: *executioner*!

And who came forth? Who had been slouching beyond the limited range of my sight? That illiterate peasant, Pikuli. Pikuli, the wretch who swept the floor of my museum. I saw he too had joined in the orgy.

Serov made the Uzbeks line up my pitiable ruined family

against the front wall of the byre, where I could no longer see them. I could see Pikuli. I could see his great dumb face, streaming rain and sweat, as he turned his dull glance to Serov and nodded his head in comprehension as he received a word of command. He lifted a revolver and moved in to obey.

I heard his first shot. I knew beyond doubt what he was doing. Frantic, I scrambled to escape from my prison. Heaving the old wine keg against a wall, I was able to climb up and seize a rafter. As I attempted to squeeze through a gap in the broken roof, a section of the wall beneath me collapsed inwards under my weight. Down I went, amid a shower of stones.

They heard that. They came for me. The door was slammed open. In they rushed – men transformed into brutes! Half a dozen of them dragged me out into the muddied field where my wife's clothes were strewn. All around me were hostile faces, some of them belonging to men I once called friends. Behind them was the neutral green of the valley. Almost at my feet . . . can I say the words? – There lay the bodies, naked and defiled, of my beloved Ranisa and my children, all shot, Ranisa with more than one bullet. The children's heads had been almost blown from their shoulders. The swift-falling rain diluted their blood into a brown puddle collecting beneath them.

Oh, that dreadful day, my friends! The hurt of it!

Pikuli stood before me. He thrust the muzzle of his revolver at the bruise on my temple. His hands were still bandaged from the burns he had suffered – bandages I had bound there myself the previous day.

I managed to speak. 'Why – how can you do this? I was your protector, my wife fed you. She pitied you.'

His expression never changed. All he said was, 'I have an important job now, you scum. No more pity for Pikuli. I'm the Executioner.'

Into his words he packed all the resentment of someone who has been condescended to since birth. He had no sense of what was just, having lived injustice. Now the social order had collapsed, he had seized his chance, like a lot of other wicked men. Civilization is a habit which protects us all from wickedness.

When it fails, women and the weak are the first to suffer. The well intentioned go to the wall.

Now that the reinforcements of legality and public opinion had crumbled, something terrible in humanity emerged: that lust for survival at whatever cost. It was in me as well as in Pikuli. But as he rammed the revolver muzzle against my forehead, my agonies were only for Ranisa, to think that she and our dear children could have suffered such a vile fate. Then this beast, this Uzbek *executioner*, squeezed the trigger.

This was an illiterate who could neither spell nor count. He had already used all his six bullets on my family, and failed to reload. I remained standing after the hammer fell.

In my right hand I was clutching one of the stones which had come loose when the byre wall collapsed under me. I swung it and struck Pikuli full in the face with it. Blood burst from his nose and mouth. He dropped the gun and fell away, roaring in pain and anger.

And the drunken company burst into laughter to see him hurt. One ran to him and kicked his behind, to guarantee his discomfort. Executioner or not, Pikuli the illiterate remained the object of their barbarous contempt.

Turning, I ran for the cover of the forest. Not a single bullet followed me. I can't say why. They were too busy with Pikuli, maybe. Would they had finished me off there and then! I had no further reason to live, certainly. All that I had lived for had died with the morning, in the rainstorm . . .

When he had finished this terrifying recitation, Dr Haydar covered his face. He sat immobile, clutching the contraband bag to his massive frame with one hand.

The express rattled on its way.

In the train compartment, silence prevailed. The two boys had fallen asleep with their arms round their mother's neck, whereupon Elmira, under the contagion of sleep, had fallen into a doze against them. The two Russians had closed their eyes. The man was no longer smoking: otherwise, it was impossible to tell whether or not he was awake.

Burnell alone remained alert, staring out at the desert with fixed glare. The snow had died away, leaving only the grey Asian night and the desolation.

He thought to himself, 'If the memory is false, the sorrow is real enough; I can't criticize. Yet for all that . . . For all that, despite the vast hole in my life, I am sure of my own identity, with all its imperfections. This unfortunate man must have met up with Nastiklov's Devil – he does not know who he is.'

Some while after the recitation had finished, he turned his head towards his neighbour and spoke in a low voice. 'But your wife is alive and living in Ashkhabad, Dr Haydar . . .'

Haydar made no response beyond a slow nod of his great head. He remained monumentally still. Burnell continued wakeful, his eyes red, as light re-entered the outside world, and he caught his first sight of a line of Caspian Sea smudged by distance.

The express, weary now, crawled at last like a wounded creature through the disorder of Krasnovodsk's suburbs and the filth of its streets, into the terminus.

On to Number One Platform poured the passengers of the Ashkhabad train. Some left eagerly, pushing to get through the barriers into the town. Others proceeded at a slower pace, because of infirmity, because they were impeded by luggage, or simply because they knew no reason to hurry.

Elmira was hustled away by her two sons, excited to be free. Burnell was some way behind her in the throng. As he struggled with his astrakhan coat, Haydar had indicated that he would remain to assist the Russians, who were almost the last to leave the train. So Burnell and the Syrian shook hands briefly, embraced, and parted. Haydar stood wordless, his Nieman Marcus bag under one arm.

Shouldering his baggage, Burnell looked about him as he pushed his way along among the crowd. Announcements in Russian, bellowed over loudspeakers, competed with the cries of seagulls which swooped overhead.

It could be said of all the passengers, who had now disembarked on the western fringes of Central Asia, that they confronted a new phase of their existence. For some, much that lay ahead held promise and adventure or, at worst, profit. For others, the new phase would be but a repetition of old ones.

Above the iron arches of the station, fragments of blue sky showed. Pushing into the ticket hall, Burnell saw a kiosk which sold a postcard of the Main Square, Krasnovodsk. He bought one to send to his divorced wife. Then the tide of people carried him out into the muddy street.

He looked hopefully for a taxi to take him to the airport.

27
Squire Ad Libs

Twelve noon was sounding, chiefly in chirps from wristwatches. In many cases those watches gave off a green blink, reassuring their owners that they were not HIV-positive; for others, the game was up.

Of the two point two million (daytime) inhabitants of Soss City, thirty of them were gathered in the discreetly gloomy entrance hall of the Amanda Schäfer *Bienenhaus*. Eighteen of this small crowd were women, the rest men; no children. The men were mostly aged between forty-five and sixty-five, with one old fellow of eighty. The women formed a younger age group, being mainly in their twenties; they had recently discovered the poetry of Amanda Schäfer.

Outside, a passing shower was sousing FAM. Inside, rain was being used as an excuse for a poor turn-out. Umbrellas predominated over the floral arrangements considered mandatory on such occasions. People looked about and smiled at each other, aware that a local TV station was covering the event, hoping to be seen looking at their best on the evening's local news.

When the director of the company owning the *Bienenhaus* mounted an improvised podium, he made reference to the weather. A trickle of polite laughter followed his remarks.

The director said the board of management had decided to defy the autumn weather and celebrate the German poet after whom the apartment block was named, Amanda Schäfer, the favourite aunt of the founder. The morrow, Sunday, would mark the forty-fifth anniversary of the publication of Amanda Schäfer's lovely novella, *Rosenstrauch-maria*. The board of control agreed to hold this pleasant little ceremony to remind those fortunate enough to live in Soss City of this auspicious date.

'Some of you may think of us businessmen as hard-hearted and philistine, and not interested at all in things of the spirit, but . . .'

After ten minutes in this vein, he said, 'We are fortunate in that we have a distinguished architect and writer in our midst, Dr Roy Burnell, who happily has recently returned from abroad. He has agreed to address us on this occasion. Ladies and gentlemen, Dr Roy Burnell.'

Burnell stepped on to the platform and smiled into the television lights. He was looking dishevelled, and tugged at the tie he had put on in his apartment only ten minutes earlier.

'It is our good fortune,' he said, clearing his throat, 'to have two lines from Amanda Schäfer's poems inscribed in stone above our heads, of which we are reminded whenever we enter this building. They read, in English:

"'Leave the Valley of Darkness,
Walk in my Sphere of Light . . ."'

'Beautiful and simple words, inviting us to change our ways. Indeed, we all should change our ways, to seek a better one. Because we live in a stable part of the world, with many material comforts, it is easy to forget that we also live in a spiritual world. We do need constantly to seek the light, and enlightenment. So these words carved in stone carry a religious meaning, and, beyond that, a psychological one. We must not stay still. Staying still implies being in the Valley of Darkness, the Valley of the Shadow of . . .'

As he was speaking, Burnell observed a tall elderly gentleman entering the foyer, who mounted the shallow steps to stand unobtrusively to one side. Removing his spectacles, he wiped the rain from them with his handkerchief. Burnell continued to talk almost automatically, searching his memory for who this man could be. Something about him filled Burnell with dread. His face was familiar. Perhaps he belonged to the lost years, the stolen years.

Climbing down from the podium to thin applause, Burnell found himself face to face with the latecomer.

The latter extended a hand. 'Apologies for lateness. If the WACH offices had been farther away, no doubt I'd have been earlier. I thought I'd come over and say hello. Tom Squire, British head of WACH.'

Directly he heard the name, Burnell remembered. He had seen a photograph of Sir Thomas Squire only yesterday, when getting a wigging from his superior, Karl Leberecht. The portrait had shown a younger Squire, unsmiling, perhaps rather gloomy; and Leberecht had pointed to the photograph, saying that Squire would be in FAM the following day. Confronting Burnell now was a rather grand man in the steeper end of his seventies, still very upright, and with a commanding presence, though his skin was stretched thin, and mottled about temples and cheekbones. He appeared more approachable than his picture had indicated, his manner informal.

'I'm over here to look at a few museums. The little Schach Gallery in Munich is threatened with closure and I don't quite see eye to eye with our office here regarding that.'

Burnell struggled to remember what else he knew or had known about this man. He could recall only that Squire liked to hold forth, laying down the law when possible.

'I'm just back from Central Asia. In fact, I'm packing, preparing to go over to England for a few days.'

'Is your father well?'

'As far as I know. I must phone him.' He was looking about for a way of escape, feeling himself at a loss. 'Perhaps I'd better speak to the TV interviewer.'

'I don't wish to keep you, Roy. But I did think I might say a word to you about e-mnemonicvision, since our paths have happened to cross.' He was not the sort of man on whom one would turn one's heel. After scrutinizing Burnell to make sure that he was not about to do so, Squire said, 'I know more about fashions than about antiquities. EMV is a fashion. It will pass, like the vogue for the removal of the colon or tonsils, or the craze for the Twist, the lust for unilateral disarmament or, indeed, any numbers of Great Leaps Forward. It will pass.

'It will fade away because there is basic good sense in humankind which always reasserts itself. However, that may not happen before lives have been ruined. That was where I hoped you might permit me to offer advice.'

Burnell was frowning. 'It's not really advice I want, thanks. Nor is it a craze, as you call it, to want my memory back. I am incomplete without it.'

He made as if to get away, by moving over to the drinks table which the management had provided, where a small-scale struggle for supremacy was going on among the visitors.

Unperturbed, Squire joined him, saying, 'Yes, yours is a loss, Roy, of course. Such losses are serious, disrupting the personality. But world health figures show that what is even more damaging to sanity than loss of a period of memory is the injection of false memory, or someone else's memory – permanently, I mean.'

A woman in her forties, just ahead of them in the genteel scrimmage for wine, turned her head and said, 'Oh, I must agree with you. I have overheard what you said. To enjoy transient memories of others, as we enjoy videos, that enlarges life, is it not? But to insert permanently, it causes dissociation of the personality, leading in many cases to psychiatric illness.'

'Quite so,' said Squire, looking put out. Having secured her glass, the woman turned fully to them, saying in her near-perfect English, 'Forgive me when I butt in on your conversation. I speak of my son. He inserted permanently a year of memory of a singer he admired. It was done professionally, but the result is his complete – what to say? – disorientation. He does not know who to be.'

'That's not my problem,' Burnell said, reaching forward and seizing up two glasses, one of which he passed to Squire.

Squire took Burnell's arm and led him to one side, away from the lady, who gave every indication of following. 'How much memory was stolen from you?'

'Tom, I have to ask. Why your interest? How do you come to know of my problems?'

'Well, the family interest. And I was shown your records yesterday, in WACH. Frankly, your work has not been satisfactory lately, and they are even considering releasing you. I thought I should warn you. Your entry shows a brief stay in a mental institution, here in Frankfurt.'

'That's purely my business. It is a breach of confidence to allow you access to my file. I'm not even in your department.'

'That is so. But you know – or perhaps you cannot remember – I have always taken a personal interest in your career. I used that information to suggest to Karl that you should be allowed to return to England and rest. I produced certain figures to show how serious is the effect of memory-theft.'

The intrusive woman moved in on them, easily circumnavigating their turned backs. Her face was plain and pleasant, her dyed blonde hair swept back over a wide forehead. 'You see, gentlemen, memory-theft is rape, breaking and entering, assault – I know not what. It must be eradicated, together with insertion of false memory. I see you are powerful men. You must campaign for an EU law against these innovations. They're barbarous! I cannot express the misery of my son, and to see him deteriorate because of this cancer of the imagination . . . Although I write to the papers, nothing has been done.'

Squire nodded sympathetically. 'I agree clear guidelines for the regulation of EMV should be formulated.'

'It should be banned entirely,' the woman said indignantly.

'If you'd like to give me your name and address, I can perhaps put you in touch with people here who can help you and your son.'

While the woman was busy with the pen and notebook Squire handed her, Burnell seized the opportunity to turn and speak to a young woman who happened to look in his direction. She was evidently shy, and backed away. Again he found himself facing Squire.

'Well, thanks for speaking to me. It's good of you to intercede with Karl on my behalf, though I think I can handle my problems. I'm going back to England in any case – a few days' leave.'

'Medical advice on abuse of EMV is more authoritative in Germany than England. In Munich there's an institute –'

'As I said, I'm going to England. The clues are there, not here. I have to regain my memory. It was ten bloody years, if you wish to know. The last ten years.'

The woman was still standing with them. She said earnestly, 'Sir, if it had been your first ten years that is stolen, then you would be totally incapacitated. That's been proved.'

'Oh, piss off, dear, will you? We're trying to have a private conversation.'

While looking shocked, the woman stood her ground. 'I understand you are disturbed. It is expected. I belong to a group of professional women who could help in your difficulty.'

Stepping into a tense silence, Squire said smoothly, 'I must be off, Roy. Perhaps you'll see me to the door. Good day, madam. I am happy to have spoken to you.'

The woman clutched his proffered hand and gave him a sad smile before they broke away. 'Don't forget,' she said. 'I would have liked to introduce myself, Mr Squire, if it had not been for this rude man with you. You see, I am a friend of an old friend of yours from long ago, the charming Jacques d'Exiteuil, just now who has retired from a responsible post in Bruxelles. I am sure you remember him, *n'est ce pas?*'

Producing something between a frown and a smile, Squire murmured that one met so many people in life.

The lady broke into French. '*Mais naturelment, m'sieu, mais . . .*'

Squire put a hand up to the hollow at his right temple. Perhaps she interpreted the gesture to mean his was a failing memory. Breaking off what she was going to say, she flashed an angry look at Burnell and turned away, to mingle with the crowd.

Burnell and Squire looked at each other. Squire smiled rather sadly.

'It's true, I was rude to her. I am a bit demented. I shall find plenty of reminders of the past in my room at home. Letters, videos, suchlike. Perhaps I kept a diary . . . All sorts of things – they should help fill the void . . .'

Giving him an understanding look, Squire said, 'Let me utter a warning. I'm sure your Mrs Rosebottom and many others with professional experience would tell you the same thing. Just suppose you retrieve that missing period of your memory. You would then be bound to scrutinize it.'

'Of course. That's why I want it back, for God's sake.'

Squire pulled up the collar of his coat. He stood by the glass door, contemplating the drizzle outside. He sighed. 'I know of two cases where people have had their memory reinstated. It comes as a shock – one can readily understand this – to have irrefutable evidence of how foolish one was previously. Hindsight is not the easiest lens with which to look back over the past.'

'I must do it, I must. I don't want your advice. I want my wife back.'

'Well, I hope there's been no harm in speaking to you. Please give my regards to your stepmother when you see her. And your father, of course.' Still he paused, as if hoping the rain would cease, while Burnell shuffled impatiently.

'Supposing we all had to relive a year of our lives, Roy. Not just remember but *relive* – relive everything just as it happened previously. That would be hell. Perhaps you've come across a novel by Ouspensky, *The Secret Life of Ivan Osokin*. Something of the kind happens to Osokin. I was scared by that story when I was a boy.'

As if aware that Burnell was fidgeting, Squire changed tack and said, with rather more vigour, 'Well, let's suppose that actually happened, and we had to relive our past life, unchanged, and unchangeable. How do you think we should fare? Happy moments, yes, of course. Good friends, good lovers, of course . . . Music, books – worth a rerun. But they would occupy a small proportion of the years, we'd find.

'Have you ever listened to a few taped hours of your own desultory conversation? It's startlingly dull . . . How about knowing that, through your own carelessness, tomorrow would be the day you fell down a flight of steps and broke a leg? Or that the friend you trusted was going to betray you in some way on such and such a date? Would you be willing to survive much of life's tedium, its second-rateness, a second time around?

'Possibly you think these are an old man's questions. I know you're impatient to get rid of me, Roy. I know you have a kind of hatred for me, possibly based on jealousy . . .

'All the same, it is as a benevolent if presumptuous friend of an earlier generation that I assure you hell is not forgetting but remembering. Remembering what asses we were – and therefore still are.'

'Look, Tom –'

But a hand was raised against him. Sir Tom Squire was unused to having his speeches interrupted. 'The trouble with what we call life – unlike "life" on stage or in a novel – is that we are forced continually to ad lib. And to gain the facility to see clearly what kind of performance we have put on is to be, for the most part, shamed out of our socks.'

It was Burnell's turn to sigh. 'Sorry, Tom. I hear you but I want my Stephanie back if possible. There may be some truth in what you say about making mistakes. I want to see my mistakes and put them right. I grant my personal past may prove awful, but that's a journey I intend to take.'

He glared at Squire's retreating back, as the old man made his way slowly through the light rain, shoulders hunched, in the direction of the WACH offices. In the foyer of the block, ten little girls dressed in white, imported from a local school, were reciting poems by Amanda Schäfer.

Up in his apartment, Burnell burst into fury, taking a running kick at his luggage. Why had Squire appeared? What the hell did the old bugger mean by saying that Burnell had 'a kind of hatred' for him, possibly based on jealousy? Why should Burnell be jealous of the old fool? Why had he presumed to give advice?

Part of his anger was directed against his own inability to recollect what role – if any – Squire had played in his previous life. He concealed that piece of self-knowledge in an outburst against the interfering older man, and kicked his suitcase again.

Next day, he arrived at the international airport in good time for the twice-weekly direct flight from Frankfurt to Norwich. His plane was delayed. A vague explanation was given: catering facilities had been disrupted. The Euro-Berlin Flight 02 would depart an hour later than schedule. Euro-Berlin wished to apologize for any inconvenience caused.

In a penitent mood – and partly to kill time – Burnell decided to apologize to Squire for his impolite behaviour. He had made an ass of himself the previous day. A secretary in the WACH offices announced that Squire had already left by rail for Munich. She gave him the phone number of Squire's hotel in Munich. Burnell called the number and was fortunate enough to catch Squire as the old man was going out to an appointment.

After Squire had accepted the apology with good grace, Burnell asked, unpremeditatedly, 'Do you have friends in Munich? Are you ever lonely?'

It was the second question to which Burnell hoped to have an answer, but Squire merely replied that some old friends of his were taking him to *Götterdämmerung* that evening. Burnell said he had no fondness for opera.

'Oh, such things improve on acquaintance and become addictive. The more you see *The Ring*, the more you see in it. As in life, really. In Wagner, proceedings are so long-drawn-out that one has time to wonder if, for instance, Brünnhilde's destruction of the gods is such a good idea after all.' He chuckled, distant, voice remote and dry, hardly audible above the clatter of the airport lounge where Burnell stood. 'But much of the *Götterdämmerung* music is lovely, even if the plot creaks a bit. It's always a touching moment when Siegfried swallows the love potion and forgets Brünnhilde in a false passion for Gutrune. One fears for Siegfried, even while envying him that wholehearted passion.'

As he went aboard his delayed flight, Burnell wondered whether Squire had been in fact answering his second question or uttering a veiled warning.

28

Open to the Public

The seasons were in retreat. From the snows of Turkmenistan and the chilly showers of Germany, Roy Burnell emerged into the mild warmth of a Norfolk October. The Burnell home, Diddisham Abbey, lay sixteen miles from Norwich airport in flat bland agricultural country. The sunshine was hazy, non-committal.

The gates of Diddisham, which had stood open throughout Burnell's boyhood, were reinforced, and now operated electronically. As his stepmother's car swept up the drive, along the avenue of lime trees planted in his grandfather's time, Burnell saw Tarquin Burnell at the far end of the avenue, escorted by Burnell's sister, Clementine.

Tarquin waylaid his son before Burnell could enter the house. What he wanted to talk about was the drought, the rotten state of the nation, the riots, the difficulty of obtaining reliable help in the garden and, by a circuitous route, the drought again.

Despite what Tarquin described as the appalling state of the garden, the grounds of the abbey were open to the public this Saturday. He described this as the only way to make ends meet.

Burnell walked along beside his father's wheelchair, murmuring occasionally in agreement, casting curious looks at his sister, who was saying even less than he. No doubt she had heard the tirade many times before. What memories had she worth mourning? Burnell wondered.

Finally Tarquin asked what Burnell had been doing. When Burnell replied that he had merely been working here and there at his profession, his father interjected, 'I was told you'd been killing off heads of state.'

'Only one, Father.'

'Wasn't that rather against the law of the bloody country?'

'There was no law in that bloody country.'

'Oh well, England's getting almost as bad.' Tarquin pursued this theme for some while, punctuating bad news with barks of something like laughter, before changing the subject. 'We're open to the public for one more weekend. Since we have this freak mild autumn – not a drop of rain for months – we must take advantage of it. Of course there's a hosepipe ban. But we'll collect a few more pennies from the peasantry. Though by the time you've paid off the tea ladies and the security staff there's little enough in it. Come on, I'll give you a look round. You'll have to forgive the electric chair.'

Although Burnell suggested he might dispose of his luggage and have a wash first, his father would hear nothing of it, warning his son that the abbey was full of weekend guests.

'Get some English air in your lungs. You see I'm still going strong, despite your absence,' said Tarquin, darting up one of his hard glances. His face could be summed up, Burnell thought, in the word 'wasted'. Tarquin's skull was part-visible beneath the fleshless skin, part-concealed by tufts and shadows of hair growing about cheeks, lips and other unexpected places, and by the flakiness of his skin, lichened over with moles and rusty blotches and broken veins. Tarquin Burnell's face resembled an old wall from which creeper had been brutally stripped.

The old wall was held together by the mortar of a fierce spirit. Tarquin had been confined to his chair for almost fifteen years. As ever, his autocratic manner, which his son had learnt to see behind, presented a challenge to those who, loving him, might be tempted to show pity.

Before them lay the major target of his attentions, the grounds of the abbey. Tarquin patrolled the grounds every day, snatching as he passed at weeds and plants which offended him, shouting orders to his two gardeners, cursing his trees into leaf, defying his grass to grow.

'It's at its worst, nothing flowering, everything rotting,' he said, speeding up, so that his offspring had to walk faster. The chair made a quiet whine, like the sound of repressed gases in a stomach.

A few visitors, probably members of the National Trust, moved out of the chair's way with various degrees of sympathy, respect, or protest.

Walking behind Tarquin's chair with a hand on the rear rail, as if she longed to push the vehicle, was a woman of thirty. Burnell's younger sister, Clementine, did not speak unless spoken to. The padded shoulders of her mauve dress gave her a hunched determined aspect which the tight set of her mouth reinforced. She used no make-up on her puffy face. When she responded to one of her brother's remarks, it was with a reserved air, and the detached look of one reading the headlines of a morning newspaper. In many respects, Clementine was Burnell's temperamental opposite.

'Don't you do visitors' teas any more, Clem?' Burnell asked, as they bowled along a gravel path.

'Min does them in the stables.' Min was a local village girl, a long-standing friend of Clementine's. It was pleasant to hear that Min remained; the horses had long since gone from the stables.

'What are you charging nowadays?'

'It's two pounds a cup. That includes a biscuit.' She spoke without irony – trying not to be amusing, Burnell thought.

'No cream teas any more? Has Mrs Parslow retired?'

'They're five pounds a head.'

'Will you be sorry when the visiting-season closes?'

'Oh, I don't know.'

'Lonely, I mean?' It was the question he had asked Tom Squire in Frankfurt two days earlier.

Clem made no reply. Perhaps she regarded the question as an intrusion into her privacy. It was impossible to know what lay concealed in that personal territory; she never told; she never mentioned their dead mother; perhaps she dreamed of her in the secrecy of her nights. Burnell's discretion, for which he cursed himself, did not permit him to probe. The three children of

Vanessa and Tarquin Burnell had responded in markedly different ways to the family situation. Burnell and Clem's brother Adrian had become schizophrenic in his teens, and was now leading a quasi-independent drugged life in a hostel in Leeds. His siblings had soon learnt not to speak of Adrian in front of their father; Adrian in consequence had faded from their lives.

Doubtless it was thoughts of this kind, prompted by the return of his older son, which moved Tarquin to ask Burnell if he was glad to be home – only to withdraw the question for fear of receiving an unpalatable answer by hurrying on, saying, 'You have to face facts, Roy, life's not as much fun as it was. We'll play "Newcastle" tomorrow – we'll enjoy that. Do you two remember that jolly holiday we had in Iceland, many a moon ago, eh?'

'I remember it,' said Burnell.

'You do remember something, then!'

Clementine said, in unemotional tones, 'I've never been to Iceland, Father. You told me I was too young. You left me behind at home.'

'You missed a damned good holiday, girl.'

All three fell silent. They were approaching the Brook Garden marked off by trelliswork constructed by a gardener long ago. Grass banks stretched where, in Vanessa's time, there had been extensive herbaceous borders. A solitary lady visitor sat on a bench, legs crossed, eating a sandwich from a little plastic box. She waved shyly to Tarquin, who waved back.

'Season ticket,' Tarquin told his son, lowering his voice. 'Here every Saturday, poor woman.'

'Who is she?'

'No idea.' The subject was dropped. Accelerating, he shouted, 'Charge!' and steered his chair on to the bridge leading to the rose garden. Saying nothing, he pointed with his stick, swinging it slowly through an arc of forty-five degrees and back.

'What do you make of that, Roy?'

Burnell was already making something of the fact that the bridge had shrunk considerably since the days when he first ran across it: which was reasonable, since it now spanned a shallow declivity instead of the chasm he remembered. He leant thoughtfully over the parapet of the bridge. A group of three visitors was strolling about in the rose garden, where an old grey gardener plied a hoe among the flower beds. He saw that the stream had died which once flowed through the grounds of Diddisham and under the stone bridge. Not even the glisten of mud shone up from its shallow bed. Rank grasses grew, black at their base, sere and yellowed at their tips.

There as a boy he had paddled, barefoot with his friends, building little bays and lets under the bridge, while reflected sunlight rippled on the arch above their heads, while the stream served as their wide Atlantic.

'The Bittering Brook. Completely dried up. Nothing. Ducks gone, of course, geese gone. Bulrushes all dead. Fish, sticklebacks . . . And the water lilies down in the pool. I blame Hitchens, mucking about with dams for his blessed cattle on his stretch of river. I'm suing him. Of course I'm suing.'

Herby Hitchens farmed the adjacent land – land which had once, in palmier days, belonged to the abbey. An amiable, lazy man was Hitchens; Burnell recalled him from childhood. He had often eaten at Mrs Hitchens's board, and played with the Hitchens sons in their sties and stables.

'Could it be global warming to blame, Father?'

'There! That's exactly what the local council claim. Idiots. Even they're against me.' Tarquin struck the parapet of the bridge with his stick, indicating the way he would deal with the world of idiots. Clementine turned and offered her brother a smile which got about halfway to him before fading out. It was an inducement to him to humour their father. Burnell recognized the signal of old.

They crossed the bridge into the rose garden. A breeze strewed brown petals in their path. The rose garden was partially surrounded by a fine old brick wall, much of which was still standing. Stone busts looked unsympathetically out from arbours along an arcaded walk. The gardener straightened up and nodded politely to his boss.

'My son's back, Ray,' Tarquin called to this withered figure. 'Been God knows where.'

'So I see,' said the gardener, grinning but not shifting his ground. He gave Burnell a combination of nod and wink. 'So I see,' he repeated, in case the message had not got through the first time.

'Bit surly,' Tarquin told his son in an undertone audible afar. 'He's lame but he does his job. Give him that. I tell him, better be lame than have no legs at all worth talking about. He agrees with me.' He gave a metallic chuckle. 'He's paid to agree with me. Daughter was shot by the IRA. Fancy that – in Norfolk. No one was ever caught. I don't know what the country's coming to.'

His chair had whined him forward while he talked. They were near enough to some visitors, a middle-aged couple, neatly dressed, with a son of ten or so, to overhear their conversation. The boy, tow-haired and bespectacled, wore a sweater which said 'Cambridge University' in variously coloured letters across his chest.

The roses in the main bed had ceased to flower. Black spot had taken hold and they had not been dead-headed. The ground beneath them looked cracked and dry. The circular bed was rimmed with brick, outside which lay a collar of stone on which a verse from the 'Rubáiyát' had been carved. While the woman stood indifferently by, gazing into space, smacking her left hand with a folding umbrella held in her right, her husband and the boy walked round the bed, reading the inscription aloud to one another: '". . . the garden wears dropped in her lip – lap, from some once lovely head one sm – sm –"'

'"Sometimes",' prompted the father.

'"Sometimes think that . . ."' continued the boy. After every few words they moved round a pace or two, frowning downwards in concentration. '"That never blows so red the rose as where . . ." It don't seem to make no sense, Dad.'

'It's a poem or somethink, isn't it?' the woman called across the bed, with an extra punitive swack at her left hand. 'Shall we go and get a cup of tea and a bun or somethink?'

The man was not prepared to accept his wife's hypothesis. 'It's probably a bit of old English writing,' he said.

'But what does it mean, Dad?'

'It's something about roses, isn't it? And their colours. It's how people used to talk.'

Tarquin Burnell yelled to his gardener, 'Ray, get these intolerably ignorant folk out of here, will you? Tell them we're closing. No tea for them. Refund their money if necessary.'

He set off in anger and a high intestinal whine of motor. Clementine and Burnell brought up the rear, not daring to look back to see if eviction was being attempted.

So they returned to the house.

Diddisham Abbey had served as an abbey for a short time only in its four-century-long life, since when it had been home to various branches of the Burnell family. The ruins of the original abbey could be visited; they stood behind the present house, and were supposedly haunted, a legend which drew in a few extra visitors every year. Tarquin kept peacocks there, the shrieks of which served to perpetuate the legend. The lands of the abbey had shrunk, chipped away over the years by penurious owners. A last hundred acres of arable land had been sold to Herby Hitchens during the recession of the early 1990s. Now the house stood in a modest twenty-one acres.

The bland brick frontage of the house faced south, its back turned to the village of North Elmham. Over the years, the structure had been much added to, neglected, restored, patched. It had been sold off and bought up; in the days of oil lamps it had caught fire. At various periods in its history doors had been moved from one side of the building to another, windows bricked up, rooms enlarged or divided, new wings added, conservatories pulled down, plumbing inserted, faulty central heating ripped out, roofs patched, old features resurrected, and yet older features desecrated. Antiquarianism and modernism had fought hard battles over the bones of Diddisham.

As fading afternoon light revealed, both the brickwork and the paintwork of the façade were dry and crumbling. The abbey towards sunset resembled an old wedding-cake, preserved beyond possible nutritional value, its surface crazed like a piece of porcelain, subject to a sentiment of squirearchy itself desiccating through age.

On the top step outside the front doors, Burnell's luggage stood awaiting him. He had not had time to take it into the house before his father buttonholed him. He had been met at Norwich airport by Laura Burnell and a driver in her car. His stepmother had listened to his account of his travels as they drove, smiling affectionately if automatically.

Laura emerged from the house now, tinkling a little bell, raising it to the level of her dark svelte hair to do so.

'Teatime, my dears,' she said, in her clear precise voice, as they approached. 'You couldn't have timed it better.' She smiled widely at them, using the smile she had frequently turned to the cameras.

Tarquin whizzed up a ramp at the side of the steps without speaking, and rode past her into the recesses of the hall.

Clementine stooped to pick up her brother's bags. When Burnell protested, she deferred silently to him, and led the way inside. Entering this house of memories, Burnell told Laura he would take his things to his room, wash, and then come down to tea.

'Same old room, Roy,' she said brightly, making a slight theatrical gesture towards him, as if to touch him. She was immaculately dressed as ever in a black beltless dress with gold collar which recalled at once the twenties of the previous century and something into which Nefertiti might have slipped.

Walking through the house, this old fragrant house, this dry house where his mother had died, he was surprised to find it so small. It had shrunk; for his recent memories of it had gone: what chiefly remained was a boy's memory of vast rooms and corridors.

His quarters were preserved as before, towards the rear of the house, on the second floor. This suite had been his since the age of four. An ante-room led into a bedroom, off which to one side were bathroom and lavatory; to the other side a small sitting-room containing a desk and computer. The main windows looked out on the ruins of the old abbey; shadows were drawing across their snaggle-toothed outlines.

Burnell stood looking about him, making mental adjustments. He remembered his quarters from long past, without knowing how many times he had returned here over the previous ten years.

The bedroom he remembered as spacious now seemed rather cramped.

Without switching on any lights, he went into the sitting-room. Here were rows of his architectural books, together with bound copies of *Architectural Review* and the WACH's own journal. Also a shelf of history, the calf-bound Gibbon, and many travel books, among them two copies with faded spines of Douglas Freshfield's *Travels in the Central Caucasus*. His mother's intrepid relation would grieve to see what was happening in the Caucasus now, long after his death.

Searching among his few novels for Hardy's *Hand of Ethelberta* and not finding it, Burnell decided to buy a copy in a bookshop and send it to Dr Hikmat Haydar in Ashkhabad as soon as possible.

Some books he remembered, some not. There was no place on earth with which he was totally familiar – not even here.

Among the framed photographs was one of himself with another man; mountains were visible in the background. Both men held the bridles of horses. Burnell thought dully to himself, so that was what Peter Remenyi looked like . . .

He was disconcerted to think he remembered nothing of this good friend – and how many other good friends, he asked himself. The photo merely reminded him there was nothing to mourn; he feared that into the vacuum would seep a pervasive melancholy.

'How much of my dislocation,' he wondered, 'is mine alone and not part of a general global malaise. People rejoice everywhere in their youth, and the hopes which are the very bloodstream of youth: yet when all that fades, the general state of affairs is seen to be no better, the sum total of human happiness no greater. Why should I care for Steff if she has ceased to care for me? Perhaps it's not she but simply my youth I am longing to regain.'

Muttering to himself, he pottered about the room.

'Still, I'm not old yet, not forty. I must go to Blanche before I miss the bus entirely,' he said aloud in the silent room. 'Time enough to worry about the state of the world later – that's an old man's job.'

With a wry smile he said to himself, 'I get the feeling you're always hanging about, Burnell. How about doing something for the common good? Anything.'

He avoided the photographs of Stephanie. Instead, he took a double snort of slap and went briskly to consider the oil painting of his mother, Vanessa. He smiled up at the sacred image. It hung over the mantelpiece. Its colours were brighter than he had anticipated, the brushwork more lively. It was – he had always regretted the fact – a portrait of no great distinction, showing her head and shoulders. Vanessa was looking wistfully over the viewer's right shoulder. He had always considered that, while the picture had captured a likeness, it lacked any psychological understanding of its subject; yet, regarding it anew, he recalled the Madonna of Futurity. Here too, perhaps, was a woman looking with anxiety into the future. The portrait had been painted the year before she died.

Walking with Clem and his father in the garden a few minutes earlier, he had noticed that his father, in a slightly old-fashioned way, wore two gold rings on the fingers of his right hand. One was a wedding ring, the other a mourning ring. As Tarquin had clutched his stick on the bridge over the dried brook, Burnell had noted the engraved design of the mourning ring: a tomb with an urn on it and a woman standing by the tomb, while a weeping willow overhung the scene.

For the first time, he realized that his father too, though silent on the subject, might also still secretly mourn Vanessa. This insight he found touching. Perhaps it would be possible to be on better terms with Tarquin in future. He could at least try.

The daylight was at a low ebb. He switched on a table lamp that stood on his old writing-desk.

In one corner of the room stood rows of video cassettes. Some were professional tapes, some he had filmed himself. Most of them he remembered: slivers of the past were recorded there.

He saw by the date printed on one cassette that it contained a record of his mother's funeral, filmed by his well-meaning Uncle Ben. He had only once had the courage to view it. Away at school on that solemn occasion, he was all unknowing even that his mother was dead. In the film, a small Clementine, then aged ten, stood by the graveside clutching her father's hand, standing on one leg, looking up questioningly at Tarquin. The image returned poignantly to him now as he paused in the dusk of the old room.

Poor sister, poor little Clem! She had suffered most from that death, and continued to suffer. He had got away. Clementine stayed, and had become her father's vassal. He wondered if she had ever had a lover, had ever been kissed by a man, her father's goodnight kiss apart.

After the funeral of Vanessa Burnell, Tarquin had fairly promptly taken up with another woman, as if anxious to throw off the lingering months of his wife's cancer. Great excitement had animated peaceful Diddisham when an American film unit moved in to make a film called *Kindred Blood*, with the abbey as its main setting. Not only had the location fee paid for repairs to the main roof, Tarquin had encountered a younger woman.

Involved in the plot of *Kindred Blood* were two sisters. The more beautiful sister was played by Laura Nye, an actress then blossoming in her early thirties. In spite of the discrepancy in their ages – Laura saying that she preferred older men – she and Tarquin had married in 1990, while Roy was at university. Again he had been absent at a crucial date in his father's life. He had come down from Cambridge for the Easter vacation to find the new wife – his stepmother – installed in all her glory.

'She's famous. Ain't she beautiful? You'd better get on with her somehow.' Thus had his father introduced the shy student to the attractive actress; tact had never been a strong point with Tarquin, even before his accident.

Among the old video cassettes were the two or three films in which Laura had acted. Burnell had also kept recordings of her first appearance, in a long television documentary series made in the 1970s, called 'Frankenstein Among the Arts'. She had then played an almost heraldic role, as Sex Symbol. Very appropriate, Burnell thought.

That tiresome quest for happiness . . . Well, it had eluded his father. It would elude him unless he pursued it. He must ring Blanche in Madrid this very evening.

Dimness had piled up, flooding in from the corners of the room. Outside, night made its meditative approach over the ruins of the abbey, shutting down the world for another day. A peacock cried.

When someone tapped at his door he called to them to enter.

Laura came in, closing the door softly behind her. She stood in the main room, hands slightly extended as if bewildered to find the room unlit. With Laura, Burnell found, there was always a slight 'as if'; not for this reason alone, their relationship had always been full of approaches and retreats. 'You've no light, Roy, dear. I came to see if you were comfortable. Is everything to your liking?'

'Nothing's changed. Thanks.' He caught the fragrance she was wearing. In the dusk, backlit from a glow on the landing, Laura looked no more than twenty. Her figure had remained trim although she was approaching her fiftieth birthday. He distinguished the oval of her face, her lips, her eyes; the power radiating from her, which had first overwhelmed him as a student, came strongly to him. She was a magical person; allured by her, he fought against the allure. That allure, he told himself, as he had ineffectually done many times before, was synthetic.

'You're feeling somewhat strange, I expect. May I put a light on?'

The light eroded the illusion of youth. The power remained of a woman who had always been attractive to men.

As they regarded each other, she told him that he had lost some weight, which made him look more elegant than ever. Since she had made a similar remark when they met at Norwich airport, Burnell was embarrassed. He told her he was preparing to go downstairs and join the company.

'Is it pleasant to be home again? The rooms are spring-cleaned. Your bed's aired. And, Roy, dear – I'm so worried about the theft of your memory. You should have returned to Diddisham when you left that hospital in Swindon, instead of rushing off back to the Continent.' Her sentences were delivered lightly, robbing them of real involvement.

Before he answered, she took a step nearer. With an attractive gesture of invitation, she asked him to escort her downstairs. 'We're still friends, aren't we, dear?'

Looking at her seriously, trying to reach her, he explained how much at a loss he felt at present. 'I know,' she agreed – too facile an answer to please Burnell. Impatiently, he said he found all relationships difficult when he hardly knew who he was talking to; who, for instance, was Tom Squire? What had he to do with their family?

To which Laura replied that yes, she had acted with Tom in her first TV appearance. Had he seen any TV in Central Asia? – if so, what on earth was it like? He said it was 'Dallas', and they both laughed.

'Yes, we are friends, I see. I'm so glad. I care about whatever happens to you. You know that, dear. What did Tom have to say?'

'Oh, he just said that to review the last ten years would be painful.'

'Was that all? . . .' She sounded disappointed. 'Anyhow, this weekend is going to be such fun.'

Laura explained that a few guests were staying at Diddisham. Friends and family. His Uncle Ben was due soon, as well as his Aunt Sheila with her friend. It was nice to have the house filled; they had so many empty rooms. She had run out of dustsheets. She expected Burnell knew what this special weekend was all about. Tomorrow was Tarquin's seventieth birthday.

He closed the door behind them as they moved together on to the rear landing. As they made for the stairs, Laura paused to pull the curtains across a landing window. Outside in the darkness, a peacock shrieked.

'As it happens, I've brought Tarquin a present from Germany.'

'How exciting! He will like that!'

'Doesn't he dislike Germans?'

'You're such a good son, Roy! It's sad about Adrian. Tarquin is so pleased to have you home, if only for a little while. Are you planning to stay with us for long, dear?'

'How is he, Laura?' It was absurd that he should still take pleasure in pronouncing her name, and in feeling her warmth against him as they descended the stairs; almost as many years lay between Laura and him as between her and his father.

'Oh, Tarquin is quite well, don't worry. You know he has equipped a little gym for himself, where he exercises to keep fit and not grow too heavy. Of course, he'll never walk again.'

'And you? How's your film-making career?'

Her laugh was self-deprecating. 'Oh, it's over, such as it was. I stay here now.' She paused. 'Except I'm having a mini-revival in Paris. The French have rediscovered me, bless them. *Film Soleil* is all the rage. I'm going over there in six weeks time to the opening of their retrospective. Isn't that fun? Isn't life amazing? You can come with me, if you like.'

She gave him a hug.

Attempting an equal playfulness, he said, 'Goodness, Laura, you must be a millionairess by now!'

She replied in an unemphatic way that she was always paid in peanuts. 'You don't know Tommy Squire's two daughters, Jane and Ann, do you? They live in California. They're now heads of a multi-million dollar industry, *coining it*, my dear! They own Loveranger.'

He paused on the half-landing. Through the window, the grounds radiated darkness. One distant light could be seen.

'He's got daughters? You know Sir Thomas Squire's daughters?' he asked, puzzled.

'Only at second hand, I'm afraid.' She looked searchingly at his face, not without, he thought, a certain kind of sadness he had noted previously. Was there, he asked himself, something you might call a blithe sadness?

'Laura, I'm back in the real world after the fabrications of Central Asia. And what do I find? In you – an unfathomable mystery . . .'

She had looked away. Now she faced him, giving a pert little smile and fluttering her eyelashes. 'You're a tease, Roy. We really must join the others in the drawing-room, what Vanessa used to call the Cream Room. Tarquin and I stick together like two old . . . chums. We're not like you and Stephanie, you know, dear!'

Trying to negotiate her evasive responses, he said, 'How's Tarquin really?'

In her usual calm voice, she said, 'Tarquin hates everything, including himself. He's often suicidal. What the hell do you expect? Now, come and meet everyone. Some you'll know, even if you don't remember them . . . I'll prompt you.'

They had paused outside the doors of the Cream Room. Burnell caught hold of Laura and said, angrily, 'Why did you mention Stephanie? Have you seen her lately? I hate all this secrecy . . .'

She lifted a finger in a dated gesture, and shook her head slightly. 'Now, now! There are some nice people for you to meet. Remember, the great secret in life is to behave properly – whatever you really feel inside.'

29
'Newcastle'

'"Newcastle", everyone! Time for "Newcastle"!' The cry rang out through the front hall of Diddisham Abbey, accompanied by the vigorous beating of a gong.

Burnell said to Blanche, 'I shall have to hang up. It's Tarquin's birthday. He's had his presents and now we're all going to have to play our dreadful family game. I must go.'

Her voice came clear from Madrid via satellite. 'Ring me again tonight. I'm sorry I wasn't in yesterday to take your call and I'm glad you're safe back in England. I'm longing to hear about the horrors of Ashkhabad. You're going to fly down and be with me, aren't you?'

'I told you I don't speak Spanish.' But he regretted the old joke as soon as he'd made it, and added swiftly, 'I'll ring you after dinner this evening. I want to hear more about the excavations. They've unearthed wooden platters, you say? It's amazingly rare for wood to be preserved that long. So we shall have to revise our opinion of Neanderthal culture.'

'I ask myself, have Neanderthals been victims of racist thinking?! Maybe that maligned sub-species sat up at table and ate breakfast cereal like the rest of us . . .'

'Maybe they said grace before meals. When your team finds wooden toys in the cave, you'll –'

'Roy, forget the past.' He heard the tinkle of laughter in her voice. 'Are your family making you suffer? Norfolk sounds so Neanderthal. I don't want you to be there – I want to see you here. We can discuss Neanderthal breakfast cereals in bed together. Madrid's gorgeous. So are the mountains.'

'So's your bed, I'm sure.'

She pantomimed excessive relief. 'Thank the heavens! You haven't forgotten our last meeting, then, have you?'

He laughed. 'I'm quite clear about that, and the way you look and smell and feel and clasp me. And if I were an archaeologist, I'd be digging into you immediately, potholing, exploring every nook and cranny of that inconceivable structure.'

'Not literally inconceivable, darling. Nor impregnable.'

'Well, I certainly didn't mean unbearable.'

'Ring me this evening, tell more to me, you flatterer. Go and play your absurd family game.'

Burnell set the phone down, to stand where he was, gazing abstractedly out of the window. The colder turn of the weather this morning rendered the countryside uncertain, subdued, awaiting a plunge towards winter. Before so long, the chill east wind would be blowing off the North Sea.

I did not have my memory stolen, he told himself. It's sickness that makes me believe such nonsense: a sickness brought on by the failure of my marriage. People fall ill when relationships die. I have lost the will to know what to do. Wishing to erase the past, a part of my mind has raised up a barrier which cuts me off from my earlier self.

He knew it was nonsense. Or did not.

When he phoned Blanche in Madrid, he had set down beside the instrument, delicately, as if it were a fallen leaf, an old diary. There, in its hastily scrawled pages, he had read something of the deterioration of his life with Stephanie. It was another person's existence which rose before him. He saw no faces, not even his own. He did not hear his own voice echoed in the writing.

He could not interpret what the mind behind the pen had been thinking. Such revelations as there were merely twitched at the curtain of what had passed. If there had been a week when Steff had not spoken a word to him, as a May date indicated, no hint was given as to what had caused her silence, or where the blame had lain. Or even if he had spoken to her during that week.

'Read Carpentier's *The Lost Steps*' was all it said on that issue. Whose had been the blame? How much had he cared? Why was the date 23rd May ringed about in red? The diary threw up questions, not answers.

What he felt was something more than guilt, more than loss. He wished to get hold of Stephanie and shake the truth out of her. Who were we? Why did we do what we did? Where exactly were we mistaken – about ourselves as well as each other?

So to press the pages shut was to seal up an Egyptian tomb full of inscrutable personages and attitudes. Only then, with the diary closed and put away, had he phoned Blanche.

From the hall below, distantly, came the second gong for 'Newcastle'.

Reluctant to face the rest of the family, Burnell left his room and walked to the front stairs. As he descended to the floor below, dragging his steps on the thick carpet, letting the palm of his hand squeak against the balustrade as he had done when a boy, he heard the faint strains of music, and paused. Lively and exuberant, it teased him to be identified.

The music came from the room his Aunt Sheila was occupying. He tapped and walked in. 'Auntie,' he called. 'Time for the game!'

Sheila Lippard-Milne was nowhere in view. He remembered what a pleasant room this one was, with its windows facing out over the parched garden embrasured in deep recesses, their shutters still functional. The room was predominantly white, with lemon cushions pillowing the window seat. This had been his mother's, Vanessa's, favourite room, where she had painted. Some of her watercolours hung framed on the bamboo-patterned wallpaper, where direct sunlight could not reach them.

A door to the left hung open, giving a view of the bedroom. Two single beds could be seen; both had been slept in, their duvets thrown carelessly back. As Burnell took in these details, his aunt emerged from the room, securing a comb into the back of her hair, which was drawn into a bun. He realized he had never seen his aunt looking less than immaculate.

She gave him one of her sharp looks, not unkindly but certainly taking his measure.

'Roy, we had no chance to talk last night, and probably will get none today. Why did you come in here? I'm a *late* riser, as you see. Are you better? You look – may I say it? – weary, forsaken. Possibly even God-forsaken.'

'Perhaps you'd like a turn outside, Auntie? Before we join the others. I heard your music.'

'Switch that thing off, will you?' But as she spoke she crossed to the machine and silenced Rimsky-Korsakov herself. Her way of speech was similar to her brother's, her bossy manner only a slight modification of Tarquin's. She was dressed in what he considered a London fashion, her blouse and jacket set off by black velvet trousers.

'Do get your hair attended to. Lawns look better for cutting. Weren't there any hairdressers where you were? *Where* exactly were you? Tarky didn't seem to know. What are you doing with yourself?'

He laughed. 'How you do go on at me! Everyone gets lonely at times. I've been stung by a scorpion and survived.'

'How unpleasant. You do go to some rum places.'

Round her neck she wore a pair of spectacles on a gold chain. These spectacles Sheila perched on her nose, the better to scrutinize her favourite nephew. She nodded to herself, as if a private suspicion was confirmed.

'Vanessa dying when you were so young. That's half the trouble. It's upset your whole life, just as it has ruined – absolutely *ruined* – Clem's. We'll say nothing about poor old Adrian. It's tragic, really. If you don't mind my saying this, Roy –' she turned away, as if not wishing to see the response her words might waken in him – 'I don't think Stephanie was understanding enough. Of your situation, I mean. Find someone else, *vitement.*'

Shaking his head, Burnell tried out a small chuckle. 'Don't criticize Steff, please, Aunt. We all make – you know the old saying – we all make mistakes. You probably know I'm hoping she'll –'

She turned back towards him and held one of his hands. 'I've often intended to say this to you, so I'll say it now, before we play that stupid game. I should have stood in for Vanessa and mothered you a bit more than I did when you were young. I'm sorry about that now. After all, you are the son I never had. Never *wanted*, come to that. Dreaded the very idea of pregnancy.' She spoke hastily, looking at him through her spectacles. 'I was quite mixed up until I was middle-aged. Bad upbringing. Unfortunate friends. Mad lovers. All the . . . all the usual excuses people like me make.'

'Oh, there are no people like you, Aunt.' To himself he thought, 'But that's exactly how people are: intending to give comfort, they talk about themselves instead. I suppose it's pain more than egotism.'

'Do you understand what I'm saying?'

'I'll have to be off again soon,' Burnell thought. 'Diddisham's too full of memories I don't need . . .'

The gong rang down in the hall for a third and final time.

Still conscious of the two rumpled beds in the adjoining room, Burnell said, as he and his Aunt Sheila made to leave the room, 'So how's Uncle Leslie? Why hasn't he come with you?'

His aunt's expression changed. She dug sharp nails into his hand. Just for an instant, he saw in her face a savage bird, a vulture, something about to alight on carrion. Then she smoothed the look away, hid it from him, from the world.

In a harsh voice she said, 'Oh God, you don't remember, do you?' She backed away from him. 'This is *spooky* . . . It's like suddenly finding you're conversing with a corpse. You must surely remember that tender *sympathetic* letter you wrote me when Leslie died! No . . .' She gestured in despair. 'I shouldn't be angry. I'm sorry, I'm sorry I was angry. It's not your fault. Your old aunt – well, the others will tell you if they haven't already. Your old aunt has gone gay.'

'What are you talking about, Auntie? Is everyone in the family mad?'

'I'm only telling you what you might have guessed.' Involuntarily, she glanced through the door at the rumpled beds. 'I've *found* myself, Roy. Late in life, I've found myself. Like Nora in Ibsen's *Doll's House*, you know? I walked out on your Uncle Leslie *four years ago*. It's over four years. And, well – I had tried to make him happy. I did, I loved him in my way, but perhaps I never made him happy – left something unsatisfied. And he went and drowned himself when I walked out. I never for a moment expected . . .'

'Oh, Auntie, dear, I didn't know.'

'You *did* know.' Again she drew back, but the anger had gone from her tone. In her ordinary voice, she said, 'You did know. You sent me that wonderful letter. Very sensitive and understanding.'

'Shit. I'm sorry. Auntie, I –' He clutched his head, lost for words.

'I wrote back to you. Later on, you sent me an obituary of Leslie from one of the newspapers. "Author of *The Sower of the Systems*", and all that. Surely you must remember? Your own uncle's death?'

He pressed fingers up to his temples, protesting. 'That's enough. I'm maimed, can't you get that? I'm full enough of guilt as it is.'

'So we all damned well are. I tore up the obit you sent me. It must have been rage or grief or something, but I tore it into shreds. I've always felt bad about that – like killing Leslie twice.' She took Burnell's hand. 'Come on, let's go and play Tarquin's bloody game . . . And I'm hanging out with Jenny now, in case you hadn't gathered that.'

As they went downstairs he said, almost in a whisper, 'I'm sorry, Auntie, dear.'

'To think you can't remember . . . Do you imagine I can forget?'

The way to the Dairy led through the rear hall, past the kitchen/breakfast room, the cloakrooms, the Flower Room, and the Gun Room – the latter nowadays bereft of all but two sporting-guns, though well stocked with Wellington boots, riding boots, hard hats, riding-crops, and Barbours.

Tarquin wheeled about excitedly in his chair, in and out of the Dairy. Burnell apologized for lateness as he and his Aunt Sheila entered the room. His father reached up and patted him in the small of his back.

'We're waiting for Laura. Don't know where she's got to. Where's the woman? Start without her in a minute.'

Other guests at the abbey, obedient to the gong, were already assembled. They were sitting with various degrees of expectancy in old battered Lloyd Loom chairs, as custom demanded. Sheila Lippard-Milne's friend, Jenny, was Jennifer Binns, a short fat lady with heavy eyebrows, fidgeting in her chair. After many years working in the film industry in England and Australia, Jennifer Binns was currently enjoying some success as a film director. She had reserved the chair next to her for Sheila, and patted it enticingly with a beringed hand as Sheila entered the Dairy. She blew Burnell a kiss.

'I'm no good at games,' she told Sheila, and giggled, as Sheila settled herself among the limp cushions. 'But I mean to win this crazy thing. I can be ruthless, as you know, darling.' The two women had worked together for some years. Sheila had begun her career as an art historian before becoming a professional set-designer. She had designed the interiors for Jennifer Binn's latest movie, *Smoke in the Streets* – in which Laura played the vital role of the psychotic mother, under her stage name of Laura Nye.

On Sheila's other side sat Clementine, wearing slacks and one of her father's old cricket blazers. She spoke to no one and clutched the wicker arms of her chair while following her father's every gesture with her eyes. Burnell took the seat beside her and exchanged a few words. His sister was, as ever, uncommunicative.

'Are you prepared to play a tough game?' he asked in an undertone. 'Looting ports? Cheating customs officials?'

'We'll see,' she replied – not without a note of grimness in her voice. 'Newcastle' was traditionally one way in which she got her own back on a hard world. Of the nine players, Clem and her father were always the keenest participants.

Ranged along the opposite wall were the other four people waiting to play 'Newcastle': Tarquin's younger brother, Ben, and his grand malevolent wife, Violet; a journalist and critic, Frank Krawstadt; and a hard-drinking poet and musician, Jack Gibson, busily running his fingers through his lank dark hair. Only Gibson lived nearby, in the village. The rest had driven up from London for Tarquin's birthday weekend.

Krawstadt, yellowy of complexion, withered of cheek, was dressed in an old faded blue shell-suit. He had been talking rather loftily about the art of the cinema, pitching his sentences across the room at Jenny Binns. He was buttering her up.

'Your successful career won't help you win "Newcastle",' Krawstadt warned Jennifer. 'There's stormy weather ahead, and dirty work on the quarter-deck.' He tittered.

The Dairy had ceased to function in its original capacity for about sixty years. It consisted of three rooms leading one into the next. From the farthest room, a door opened – or had once opened – into the stable yard, where a dozen semi-nomadic poultry still strutted. In these damp rooms, the clang of milk churns had once competed with the cries of milkmaids locked in the arms of robust prayerful men. The Burnells had been known for their robust qualities. Now all lay silent. Wooden shutters closed off the windows. The old days had gone, and milk was not likely to stage a comeback.

The two inferior rooms were clogged with old metal machineries and deep stone sinks. Wooden dollies rotted in bathypelagic damp. But the largest room of the three, in which the company assembled to play, had been wired for light and heat and converted into the 'Newcastle' room.

Vinyl flooring formed an important element of the game. It was blue and squared, each square representing a league of sea. Newcastle itself was represented by a sea chest in one corner of the room. Each of the players had a port at their feet, variously designated 'Genoa', 'Aden', 'Bombay', 'Singapore', 'Bilbao', and so on. A bucket full of coins stood in the middle of the room. The coins were pennies and silver threepenny bits dating from the early years of the twentieth century. They served as the game's currency. 'Newcastle' had been invented by Roy Burnell's great-grandfather, in part to keep his children amused in those prosaic years round about the old Queen's death, in part to commemorate the drowning at sea of his beloved brother, Gabriel.

A man-servant brought in a box full of old shoes. Tarquin asked Jack Gibson to distribute them.

'"I must go down to the seas again,
To the lonely sea and the sky,"'

shouted Tarquin, excitedly.

'And all I ask is an old boot
And no cheating on the sly . . .'

'Here you are, Roy,' Gibson said, pushing a green-and-white tennis shoe over to Burnell. The tennis shoe would serve as his ship. Some of the shoes were almost a century old, laceless and polishless, to be dragged out every year, at Christmas and on Tarquin's and Ben's birthdays.

'Do you think the general public will understand *Smoke in the Streets*?' Krawstadt asked Binns, keen to show his lack of interest in the unintellectual aspects of the game, which were many.

'My movie represents the imperfections of life, and therefore is itself designedly imperfect,' Jenny Binns replied, accepting an old brogue as her ship. 'Life has become a great deal happier since we rejected the idea of perfectionism. The craze for EMV proves, I'd say, just how unsatisfactory is the linear event of life as normally experienced.'

'So you set out deliberately to make an unsatisfactory film? Come, now, Jenny, darling, you're not saying that? The critics won't love you for it.'

'Critics have no love of love,' Jack said, handing Clementine a velvet slipper.

'Oh, art doesn't have to mimic life –' Jennifer Binns began.

But she was cut short by Tarquin, who said, 'No, but "Newcastle" mimics life in all its ghastly unfairness. I'm going to swing the Albert clock and we'll start without Laura. Remember, you have three items to trade in the port of Newcastle, stones, apples, and ELCs.'

Although the game had changed little since his grandfather's day, the goods to be traded had been altered by family consensus. Where once coal, eggs, and empty cartridge cases had represented the exports, now stones were substituted for coal and apples for

393

eggs. The cartridge cases had been replaced by Empty Lipstick Cases, always referred to as ELCs.

The Albert clock on one wall, together with the Winifred clock on the opposite wall, governed various moves that could be made. Some players loaded their shoes with goods and set out across the squares of sea, knowing that a cross-reading on the two dials could mean their cargoes were declared contraband and impounded, their captains imprisoned for two whole turns. Another danger was that of hurricane-force winds, which blew every five turns, sinking all ships loaded with cargo.

'Art doesn't have to mimic life,' Binns repeated, stubbornly. 'At its best it creates its own *umwelt*, a parallel world recognizable but distinct. Films, novels, surely do that. We now know – thanks to EMV – how subjective are all our interpretations of events in the real world. One may find it attractive to incorporate the sheer *untidiness* of life into one's work . . .'

It was Clementine's move. She decided to compound interest her score, kept her velvet steamer in port, and obtained a Docket. Burnell moved next, sailing his shoe diagonally across the board towards London from his home port of Ullapool (the initial letters of the ports spelled out the name of the long-dead nautical Gabriel, known as 'Gabs', Burnell).

'What would you consider a tidy life?' Burnell asked Binns.

His Aunt Sheila answered him. 'Oh, come now, Roy. We're too *modern* to expect tidy lives. Monastic life in the Middle Ages was probably *tidy*. Compartmentalized, regulated, ordered by the hour, the calendar. However, I see the challenge in your eyes, so I may say that since I became an independent lady, rather late in life, and followed my own desires, my life has been much neater, much more pared down.'

Seeing she patted Jenny Binn's arm, Burnell asked, 'Do you spell that "p-a-i-r-e-d"?'

'Spell it how you like, and it's Jack's turn.'

'I know it, I know it,' Jack said, with only partly simulated gloom.

'Well, buck up, then,' urged Tarquin.

'. . . And I'm not leaving port. I'm buying five ELCs in the hope they'll increase in value next round.' He looked at the Winifred clock to estimate his chances before producing his money. 'There, that's my go. Violet, your turn!'

Violet made no answer, merely leaning forward heavily in her chair and dropping one apple into her galosh. She fixed a calculating eye on the chest which represented Newcastle. A church had been painted on its side. Players could trade for rings in Newcastle, and marry there, forming transitory alliances with other players which enabled them to avoid some of the more crippling turns of fate the game regularly threw up. Violet, as mariner, was a renowned marrier.

'It's three years since I won this game,' Tarquin said. 'When it's a man's birthday, he ought to be allowed to win.'

Sheila said, 'We're talking about *art*, not about me. Just for once. The story of *Smoke in the Streets* is deliberately confused. Nothing is resolved – who did what et cetera. It's terribly clever. So I've designed the sets with a deliberate simplicity. Lots and *lots* of Tarkovsky muslin curtains blow about at long windows in long bare rooms.'

'You'll have to remind me of the absurd rules,' Violet said in her deep voice, looking about at everyone except her husband for assistance. 'I never liked Esbjerg as a port. It's so far from Newcastle. Am I allowed to carry three apples in my hold after my maiden voyage? How many apples does a wedding-ring cost?' She looked round the company with her dark sunken eyes. 'Who wants to marry me? Could we have some coffee? We always have coffee when we play.'

The first hurricane came, and only Ben capsized. The symbolism of the game was impressive.

'Sounds like early Rouben Mamoulian – Garbo and all that, Sheila,' mocked Krawstadt, in a tone indicating he was not to be taken seriously.

'Never mind Garbo, let's get on with the game,' barked Tarquin. He abused them for land-lubbers, and they played in silence for several turns. Ben sailed into his wife's port and deposited an ELC. The housekeeper brought in coffee on a tray.

'What I had in mind,' said Sheila, 'was an approach to abstraction. The results are mystical and really quite –'

'Come on, old girl,' said Tarquin impatiently. 'Concentrate, will you? It's your bloody go. No wonder women don't make good sailors!'

Sheila stared at the board through her glasses. 'Well, I'm coming out of Bilbao and I'm going to block the sea lane, because I can see Clem is heading straight for Newcastle with her stones.' She pushed her old cracked sandal forward, square by square.

'Every life is "mystical and really quite –", Auntie,' Burnell told her. 'When seen in the right perspective, that is. It's a question of interpretation.' Restless, he rose from his chair and went to stare out of the window at the side terrace. It was definitely colder today. Something in the chill oppressed him; God was on his trail, stealthily, like the approach of winter, and would get him one day. The autumn was here already, the autumn which eluded Ashkhabad: the garden was wearing no hyacinths: soon he would have to accept another commission from the WACH. The passport, the suitcase, the real travels across the real seas . . . When this game was over, he would phone Blanche again. He suffered from an impression that none of these people, even his father, really remembered who he was, or cared; though he sought to ascribe this feeling to his own introspection.

'You're stuck, aren't you?' Jenny Binns said, turning round in her chair towards him. 'Why not marry me and we'll block Newcastle?'

Jack Gibson had said something to Sheila and was laughing at his own remark. She asked him, tartly, 'Don't *you* experience anything mystical, *ever*? Isn't mysticism – being aware of otherness – really the best thing in life?'

'The best thing,' Jack said, 'is getting your hand up a girl's skirt.' The others laughed. Except Sheila, who gave a scream.

'Oh, look at that! Clem, you wretch, you've done a Lutine on me!'

At this moment of crisis – for Lutines could change everyone's fortunes – Laura walked into the room. Laura looked at her icy best, in a long puff-skirted dress of deep blue, her hair elaborately curled about her face, minute pearls studding the lobes of her ears. The players in the Dairy fell silent. Laura spoke in an undertone to Tarquin, who snorted and puffed; whereupon, she placed a calming hand on his shoulder. Burnell saw the flawless hand with its red fingernails sink into his father's shoulder. It was quite a firm grip. He was a horse soothed by its rider.

Looking across the shoe-studded floor, head raised, she beckoned Burnell over.

'There's someone called to see you, Roy, dearest.'

He let his sister take over his port. In the front hall, Stephanie was awaiting him.

'She wants you back, Roy, dear,' Laura whispered, giving Burnell a slight push by way of encouragement.

He could see Stephanie was nervous. She hesitated to come forward. Her tall figure was framed in the rectangle of the front door, the two side windows with their stained glass contributing to a triptych effect. Stephanie wore a light fawn coat draped over her shoulders, underneath which was a brown jersey suit. As he approached, she put a hand up to pat her fair hair, smiling uncertainly in greeting.

Laura said, 'I'll get you some coffee, dear Stephanie and Roy. There's a fire in the blue room – you can sit in there and talk and be absolutely private.'

But directly Laura was gone, retiring in the direction of the kitchen, Stephanie said in a low voice, 'Roy, can we go outside? I don't really wish to remain in this house. We need to talk without interruption.'

Burnell was not certain that was the case.

To be with her again, taking in that almost pretty face, was disconcerting. It was with startlement he saw she had aged; in his self-absorbed state in hospital, he had not noticed the wrinkles under her eyes. To take in her presence at all was one thing; to have evidence that she was growing old quite another. Burnell felt his words to be slow and heavy as he said, 'It would be warmer in the blue room.'

She gestured as if to dismiss his objection, turned, and made for the front door. She opened it, fumbling with the latch. In a low voice, as if she had answered him, he said, 'You're right. Laura was manipulating us, as always.'

Walking down the shallow steps beside her, he saw a black limousine drawn up in the drive a short distance from the house. A small hand waved from the car's rear window.

'Your son?' Burnell asked.

'I didn't exactly aim for you to see him.'

'Oh no. I wouldn't have seen him if we had gone in the blue room . . . I suppose Laura arranged this meeting, did she? How else would you know I was here? I sensed there was something in the air.'

'You remember Laura and I always were close . . . or perhaps you can't.' He noticed her faint American accent.

He forced himself to ask, 'So that's your boyfriend in the car with your son? You've brought all the family along for the outing?'

She sighed as they began to crunch their way over the gravel. 'Humbert's in Europe on a business trip. Rather an important one, he says.' Her voice expressed either over-emphasized patience or weariness. 'He's often in the UK. He travels a lot. The Far East, Hong Kong, everywhere . . . But that's not what I want to talk about.'

'Thank God for that! What do you want, Steff? Why exactly are you here?'

Then she gave him her first faint smile, as if life had become less unpleasant. 'Gosh, it's great to hear you call me Steff again, after all this while.'

'Habits are hard to break. Last time we met, you told me to call you Stephanie. You couldn't stand "Steff".'

Her response puzzled him. If she had come here merely to annoy him, the presence near the house of the man Humbert, sitting in his black Mercedes with the child, Steff's child, was provocation enough. Her small approach to familiarity seemed to him merely contradictory; he failed to understand it.

Being annoyed too at her insistence that they walk outside on a rather chilly morning, he hunched his shoulders and looked glum.

The gravel crunched under their feet. Her reply was delayed, but she put on a bright tone to say, 'Can we go round by the ruin? That little objection of mine was a while ago. A lot has happened since then. Does Tarquin still keep peacocks? I just hate the way those things shriek.'

He sighed. They turned the corner of the house. Passing the summerhouse, they walked along a curving path under a pergola of entwined clematis. Twice on the way Stephanie glanced back at the waiting car, until they came to a holly hedge. Filing separately through a narrow kissing-gate, they entered the precincts of the old abbey. The abbey's remains were partly concealed behind a crumbling stone wall, built in the Norfolk fashion of knapped cobbles. The sky overhead had become as grey as the wall, and as unyielding in appearance. The growl of a lawnmower grew louder as they approached through an ivy-covered archway.

'I suppose you got my card from Ashkhabad?'

More annoyance for him when he felt her answer was deliberately casual. 'Ashkhabad? Is that in India?'

'It was a view of the railway station. They have a great railway station in Ashkhabad.' He tried a laugh which sounded false even to himself.

'I mustn't keep Humbert waiting too long. He's not at his best with children, not really . . . Roy, I have to ask you – I don't know how to put this. I guess you feel pretty grumpy about me, right?'

The grass was brown among thick low lines of stone, which were all that remained of walls once dividing the rooms of the old religious edifice. For the convenience of visitors, these phantom rooms had metal notices attached: Church, Lay Brothers' Room, Buttery, Cloister Garth, Sacristy, and so on. As they walked along a passage labelled Passage, Tarquin's gardener rode his ride-on mower up and down among the grass banks, turning amid the flinty skeleton of the abbey. This would be the last cut of the season, and a sparse one at that.

Burnell asked himself if his wanting her had not been a mere fossil habit. Glancing at her set expression, he felt he detested her. Certainly their old way of life, whatever it had been, was as dead and gone as the order of men who had once lived and worshipped on this spot.

'Ask what you like.' Burnell was unable to keep a note of bitterness from his voice. 'You're a Hillington again now, aren't you, not a Burnell? Or so you told me, I seem to remember – when you said you didn't wish to know about me any more.'

She turned to face him, looking earnestly into his eyes as if seeking a way to proceed. Under the inhospitable sky, wrinkles were more evident. 'Let me tell you this. I didn't know how to behave when I was younger. Perhaps I still don't. I don't know what you're – what anyone's – supposed to do. With themselves.'

'You didn't come here to discuss your behavioural problems, did you?'

His remark silenced her for a few seconds. Feeling sorry for what he had said, he prompted her to go on.

'On a day-to-day basis, I mean. I used to be so fussy and precise.'

'Oh no,' he said. 'Your neat airing-cupboard! I admired it.'

'You don't remember,' she said, dismissively, needing to make her confession. 'Everything had to be just so with me in those days. It was the way I was brought up. You were irritated. I didn't realize how or why I irritated you. I didn't know it was *me* all the time . . .'

He did not respond, seeing that more was to come. They paraded among the ancient slabs, plunging hands in coat or trouser pockets against the cold. Apart from occasional glances at each other, to judge the level of hostility between them, they kept their gaze on the ground, to see where they walked. Stone steps had to be negotiated here and there. The flinty ground plan of the ancient buildings formed a labyrinth to amuse child visitors, freed of its religious significance. The mower's roar faded, growing again as the machine turned and charged in their direction.

Stephanie tugged her coat more tightly round herself. Her voice came suddenly, as internal argument broke to the surface. 'But at least ours was a passionate marriage. Do you remember that? I never knew until recently how passionately you felt about me, under that cool surface of yours. How, I mean, you *desired* me . . . No one else ever . . . well . . .'

'It would have been quieter in the blue room. I can hardly hear what you say for this chap on his bloody tractor.'

'Oh, shut up about the blue room. Buddies Laura and I may be still, but I wasn't having her listening in to what I had to say.' Her voice rose to a shout. 'I was saying it was all my fucking fault!'

'Come to that, Steff, I might also have something to say . . . God knows what quarrels we've had in the past – they're stolen from me, the bad things along with the good. I feel wretched about this whole thing, this whole situation – and particularly about your leaving me. I've wanted you . . . I've travelled here, there, everywhere, wanting you. But just recently –'

The mower came roaring by again, drowning their voices. There was nothing for it but to retreat. They moved into the shelter of what had been the church, one end of which still remained standing, together with some evidence of the chapel at its east end. Above them an empty window frame gaped to the sky. Not a peacock was to be seen.

Looking at Stephanie, realizing that this meeting entailed as much pain for her as for him, Burnell found himself – it was hardly a conscious decision – relenting, telling her that if they were going to be penitent, then it was all as much his fault as hers. 'I know my attitude to life is to blame. I've always been like it, since I was a schoolboy. I think you know what's behind it, behind my chilliness. My sense of having been cheated. But not by you, no, I don't mean by you . . .' He jerked his head upwards, with a half-sneer at the clouds grinding along above them.

Stephanie looked at Burnell, at the wall behind him, and back at him, as if perplexed, as if thrown from her line of argument by his admission.

'Why did I leave you?' she asked, without particularly directing the question at him. 'Why did everything have to happen as it did?'

She tensed her hands at her side, bursting out with sudden venom, 'Jesus, here we are talking so quietly and half our life's already over! Why? Why are you being so bloody English and decent to me? You make me come over all English too. Why don't you shout and rave? Why don't you hit me about, for God's sake, the way Humbert does – show me you're angry and hurt?'

He leaped into her words before they had died on her lips.

'Because Humbert's a shit and a phoney and a creep and a mean little arsehole who probably loves any excuse to knock a woman about. I hate him, I hate to know you've had a son by him, I hate the way you connive with Laura to drive up and park that scumbag in the family's drive, sitting there like a gangster, waiting impatiently for you to shut up and hop back in the car with him. And a whole lot more things I hate, if you want to hear them. I have a little self-control. That doesn't mean to say my life isn't fucked up. All the while I was away, I was thinking of you with longing. Now I have you here, and a boyfriend waiting for you, and your kid, I'm just not so sure how I feel. And I'm cold.'

Despite her recent protest, she disliked this outburst. Saying nothing, she thrust her hands deep into her pockets and went to stare down the nearby well, the circular mouth of which was protected by a heavy iron grating.

'This isn't going to work,' she said aloud, addressing herself. Despite the drought, the well retained its water. She looked down at her dark reflection, while Burnell stood apart, watching.

'When we were first married, I felt inadequate, a child still. I used to think about drowning myself. I could see quite clearly the fish devouring my body. I could almost watch myself disintegrating. You made me feel so – oh, insignificant.'

She dropped a piece of mortar down the well, waiting for the delayed splash, watching her reflection disintegrate.

Looking across the stony distance between them, she spoke quietly but intensely, as if from a witness box.

'You've forgotten when we were staying in Holland that time and what you did to me. It's very nice for you not to remember, but don't think I forget. The WACH conference in The Hague and I was made to feel like nothing, nothing, in public, while you went off with that dreadful French creature Blanche who –'

'Wait. Hang on a minute.' He raised a hand, scowling as he did so. 'Maybe you really don't know how to behave! If you persuaded this boyfriend of yours to drive you up here – with Laura's connivance – so that you could pitch into me, I'm not taking that. If I hurt you in the past, I'm really sorry, but I'm not going to hang

402

around out here in the permafrost and listen to a diatribe about something I don't –'

'You used to listen! You used to listen!' Stephanie turned from him and clasped her hands up to her face. 'Listen now, will you, to what I'm trying to say. I'm not trying to quarrel – I'm trying to make it up. I'm not blaming you because you had an affair, Roy, I'm just telling you. Believe me, Humbert goes with other women all the time, everywhere. Humbert the Mad Humper . . . I hate it and I've put up with it for long enough. I've had affairs too. Maybe it's important, maybe not – that's the sort of thing every-one has to make up their minds about.

'I've submitted to insults and beatings from him because I was so selfish when you and I were a twosome. I now understand exactly what you put up with.'

Burnell shook his head impatiently. 'What are you saying? This penitence. It's a bit late for penitence, isn't it – from either of us? Steff, I can't trust what you say because I don't know what hap-pened between us.'

'But I do!' As she swung round to face him, he saw that at last she had gained the anger, or perhaps the courage to deliver what she had come to say. In her expression, her impassioned look, he was reminded of something he had merely mislaid, buried too deep to be stolen, and without thought he leant forward to receive it.

'I do! Oh, Roy – I've ventured inside your head, into your very heart. A rare and uncomfortable privilege . . . I've got hold of one of your EMV bullets and I've played it through in my own brain. All through, all those years. And the insight nearly killed me. The shock of it!'

She suddenly flung her arms round his neck. Without volition, he wrapped his arms about her waist. The gardener roared near by on his machine, eyes rigidly averted.

Burnell pushed her away. 'You found the bullet? How? I was in the wrong country?' He was incoherent. 'You can't – you've brought it with you? Give it me! That's all I want.'

She explained. He broke into her explanation then begged her to go on. She told him that Humbert's firm, Stuckmann Fabrics, had contacts and a chain of dealers in carpets and costumes in Central Asia. By putting pressure on his dealer in Tashkent, she had got him to trace one of the missing EMV bullets. This was after she had seen Burnell in the Swindon hospital. Her intention had always been to restore Burnell's memory to him.

Once the bullet had come into her hands, she had been unable to resist the impulse to view it herself. She said it was a woman's curiosity. When she played it, when those episodes from the past had again come to life, she had been forced to experience Burnell's side of their marriage. There, undeniably, was her younger self, preserved, seen from a loving but analytical perspective. For weeks she had been overwhelmed with the pain of new insight into herself.

'I just want the bullet,' he said, but she was in full spate.

She had had to leave Humbert for a week, to go to a sanctuary for women and think things over. He had beaten her when she returned.

'He was too insensitive to see I had changed. It was so *hard* for me. What's that poem we learnt at school? "Would God the gift to others gi'e us, To see ourselves as others see us"? It was so *hard* . . . I had to accept that I was so immature. I followed the daily activities of a trivial little person. I saw all that impartially, through your loving eyes.

'Oh, we were fine in bed, screwing, so I had reckoned that was enough. I was so superior, so prissy, so precise, so *juvenile*. My clothes! My God! But I never conversed with you, never responded to your jokes, was bored by your insights into life, hated architecture . . .'

He took her hand, halting her flow of words and tears that were about to fall. 'I was probably just as insensitive. Aren't people like that? Perhaps I wanted you that way – did you ever consider that possibility? If, indeed, you were as you claim. When you're young it's really hard to . . . Anyhow, forget it. Just give me that bullet. You have brought it?'

She hesitated. 'Your hands are cold. The bullet's in the car. Humbert's got it. He paid for it. He wants to hand it over to you.'

'What? You're mad! It's none of his business. I will not speak to

Humbert.' He was immediately angry. 'I suppose you've let him have a look at the bullet, too, just to make him randy, eh? Steff Hillington when young and naked . . .'

Stephanie turned away and began to walk slowly towards the kissing-gate. She said, without looking round, 'You are chilly, you are cold, if you imagine that. I wasn't going to let Humbert in on our past life, no way. Then I found he just wasn't interested.'

He caught her up, grasping her arm to detain her by the gate, asking her why she did not talk straightforwardly: why should Humbert decide to hand over the bullet? What kind of power-play was it?

They were beside the holly hedge. She pulled at a leaf absent-mindedly, pricking a finger; he saw the bright speck of her blood, no bigger than a pinhead. Motives were always mysterious; had she drawn blood accidentally, or with the intention of allowing some physical sign for her troubled state of mind? Whatever had been her intention, he was moved by the sight of that bright red spot on her pale finger.

'Roy, please don't be like this. I can't take it. OK, Humbert wants to hand over the bullet. It's kind of a ceremony — I don't know what goes on in his mind. You see, he wants to hand me over too. He and I have come to the end of the road.'

'Hand you over?'

'Hand me over.'

In a quiet voice, he said that could not be. 'I'm planning to go to Spain immediately. There's someone in Madrid I love and need.'

After scrutinizing his expression, she made a *moue* of resigna-tion. Pulling a wisp of handkerchief from her brassiere, she twisted it round her finger, beginning to walk slowly back in the direction of the house.

'Oh well, if that's the way it is . . . OK, somehow I didn't . . .' She choked back tears before saying in a more formal voice, 'In any event, I couldn't really have expected you'd take me on a second time — me and the boy. After everything. You're not really made like that.'

'Like what?'

405

'Laura thought it was worth trying.' She spoke indifferently. 'Okay, I'll get the bullet for you. Humbert will give me a lift into Norwich. He's quite obliging in some ways, the old bastard.'

Burnell stood on the edge of the path by the summerhouse, watching her go. The breeze was getting up, so that her fawn coat fluttered about her legs as if to detain her.

'Steff,' he called. 'Wait a moment. Don't just walk off. I . . . I don't know any Spanish . . .'

Her shoes crunched as she crossed the gravel towards the waiting black car. She had not heard. He had called too faintly.

He wanted to say to her, 'Look, you score more points than you know for gaining self-knowledge. Of course it was painful – it's meant to be, so you remember the lesson. And we live in a world where love is scarce and almost always has to be earned and re-earned, and besides . . .'

But all he managed to do was to call her name again, much more loudly this time.

Inside the old house, the old contest was still being played. Shoes were shuffling across the treacherous floor. As the game progressed, discussion of artistic matters fell away. Fruit and stones were traded. More coffee was ordered and brought. They played competitively.

Jenny Binns fell into a passion when her port was sacked by Tarquin, and threatened to leave the game entirely. She was comforted by a stiff gin and tonic. Other players demanded the consolation of alcohol. The opposed clocks brought their mixtures of good fortune and havoc.

Clementine Burnell seemed to be winning. She played her game alone, marrying no one. Violet Burnell married her husband and Sheila Lippard-Milne in quick succession. Money poured out of the bank. Old scores were settled. The Empty Lipstick Cases piled up in Newcastle.

When time came for a lunch break, some players were delighted. Others, like Ben Burnell, were reluctant to leave the board and face reality, even the reality of game pie followed by fresh fruit salad and cheese. Laura presided over the lunch table as they talked over past games. Punctually at two-thirty, Tarquin ordered them all back into the Dairy, where he promptly Lutined his brother's wife.

When dusk began to gather, it was still difficult to judge who was ahead of the game. One of the horrors and delights of 'Newcastle' was that the outcome was uncertain until the bitter end. They agreed to play on until the very stroke of midnight and hold a reckoning then.

It was only over port and liqueurs and a late-night tongue sandwich that anyone remembered to ask where Roy had gone.

Author's Note

Somewhere East of Life is the fourth volume in the Squire Quartet. These novels set the difficulties and pleasures of family life against a changing political background and a world-wide scene which stretches from the USA and Sicily to Turkmenistan and Singapore, while always returning to East Anglia. Some of the characters disappear, only to reappear in later books in subsidiary roles.

The sequence runs as follows:

Life in the West
Forgotten Life
Remembrance Day
Somewhere East of Life